Naturally Sweet Desserts

The Sugar-Free Dessert Cookbook

Marcea Weber

AVERY PUBLISHING GROUP INC.

Garden City Park, New York

Photography by Michael Cook
Illustrations by Amanda Upton
Designed by Steven Dunbar
Edited by Margaret Olds

Reprinted by special arrangement with Transworld Publishers.

ISBN 0-89529-443-5

Contents

1. NATURAL NECESSITIES:
Equipment, Techniques and Ingredients 15

2. LAYER AFTER LAYER:
Cakes for All Occasions   31

3. THE FINISHING TOUCH:
Icings, Glazes, Purees, Fillings, Creams and Toppings   65

4. SHAPING SIMPLY:
Pastries, Tarts, Pies and Strudels   99

5. HIGHER AND HIGHER:
Yeasted Pastries   139

ACKNOWLEDGEMENTS

I would like to express my gratitude and deepest appreciation to my teachers: George and Lima Ohsawa; Michio and Aveline Kushi; Herman and Cornelia Aihara; Oki Sensai. Also to Leslie Gillet – who shared her experiences and gave support in tasting and testing; my mother and father, Rose and Paul, for always being there – no matter what; my friends who became my students; Masako Kuneno and Catriona MacMillan – photo stylists who gave support, patience, understanding and constant love; Vivian Broughton – typing; my students who became my friends; Cathy DelFaunte – support, understanding, research, love and clarity; Libby Wertheim – for working with me, sharing her youth, vitality and love; Angela – who minded my son so I could get on with it; and Daniel – my husband, tester and best critic, and always understanding.

FOREWORD

A typical day for this particular patient of mine started with black coffee and two sugars, then a cheese sandwich for lunch and usually a mixed grill when she came home. 'Oh, I do have a bit of a sweet tooth,' she admitted. 'I often buy chocolate or ice-cream, but the worst time is after dinner. I just have to have something sweet. Sometimes I eat half a carton of ice-cream at one sitting or a whole packet of chocolate-coated peanuts – I just can't help myself. I actually have a kind of craving for these things.'

In fact, most days she averaged around six cups of coffee, 1 litre of milk, large amounts of cheese and ice-cream, up to half a kilogram of confectionery (notably chocolates) and around 12 teaspoons of added sugar. She came to me complaining of chronic fatigue, catarrh, breathlessness with heart pounding, daily headaches, painful joints, sore muscles and severe symptoms of premenstrual syndrome including enlarged breasts and fluid retention. These are frequently manifestations of excessive intakes of sugar, caffeine and dairy products.

After learning that she developed eczema as a child after drinking cow's milk I suggested that we eliminate dairy products from the diet for three to four weeks to see what would happen. Her reaction was immediate. 'But what can I eat?' She liked even less the suggestion that she should try alternatives to sucrose (common table sugar) and coffee. The craving, the addiction, the ups and downs in energy levels and mood swings were all too familiar and the mere mention of alternative foods and drinks such as tahini, nut butters and mu tea produced a predictable bewildered look. Nevertheless, six weeks later she bounced back into my office ready to conquer the world. All of her symptoms had miraculously disappeared after she removed the 'empty calories', caffeine and dairy products from her diet. She was now enjoying a wide variety of foods with high nutrient density and free of additives.

Clearly, our bodies like to get the full range of micro-nutrients and other food factors that are naturally associated with foods. If these vitamins, minerals, fibre, enzymes, oils, etc., are removed during the refining process, we cannot metabolize our foods adequately, which subsequently affects the normal functioning of our body. Eating refined sugar and flour is like filling up the car with petrol while forgetting to fit the spark plugs. The caffeine and other related stimulants in chocolates and colas merely add fuel injection when the car is out of tune.

Fortunately, there are many natural sources of sugars for those with a 'sweet tooth'. Refined white sucrose is by far the most prevalent but not the most nutritious sugar. Similarly, cow's milk is thought to be the only major supplier of calcium in the diet. Other good sources, however, include sesame seeds (1250 mg calcium per 100 g), almonds, hazelnuts and soybeans (which contain 250 mg/100 g).

We have an abundant supply of foods on our planet with an enormous variety of different nutrients. We only use a fraction of these in our daily diet. We must start moving away from our preoccupation with three or four foods in our daily diet (dairy products, white flour, sugar and meat) and start selecting from two hundred or more foods (as they become available throughout the year). This would not only provide maximum nutrition but also maximum enjoyment.

Marcea's splendid book of different and exciting new approaches to desserts is a good starting point for those 'sweet toothers' who want to increase their enjoyment of foods without sacrificing nutritional content.

Robert Buist

Introduction

We all love sweet, rich, creamy, tantalizing desserts, and why not? Of all the five primary tastes – salty, sweet, sour, pungent and bitter – sweetness is often said to be the most popular, and according to ancient Chinese philosophy it is the 'mother' of all the others. Can you imagine what Christmas would be like without the traditional pudding and fruit cake?

Can you imagine a birthday party without cake and ice-cream? Let's face it, our Western palate is definitely 'hooked' on sweets, especially at the end of a meal (of course we don't celebrate with cake and ice-cream every night!) or in between meals especially at 1.00 a.m. or 4.00 p.m. which is considered to be 'low blood sugar time', a period when the body is craving a boost of energy of some sort. This leads to a snack, usually in the form of sweet cakes and pastries, and so the pattern establishes itself.

Desserts, however, don't have to be considered the least nutritious, most indulgent and fattening part of our meal anymore. Using natural, unrefined foods like wholemeal flours, fresh or dried fruits, unprocessed and unrefined oils and sea salt, untampered-with flavourings and the other ingredients used in these recipes, and avoiding refined sugar, can help to provide us with an excellent source of fibre, vitamins and minerals and still allow us to enjoy desserts without being fanatically worried about kilojoules and our state of well-being.

If you're overly concerned about your weight, you'll be happy to know that one cup of chopped, fresh fruit has only about 11 per cent of the kilojoules in an equal measure of sugar! If you're concerned about nutrition as well, honey, compared with apricots, mangoes and rock melons, has no vitamin A, while these fresh fruits or dried ones are all good sources. Did you know that one cup of honey has more kilojoules than one cup of sugar, and that various minerals found in limited quantities in honey are more abundant in many fruits?

I remember watching my mother make desserts, using only fresh or dried fruits, home-made baking powder, fresh yeast when available, never refined sugar, canned fruit, white flours or foods containing additives, preservatives or refined sugar. She would fill the air weekly, usually on Fridays, with the aroma of her home-made apricot cakes, pear breads, apple-raisin pies, orange biscuits and prune danishes in the winter and in the summertime she would elaborate and vary her desserts by creating fresh pineapple-cherry upside-down cakes, melon cheesecakes, blueberry pies and peach pastries. There was never an end to her creativity. As the seasons changed, so did the ingredients she used.

Not only did I learn how to shape, roll and bake these delights, but unknowingly how to use fruits, nuts, seeds, spices and cooking techniques seasonally. Of course, I never realized how much she shared with me, as I was usually too preoccupied with licking the bowls clean.

When I finally began preparing desserts on my own, I began to innovate and embellish my mother's themes unconsciously. What came out were delicate pastries, cakes, pies and fresh fruit desserts, and not only were they gobbled up the minute they came out of the kitchen, but reflected the seasons as well. I began to first rely heavily on fruits, honey, fruit purees or concentrates, brown sugar, seeds and nuts for my basic ingredients. Slowly the white flour and refined sugar and even brown sugar and honey began to disappear from my pantry, as I was told that I needed to make a shift in my diet and eliminate all sugar, honey and dairy foods to improve my health at the time.

I began to search around for ingredients that would support my health and began to experiment with wholemeal flours, organic whenever possible, untreated seeds, unrefined oils, nuts, dried and fresh fruits, free-range eggs, soy milk and tofu (a soybean cheese).

Little did I realize how addicted to 'sugar' I had become, until I stopped using it and experienced 'withdrawal' symptoms otherwise known as 'sugar blues'. Many years later, when I successfully kicked the 'sugar habit' I experienced the loss of 15 kg (30 lb), a clearer complexion, more vitality, less depression, improved disposition, and less tiredness, emotional upsets and nervousness.

When we take refined sugar in any form into our bodies, it is so close to our own internally produced glucose it escapes the ordinary digestive process and passes right through to the intestines and is readily absorbed into the bloodstream. This then leads to a rapid rise in the glucose level and this imbalance calls for more hormones which are secreted directly into the blood.

This in turn affects your metabolism, the blood sugar level drops, and we feel a 'high' or sugar 'rush'. But then very quickly, it drops and low blood sugar results and no more insulin is produced. Then a signal is sent to the adrenal and pancreatic hormones to raise the blood sugar to a homeostatic level. This withdrawal, or tired, down feeling, occurs while the body tries to get back into balance.

Of course, sugar-bearing foods such as grains, vegetables and fruits do play an important role in our diet. They provide essential nutrients, add flavour, fibre and energy to our meal. Adequate carbohydrate levels in the body must be maintained to prevent excessive breakdown of fat and protein and other undesirable metabolic changes. The more unprocessed and unrefined sweeteners we use, as well as our daily foods, the less of an adjustment and dramatic shift our bodies must make, as they are the way nature intended them to be with all of the nutrients prescribed intact and in the form in which our bodies can assimilate and digest them without depleting our system. The same way the sweetness of cane juice was used by primitive man who chewed the *whole* sugar cane as part of his regular diet, we should now use whole fruits, juices and unprocessed sweeteners.

The more refining we do, the fewer micro-nutrients are left for us to use without causing dramatic changes in our blood fat levels as well as our blood sugar levels. Micro-nutrients help us to metabolize any kind of food more naturally into our bodies without robbing our system.

The key to a proper balance in your diet is moderation. Fats, proteins and sugar-bearing carbohydrates all have a place in our daily diet; the key is to eat them in proper proportions. Dr James H. Shaw, Professor of Nutrition at the Harvard School of Dental Medicine, believes that man's taste for sugar is not a natural desire, but rather a programmed desire. He explains, 'With the heavy usage of sugar in the preparation of baby foods where the sugar is not essential for preservation or even for a good natural taste, we are conditioned throughout life to sweeten foods more than nutritionally desirable.'

There have been some other studies done where nutritionists have found that men tend to be more fond of sugar than women are and that maximum intake occurs around the age of twenty. They also discovered that low-income families consume twice as much refined table sugar as those with moderate or high incomes, but that the wealthy buy twice as many prepared sweetened products, according to Dave Schwantes in *The Unsweetened Truth About Sugar and Sugar Substitutes.*

Over the years we, as a society, have become increasingly dependent on sugar, to the extent that the average per head consumption has risen from half a kilo in 1588 to 4 kg in 1720, 7 kg in 1850, 36 kg in 1900 and 54.5 kg in 1978 (more than a kilo per week!) according to Peter Meier (newspaper columnist for the *Sunday Telegraph*). According to the latest figures from the Australian Bureau of Statistics, we consume about 52 kg per head per year.

Slowly but surely, Australians and Americans are going sour on sweets. We all still adore desserts, of course, and most of us have not banned the occasional treats from our diets, but a growing number are cutting back on sugary stuff in a move towards healthier diets.

If you're a dessert lover like me, you can still have your cake and eat it too – without a granule of sugar, a drop of honey or artificial sweetener. The secret is using fruit as a sweetener, in any of the various forms mentioned in Sweeteners: Sweetness Equivalency Chart on page 12. Relying on foods of natural sweetness is not a new idea. Sugar was considered to be a luxury until the 1800s when sugar refining was established.

Fruit is an ideal sweetener, and it's an excellent source of fibre, vitamins and minerals, as opposed to white sugar (sucrose) or raw sugar, raw honey and corn syrups which contain few, if any, other nutrients. Besides being more nutritious and lower in kilojoules than sugar, fruit provides a remarkably versatile sweetener available in many forms.

Of course enjoying foods that contain no additional sugar takes some 'conditioning' and people who have consumed a lot of sugary foods may have to gradually decrease their sugar intake before they are able to enjoy sugarless desserts.

When I discovered that I needed to eliminate sugar completely from my diet to improve my health, I had to make major ingredient changes, eliminating sugar and substituting fruit juice in place of milk or other liquid, and very often the end product was inedible. So I decided to develop recipes from scratch. After many frustrating attempts, sometimes testing a cake recipe more than ten times, and after creating, experimenting and tasting for two years I had enough recipes for this cookbook.

My basic aim is to make desserts that taste and look as good as they can without using sugar and butter as ingredients. I've tried to produce a collection of the highest quality desserts to serve for special occasions as well as for everyday ones. Also being aware of certain dietary requirements, such as gluten- or egg-free, I have included a key to guide you to these recipes. Recipes are also included for those of you with sugar sensitivity, food intolerances, or hyperactivity, and for those of you who are watching your weight and reducing cholesterol intake.

Fruit sweetening, organic, preservative-free and pesticide-free wholefood ingredients can open up a whole new vista for your dessert making. You can transform your sugar-laden desserts into sugar-free, healthy and light, low-kilojoule, allergy-free delights, to complement any meal. The simplest dessert can be turned into a fancy one that will surprise your family and friends alike!

Essential Reference

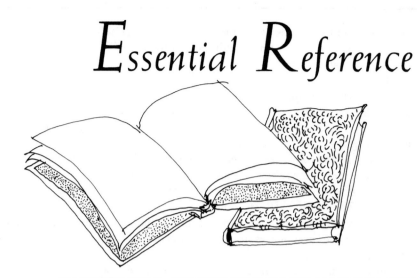

SWEETENERS: SWEETNESS EQUIVALENCY CHART

Usually when I prepare desserts, I choose a sweetener according to what kind of taste I would like: very sweet or less sweet. I like to vary the sweeteners and to try to get different effects in taste, texture and degree of sweetness.

When I am cooking for my family (they don't like their desserts very sweet) I use rice syrup, maltose, barley malt or less sweetener than called for, but when I have invited guests I tend to use more maple syrup for extra sweetness.

This list is designed to help you substitute one natural sweetener for another, and begin to understand the relationship among them in terms of sweetness. Remember, always decrease or increase the amount of liquid or flour in the recipe according to the liquid content of the sweetener.

In all recipes, ½ cup sweetener =
½ cup maple syrup
½ cup honey
⅓ cup molasses
½ cup black sugar
½ cup coconut sugar
1¼ cups maltose*
1½ cups barley malt extract*
½ cup fruit juice concentrate
1 cup sugarless fruit jam or jelly*
1¼ cups dried fruit puree**
1¼ cups rice syrup*
2 cups fruit juice or ½ fruit and ½ carrot juice*
½ cup unsweetened frozen juice concentrate (e.g., orange juice)*

*If these sweeteners are used, the amount of liquid will have to be reduced or the amount of dry ingredients will have to be increased. Add ground nuts, seeds, coconut or carob flour or arrowroot for best results.

**Includes the following: nectarines, peaches, apricots, prunes, pears, apples, mangoes, paw-paws, raisins, sultanas, currants, figs, dates, Chinese dates, pine-apples, and bananas.

- These sweeteners are all gluten free, except for the maltose and barley malt extract which cannot be used if following a gluten-free diet.

- When using any sweetener in place of sugar in an ordinary recipe, reduce liquid content in recipe by 1/4 cup or more, depending on the sweetener you choose. If no liquid is called for in recipe, add 3-5 tablespoons of flour for each 3/4 cup of sweetener.
- Be sure to heat maltose, malt or rice syrup before working with it.
- Oil the measuring cup and spoon before measuring liquid sweeteners.
- When maltose, rice syrup or barley malt extract is used, it may liquefy the consistency of the mixture. This is more likely to occur when eggs are not used. To compensate, use more dry ingredients.
- Those liquid sweeteners which have an acid factor (honey, molasses) need neutralizing by the addition of baking soda.

SUBSTITUTE THIS FOR THAT

There are certain recipes that call for ingredients that you may not have, or are not familiar with. Here is a handy reference chart, to bridge the gap.

1 tablespoon miso = 1/2 teaspoon sea salt
2 tablespoons *shoyu* = 1 tablespoon miso
1 cup whole wheat flour minus 2 tablespoons = 1 cup white flour
1/4 teaspoon dried herbs = 2 teaspoons fresh herbs
2 teaspoons dried yeast = 30 g (1 oz) compressed fresh yeast
1 bar agar-agar = 4-6 tablespoons flakes
1 bar agar-agar = 1/2 tablespoon powder (not recommended)
1 cup carob = 1 1/2 cups cocoa
3/4 tablespoon carob = 1 square chocolate
1 cup peanut butter = 315 g (10 oz) peanut butter
1 cup tahini = 250 g (8 oz) tahini
3 1/4 teaspoons kuzu = 1 tablespoon arrowroot flour

When using tahini in recipes (especially in confectionery), it may be necessary to decrease the liquid content of the recipe by 1/4 cup, or add a few tablespoons of dry ingredients (carob, spices, crushed nuts) to absorb excess oil from tahini. Other nut butters tend to be less runny.

When a recipe calls for miso, use only the rice, buckwheat or soybean miso if following a gluten-free diet.

KEY TO ABBREVIATIONS

EF denotes that the recipe is egg-free.
GF denotes that the recipe is gluten-free.
When either EF or GF appears at the beginning of recipe, the entire recipe is egg/gluten free, unless otherwise stated. When the abbreviations appear against elements of the recipe (e.g., topping, filling etc.), only those ingredients are exempt.

FOOD INTOLERANCE CHART

Allergy To	Substitution Suggestions
Chocolate	3 tablespoons carob powder plus 1 tablespoon oil for every 30 g (1 oz) square of chocolate
Cocoa	Carob powder in equal measure
Cornstarch (1 tablespoon)	4 teaspoons whole wheat flour, or 1 teaspoon arrowroot or kuzu. In sauces use $\frac{1}{3}$ cup arrowroot for 1 cup cornstarch
Gelatine (2 tablespoons)	2 tablespoons agar-agar flakes
Milk	Soy milk, nut milk or oat milk (pp. 232-4) Coconut milk (p. 233)
Cream	Basic Tofu Cream (p. 93), potato puree
Sour Cream	Tofu Sour Cream (p. 95) or yoghurt
Baking Powder (1 teaspoon)	$\frac{1}{3}$ teaspoon baking soda and $\frac{2}{3}$ teaspoon cream of tartar
Eggs (white acts as leavening, yolk as a binder)	Binders: Nut butters – 1 teaspoon nut butter with water or fruit juice to consistency of whipped egg, or 1 part soy flour and 2 parts water blended and heated, thickens as it cools Leavening agents: 1 teaspoon baking powder substitute for omitting one egg from recipe Substitute $\frac{1}{2}$ teaspoon arrowroot and $\frac{1}{4}$ teaspoon baking soda for one egg Binder and leavener: 4 tablespoons almond or cashew butter with 2 tablespoons lemon juice
Eggs	1 tablespoon vinegar
Eggs	For cookies or biscuits – 1 tablespoon oil, 2 tablespoons baking powder substitute and 2 tablespoons water or fruit juice
Wheat Flour (1 cup)	$\frac{1}{2}$ cup arrowroot and $\frac{1}{2}$ cup soy flour OR any ONE of following: $\frac{3}{4}$ cup brown rice flour 1 cup cornflour $1\frac{1}{4}$ cups barley flour $\frac{3}{4}$ cup potato flour $1\frac{1}{3}$ cups oat flour $1\frac{1}{3}$ cups soy flour
Peanut Butter	Almond, cashew, sunflower, hazelnut, sesame butter or tahini
Chestnut Flour	4 parts brown rice flour and 1 part soy flour OR 4 parts oat flour and 1 part soy flour OR 4 parts barley flour and 1 part oat flour

1. NATURAL NECESSITIES:
Equipment, Techniques and Ingredients

NECESSARY EQUIPMENT

*J*UST as good natural foods make more nutritious desserts, proper kitchen tools are necessary for the preparation of good quality culinary delights. By using the cooking and baking utensils suggested, you will find that your desserts are not only more delectable, but truly wholesome as well.

J. P. Beach, editor of the magazine *You and Your Health*, has pointed out that aluminium 'exerts an irritating action on the mucosa of the entire gastrointestinal tract before absorption, and, as aluminium salts, on the tissues and organs of the body after absorption. Thus, it is a common cause of constipation, colitis, and ulcers...'

If you boil ordinary drinking water in an aluminium dish or pan for half an hour and immediately pour it into a clear glass container, you can see the aluminium compounds, mostly aluminium hydroxide. In cooking, more of these particles are released from the aluminium, enter into the food, and are absorbed by the body as well.

Choose baking and cooking utensils made of tin, stainless steel, earthenware, stoneware, porcelain, cast iron, enamel or glass. Avoid aluminium and all synthetically coated equipment. For the same reason, avoid wrapping food in aluminium foil for baking, cooking or storing.

Mixing
Glass or porcelain mixing bowls
Wooden spoons
Measuring cups, stainless steel or tin for dry ingredients, and glass for liquids
Measuring spoons
Flour sifter or strainer
Wire whisk
Rotary hand beater or electric mixer
Rubber spatulas
Suribachi (see p. 174), or mortar and pestle

Decorating
See p. 66.

Cooking
Double boiler
Saucepans
Confectionary thermometer
Flame spreader (metal heat distributor)
Wok, or deep fryer
Oil skimmer

Shaping
Flute-edge pastry wheel
Cookie cutters
Rolling pin
Pastry cloth
Knife
Baker's scraper (to clean pastry cloth and cut sections of dough)

Baking and Cooling

Swiss roll pan (low sides)
Pastry brushes (to oil pans and brush top of pastries)
Baking sheet, 5 cm (2 in) smaller than the size of your oven
Bread tin
Fluted cake tin
Tube pan
Rectangular baking tray
Layer cake pan
Springform pan*

Tart tins
Cupcake tins
Assorted tins and moulds
Greaseproof paper
Cake racks

*A springform pan is best because it is easy to remove the cake without disturbing the shape.

BASIC TECHNIQUES

*E*VERYONE has his or her own way of explaining how to beat, sift, fold, mix, and when to boil, bake, steam or fry. Directions will always vary regarding baking terms and techniques used, as well as ingredients called for. The following are some tips that I hope you will find helpful.

Along with these techniques, there is one ingredient that I feel is most essential – *intuition*. For me, baking is an art that I have translated into measurements and step-by-step instructions. I feel that one should come to it with the same enthusiasm and creative spirit that one would bring to any art form, be it painting or writing or making music. What could be more creative than the preparation of food that is both attractive and delicious?

So, please experiment with these recipes, suggestions and methods. Find your own way and bake according to your own good judgement, intuition and need.

Beating

Depending upon what you want to accomplish, there are two ways to beat.

1. The first way is to fill the eggs with air. This method uses a rotary hand beater, wire whisk or electric mixer and is mainly used for cake batters.

2. The second type of beating is for mixes that are fairly stiff and already combined. It is best done with a wooden spoon, rotary hand beater or electric mixer. This method is used for eclairs and yeasted batters or dough.

Folding

Folding is perhaps the most important technique for working with batters that use only eggs as a leavening agent. It is the gentlest way of combining two or more ingredients to retain the air that you have beaten into them.

It should be done with your hand, preferably; or, if you wish, with a rubber spatula.

1. If you are folding in dry ingredients, sift them on top of the mixture. If the ingredients are liquid, pour them on slowly, gradually folding them in.

2. Folding with your hands allows you to feel how light and delicate the mixture really is. Spread your fingers open and cut through the mixture to the bottom of the mixing bowl.

3. Move your hands across the bottom of the bowl and up the side.

4. Bring your hands up, holding some of the batter. Rotate your hands so that you release the mixture.

5. Repeat the whole procedure until all the ingredients are combined but still feel light and delicate.

COOKING METHODS

Boiling
Boiling in a saucepan over direct heat is a good method for heating up liquids that do not contain any flour.

A double boiler is needed to cook custards, creams or any delicate flour-liquid or egg combination. These may overcook or scorch if left directly on heat.

It is not necessary to stir as often when cooking in a double boiler, but the cooking time must be increased.

Steaming
This is a very old, but popular method for preparing bread puddings, pastries, and even cakes, allowing the flavours to permeate more evenly through the dessert. When women spent more time in the kitchen, they didn't think twice about steaming something for 2 to 3 hours.

Oil a coffee can, cake pan or mould. Fill two-thirds full with batter and cover tightly with foil. Place on a rack in a large heavy pot filled with enough boiling water to come one-half to three-quarters of the way up the side of the mould.

Cover the pot and steam on a medium-low heat 2 to 3 hours or longer, keeping the water constantly boiling. If the cake is too moist on top after steaming, preheat the oven to 180°C (350°F) and bake uncovered 10 to 15 minutes to remove excess moisture. Best for fruit cakes or puddings.

Deep-frying
(For unrefined oil, see 'Preparation of oil'.)

1. Heat oil on a high heat. To test readiness drop a few grains of salt or batter into oil. If salt or batter rises to the top immediately, the oil is ready. Or, place the handle of a wooden spoon in the centre of the oil.

When the oil starts to bubble around the wood it is ready.

2. Place several pieces of food into a wok or deep fryer. Do not overload. This can lower the temperature, making the oil bubble and preventing the food from cooking properly.

3. Deep fry, turning pastry over and removing when bubbling almost stops.

4. Drain on egg cartons, white paper towels, or unwaxed brown paper bags.

5. Immediately after removing pastry from oil, replace with another piece. If you leave the oil empty, its temperature will rise and it will burn.

6. Remove excess particles from the oil with an oil skimmer. Strain through cheesecloth into a glass jar and refrigerate.

Preparation of oil: (This step is necessary for unrefined oil which usually bubbles.)

Place 5 cups oil (one-third sesame to two-thirds safflower, or all safflower) in a wok or deep fryer. Cook over medium heat until oil begins to move. (If oil is overheated, it will smoke and be unfit for use in cooking.) Turn heat off immediately, and cool.

Unrefined oil often contains naturally occurring liquids which can be boiled off prior to cooking. This accounts for the bubbling often seen when first cooking unrefined oil.

Baking*

Preheat oven to suggested temperature 15 minutes before baking (use an oven thermometer to ensure correct temperature).

*Seeds and nuts can be toasted in this way.

If the oven is too warm, leave the oven door open for a few minutes to lower the temperature.

Never overload an oven. When both racks are filled, the heat cannot circulate evenly around the pans.

The top rack of an oven is used only for last minute browning. Placing baked goods on the top rack will often result in a browned top and a bottom only half baked.

Roasting

Roasting flour, oats and seeds improves the flavour of desserts and toppings in which they are used. Use only a dry skillet for seeds. Prepare as follows.

1. Cover the bottom of a dry or oiled heavy skillet or frying pan with the rolled oats, flour or seeds and heat over a low heat.

2. Move the ingredients from side to side, in a clockwise or anticlockwise motion until they are lightly browned and have a strong sweet aroma (when roasting chestnut flour, roast until the flour is a medium shade of brown).

3. Remove from the pan, and place on a plate to cool before using. Never add warm flour to cool liquid or it will get lumpy.

Roasting flour adds more flavour, but overroasting can add a bitter taste.

Blanching

Sometimes a recipe calls for 'blanched nuts', used mainly on the top of a cake for decoration, for making almond milk, or as a flour substitute in cakes. Fresh fruit can also be blanched by the same method.

Drop nuts or fruit into boiling water. Turn off heat and let sit about 1 minute. Drain immediately and rinse under cold water. Peel and use as desired. (If the fruits are organic, save the skins and use them in salads or fruit compotes, or to flavour other desserts.)

NATURE'S NECESSITIES

Agar-agar

Agar-agar (also known as *kanten*), a vegetable gelatine made from seaweed, is a rich source of essential minerals. It is used mainly as a thickener, adhesive or emulsifying agent. Having the consistency of gelatine, it will set in approximately half an hour without refrigeration.

It can be purchased in bar form, strands, flakes or powder. (The powder is not recommended.)

Amazake

Amazake is brewed from sweet brown rice, koji (starter) and water. It can be used as a sweetener, drink or leavening agent, depending on how long you let the mixture ferment. It is a delicious substitute for alcohol in fruit cakes (before blending), or can be boiled and blended with lemon juice and vanilla as a cream puff or eclair filling.

Apple Butter

Made from fresh apples which have been cooked down to a soft, butter-like consistency, apple butter can be used as a sweetener or filling.

Apple Cider (see also Hard Cider)

Cider is the fermented or partially fermented juice of apples. Organic apple cider has no preservatives, so it must be refrigerated at all times to retard natural fermentation.

Apple Cider Jelly

Apple cider jelly is a concentrated form of apple cider, produced by boiling down the cider until it gels.

Arrowroot

Arrowroot was named by the South American Indians, who used its fresh roots to heal wounds made by poison arrows. Arrowroot is used as a thickening agent in place of flour in many instances, because it does not lose its thickening power when combined with very acid fruits. If overcooked, it has the tendency to lose this good quality.

This thickening agent has properties very similar to those of cornflour, but it is of better quality. It is a light starch used in glazes, cake batters, doughs, pudding and pie fillings and other dessert mixes. It is very helpful in holding dough together while rolling it out; just sprinkle some on the cloth before you begin to roll. Arrowroot can also be used as a food for sick people and children because it is easily digested.

Baking Powder

In all baking powder there must be an acid and an alkaline material (bicarbonate of soda and cream of tartar) reacting with one another in the presence of moisture to form a gas – carbon dioxide – which takes the form of tiny bubbles in the dough or batter. In baking, these quickly expand the batter which is set by the heat to make a light textured crumb.

Baking Soda (Bicarbonate of Soda)

Baking soda is used as a leavening agent in baking powder and also on its own to lighten or raise dough in bakery products like biscuits, crackers, cookies and cakes, muffins and even breads. It is produced by mixing carbon dioxide with soda ash, a white powder sometimes extracted from sea water or produced commercially. The amount of sodium is rather high (821 mg per teaspoon) so if you are watching sodium intake please use *carefully*. You can make your own baking powder by mixing 1/3 bicarbonate of soda with 2/3 cream of tartar. This combination gives one of the tenderest crumbs.

Too much too often destroys vitamin C, so use sparingly and only on special occasions.

Barley Malt

Malt is naturally processed by sprouting barley in water. When the sprouts are ready, heat is applied to stop the sprouting and dry out the malt. Use it as a sweetener in or on any dessert.

Bean Curd

See Tofu.

Beetroot Juice

Boil beetroots in salted water until soft. Strain off water and use for tinting icings, tofu fillings or biscuits.

Bicarbonate of Soda

See Baking Soda.

Bulgur

To make bulgur, whole wheat is roasted, cracked, parboiled and dried. Bulgur can be used to give a fluffy, light texture to cakes. It is available in natural, health and Middle Eastern food stores, and can be used in place of couscous, semolina or ground nuts.

Carob Flour

Otherwise known as St John's Bread, this food is an ideal natural substitute in recipes calling for the use of cocoa or chocolate. The flavour and colour it imparts is similar to that of chocolate, yet without the detrimental effects of calcium oxylate, theobromine and caffeine contained in products from the cocoa bean.

Corn Flour

Also known as maize flour; not related to the thickening agent.

Couscous

This is made from the middle of hard semolina wheat which has been precooked before being dried to make it easier to prepare and to give it a lighter, fluffier texture. It is similar to bulgur and is a staple food in the Middle East, and served steamed with other food and condiments in Tunisia, Morocco and Algeria.

Couscous is available at natural, health and Middle Eastern food stores and may be used flavoured, as a separate dessert, or combined with flour and other ingredients to add lightness to cakes.

Cream of Tartar

Cream of tartar, which is an essential ingredient in baking powder, is a purified form of tartaric acid. This acid is an organic colourless crystalline compound that is found in grapes and other fruits. It is usually obtained from the hard deposits in casks of wine not completely fermented. The cream of tartar is obtained from this crude form.

It provides the acid necessary to react with an alkaline factor (bicarbonate of soda) in home-made baking powder. These two elements together in the presence of moisture create carbon dioxide which is responsible for the tender crumb of cakes and biscuits.

Dried Fruit

Sun-drying is the only natural way to dehydrate food. This drying process evaporates the water from the fruit, so that there is not enough moisture to support bacteria.

The fruits are first picked, washed and peeled, then blanched with steam and spread out on a large tray to dry in the sun. The contact with the air tends to darken the pulp. If the dried fruit you purchase is not darker than the fresh fruit of the same kind, it usually shows that sulphur dioxide was used to preserve the colour.

It takes about 2.5 kg (5 lb) of fresh fruit to produce 500 g (1 lb) of dried fruit.

Dried-fruit Juice

Cover dried fruit with four times as much water or juice. When soft, cook soaked fruit plus soaking liquid, ¼ teaspoon sea salt, 1 cup more liquid as needed, a vanilla bean or 2 tablespoons orange rind, for 20 minutes. Strain. Use in place of fruit juice.

Dried-fruit Puree

This can be made from any dried fruit by soaking (if necessary) in enough water or fruit juice to almost cover, overnight or for several hours. Then simmer the fruit in liquid to almost cover, with a pinch of sea salt, until there is no liquid remaining. Stir occasionally to prevent from sticking to the bottom of the pan.

Fruit puree can be made from nectarines, peaches, apricots, prunes, pears, banana, apples, mango, paw-paw, raisins, sultanas, figs, currants, dates, Chinese dates and pineapple.

Eggs

See Eggs, p. 32.

Flour (See also Flour p. 45.)

There are many different types of flour available in health and natural food stores. It is important to know how they differ from each other, so that you will be able to work successfully with each of them. All flour should be refrigerated to preserve nutritional value.

Brown Rice Flour: This is the most suitable flour to use to achieve a crunchier, sweeter taste and texture.

Chestnut Flour: Ground from dried chestnuts, this flour is sweet enough to be used, without any additional sweetener, especially if cooked for a long time, as a cream, or for toppings or fillings. Chestnut flour can also be used in combination with whole wheat pastry or cake flour in pastry to add crunchiness to pie crusts and biscuits, and to lend a distinctive flavour. It is obtainable at natural food and Italian food stores.

If chestnut flour is difficult to obtain, substitute one of the following:

1. 4 parts brown rice flour and 1 part soy flour
2. 4 parts oat flour and 1 part soy flour
3. 4 parts barley flour and 1 part oat flour

Cornflour (Maize, yellow): Made from corn, this flour has a sweet flavour and a delicate quality. It is more finely ground than maizemeal, and is used mainly in fillings, and bread.

Cornflour should be used as fresh as possible because it can develop a bitter taste if kept too long.

Sweet Brown Rice Flour: This flour is sweeter than brown rice flour, and is best used to make confectionery, steamed desserts, crunchy biscuits or mochi. (The Chinese use sweet rice flour mostly in their desserts, which are usually steamed.) This flour may be difficult to buy in Australia and New Zealand; use sweet white rice flour instead.

Whole Wheat or Whole Meal Flour: Whole wheat flour is mainly used in breads, although a small amount can be used along with whole wheat pastry or cake flour in yeasted pastries. Because it absorbs more liquid and contains more gluten than whole wheat pastry or cake flour, it can make dough tough if overworked, but it can also provide a greater rise for certain yeasted products.

Whole Wheat Pastry or Cake Flour: This flour is made from a different species of wheat, known as soft wheat. It is a low gluten variety of wheat. It may be called cake flour – 20 per cent whole wheat, 80 per cent unbleached white. Some of the best, lightest and most delicious cakes are made from whole wheat pastry or cake flour. Because it contains the bran from the outside of the wheat kernel, it is slightly brownish in colour and a great deal more nutritious than unbleached white flour.

Fruit Jams, Jellies and Butters

Made from fresh fruit, fruit juice and sometimes pectin, these concentrated sweeteners have a smooth consistency, and can be used as a filling, topping or sweetener.

Fruit Juice Concentrates

These concentrates are made from fruit that has been pressed into juice, then reduced down for a long time. It is so concentrated that ¼ cup of juice concentrate will make 2 glasses of fruit juice. Fruit juice concentrates can be made from apples, grapes, etc.

Grain Coffee (Coffee Substitute)

*Dr Irwin Rose wrote in *Science Digest* that caffeine, found in all coffee, has the ability to make your heart beat 15 per cent faster, make your lungs work 13 times harder and make your stomach secrete up to 400 per cent more hydrochloric acid. Coffee has been linked to ulcers as well as heart disease. Caffeine naturally occurs in coffee beans, cocoa beans, tea leaves and cola nuts.

Because of the harmful effects caffeine may have on our systems,* more and more people are discovering 'grain coffee'. This tastes very much like coffee but contains cereals, fruit and roots. It is available in both instant and regular form. The instant is most convenient in dessert making. All recipes when listing grain coffee refer to the instant kind.

When a recipe calls for at least ½ cup additional liquid, regular grain coffee may be substituted for the instant.

To prepare regular grain coffee: Bring liquid to a boil, add grain coffee and percolate or simmer 10 minutes. Strain. Substitute for the liquid called for in a recipe.

Grain Syrup

Grain syrup is a natural sweetener that can be made at home. It can be used as a topping for a cake, or in the same way as maple syrup or honey. Make a large quantity so that you can try it in various ways to see which suits you best.

To prepare, see p. 98.

Hard Cider (see also Apple Cider)

Hard cider may be made by keeping cider in a loosely closed container at room temperature for two to three days. Leave until the top of the cider is foamy and it has a sharp fermented taste.

Kanten

See Agar-agar.

Kuzu

Kuzu (not to be confused with arrowroot) is the powdered root of the wild

arrowroot. It is gathered in the high mountains of the Far East. Used medicinally for many years in the Orient, kuzu is traditionally taken as a thick beverage to soothe and strengthen the intestines and other internal organs. It is available at most natural and health food stores. Kuzu can be used as a thickening agent in place of arrowroot. When substituting, use two-thirds the amount of kuzu as arrowroot.

Maltose

Maltose is a combination of sprouted wheat and freshly cooked sweet rice. It is allowed to ferment at a high temperature until the starch turns into sugar. At that point, it is cooked, strained and cooled. As it is highly concentrated and sweeter than barley malt extract, I recommend it as a sweetener for all types of baking and cooking. Usually found in Chinese or Asian food stores.

Maple Syrup

Maple trees are native to the north-eastern part of the United States. The Indians used the sweet sap of the tree for making sugar and syrup. The sap of the maple usually flows in early spring, for three to four weeks.

The Indians tapped the tree by cutting through the bark and guiding the sap into containers, using curved pieces of bark. The sap was concentrated by dropping hot stones into it, thereby boiling out the liquid. Freezing this and removing the ice that formed on top produced sugar.

Today, maple syrup is extracted by drilling holes into the side of the tree and inserting wooden taps to let the sap flow out into buckets.

The sudden change in temperature from a warm day to a freezing night stops the sap from flowing, and the warmth starts it again in the morning.

After the buckets have been filled, the sap is taken to a 'sugar house', poured into large containers and cooked over fires, which boil the sap down and concentrate it. It takes 150 litres (about 40 gallons) of sap (the sap of about 9 maple trees) to make almost 4 litres (about 1 gallon) of syrup.

Unfortunately, today many trees are being injected with formaldehyde so that the sap will not coagulate. Formaldehyde not only feeds into the syrup that is sold, but is harmful to the tree, shortening its life by many years.

Syrups are graded A, B and C, depending on the temperature and length of boiling. Grade A Extra Fancy is made from the sweetest sap and has been boiled the longest amount of time. The lighter the colour, the better the quality.

Rich in minerals, maple syrup is one of the few naturally occurring sweeteners found today. Because it is so concentrated, it goes a long way. So remember, use maple syrup sparingly.

Miso

Miso is a paste made from fermented soybeans, sea salt, *koji*, spring water, and sometimes a grain. It can be used in the place of sea salt, but mainly it is used as a protein supplement in salad dressings, soups, sauces and sourdough breads. Miso should never be boiled, since boiling destroys the vital enzymes. Simmering reduces its lactic acid content. Natto miso also has ginger and barley malt added which makes it even more delicious in desserts. White miso is a sweeter, younger and lighter coloured miso which complements many desserts such as apple pie.

For a richer flavour in desserts, try using miso in place of sea salt (1 tablespoon miso equals ½ teaspoon sea salt).

Molasses

There are at least four kinds of molasses available today. 'Unsulphured' molasses is said to be made from the juice of the sun-ripened cane. 'Sulphured' molasses, believed to be a by-product of refined sugar, picks up sulphur from the fumes used in the process of converting sugar cane into sugar. 'Black-strap' molasses, another by-product of the sugar industry, results from boiling down the sugar several times during the refining process. It is the discarded residue of the cane syrup, after the sugar crystals have been extracted.

Sorghum molasses is the concentrated juice of sorghum, a relative of the millet family, a corn-like cereal grain. The sorghum stems are crushed in a way similar to sugar cane, and boiled to obtain sorghum molasses.

Corn syrup or corn sugar is a product of cornstarch produced by treating corn with sulphuric or hydrochloric acid, then neutralizing and bleaching it with other chemicals. Because it costs less to produce than cane or beet sugar, it is used in tremendous quantities in canned fruits, juices, pastries and other processed foods.

Mu Tea

Mu tea, popular for its strengthening qualities as well as its unusual taste, is a blend of 9 or 16 herbs. It may be served either hot or cold, plain or mixed with apple juice. Because of its delicate flavour, it may be used as a liquid in various desserts, in place of, or in addition to, other spices. It adds zest to fillings, pie crusts, pastries, biscuits and even cakes. Try substituting it for part of the liquid suggested. To prepare, boil 1 bag of mu tea in 4-5 cups of water for 20 minutes. Let simmer for 10-15 minutes. You may re-use the bag to make a weaker tea.

Nut Butters

See Seed and Nut Butters.

Nut Milk

You can make your own nut milk by using any nuts such as blanched almonds, roasted cashews, hazelnuts, sunflower seeds, etc., and hot water or apple juice and a blender. (See p. 232.) The skins of almonds are rather bitter and contain a large quantity of prussic acid which should be

avoided. Before roasting, cashew nuts contain a burning acid from which indelible ink is made.

Nuts (see also Seed and Nut Butters)
Various kinds of nuts can be used creatively to enhance texture as well as flavour in dessert making.

Shells of walnuts or almonds are sometimes bleached, and shelled nuts sometimes bathed in chemicals to help dissolve the outer skins. However, it is possible to find nuts that are organically grown and not adulterated with chemical preservatives.

Roasting imparts a richer taste to any dessert which uses nuts, and is essential for cashews. Prepare as follows.

Place the nuts on a baking sheet, giving them plenty of room. Preheat the oven 10 minutes at 160°F (325°F). Bake nuts, stirring once or twice, until lightly toasted. Over-roasting will make them bitter. Cool and store in the refrigerator in an airtight glass jar if not to be used immediately.

Do not roast nuts too far in advance because they tend to get soggy and stale. Nuts that are to be crushed, chopped or ground should be roasted just before using. Crushing the nuts releases their oils, enhancing their flavour.

Oats or Barley (Rolled)
Rolled oats or barley are not just a popular breakfast cereal. They are used in many cakes, biscuits, pie crusts, fillings and toppings as well.

Use only 'rolled oats', or 'old-fashioned oats', as 'instant oats' or 'quick cooking oats' may have been heavily processed.

Oil (see also Oil, p. 50)
The best oils for baking and dessert making are expeller pressed unrefined safflower, sesame or corn oil. They are nutritionally rich and unprocessed, giving a delicate, almost butter-like effect in cakes, and making the flakiest pastry dough imaginable.

Keep refrigerated after opening.

Orange Flower Water
A fragrant liquid distilled from orange blossoms. It is used to flavour syrups, cakes and biscuits.

Rind
Rind is the grated skin of an orange, tangerine or lemon.

I searched many health food stores for organic flavourings in the form of dried orange, tangerine or lemon rind when I began to bake commercially. The only rind available was coloured, sugared and chemically treated, so I had to make my own. Here is a quick and easy method for making your own rind. Made this way, rind can be stored indefinitely, so make extra.

1. Slice an organic fruit into quarters.

2. Peel off the skin and discard the white pulp beneath the skin (this white is very bitter and should not be used).

3. Dry the skin outside in the sun on a bamboo mat so that the air circulates all round until hard and dry.

4. Blend the skin in a blender 3 to 5 minutes until it turns into a fine powder, or grate the rind on the smallest side of a grater.

5. Store in a tightly sealed container or a paper bag in a cool, dark place.

Rolled Oats or Barley
See Oats.

Rose Water
Distilled from fragrant rose petals, rose water is used for both savoury and sweet dishes.

Sea Salt
See Salt, p. 230.

Seed and Nut Butters (see also Tahini)
Seed or nut butters are made by grinding roasted or unroasted seeds or nuts to a creamy texture. The most commonly used are peanut butter, almond butter, cashew butter, sunflower butter and tahini (sesame).

Tahini is made from hulled sesame seeds whereas sesame butter is made from whole, roasted sesame seeds. Substituting one seed or nut butter for another can enhance flavour and add variety in texture to your desserts.

Seeds
Sesame seeds not only provide us with sesame oil, sesame butter and tahini, but also lend a decorative effect to glazes and any pastries, as well as a crunchy texture to biscuits. They are a rich source of calcium, vitamin E, and protein. Sesame seeds should be lightly roasted before using.

Sunflower, poppy and pumpkin (pepita) seeds are also rich in oil and delicious in biscuits, cakes, breads, confectionery and pastries. They make a fine snack that is rich in vitamin E, and can lend an attractive finish as well. Sunflower and poppy seeds, too, should be lightly roasted before using, to aid digestion.

Semolina
Semolina is only the endosperm part of the wheat. It can be used in cakes, puddings, biscuits or cereals. It tends to make cakes lighter when it is substituted for part of the whole wheat flour.

Soy Milk
Increasing in popularity in the West, it has been a staple food for many hundreds of years among Asian people. Rich in protein, low in fat, it has

served as the backbone of most Eastern diets as a daily source of protein (see p. 233) and is increasingly popular for infants and allergy prone individuals.

Tahini

Tahini is made from hulled sesame seeds which have been lightly toasted, and contains lecithin, phosphorus, calcium, iron and vitamins B and E, and protein. Tahini that appears loose and liquidy may have been adulterated with poor quality oil and chemicals.

It can be blended with cooked oatmeal, raisins and vanilla, used as a milk substitute, spread on bread or crackers or used in baking as a flavouring, filling, icing or topping.

If tightly covered and stored in a cool place, it should keep for many months. Natural separation should occur. Stir before using.

Tofu (Soybean Cheese)

Tofu (pronounced 'dofu' in Chinese) can be purchased at most health, Asian or Oriental food stores. It is made from soybeans by soaking, grinding and boiling. Then it is strained through a fine cloth bag, separating the outside of the bean from the milk. To this liquid (soy milk), lemon juice, vinegar or natural *nigari* (seawater extract) is added, which acts as a coagulant. The liquid is covered and set aside for several minutes. The whey is removed and the tofu is placed into settling boxes which have holes to allow the excess whey to drain off. It is pressed until a solid block is formed and then cut under water and allowed to soak 1 hour before being packaged.

Tofu is high in protein, has no cholesterol and is low in kilojoules and fats. It is used daily in the Orient as a staple form of low cost protein. Its light, delicate texture embellishes any dessert as a cream, filling, or custard.

Remember to keep tofu refrigerated and covered with water. Change the water when cloudy, or every other day.

Vanilla Essence or Extract

Vanilla is a natural flavouring found in the form of a bean or liquid. Most of the vanilla available in supermarkets today is artificially produced with chemicals and boosted with vanillin, which is made from a coal derivative.

There are two different 'natural' vanillas available: vanilla essence and vanilla extract. These differ only in the way that they are made. Vanilla essence is made by an extraction method that first soaks the bean in an alcohol based solution, then drains off the liquid and adds caramel colouring to it (to stabilize the colour because each batch can come out looking different).

The second process begins by boiling down vanilla beans with water. The same colouring is then added to the mixture to standardize it. This is known as vanilla extract.

If pure vanilla is unavailable, substitute a bean for the liquid and pre-pare as follows.

Slit the bean lengthwise on one side only.

Add water to cover, simmer at least 15 minutes. (The longer you cook it, the better the flavour.)

Remove the bean and use the liquid. Dry the bean and re-use it again.

If neither bean nor extract is available, substitute grated orange or lemon rind, brandy or rum, orange flower water or rose water to taste.

Yeast
See p. 140.

2. LAYER AFTER LAYER:
Cakes for All Occasions

*At the end of a meal, when our appetite is usually more than satisfied,
the surprise dessert awakens an unknown desire for a little bit more. Cakes usually
reserved for special occasions such as birthdays, weddings or anniversaries,
can be used any time for any occasion. It's the icing or glaze that can adapt
the dessert to any kind of meal. Any leftover cake can be re-dressed and
served the following day or cooked up into a delightful fruit pudding.
Whatever the reasons, you will find a cake for all of them here and you may even
bake a cake and then look for an excuse to serve it!*

LEAVENING *(how cakes rise)*

MOST of these cake recipes rely on eggs, home-made baking powder and/or yeast for lightness in texture. Because the flour that is recommended has not been pre-sifted, bleached, bromated or stripped of all the bran, it reacts differently with other ingredients. Most of the cakes will not rise 10 cm (3-4 in); they will be lower than the normal 'layer cake'. If you wish a higher cake, bake three layers instead of two, or increase the amount of yeast suggested by half, or double the amount of eggs.

Yeast
See p. 140 'Higher and Higher' for instruction in using yeast in baking.

Baking Powder
Sift with flour or dry ingredients.

EGGS

How Old Is That Egg?
A *very fresh egg* has a tiny air pocket. It will sink and lie horizontally on the bottom of the bowl. When cracked open, the yolk will stand high and the white will be compact. These eggs are the most desirable where appearance counts. They poach and fry especially well.

In a *week-old egg,* the air pocket has expanded, and the egg will lie tilted in the water with its rounded end up. The white will be more fluid and less cohesive, making the egg easier to separate. Because the white no longer adheres too closely to the shell, a hard-boiled week-old egg will be easier to peel.

A *2- to 3-week-old egg* will stand upright in the water. When cracked open, the yolk will spread out and the watery white will run. These eggs are best used where appearance is less important – in baking or sauces. After four weeks, the egg will completely float. If it does, throw it out.

In all recipes, eggs should be used at room temperature. If they are cold, they should be warmed as follows. Combine eggs and sweetener in a mixing bowl. Stir for 1 minute. Set the bowl over a pan of hot water on low heat until contents are lukewarm. Stir occasionally to prevent them from cooking or sticking. Take off heat.

To use whole eggs in baking a cake, beat with a hand beater, wire whisk or electric mixer until the eggs have almost doubled in volume, and are thick, fluffy and filled with air. Do not overmix when folding in with other ingredients, or you will force the air out of the eggs, and the result will be a heavier cake.

Separated Eggs
If you separate the eggs, the batter will usually be lighter.

Crack the egg and let white fall into a mixing bowl, catching yolk on half of shell. Transfer yolk to other half of shell, alternating back and forth, letting remainder of white fall from shell into bowl.

Place yolk in a separate bowl. Mix with a fork and add the other ingredients called for.

Using hand beater, wire whisk or electric beater, beat egg whites and sea salt together until whites stand up in firm peaks.

Fold whites carefully into batter by hand (p. 18), or with a rubber spatula, to retain as much air as possible.

Bake batter as quickly as possible without banging or opening the oven door until at least half of the baking time suggested has elapsed.

SWEETENING

MOST of the recipes call for a minimum amount of sweetener, allowing the flavour and taste of the other ingredients to come through. However, you may want to use more sweetener than is suggested.

Add as much sweetener (maple syrup, fruit juice concentrates, rice honey, molasses, barley malt, maltose) as you like, or supplement with apple butter, apple cider jelly, amazake or fruit puree, decreasing the amount of liquid proportionally. Oil the cup before measuring. (See Sweetness Equivalency Chart, p. 12.)

READY OR NOT?

1. Insert a thin wire cake-tester or metal skewer into the centre of the cake. It will come out dry when the cake is ready.

2. Press a fingertip lightly in the centre of the cake. The centre will spring back when the cake is done.

3. A leavened cake will usually pull away from the sides of the pan.

REMOVING CAKES FROM PAN

RUN a knife around the edge of the cake. Place a wire rack on top of the cake in its pan. Invert rack, pan and cake simultaneously. Let stand until the cake begins to contract away from the sides of the pan. If cake does not begin to slip down out of the pan and onto the rack, take a cold damp sponge and run it over the bottom of the pan several times. Then with the handle of a wooden spoon, tap the bottom of the pan gently.

Egg cakes should be left to cool in the oven with the temperature turned off and the oven door ajar. This helps prevent cake from sinking.

If you are using a baba form (pan with a hole in the centre), set the tube on the neck of a bottle so that air can circulate around it while cooling.

FRUITS RANKED ACCORDING TO SWEETNESS (NATURAL SUGAR CONTENT) GRAMS PER 100 GRAMS

	Sweetest
Dried fruits (e.g., dates)	63.9
Bananas	16
Grapes (white)	16
Grapes (black)	16
Mangoes	15
Nectarines	12
Cherries	12
Apples	12
Pineapple	12
Pears	11
Figs (green)	10
Peaches	9
Oranges	9
Tangerines	8
Apricots	7
Currants (black)	7
Blackberries	6
Quinces	6
Strawberries	6
Currants (white)	6
Raspberries	6
Grapefruit	5
Cantaloupe (rock melon)	5
Watermelon	5
Honeydew	5
Currants (red)	4
Cranberries	4
Lemons	3
Rhubarb	1
	Least Sweet

When using a springform pan, place it on a wire rack and let stand until the cake begins to contract away from the side of the pan. Run a knife around the side of the pan, unclip and remove the side. Allow to cool before removing the bottom.

Cake Baking Advice

A cake may have:	Oil Cakes	No-Oil Cakes
A hard top crust	Temperature too high Overbaking	Temperature too high Overbaking
A sticky top crust	Too much sweetener Insufficient baking	Too much sweetener Insufficient baking
A humped or cracked top	Too much flour or too little liquid Overmixing Batter not spread evenly in pan	Too much flour or sweetener Temperature too high
One side higher	Batter not spread evenly Uneven pan Pan too close to side of oven Oven rack or range not level Uneven oven heat	Uneven pan Oven rack or range not level
A soggy layer at bottom	Too much liquid Underbeaten eggs Undermixing Insufficient baking	Too many eggs or egg yolks Undermixing Underbeaten egg yolks
Fallen	Too much sweetener, liquid, leavening or oil Too little flour Temperature too low Insufficient baking	Too much sweetener Overbeaten egg whites Underbeaten egg yolks Use of oiled pans Insufficient baking

Coarse grain	Use of whole wheat bread flour
	    instead of cake flour
	Too much leavening
	Insufficient creaming
	Undermixing
	Temperature too low
		Use of whole wheat bread
		    flour instead of cake flour
		Omitting cream of tartar
		Undermixing

Tough crumb	Too much flour Too many eggs Too little sweetener or oil Overmixing Temperature too high	Too little sweetener Overbeaten egg whites Underbeaten egg yolks Omitting cream of tartar Overmixing Temperature too high Overbaking
A heavy, compact quality	Too much liquid or oil Too many eggs Too little leavening or flour Overmixing Temperature too high	Overbeaten egg whites Underbeaten egg yolks Overmixing
Crumbled or fallen apart	Too much sweetener, leavening or oil Undermixing Improper pan treatment Improper cooling	
Fallen out of pan before completely cooled		Too much sweetener Use of oiled pans Insufficient baking

FORGET ME KNOTS

1. Liquid content will vary according to the temperature of the room, the moisture and milling of the flour, and the general weather conditions of the day.
2. Preheat the oven 15 minutes before baking. An overheated oven may produce a cracked, heavy cake, and an underheated oven will produce a soggy cake.
3. Use all ingredients at room temperature so that they will blend more evenly.
4. Unless otherwise specified, the best oils to use for all baking are expeller pressed unrefined corn, sesame or safflower oil. Too much oil may cause the cake to be too crumbly to handle.
5. Sift flour before measuring, never shaking the flour down into the cup after sifting; sift only to get out the lumps. Do not separate the bran from the wheat except for very delicate cakes or pastries. Add the bran back to the sifted flour (or reserve for puddings, breads), before folding it into the batter.
6. Too much flour (or too little liquid) will make the cake uneven and dry.
7. Bulgur wheat, ground nuts or couscous add lightness to unleavened cakes.
8. When adding eggs to an eggless recipe, decrease the amount of liquid accordingly (1 egg = ¼-⅕ cup liquid).
9. When using fewer eggs than called for, substitute 1 teaspoon arrowroot or 2 teaspoons whole wheat pastry or cake flour for each omitted egg.
10. Use ½ teaspoon lemon juice to every 3 egg whites to make a stiffer white, with larger volume and greater stability.
11. When measuring liquid sweeteners, oil the measuring cup to prevent the sticky liquid from adhering to the cup.
12. Wooden utensils are preferable because metal can alter the taste.
13. When using a hand beater, extra time should be allotted for beating.
14. Overbeating will break down air bubbles after they have been formed, leaving a heavy, dry cake (yeasted batters excluded).
15. To prevent cake from sticking to the bottom of the pan, dust a little flour over the oiled bottom and sides of the pan.
16. When placing batters containing eggs in a pan, *do not pat down* batter or bang pan; this will cause the air in the eggs to escape.
17. When a cake sticks to a pan, wrap a cold damp cloth around the pan for a few minutes, and it should come out more easily.
18. To keep a cake from drying up, place an apple or orange in the cake box, and keep it in a cool place.
19. An old-fashioned way to preserve fruit cake up to one year is as follows. Pour 1 teaspoonful of brandy over the underside of the cake, and let it soak. Wrap it up in a clean cloth which has been sprinkled with brandy. Place it in an earthenware crock with a tight lid; place a fresh apple on top of the cake, and cover. Once a week, set the crock on a range until it is warmed, taking out the apple before warming. Place a fresh apple in the crock every 2 weeks and renew the brandy application as well. (Hard cider may be substituted for brandy.)
20. Do not oil cake tins when preparing sponge cakes as they need to cling to the sides of the pan to rise.
21. Cool all cakes, pastries, pies and tarts on a rack so that air can circulate completely around them. This prevents moisture from accumulating on the bottom.

OIL CAKES

ALMOND CAKE

¹/₂ cup sweetener (p. 12)
6 eggs, separated
¹/₂ cup oil
1¹/₂ cups sifted whole wheat pastry or cake flour
2 teaspoons cinnamon
1 teaspoon ground coriander
1 cup roasted, crushed blanched almonds
2 teaspoons lemon rind
Pinch of sea salt
1 teaspoon lemon juice
Pinch of sea salt
1 teaspoon almond essence
1 quantity Chestnut Icing (p. 37)

1. Beat sweetener and yolks together until the mixture resembles thick cream. Slowly drip in the oil and continue beating until fully absorbed.

2. Sift together next three ingredients three times. Add almonds, rind and salt, and fold into first mixture.

3. Beat egg whites with lemon juice and pinch of sea salt till peaked. Gently fold about ¹/₃ of the egg whites into the batter and then add almond essence and the remaining whites to batter, folding gently. Preheat oven to 180°C (350°F).

4. Bake in oiled and floured cake tins for 45-50 minutes or until cake tests done. Turn off oven and leave door slightly ajar. Leave cake there until cool. Remove from tin when cool and ice. Prepare icing.

VARIATIONS

Special party cake: Add to basic recipe 3 eggs and ¹/₂ cup more toasted crushed nuts or coconut. This will yield a larger layer or 3 smaller ones.

Poppy seed: Add ¹/₂ cup roasted poppy seeds before folding in flour. (Decrease flour by ¹/₂ cup.)

Nut: Add ¹/₂ cup more roasted crushed nuts – blanched almonds, walnuts, pecans or cashews – before folding in flour (use ¹/₂ cup less flour). Or prepare ¹/₂ cup cooked chestnuts (follow instructions for Chestnut Cream, p. 90). Add to mixture before folding in flour.

Dried fruit: Marinate ¹/₄ cup dried fruit in fruit juice or cider to cover overnight. Squeeze out liquid; dice fruit and toss with flour before folding into rest of ingredients.

Spice: Sift in the flours before adding to egg mixture 2 teaspoons cinnamon or dried mint, ¹/₄ teaspoon cloves, 1 teaspoon ginger and 1 teaspoon coriander.

Coffee: Add ¹/₂ cup instant grain coffee to dry ingredients before folding into eggs. Decrease flour by ¹/₂ cup.

CHESTNUT ICING

EF   GF

1 cup tahini or any nut butter
³/4 cup Chestnut Cream (p. 90)
1/2 cup sweetener (p. 12)
1 tablespoon grated orange rind
2-3 tablespoons carob flour
1 teaspoon shoyu or tamari or pinch sea salt
2 teaspoons vanilla or rum
1 cup roasted crushed hazelnuts
Fruit juice as needed
Fresh fruit for decoration

Blend all ingredients together slowly, adding hot water or fruit juice until desired consistency is reached. Spread some of the icing between layers and sandwich cake together. Spread icing around sides of cake and then roll cake sides in crushed nuts. Cover top with remaining icing and decorate with fresh fruit.

VARIATIONS

Chestnut marzipan icing: To make a marzipan that you can roll out, do not add too much liquid to Chestnut Icing. (It may not be necessary to add any at all.) Roll out on greaseproof paper to desired thickness and size. Place on top of cake, then cream the rest of the icing with hot liquid and pipe it around the sides of the cake. Press almonds around top. Decorate with fresh fruit.

Tofu sour cream: Combine Tofu Sour Cream (p. 95), 1/2 cup apples and 1/2 teaspoon cinnamon or ginger. Spoon this topping over the cake 10 minutes before the cake is done. Lower temperature to 150°C (300°F) and bake until browned.

Vanilla: Increase vanilla to 2 tablespoons.

Tangerine, orange or lemon: Add 2 teaspoons more of tangerine, orange or lemon rind, and 3 tablespoons juice of fruit; or add juice and rind of half a grated orange, lemon or tangerine.

CAROB SOUR CREAM CAKE

Follow recipe for Almond Cake (p. 36), adding 2 tablespoons extra sweetener and 1/2 cup carob flour to dry ingredients before folding in eggs. Prepare 1 cup Tofu Sour Cream (p. 95) and spoon on top of cake 10 minutes before baking time has elapsed.

COFFEE SOUR CREAM CAKE

Follow recipe for Almond Cake (p. 36). Combine 1 cup Tofu Sour Cream (p. 95) and 1-2 tablespoons extra sweetener. Add this to eggs or egg yolks in basic recipe. Also add ½ cup instant grain coffee (p. 24) and ¼ cup additional whole wheat pastry or cake flour to dry ingredients before folding into egg mixture.

CRUMB COFFEE SOUR CREAM CAKE

Prepare 1 cup Crumb Topping (p. 96). Follow recipe for Almond Cake. Add grain coffee and sweetener as in method above. Pour half of the batter into pan, sprinkle half of topping over it and cover it with remaining batter. Spoon Tofu Sour Cream on top of cake and sprinkle remaining Crumb Topping over it 10 minutes before baking time has elapsed.

PETIT FOURS

Petit fours are made by cutting large cakes into smaller, different shapes – diamond, square, round, triangular or rectangular, or use large biscuit cutters. They are delightful to serve at children's parties or as small dessert cakes for unexpected guests. It is a great way to 'dress up' leftovers and serve as a new dessert to friends and family. For example:
METHOD A
 1. Cut cake into thirds.
 2. Cut one part into eight squares.
 3. Cut another section into small rectangles.
 4. Cut remaining third into triangles and diamonds by cutting diagonally in strips, then cut again diagonally.
 5. Dip squares into any glaze (p. 79), sprinkle crushed nuts on top.
 6. Spread any icing (p. 74) on top of rectangles.
 7. Decorate with raisins (features of a face), orange, tangerine or lemon rind, crushed roasted nuts, seeds, mint.
 8. Spread any cream (p. 89) on top and sides of diamonds and trim the edges with seeds or crushed nuts.
 9. Spread with Basic Tofu Cream (p. 93).
METHOD B
 1. Cut cake into 6 mm (¼ in) slices.
 2. Spread five slices with Fruit Puree (p. 85).
 3. Stack six slices to make six layers.
 4. Cut into 2.5 cm (1 in) slices and then cut slices into 5 cm (2 in) cubes.
 5. Top with any crushed, roasted nut, seed, lemon, orange, or tangerine rind or shredded coconut.

FORBIDDEN FANTASY CAKE

GF*
4 cups dried apricots soaked in fruit juice to cover
grated ginger to taste (optional)
1/2 cup oil
12 eggs, separated
1-1 1/2 cups maple syrup
3 teaspoons vanilla
1 cup carob flour
6 cups ground nuts
*5 cups desiccated coconut or 3 cups semolina **
1 1/2 teaspoons cream of tartar
Pinch of sea salt
Fruit juice as needed
CAROB ICING
EF   GF
1 1/2-2 cups fruit juice
3/4-1 cup maple syrup to taste
3 cups carob flour
1 cup tahini or other nut butter such as cashew or hazelnut
2-3 teaspoons brandy or rum for flavouring

* Gluten free if using coconut.

1. Bring apricots and juice (soaking) to the boil. Simmer uncovered until there is no liquid remaining. (You may stir in a few teaspoons grated ginger after cooking for a more exotic flavour.) Set aside to cool.

2. Beat together the oil, egg yolks, and maple syrup for at least five minutes or until fluffy and light. Add flavouring.

3. Mix together the carob flour, ground nuts and coconut. Beat egg whites until fluffy, add cream of tartar, sea salt and beat again till peaked.

4. Combine the yolk mixture with the dry one, then fold in one-third of the egg whites until they are no longer visible. Fold in the remaining egg whites adding fruit juice if necessary until mixture has a thick batter-like consistency.

5. Oil and flour three 19 cm (8 in) round springform tins. Preheat the oven to 180°C (350°F).

6. Spoon the batter into the three tins, and bake 30 minutes. Test with a cake skewer to see if the centre is done. Turn off the oven and leave the cakes in the oven with the door slightly ajar. When they are cool, remove from the tin. Cool before filling.

DECORATING THE CAKE

1. Combine all the carob icing ingredients and mix till creamy and smooth adjusting the consistency with fruit juice. Flavour with brandy or rum.

2. Ice cake, put extra tahini in pastry bag and pipe in rows onto the top of the cake about 2.5 cm (1 in) apart. Run a skewer across the cake in the opposite direction to that which you piped in.

3. To decorate the cake use fruit in season. We used strawberries, rock melon, pineapple and kiwifruit as it was summertime. Choose fruits that appeal to the eye as well as the palate. Cut them into decorative shapes and place around and on the top of the cake just before serving.

CUPCAKES

Use any cake recipe. Fill oiled cupcake tin half full with cake batter.

Put 1 tablespoon fruit puree, cream or custard in centre. Cover with remaining batter and bake.

CUPCAKE SURPRISE

1. Bake cupcake. Cool and cut a thin slice off the top.
2. Scoop out the centre and fill with custard, cream or puree. Replace the top, glaze, and serve.

MANGO-ALMOND LEMON CAKE

EF

1 1/2 tablespoons dry yeast
4 cups fruit juice
1/2 cup sweetener (p. 12)
3 cups sifted whole wheat cake or pastry flour
1 cup arrowroot flour
1/4 cup oil
2 blended lemons, including skin
1 tablespoon vanilla
Pinch of sea salt

1. Dilute yeast in 1 cup warm fruit juice and let sit until bubbly.
2. Add enough flour to form a thin batter. Cover and let rise in a warm place until it doubles in size.
3. Add the rest of the ingredients including 3 cups fruit juice, and beat well. It should resemble a thick pancake batter in consistency, thick enough to drop from a wooden spoon with difficulty (adjust flour-liquid content accordingly).
4. Preheat the oven to 180°C (350°F) and oil a small round or square cake pan. Place batter in pan, cover and let rise in a warm place until batter almost doubles.
5. Bake about 30-40 minutes, or until cake is springy to the touch and pulls away from the side of the pan. Remove from oven and place on a wire rack to cool.

Opposite: Forbidden Fantasy Cake (page 39)

MANGO-ALMOND TOPPING

EF   GF

2 tablespoons oil
2 cups sliced and cored mangoes
1/2 cup roasted chopped blanched almonds
1/2 cup raisins or currants
1 teaspoon ground ginger
1 teaspoon cinnamon
Pinch of sea salt

Heat oil in a skillet. When oil is hot, sauté mangoes lightly. Add nuts, raisins or currants, ginger, cinnamon and salt. Cook on a low heat for 5 minutes. Spoon over cake.

PECAN APPLE CAKE

2 teaspoons dried yeast
1/2 cup maple syrup
1 1/2 cups whole wheat cake or pastry flour
1/4 cup oil
2 eggs, separated
Juice of half lemon
Pinch of salt
1 teaspoon cinnamon
1/2 cup roasted, crushed pecans
4 apples, peeled, cored and halved

1. Dissolve yeast in 2 tablespoons warm water and 1 tablespoon maple syrup. Cream until there are no lumps. Add 1 tablespoon flour, stir and set aside in a warm place. Cover and wait 5-10 minutes or until yeast mixture bubbles.

2. Meanwhile combine oil and the rest of the sweetener together and beat until creamy and fluffy. Add egg yolks and beat until mixture resembles cream. Add juice of lemon, salt and cinnamon. Slowly drip in yeast mixture.

3. Sift flour over first mixture and fold into batter, along with pecans. Whip egg whites with a pinch of salt until peaked and fold into flour combination, mixing only enough to combine the ingredients.

4. Spoon batter into an oiled cake pan. Slice the apple halves crosswise into fan-like shapes leaving the slices attached at the bottom. Arrange the fans on top of the batter. After cake has risen at least a third in size, bake in a 180°C (350°F) preheated oven 45-50 minutes. Remove from oven and cool on a wire rack before removing from pan.

Opposite: Carrot Pecan Cake (page 46)

BLACK AND WHITE CHERRY CAKE

This makes a wonderful birthday cake, but you needn't wait till you have that excuse to make it.

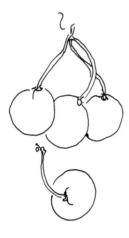

WHITE LAYER
3 eggs, separated
1/2 cup oil
1 teaspoon vanilla
Pinch of sea salt
1/2 teaspoon lemon juice
1/2 cup sweetener (p. 12)
1/2 cup sifted whole wheat cake or pastry flour
1/2 cup ground nuts
Fruit juice if necessary
1/2 cup pitted, finely diced cherries
BLACK LAYER
3 eggs, separated
1/3 cup oil
2 teaspoons orange rind
Pinch of sea salt
1 1/2 cups Raisin Puree (see Fruit Puree, p. 85)
1 cup sifted whole wheat cake or pastry flour or 1/2 cup whole wheat pastry or cake flour, 1/3 cup carob flour and 1/2 cup maple syrup (omit Raisin Puree)
1 cup ground nuts
ICING
2 cups Rich Icing (p. 75)

WHITE LAYER
   1. Combine yolks, oil and vanilla. Stir and set aside.
   2. Oil and lightly flour two 18 cm (7 in) round springform pans.
   3. Beat whites gradually, adding sea salt and lemon juice, until they are stiff. Add sweetener slowly, beating continuously until whites peak. Fold a quarter of the whites into the yolks. Pour this mixture over the remaining whites.
   4. Fold in the sifted flour and nuts gently until the whites are no longer visible. *Do not overmix.* Gradually add diced cherries.
   5. Preheat the oven to 180°C (350°F).
   6. Pour into pan. Do not pat down. Bake 30-40 minutes at 180°C (350°F), or until cake is puffy and pulls away from the sides of the pan. Turn off oven, leave door slightly ajar until cake is cool.
BLACK LAYER
Follow the directions for white layer, substituting in appropriate places.
PUTTING IT ALL TOGETHER
When both layers have cooled, place the black layer top side down, and spread icing over it. Place the white layer on top and ice the sides of the cake. You may wish to roll the sides in crushed nuts, rind etc. Cover top with icing and decorate as desired. Refer to Chapter 3 for other decorating ideas.

VARIATION
Substitute 1 cup arrowroot for whole wheat cake or pastry flour, in black layer. Bake at 180°C (350°F) 10-12 minutes or until almost solid. Over-baking may make the cake rubbery.

APRICOT HAZELNUT FANTASY

Souen is a small Japanese natural food restaurant, located on Manhattan's upper West Side. Many years ago when my friend Taki decided to open this restaurant, he asked me to be the baker. This was my first venture into the world of professional dessert making.

In memory of Taki.

EF

1 tablespoon dried yeast
1-2 cups warm fruit juice
2 cups whole wheat cake or pastry flour
2 tablespoons oil
1 teaspoon vanilla
Pinch of sea salt
1/3 cup sweetener (p. 12)
APRICOT-HAZELNUT TOPPING
2 tablespoons oil
4-6 apricots sliced and pitted
1-2 tablespoons sweetener (p. 12)
1/2 cup roasted chopped hazelnuts
1/2 cup raisins or currants
2 teaspoons cinnamon
Pinch of sea salt

TOPPING
Heat oil in a skillet. When oil is hot, sauté apricots lightly. Add sweetener, nuts, raisins or currants, cinnamon and sea salt. Cook on a low heat for 5 minutes. Set aside.

CAKE
1. Combine first two ingredients. Set aside until it bubbles. Mix. Add half the flour and beat. Cover and set aside to rise.

2. Preheat oven to 180°C (350°F). Oil and lightly flour a 20 cm (8 in) cake pan or two small ones. After batter has doubled, add the rest of the ingredients, and beat with a wooden spoon about 10 minutes. The consistency should be that of a thick pancake batter (adjust flour-liquid content accordingly).

3. Place topping in the oiled cake pan. Pour batter over topping. Cover and let rise in a warm place, until almost double in size.

4. Bake about 30-45 minutes, or until top is slightly browned and springy to the touch. Remove from oven and place on a wire rack to cool. Serve upside down, with Basic Tofu Cream (p. 93).

CHERRY ALMOND SURPRISE

EF

2 cups uncooked couscous
4 tablespoons oil
1/2 cup blanched, roasted, crushed almonds or hazelnuts
1 teaspoon sea salt
5 cups boiling fruit juice
6 tablespoons agar-agar flakes
1 tablespoon dried mint
Cherry Almond Glaze (p. 80)

1. Sauté couscous until well coated with oil (2 tablespoons oil for 1 cup couscous). Place in a mixing bowl, add nuts, sea salt and 3 cups juice. Stir well. Set aside.

2. Combine agar-agar with remaining juice. Bring to a boil, lower heat and cook together with mint until agar-agar dissolves. Add couscous to agar-agar mixture and stir until well combined.

3. Rinse a mould under cold running water; dry well and oil. Place couscous into mould immediately after cooking (if too much time elapses, the mixture will begin to set). Cool. Prepare Cherry Almond Glaze. Spoon over cake just before serving.

DATE PINE NUT CAKE

GF

1 cup hot fruit juice mixed with 2 tablespoons carob flour
1 cup chopped dates
1/3 cup oil
1/2 cup maple syrup
3 eggs, separated
1 tablespoon vanilla
1 cup brown rice flour
1 cup lightly roasted, ground pine nuts
Pinch of sea salt

1. Pour the hot fruit juice – carob combination over the dates and set aside 10 minutes.

2. Cream the oil, maple syrup and the egg yolks until light. Add the vanilla and carob date mixture. Add the brown rice flour and nuts.

3. Beat the egg whites with sea salt till peaked and fold into the cake. Oil and flour cake tin. Spoon batter into tin. Bake in preheated 180°C (350°F) oven 30-40 minutes.

4. Turn off oven and leave door slightly ajar till cake cools. Remove to wire rack and cool completely before removing it from tin.

Flour

In prehistoric times, flour was milled by the pounding of grains between two stones. In time, the lower stone became hollowed out and the upper one rounded, making the mortar and pestle or saddlestone. About 300 B.C., the rotary mill or quern was developed. This mill enabled the grain to be poured down through a hole in the upper stone, slowly feeding down to a lower stone and a stick. This stick, serving as a lever, turned the upper stone against the lower. Slaves or strong animals turned the larger millstones to grind the grain into fresh flour or meal.

A hundred years ago, most people made their own breads, cakes, biscuits, pastries, pies and puddings using freshly ground whole wheat or other whole grain flours. Much of the bread available today is no longer the 'staff of life' which nourished and sustained our grandparents. It is largely made from 'refined' white flour, either bleached or bromated or both, sometimes with preservatives and vitamins added.

In the past century, commercial wheat flour has been stripped more and more of natural vitamins and minerals. To begin with, most wheat today is grown with chemical fertilizers, pesticides or herbicides. These lower the protein content. Then, in the refining process, the outer coating, or bran of the wheat, is removed and the flour is usually bleached to make it 'white'. The outer bran is the part of the grain which contains most of the proteins, minerals and vitamins. It is one of the richest sources of vitamins B and E. This coating, which also provides roughage or lubrication for the intestinal tract, is broken up in the milling of the whole wheat flour. Thus, the digestion of foods made with this flour is actually more difficult than that of unmilled whole grains.

Moreover, the grinding itself exposes the grain to oxidation which quickly destroys a great deal of nutritional value. Finally, commercial processes to make the flour store longer (have a longer shelf life) destroy almost all of the wheat, or add chemicals which are easily absorbed by the starches inside the kernel. In this way, flour can be stored for years at any temperature and shipped to all parts of the world with never a rancid taste to spoil it. Synthetic vitamins and minerals are added not to 'enrich', but actually to restore some of the nutrients that would ordinarily be present in the whole grain. No wonder bread and other flour products sold today all have the word 'enriched' on the label, for almost all the valuable natural nutrients have been removed.

During the First World War, a doctor by the name of Sir William Wilcox discovered that an epidemic of beriberi (an extreme deficiency of vitamin B) which had been destroying the British troops in India did not affect the Indians. Sir William found that the Indian troops had been fed their native stone-ground whole wheat flour, while the British troops had been fed a white flour.

If flour is allowed to sit on the shelf more than 10 days after milling, it may lose all nutrients. Since it is usually necessary to keep flour at least several days after it has been milled, be sure that the store, as well as you, keeps it refrigerated and away from light. A cold temperature does not eliminate nutritional loss completely, but it does slow it down considerably.

CARROT PECAN CAKE

2 1/4 cups whole wheat cake or pastry flour
2/3 teaspoon cream of tartar
1/3 teaspoon bicarbonate of soda
2 teaspoons cinnamon
Pinch of sea salt
1 teaspoon ground ginger
1 teaspoon ground coriander
1/4 teaspoon ground cloves
1 cup Nut or Soy Milk (pp. 232-3)
2 teaspoons vanilla
1/2 cup oil
1/2 cup maple syrup to taste
3 eggs, separated
2 1/2 cups finely shredded carrots
1 1/2 cups finely chopped pecans
1 cup desiccated coconut or 1 extra cup chopped nuts
1-2 tablespoons grated lemon or orange rind
1/2-3/4 cup fruit juice as needed
TOPPING
Crushed macadamia nuts
Fruit Glaze (p. 79)

1. Preheat oven to 180°C (350°F) and oil and flour a 20 cm (8 in) tube pan.

2. Sift the flour, cream of tartar, bicarbonate of soda, cinnamon, sea salt, ginger, coriander and cloves into a bowl. Combine the milk and vanilla in another bowl.

3. Beat together the oil, maple syrup and one egg yolk for 5 minutes. Add the rest of the egg yolks and one of the whites. Beat together for 3 minutes. Then add the flour mixture in three additions and the milk gradually and fold in gently.

4. Stir in the carrots, pecans and coconut.

5. Beat the remaining 2 egg whites until foamy. Add a pinch of sea salt and the rind and continue beating until firm, not peaked.

6. Fold beaten whites into cake batter carefully.

7. Adjust liquid content by adding more fruit juice if necessary until thick batter is formed.

8. Pour batter into prepared cake pan; bake 55-60 minutes or until cake tester comes out clean. Cool cake in pan 10 minutes. Turn out onto wire rack to cool completely.

9. Just before serving spoon glaze over cake and sprinkle nuts on top. For a more elaborate topping, use White Fluff (p. 75).

CARROT SPICE CAKE

1/2 cup warm sweetener (p. 12)
3 eggs, separated
1/2 cup oil
1 cup sifted whole wheat cake or pastry flour
1 teaspoon cinnamon
1/2 teaspoon cardamom
1 teaspoon ground coriander
1/2 cup ground roasted cashews
1 tablespoon lemon rind
1 cup grated carrots
Pinch of sea salt

1. Beat together warm sweetener and yolks until the mixture resembles thick cream. Slowly drip in the oil and continue beating until fully absorbed.

2. Sift together the next four ingredients. Add cashews, rind, carrots and fold into first mixture.

3. Beat egg whites with sea salt till stiff peaks form. Gently fold about one-third of the egg whites into the batter and then add remaining whites to batter, folding gently.

4. Bake in oiled and floured baking pan with shallow sides in 180°C (350°F) preheated oven 45-50 minutes or till cake test as done. Turn off oven and leave door slightly ajar. Leave cake there until cool. Remove from pan and when completely cool, cut and serve.

Carrot *(Daucus carota)*

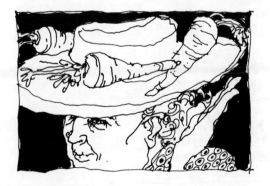

Carrots known to the Romans and the Greeks are now cultivated in every part of the world. They are a rich source of vitamin A and contain a great deal of natural sugar. There is another kind of carrot, known to many as 'wild carrot', that grows wild in some parts of the world. This is also an edible species, with a small, pale-coloured root, but there are plants resembling the carrot which are poisonous, so be careful. Because of the high amount of sugar that they contain, carrots are a wonderful source of natural sweetness that can be used in any dessert.

ELIJAH'S BANANA WALNUT CAKE

For years, I have been creating recipes on my own. When I gave birth to my son, Elijah, I was no longer able to be in the kitchen without a little companion. When he was seven weeks old, I decided that I wanted to bake a 'celebration' cake to commemorate his birth so I packed him into his baby carrier, strapped him on, and off we went into the kitchen to bake his cake.

GF*

1 1/2 *cups whole wheat or brown rice flour* *
1 cup ground nuts or seeds (I like walnuts)
2 teaspoons cinnamon
1/2 teaspoon bicarbonate of soda
2 eggs at room temperature
1/2 cup maple syrup
1/2 cup oil
2 teaspoons vanilla
1 cup mashed banana

* Gluten free if using brown rice flour.

1. Preheat the oven to 190°C (375°F). Oil and lightly flour a 23 cm (9 in) cake tin.

2. Sift all dry ingredients. Set aside. Beat together eggs, maple syrup and oil for five minutes. Add vanilla and fruit.

3. Combine wet mixture into dry, and add some fruit juice if necessary so that the batter is thick but not runny.

4. Spoon into prepared cake tin and bake 30-40 minutes. Turn off oven, open door slightly and cool. Remove from oven and cake tin. Serve with Carob Icing, p. 78.

PUMPKIN AND PEAR CAKE

4 tablespoons maple syrup
1 tablespoon lemon juice
1 teaspoon vanilla or brandy
4-5 semi-ripe pears, peeled, halved and cored lengthwise
1/2 cup oil
1/2 cup maple syrup (to taste)
1 teaspoon vanilla
2 eggs at room temperature
1 cup whole wheat cake or pastry flour
1 teaspoon baking powder substitute*
1 teaspoon cinnamon
2 cups grated pumpkin
1/2 cup chopped walnuts

* Baking powder substitute: For 1 teaspoon baking soda use 2/3 teaspoon cream of tartar and 1/3 teaspoon bicarbonate of soda.

1. Preheat oven to 180°C (350°F). Brush a 20 cm (8 in) deep pie plate with oil.

2. Combine 4 tablespoons of the maple syrup with the lemon juice and vanilla or brandy. Spoon into pie plate.

3. Cut pear halves crosswise into thin slices, and flatten slightly. Arrange the slices round side down in concentric circles in pie dish. Bake 10 minutes. Cool slightly.

4. Beat together oil, maple syrup and vanilla. Add eggs, and continue beating. Sift flour, baking powder substitute and cinnamon. Fold into egg mixture. Add grated pumpkin and walnuts. Pour over pears in oiled pie plate and bake 30-40 minutes. Cool on wire rack.

AUTUMN HARVEST CAKE

1/2 cup sweetener (p. 12)
6 eggs, separated
1/2 cup oil
1 cup Pumpkin Puree (see Basic Vegetable Puree, p. 82)
2 cups sifted whole wheat cake or pastry flour
2 teaspoons cinnamon
3/4 teaspoon cloves
1/2 teaspoon nutmeg
3/4 cup crushed roasted cashews
1 tablespoon orange rind
6 egg whites
Pinch of sea salt
1 tablespoon orange juice
1 quantity Nut Glaze (p. 81)

1. Beat sweetener and yolks together until the mixture resembles thick cream. Slowly drip in the oil and continue beating until fully absorbed. Mix in pumpkin.

2. Sift together next four ingredients. Add cashews and rind, and fold into first mixture.

3. Beat egg whites with a pinch of sea salt and orange juice until stiff peaks form. Gently fold about one-third of the egg whites into batter, folding gently. Preheat oven to 180°C (350°F).

4. Bake in oiled and floured cake tins about 50-60 minutes or until cake tests done. Turn off oven and leave door slightly ajar. Leave cake there until cool. Prepare Nut Glaze. Remove from tin, and when completely cool, glaze before serving.

Oil

Oils are usually obtained from seeds, flowers, nuts, beans, and the kernels of native and tropical fruits and grain. Seeds constitute one of the most important sources of man's food supply, because within their structures are the elements and properties essential to the beginning and reproduction of life. Most of the oils we use are pressed from oil-bearing seeds such as safflower, sesame, sunflower, and the germ of whole corn kernel.

It seems that one of the chief aims of the food processing industry today is to make food look 'pure'. Food processors remove valuable nutrients, which impart colour, odour and flavour, in an effort to make foods look whiter, brighter, lighter and clearer, and last longer. Oil is no exception.

Most of the cooking oils commonly sold today are refined so much that they are usually flat tasting, odourless and dull-looking, but according to the manufacturer, they are 'pure' and 'stable'. The refining process subjects oil to heating, the addition of acids and solvents derived from petroleum, bleaching and the alternation of extreme hot and cold temperatures. These treatments are not without their ill-effects.*

Unrefined expeller-pressed oils, on the other hand, still contain original substances which give natural colour, odour and flavour not usually present in a refined oil. As a con-sumer, you can tell if an oil is truly unrefined and pure by using your senses. An oil that has not been chemically treated will be darker, thicker, and have an odour and flavour similar to the source from which it was pressed.

It was a pleasure to discover oils that were not bland, tasteless or odourless, and that could be used for cooking as well as baking. Nutritious and flavourful, expeller-pressed unrefined oils provide vitamins A, E and K along with lecithin, which helps to break down cholesterol deposits in the tissues of the body.

Saturated fats are mainly responsible for cholesterol deposits that form in the tissues, clogging the arteries and the veins. One way to distinguish between saturated and unsaturated fats is by observing them at room temperature: saturated fats are solid, but the unsaturated fats are usually liquid, otherwise known as oils.

I recommend that you use good-quality, expeller-pressed unrefined oils, such as corn, safflower, sesame, soybean or olive when cooking and baking instead of refined oils, or butter, margarine or shortening. You will be amazed at the difference in taste, texture and aroma of your products, and, at the same time, at the improved health of the people who enjoy them.

Look for nitrogen packed oils as these stay fresher. Store your oils in a dark glass container in a cool place to ensure their freshness. Keep them well sealed in small jars, leaving very little room (if any) for oxygen to mix with the oils. This ensures slower rancidity.

---

* *Dr Roger Williams in his book* Nutrition Against Disease *outlines the dangers of refined oils. In tests which compared refined oils in relation to unrefined oils, it was shown that refined oils actually increased the cholesterol levels in the blood and increased the danger of heart disease. Refined oils are sold under nationally known brands labelled as cold-pressed. These can be easily distinguished by their light colour, and lack of odour and taste. In his book, Dr Williams suggests that all consumers take the extra time and trouble to seek out unrefined and expeller-pressed oils, and that the threat to health posed by these refined oils was too great to be overlooked.*

UPSIDE-DOWN PEACH CAKE

2 tablespoons oil
1/4 cup sweetener (p. 12)
4 stoned and sliced peaches
2 eggs
2-3 cups boiling fruit juice or cider
1 teaspoon vanilla
2 cups sifted whole wheat cake or pastry flour
1 tablespoon cinnamon
1/2 teaspoon sea salt
3/4 cup roasted chopped macadamia nuts
2 tablespoons orange rind
1 teaspoon vanilla

1. Preheat the oven to 180°C (350°F). Oil and lightly flour the bottom of a 15 x 20 cm (6 x 8 in) pan. Heat oil and sweetener together. Mix peaches into the oil-sweetener combination. Set aside.

2. Beat eggs, gradually adding juice or cider, and vanilla. Add sifted flour, cinnamon and sea salt to the egg mixture. Mix in nuts and rind.

3. Place peach mixture decoratively into the pan, pour batter over the peaches and bake 20-30 minutes, or until set. Remove from oven and place on a wire rack to cool. Turn upside-down, remove pan and serve.

VARIATIONS

1. Add 2 tablespoons orange rind to egg mixture before adding boiling juice.

2. Substitute berries for peaches.

3. Soak 1 cup dried fruit in liquid to cover until soft. Squeeze out excess liquid; dice and substitute for peaches.

4. Add 1/4 teaspoon cloves, 1/2 teaspoon ginger and 1 teaspoon lemon, orange or tangerine rind to flour and sea salt before combining with egg mixture.

Peach *(Prunus persica)*

The tree from which the peach originates is a small, deciduous type, producing small pink and sometimes white flowers from which spring forth peaches varying from greenish white to yellow. Peaches mostly grow in countries with warm climates like the United States, China, Japan, South Africa and Australia.

CHRISTMAS TREE CAKE

The most celebrated festival of the ancients occurred at the time of the year when the sun was beginning to regain its power. Called 'Yule', it was a time of mingling, feasting, drinking and dancing, with sacrifices and religious rites for all. Presents were exchanged between masters and slaves, family and friends, all of whom were then considered to be on an equal basis.

1½ tablespoons dry yeast
½ cup warm fruit juice
1½ cups whole wheat cake or pastry flour
1 cup semolina (or use 1 cup more nuts)
2 cups ground hazelnuts
1 tablespoon cinnamon
2 tablespoons orange rind
Juice of one orange
1 tablespoon brandy or rum
Pinch of sea salt
6 eggs, separated (room temperature)
¾ cup sweetener (p. 12)
½ cup oil
ICING
EF   GF
1 kg (2 lb) blanched, drained tofu
½ cup sweetener (p. 12)
½ cup roasted cashew or hazelnut butter
Few tablespoons beetroot juice for colouring
DECORATION
Glacé fruit (cherries and ginger)
Blanched almonds
Pecans
Desiccated coconut
Shredded coconut dipped in beetroot juice for colour

1. Oil and flour a 23 x 30 cm (9 x 12 in) cake pan. Set aside.

2. Combine yeast and warm juice and stir till dissolved. Set aside till mixture bubbles.

3. Beat down, add flour and set aside covered in a warm place till mixture doubles in volume.

4. Add semolina, nuts, cinnamon, rind and juice, brandy and sea salt. Stir till well mixed. Set aside.

5. Blend together yolks, sweetener, oil and yeast mixture for 5 minutes.

6. Fold into flour-nut mixture.

7. Beat egg whites with a pinch of sea salt till peaked. Fold one-third into yolk mixture until well incorporated. Add the rest of the whites, folding in gently.

8. Preheat oven to 180°C (350°F). Adjust liquid content here if necessary till thick batter is formed.

9. Spoon into prepared cake pan, and set aside in a warm spot for 30 minutes. Bake 30-45 minutes or until cake tester comes out dry. Turn off oven, open door slightly and allow cake to cool in oven.

10. Remove from the oven and from the pan.

ICING PREPARATION

1. While the cake is baking combine the blanched tofu, sweetener, nut butter and blend till creamy and smooth.

2. Add beetroot juice for colour, and if necessary some fruit juice until desired consistency is reached.

3. When the cake is cool cut it as shown.

4. Decorate with fruits, nuts and coconut as you like.

Merry Christmas!

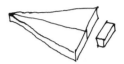

VARIATIONS

1. Add 1-2 cups dried chopped fruit (soak before adding).

2. Add 1 cup chopped roasted nuts or seeds to batter after combining the two mixtures (toss lightly with flour before adding).

3. Add 1 teaspoon dried ginger, or 4-6 teaspoons grain coffee to dry mixture.

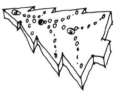

HOLIDAY MAGIC

1 baked Christmas Tree Cake (p. 52)
Cider, as needed
CUSTARD FILLING
1 1/2-2 cups grated apples, pears, peaches or whatever is in season at the time
Juice and rind of 1/2 lemon
2 tablespoons sweetener (p. 12)
1 tablespoon roasted whole wheat cake or pastry flour or kuzu flour
Pinch of sea salt
1/3-1/2 cup fruit juice
2 egg yolks (room temperature)
1 teaspoon vanilla
1 teaspoon cinnamon
2 tablespoons oil
TOPPING
Cherry Almond Glaze (p. 80)

CUSTARD FILLING

1. Combine fruit, lemon juice and sweetener together. Cook on a medium heat until mixture boils. Add rind.

2. In a separate pan, dissolve roasted flour or kuzu flour and salt in juice. Combine with fruit mixture and yolks.

3. Put this mixture back in filling, stirring rapidly. Return to heat and cook in a double boiler on a low heat, stirring constantly until mixture thickens. Remove from heat, stir in vanilla, spice and oil. Chill.

PUTTING IT ALL TOGETHER

1. Cut each layer of the cake horizontally in half. Place layer on wire rack and put baking sheet under rack to catch drippings. Drip hard cider evenly over the layers.

2. Place one layer on a plate, top side down, putting strips of wax paper on all four corners of the plate before setting down the layer. This enables you to decorate and serve the cake on the same plate.

3. Spread layer with custard filling. Repeat layering and filling, placing each layer top side down, ending with cake layer.

TOPPING

Frost sides and top of cake with glaze. Decorate cake with crushed nuts, orange or tangerine rind. See Chapter 3 'Inside and Outside', for more decorating ideas.

COCONUT CASHEW CAKE

1 quantity Christmas Tree Cake (p. 52)
White Fluff (p. 75)
1 quantity Cashew Nut Cream (p. 89)
Lemon or lime rind to taste
¹/₂ cup sweetener (p. 12)
Pinch of salt
Crushed almonds or coconut

1. Preheat the oven to 180°C (350°F). Oil and lightly flour two round cake pans, approximately 20 cm (8 in) or 15 cm (6 in) size.

2. Spoon batter into pans and bake 30-45 minutes or until cake pulls away from the sides of the pan and is springy to the touch. Cool on a wire rack.

Bake one day in advance. Moisten after cooling with cider or brandy. Store tightly wrapped in a cool place until ready to use.

DECORATIONS

1. Prepare Cashew Nut Cream, adding rind to taste after cooking.

PUTTING IT ALL TOGETHER

1. Trim the sides and top if necessary so they are level and prepare the cake for decorating. Place the layers on top of each other to make sure that they decrease in size proportionately. Spread Cashew Nut Cream between the layers and place them upside-down on top of each other. If the layers are too thick, cut them in half horizontally and spread Cashew Nut Cream between the cut layers first. Prepare White Fluff.

2. Peak icing over the entire cake.

FINISHING TOUCHES

Sprinkle almonds or coconut all over the cake.

ANGEL FOOD CAKE

1 cup sifted whole wheat cake or pastry flour
1 cup egg whites (8 to 10 eggs)
1 teaspoon cream of tartar
Sea salt to taste
3/4 cup maple syrup
3/4 teaspoon vanilla
1/4 teaspoon almond extract

1. Sift flour four times. Preheat oven 180°C (350°F).
2. Beat egg whites, cream of tartar and salt until frothy.
3. Add maple syrup in small amounts and beat after each addition. Egg whites should have fine, even texture and be stiff enough to hold a peak but not dry.
4. Add flavourings. Sift one-quarter of flour at a time over mixture and fold in lightly.
5. Pour into large un-oiled tube pan; cut through batter with spatula to remove large air bubbles.
6. Bake 45-60 minutes. Invert pan and let cake hang until cool. Makes one 18 cm (7 in) cake.

Eggs

Eggs are prepared by nature to serve as food for the growing, unborn bird. They contain all the minerals and vitamins essential to support life. Thus they can be good food for humans too, if not taken to excess. But the quality of the eggs we use depends upon the food we feed the hen and the environment in which she lives.

Commercial chickens are usually raised to yield the greatest amount of eggs or meat, disregarding the natural environment and diet of the birds. Stimulants are used to increase the productivity of the chickens.

Chemicals are sometimes put into their feed to increase their appetite so that they will weigh more and draw a better price in the marketplace. These additives result in large chemical deposits in commercial eggs and chicken meat. Furthermore, the meat and fish-meal fed to these chickens are of the lowest possible quality and full of preservatives, hormones and weight-gaining stimulants as well. Other unnatural ingredients in commercial eggs may include antibiotics, phosphates and meat steroids.

The best eggs to buy are those marked: organic, free or open range. This indicates that the birds that laid the eggs are not cooped up in pens but allowed to roam and scratch, and to mate freely, that they have been fed high-quality food without additives or preservatives, and that the eggs are complete and whole. These eggs have many natural growth-promoting hormones which can be lacking in non-organic eggs.

Healthier and happier chickens produce eggs with more vitality, which can lead to a healthier and more vital you.

CAROB ANGEL FOOD CAKE

³/4 cup sifted whole wheat cake or pastry flour
4 tablespoons carob flour
1 cup egg whites (8-10)
Sea salt to taste
1 teaspoon cream of tartar
³/4 cup maple syrup
1 teaspoon vanilla
2 teaspoons orange rind

1. Preheat oven to 180°C (350°F).
2. Sift flour and carob together four times.
3. Beat egg whites and sea salt until foamy, add cream of tartar and continue beating until peaked.
4. Keep beating and slowly add maple syrup. Add vanilla and orange rind.
5. Sift small amounts of flour over the mixture and fold in quickly but gently.
6. Pour batter into un-oiled 20 cm (8 in) tube pan and cut through batter to remove large air bubbles.
7. Bake 50-60 minutes. Invert the cake pan and let the cake hang in pan till cool.

Sweet Chestnut *(Castanea sativa)*

Originally from southern Europe, the chestnut tree has been planted in many different parts of the world.

Chestnuts grow on moderately large trees, characterised by alternate deciduous leaves with bristle-tipped margins. Their small, inconspicuous unisexual flowers are born in catkins. The fruit, a nut, born in clusters of two or three, is enclosed in a leathery husk, clothed with multibranched spines. Both the wood and the bark of the tree contain tannin, a chemical complex which is extracted in commercial quantities and used in converting rawhides into leather.

The European or Spanish chestnut (called marron) is probably the most important species. It grows in southern Europe as well as North Africa, southern Asia, England and India. During the nineteenth century, it became widely established and can be found in California and the Pacific Northwest.

The largest nuts are eaten raw, boiled or roasted. Smaller ones are dried and milled into flour. The smallest nuts are fed to livestock.

Chestnuts are used in soups, stuffings and desserts, as well as roasted and eaten hot.

Opposite: Christmas Tree Cake (page 52)

CHESTNUT CAROB CAKE

SPONGE
3 eggs, separated
1/4 cup sweetener (p. 12)
Pinch of sea salt
1 teaspoon vanilla
1 tablespoon orange rind
1 cup sifted whole wheat cake or pastry flour
FILLING AND TOPPING
1 quantity Chestnut Cream (p. 90)
1 quantity Carob Icing (p. 78)

1. Preheat oven to 190°C (375°F) and line the bottom of a 20 x 27 x 1.25 cm (8 x 11 x ½ in) baking sheet with greaseproof paper. Oil paper well.

2. Beat yolks and sweetener together until creamy and light. Set mixture aside.

3. Beat whites and salt together until stiff peaks form. Beat in vanilla and rind.

4. Fold whole wheat flour into yolk mixture.

5. Fold one-third of the egg whites into yolk mixture, then fold the rest of the egg whites in very gently.

6. Spoon into baking pan, bake 12-15 minutes or until sponge is lightly browned and pulls away from the sides of the pan. Prepare filling and topping.

7. Immediately remove sponge from pan, and place on a cloth.

8. Peel off the paper, trim the edges so that it will roll without splitting. Spread with filling. Roll up sheet tightly in the towel or cloth. Let stand on a rack to cool.

9. Ice and decorate before serving.

VARIATION

After baking sponge, cut into strips and sandwich them together, spreading chestnut cream in between each layer. Spoon Carob Icing over top.

Opposite: Melon Tofu Cheesecake (page 62)

TROPICAL KIWI-BERRY TORTE

TORTE
3 eggs, separated
1 teaspoon vanilla
4 tablespoons sweetener to taste (p. 12)
1/2 cup whole wheat cake or pastry flour
1/4-1/3 cup ground pine or macadamia nuts
1/2 teaspoon cinnamon
1/2 teaspoon ground coriander
1/4 teaspoon bicarbonate of soda
1/2 teaspoon cream of tartar
Several tablespoons fruit juice as needed
1 quantity Cinnamon Rum Custard (p. 209)
FRUIT TOPPING
2-3 peeled and thinly sliced kiwifruit, strawberries or raspberries
Nuts for garnish

1. Line two 20 cm (8 in) round cake pans with greaseproof or wax paper. Oil and set aside.

2. Preheat oven to 170°C (325°F).

3. Beat together yolks, vanilla, sweetener until light and fluffy (2-3 minutes).

4. Combine dry ingredients except cream of tartar in another bowl. Fold into yolk mixture.

5. Beat together whites and cream of tartar until they peak. Fold into yolk mixture. Batter should be thick. Adjust liquid as needed.

6. Pour batter evenly into cake pans. Spread to within 2.5 cm (1 in) from the edges.

7. Bake 12-15 minutes or until firm to the touch.

8. Cool on a wire rack 5-10 minutes. Flip out onto rack, peel off paper, turn over and cool. Prepare Cinnamon Rum Custard.

9. To assemble, place one layer on serving dish, top with half the custard, another layer of cake and remaining custard. Arrange kiwifruit slices in a ring around the top, alternating with sliced berries. Garnish with nuts.

Kiwifruit (Chinese Gooseberries) *(Actinidia chinensis)*

Originally found in China's Yangtze Valley, Chinese gooseberries were introduced into New Zealand in the early 1900s and through careful propagation the current varieties were developed. Kiwifruit require a mild climate but can tolerate light frosts. The fruits, about the size of hens' eggs with brownish hairy skin, have a light green flesh with a white centre core crowned with a ring of black speckles. When ripe the fruit has a refreshingly light and satisfying taste.

UNLEAVENED CAKES

Sometimes home ovens (gas or electric) tend to be too dry for certain batters. Those batters that do not have much leavening agent at all, such as fruit cakes, may form a hard crust on top of the cake before it is sufficiently baked on the inside. To prevent this, place a small pan of hot water in the bottom of the oven while baking. This allows more moisture in the oven to circulate around the pans and prevents a crust from forming. This method may also be used when baking yeasted batters, but allow more baking time.

ALTERNATIVE METHOD

Cover baking pan and steam for half of the recommended baking time (use a cover that is high enough to allow for rising). Remove cover and bake until cake is done.

BOSTON FRUIT CAKE

This recipe makes twelve cakes.

EF

2.75 kg (5 1/2 lb) dried mixed fruit
1.5 kg (3 lb) raisins or sultanas
16 cups amazake (p. 238) or 1/2 apple juice and 1/2 stout
8 cups whole wheat cake or pastry flour
7 cups rye flour
6 tablespoons orange or tangerine rind
12 teaspoons cinnamon
6 teaspoons cloves
2-3 teaspoons powdered ginger (to taste)
4 cups roasted chopped almonds
2 teaspoons sea salt or 2 tablespoons miso (p. 26)

1. Soak the dried fruits in amazake or juice and stout mixture to cover overnight. Squeeze out and reserve the excess liquid, and dice fruit into bite-sized pieces. Add flours to the liquid and let sit at least a few hours. Combine the fruit and flour mixture with the rest of the ingredients and beat until batter is smooth and thick enough to drop with difficulty from a wooden spoon.

2. Oil and flour 12-14 small cake moulds. Fill moulds two-thirds full, cover and steam 1 1/2 hours in preheated 150°C (300°F) oven. Remove cover and bake until cakes pull away from the sides of the moulds. Place on cake racks to cool.

To age: When the cakes have cooled completely, remove from moulds; dip a piece of cheesecloth into hard cider or brandy, wrap it around the cakes and cover tightly with a dry piece of cheesecloth and brown paper. If you have a tin can (an old coffee can will do nicely), place the wrapped cakes in the can and store them for a few weeks in a dry, cool place (also see p. 35).

DOWN UNDER FRUIT CAKE

¹/₂ cup dried mixed fruit
¹/₂ cup raisins or sultanas
1 cup hard cider or stout
3 teaspoons orange, tangerine or lemon rind
1 tablespoon rum or brandy
¹/₄ cup oil
¹/₄ cup sweetener (p.12)
Pinch of sea salt
1 cup whole wheat cake or pastry flour
3 eggs
1 cup almond paste
ALMOND PASTE
EF   GF
500 g (1 lb) blanched almonds
2 egg whites or hot apple juice
1 cup maple syrup

1. Soak dried fruit and raisins in hard cider to cover until soft. Squeeze out excess liquid and reserve. Dice fruit. Combine fruits and rind in a bowl. Add rum, oil and sweetener. Let stand for at least 30 minutes.

2. Combine sea salt and flour. Add the fruit to the flour mixture. Set aside. Beat the eggs until double in volume, then fold into fruit mixture until the eggs are no longer visible.

3. Preheat oven to 180°C (350°F). Oil and lightly flour the bottom of a 20 cm (8 in) round pan (preferably springform).

4. Blend almonds adding egg whites, till smooth. Place the mixture in a pan, add sweetener and cook, stirring constantly until it thickens.

5. Pour half of batter into cake pan. Cover with Almond Paste. Add remaining batter and bake 60-70 minutes or until cake is springy to the touch and pulls away from the sides of the pan. Remove from the oven and cool on a wire rack.

HOLIDAY FRUIT CAKE

EF

Follow the recipe for Down Under Fruit Cake, omitting eggs. Add 1 cup more flour and enough cider to form a pancake-like batter. Bake covered for the first 45 minutes, remove cover and bake 20-30 minutes longer.

COCONUT STRAWBERRY CHEESECAKE

EF
FILLING
1 cup sweetener (p. 12)
1/2 cup tahini
1 tablespoon vanilla
1/2 teaspoon sea salt
10 cups blanched tofu (p. 93)
CRUST
1 cup whole wheat cake or pastry flour
1 cup rolled oats
5 tablespoons oil, as needed
3-4 tablespoons sweetener (p.12)
1/2 cup fruit juice as needed
TOPPING
STRAWBERRY GLAZE
2 tablespoons arrowroot flour
1 1/2 cups fruit juice
1/4 cup maple syrup
4 cups chopped strawberries
Tahini or other nut butter, as needed
1/2-3/4 cup shredded coconut

FILLING
Combine sweetener, tahini, vanilla and sea salt. Blend until creamy. Add blanched tofu and continue to blend 3-5 minutes longer. (If there is not enough liquid, add enough to form a creamy consistency.) Set aside.
CRUST
1. Combine flour, oats and salt together in a mixing bowl. Cut the oil in. Add sweetener and enough liquid to form a semi-moist crust. Pre-heat oven to 180°C (350°F) and oil a 20 cm (8 in) springform pan. Press crust into the bottom of the pan and bake 10-15 minutes.

2. Pour tofu mixture into the bottom of the crust. Bake 25-30 minutes or until the pie is almost solid (shake pan). Remove from oven and place on a rack to cool. When completely cool, remove sides of pan. Cool at room temperature 3 to 6 hours longer.
TOPPING
Dissolve the arrowroot flour in fruit juice. Add maple syrup and cook on a medium heat, stirring constantly until mixture boils; add strawberries. Remove from heat. Spread nut butter around the sides of the cake. Press coconut around. Spoon over cake.

MELON TOFU CHEESECAKE

BASE
EF
¹/2 cup ground, blanched almonds or hazelnuts
1 cup rolled oats
¹/2 cup whole wheat cake or pastry flour
Pinch of sea salt to taste
¹/2 cup oil
Few tablespoons fruit juice to bind
MELON CREAM
EF   GF
1 cup pureed rock melon
¹/3 cup sweetener (p.12)
Juice of ¹/2 lemon
1-2 tablespoons arrowroot flour or kuzu as needed
Few tablespoons fruit juice for dissolving arrowroot or kuzu
TOFU FILLING
GF
750 g (1¹/2 lb) drained tofu
3 eggs, separated
¹/2 cup sweetener (p. 12)
Juice of 1 lemon or orange
Rind of 1 lemon or orange
2 teaspoons vanilla, brandy or rum
³/4 cup currants
2 tablespoons arrowroot or kuzu flour
FRUIT TOPPING
EF   GF
2-3 teaspoons arrowroot or kuzu flour as needed
1 cup fruit juice
Kiwifruit, strawberries, raspberries, blueberries, bananas, peaches, apricots
or any fresh fruit in season
Crushed nuts, lightly toasted, to sprinkle

BASE

1. Combine all the dry ingredients in a mixing bowl.

2. Rub in the oil until the ingredients are well coated and add enough fruit juice to bind.

3. Preheat the oven to 190°C (375°F) and oil a 20 cm (8 in) springform pan.

4. Press or roll the pastry out on greaseproof paper or rolling cloth, then invert both the pastry and paper or cloth into the pan. Peel off the paper or cloth and allow the pastry to fall naturally into the pan. Do *not* stretch the pastry otherwise it will shrink during the baking process.

5. Cut the sides off so the pastry is just covering the bottom of the pan and slightly up the sides to allow for some shrinkage.

6. Prick the base all over with a fork to allow air to escape during the baking, and baste with egg white and a few drops of water mixed together to seal the base.

7. Bake 15-20 minutes. Remove from oven and leave to cool.

MELON CREAM

1. Combine all the ingredients for the cream and bring to the boil,

stirring continuously until the mixture thickens and boils.

2. Cool. Spread on the base and set aside for a few minutes while you prepare the tofu filling.

TOFU FILLING

1. Drop the tofu into a pot of boiling water and remove from the heat. Drain.

2. Combine the egg yolks and sweetener together and beat till creamy. Blend the tofu, and yolk combination, adding the rest of the ingredients except the arrowroot or kuzu and egg whites and continue beating until creamy and smooth.

4. If the mixture is difficult to blend add a few teaspoons of fruit juice. Fold in the arrowroot flour.

5. Whip the egg whites with a pinch of sea salt till peaked. Fold one-third into the tofu mixture and then gently fold in the rest.

6. Spoon into pre-baked base, over the melon cream, and bake 30-40 minutes or until almost set.

7. Turn off the oven and leave the 'cake' in the oven with the door slightly ajar until cool. When cool, transfer to a cooling rack and remove from the tin.

FRUIT TOPPING

1. Combine the arrowroot or kuzu with the cold fruit juice and stir until well dissolved.

2. Place in a saucepan and bring to the boil, while stirring continuously until the mixture boils and thickens. Transfer to a bowl to cool.

3. Decorate the top of the cake with the fresh fruit, placing slices of peeled peaches or apricots at the base to create a tail effect.

4. Brush the glaze all over the fruit and drip it between the fruit.

5. Sprinkle lightly toasted crushed nuts around the edge, and sides and the melon puree which has probably oozed out during the baking. Allow to set and then serve.

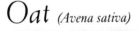

Oat *(Avena sativa)*

The use of the oat is believed to date back to the European Bronze Age. Today oats are usually used to feed livestock or eaten in the form of breakfast cereals. Oats possess a special quality: when cooked with four or five times the amount of liquid, they become glutinous and make a fine substitute for milk and milk puddings.

MARBLE CHEESECAKE

EF
CRUST
1/2 cup corn or maize meal
2 cups whole wheat flour
1/2 cup crushed nuts
Pinch of sea salt
1/3 cup oil
Fruit juice to bind
CAKE MIXTURE I
8 cups blanched tofu
1/2 cup tahini or almond butter
2 teaspoons vanilla
Pinch of sea salt
1/4 cup oil
3/4 cup sweetener (p. 12)
CAKE MIXTURE II
2 cups date puree
3/4 cup arrowroot flour
Pinch of sea salt
2 teaspoons orange rind
TOPPING
Peach Coconut Glaze (p. 81)

CRUST
Combine flours, nuts and sea salt. Beat together oil and juice and add to
the dry mixture until the dough begins to stick together. Preheat oven at
190°C (375°F) and oil a 20 cm (8 in) springform pan. Press the crust mixture into the bottom of pan and prebake 10-12 minutes.
CAKE MIXTURE I
Blend tofu, tahini, vanilla, salt, oil, and sweetener until creamy. Set aside.
CAKE MIXTURE II
Combine 2 cups date puree with the arrowroot flour, salt and orange
rind. Mix until smooth.
PUTTING IT ALL TOGETHER
　　1. Remove crust from oven and pour the first mixture into it. Swirl
the second mixture into the first, until the batter is marbled.
　　2. Lower oven temperature to 180°C (350°F) and bake 25-30
minutes. Remove cake from oven and place on a wire rack to cool. When
cake has cooled completely, remove the sides of the pan. Leave outside
until cold. (The longer the cake is aged, the better it will taste.)
　　3. Prepare topping before serving and decorate, trim, or sprinkle
with coconut.

3. THE FINISHING TOUCH:
Icings, Glazes, Purees, Fillings, Creams and Toppings

GENERAL EQUIPMENT FOR DECORATING

Pastry bag
Metal tubes in various sizes to
    use for piping or fluting
    (see p. 71)
Cake rack
Extra cake pans or cardboard
    forms the same size or slightly
    larger than the cake being
    decorated
Metal and rubber spatulas
Pastry brushes
Blender or processor

Wire whisk
Double boiler
Electric mixer or rotary hand
    beater
Brown, wax or greaseproof
    paper
Biscuit or baking sheet (to catch
    drippings when decorating)
Cake-decorating stand
    (optional)

CHOOSING A DECORATION OR FILLING

THERE are many different kinds of decorations and fillings to choose
from; each with a special look and texture of its own. Choose one or
more according to the type of cake or pastry, the look, shape, taste and
texture you want it to have, and where, when and to whom you want to
serve it.

Nut Butter Icings and Fillings
Made from a nut butter base, and embellished with fruit and spices, this
type of decoration can give a creamy effect as well as a stiff peaked look.
Try it for fillings or icings, fluting or piping, using a pastry bag for added
effect.

Creams (see p. 89)
   Egg-based: Made with the yolk, white, or whole egg, these are desirable
for fillings as well as toppings.
   Flour-based: Usually made from whole wheat cake or pastry flour, corn
or chestnut flour, they too are perfect for filling pies or pastries.
   Grain-based: Made from cooked, rolled oats, barley or rice, and
cooked, blended and flavoured, they form a delicious creamy base filling
or topping on the inside or outside of any kind of dessert.
   Tofu: This cream can be used for any purpose, such as icings, toppings
and fillings, or as a separate cold dessert.

Fruit or Vegetable Puree
Simple, but tasty, these blends of fruits and/or vegetables and added
flavouring, such as rinds or vanilla, can embellish any pastry or cake. Use
as a filling, topping or trim.

Glazes

Heated maple syrup or other sweeteners (p. 12) cooked with kuzu or arrowroot and flavoured with nuts, rind, spices or fruit, this form of topping can present a glowing appearance, as well as a delicious taste.

PRE-DECORATING TECHNIQUES

1. Cool the cake completely. Remove from pan.
2. Trim off the hard, crisp edges from the side, about 3 mm (⅛ in).
3. Check to see if layers are level. If not, trim some off top of cake, so that they are level when sandwiched together. If top layer is too irregular, level off top and invert.
4. Brush away all loose crumbs.
5. Place cake (or layer) upside-down on platter.
6. Cut four strips of wax paper at least 10 cm (4 in) wide and long enough to cover surface of the platter that the cake is being served on.
7. Lifting the cake with a spatula, insert the strips of wax paper 5 cm (2 in) underneath the bottom, extending them a few centimetres outward.
8. After decorating the cake, allow icing to dry before removing wax paper.

FINISHING TOUCHES

Before Baking
Brush or spread any glaze (p. 79) on top of yeasted and unyeasted pastries, covered pies, tarts and rolled biscuits.

During Baking
Brush the tops with oil, sweetener, or any glaze 10 minutes before removing from oven.

Decorations Baked on the Cake
Some decorations can be put onto a cake before it is baked.
Nuts: Unroasted nuts are usually easy to apply before baking and look attractive on top of a cake. For very special occasions, blanch the nuts before scattering them on top of the cake (see p. 20).
To make a glaze over nuts, you may brush a little egg white carefully over the unroasted or blanched nuts before baking.
Rind: Plain cakes look more attractive if you sprinkle orange or lemon rind on top. If baking period is long, sprinkle the rind gently on top of the cake three-quarters of the way through the baking time.
Crumb topping: If the cake has a long baking period, sprinkle the crumb topping (p. 96) on halfway through the baking time allotted.

Pastry as a decoration: Pastry can be used as a decoration, especially if you are making pastry and batter cakes on the same day. Use a lattice design of pastry over a fruit cake or any design you choose on top of any cake. Be sure that proper time is allotted to bake the pastry as well as the cake.

After Baking

Brush the top of yeasted or unyeasted pastries, covered pies, tarts, biscuits and petit fours with sweetener (p. 12) *before* the dessert cools, preferably immediately after baking. Brush glaze on cakes after cooling, sprinkle roasted nuts, seeds or crumb topping on top of glaze. (Or, the nuts, seeds etc., may be placed on the dessert before glazing, and the glaze spooned or brushed carefully over them.)

To prepare cakes and petit fours for glazing, follow these steps before proceeding:

1. Trim off hard, crisp edges.
2. Place cake on a rack.
3. Place a pan or baking sheet under the rack to catch the drippings.
4. Spoon hot glaze over the top of the cooled cake, allowing it to drip down the sides.
5. Coat sides before or after glazing. (It is good to spread a base of butter icing, cream or glaze over the cakes before putting on the final icing.)

DECORATING TECHNIQUES

Choose one of the following:

1. Spread the icing over the top of the cake. Draw a small knife across the icing to give a ridged effect.

2. Spread icing over top and sides of a cake. Mark the top with a fork, by moving it across the icing in a wavy line. Coat sides with roasted nuts or seeds, etc.

3. Spread a nut butter icing over the top of a cake rather thickly. (Use a cold icing that has been chilled.) Sweep the point of a knife or the prongs of a fork or the back of a spoon over the icing, and at the same time, lift it in peaks. Do not try to do this evenly, since it looks more effective if it is slightly uneven.

4. Place a doily on top of the cake. Shake or sprinkle roasted chestnut flour, orange or lemon rind, or crushed roasted nuts or seeds on top of the doily. Lift the doily carefully, with one upward sweep.

5. To glaze or ice only the top of the cake, tie or pin a strong band of paper around the sides of the cake. Put any agar-agar topping or pie filling on top of the cake. Allow to set before removing paper.

6. Prepare an icing or glaze that is stiffer, by using less liquid. Spread over top and sides of cakes. When top starts to harden, take the edge of a knife and go around the rim of the cake, sweeping upward.

7. A broken line effect can be achieved by spreading the butter icing roughly over the cake. It usually forms a rough-looking texture. If you want to follow a definite design, push it very gently with a knife.

8. Lattice design can be produced by using butter icing and different coloured fruit butters. Mark the lattice design on the top of the cake that has been given a thin layer of icing on top. Pipe either straight or slightly wavy lines following the marks. Fill the centres between lines with fruit butter. (The fruit butter can also be applied to the top of the cake using a pastry bag.) If the butter is too stiff, mix with a small quantity of warm liquid.

9. Smooth-looking nut butter icing can be made by using a knife that is long enough to cover the entire width of the cake, holding it at both ends at an angle and pulling it toward you.

10. Swirl the nut butter icing using a knife and a sharp upward motion after each swirl.

11. To obtain a line effect with nut butter icing, use a tea knife or very thin palette knife. Make a sweep from the centre of the cake to the edge and then follow this line all around. This is difficult to do around the sides of the cake, so straight or wavy lines are better there.

Hold a spatula, tea knife or very thin palette knife at the centre of the cake. Turn the cake slowly, and move the spatula gradually to the outer edge of the cake or sweep the knife or spatula from the centre of the cake to the edge in a semi-circular motion. (Use a nut butter icing for best results.)

12. *Peak:* Using a nut butter icing or White Fluff (p. 75), ice the entire cake. Place a spatula on the cake and pull it away to make a series of peaks.

13. *Zigzag:* Cut saw-like teeth along the edge of a piece of cardboard slightly larger than the width of the cake, move the cardboard along the top of the cake from side to side.

14. *Spiral:* First cover the cake with a dark or light coloured icing, then fit a pastry bag with a small round tube and fill the pastry bag with a contrasting coloured icing. Pipe a series of circles, working from the outer edge of the cake to the centre. Draw a thin knife or skewer lightly over the cake, as if cutting a pie into 8 or 12 pieces.

15. *Stencil:* First ice the cake with a stiff nut butter icing. Allow the icing to dry. Cut any pattern or shape out of cardboard and place it on top of the cake. Spread icing or sprinkle roasted chestnut flour, rind, mint or cinnamon over the top of the cardboard where the pattern has been cut out. (Use a contrasting colour for best results.)

16. *Feather icing:* Use any light coloured icing (tofu cream, oat, barley or rice creams) or light icing tinted with vegetable colouring and any dark icing (nut butter base is best for piping). Place the dark icing in a decorating bag. (Use a plain round tube for the pastry bag. See p. 71.) Spread light or tinted icing on biscuit or cover cake with icing. Immediately pipe onto this straight lines, circles, spirals, etc., in dark icing. Use a skewer or toothpick to create designs, drawing skewer either in straight lines, circles or swirls.

FLOWERS

Choose fresh flowers that do not have poisonous properties and place them on the cake just before serving. Open-petalled flowers that have bright gay colours give an attractive finish to any cake.

Added Touch

For an added touch, use either lemon skin or orange skin, cut into different shapes (thin, long strips, curves) and boil in fruit juice until soft. Drain immediately and keep in a bowl of cold water with a pinch of sea salt until using. Lay a flower down. Place strips or curves around the outside of the flower.

Decorating may be used on many different kinds of food such as cupcakes, petit fours, French pastries, moulded agar-agar desserts, salads, biscuits and pies. The same method is applied; the only change may be the icing you choose to decorate with.

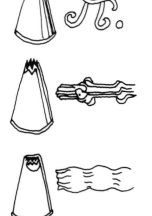

CUPCAKES

Here are a few ideas for cupcake decorations. An open-star tube was used for most of these designs.

This is another way of decorating a cupcake. Cut off the top third of the cupcake. Cut this piece in half down the centre.

Fill the bottom of the cupcake with a heavy nut butter icing or White Fluff (p. 75).

Place the two halves of the top section at an angle in an upright position on top of the icing. Decorate with the rest of the icing, nuts and dried fruit.

NUTS AS DECORATIONS

Nuts can add an attractive appearance to any cake, pie or pastry, as well as an enjoyable taste and texture.

Blanched: Blanched nuts add a certain finished look to a cake. They may be used after icing or before baking. If placing blanched nuts on top of a cake after baking use some sweetener, nut butter icing, or cream to make them adhere properly.

Whole, halved or split: Good to use for border decoration. Place them around the top edge of a cake before or after baking.

Chopped, shredded or slivered: Sprinkle them over cakes, pies or roll sides of iced cake before decorating top.

NECESSARY ITEMS

Cake decorating is fascinating and simple to do. It is something everyone can learn, but it requires perseverance, patience and practice. Once you acquire the knack of working with a pastry bag, you will be able to serve attractive and skilfully decorated pastries, cakes, biscuits and pies, which will elicit compliments not only for taste, but for looks as well.

I began to learn cake decorating when two of my friends asked me to make their wedding cake. I bought myself a pastry bag, four basic tubes, and a cake decorating book, and began to practise piping and fluting with mashed potato on upside-down bowls, baking pans, baking sheets, cardboard boxes, wax paper – anything that could be decorated. In a short time I was able to create home-made cakes that looked as lavishly glamorous as anything I had seen in a bakery store.

My mother used to take a paper bag, cut and roll it into a cone, fill it with icing, snip off the tip and squeeze. Out came 'magic' flowers, spirals, borders, even words... Today, most stores are supplied with pastry bags and various tubes which offer a greater variety of ways to fashion pastries, cakes and pies into tantalizing desserts.

In order to accomplish quick and easy decoration, the following items are necessary.

One or two 35 cm (14 in) bags: These should be large enough to use for creams, biscuit batters or fillings, and small enough to handle gracefully.

Plain round tube: There are several different sizes that can be advantageous, depending on what you want to do.
- 6 mm (¼ in) opening can be used for shaping small biscuits and for lettering or decorating the top of a cake or pie.
- 12 mm (½ in) opening can be used for making cream puffs, eclairs, biscuits and for filling tart shells.
- 18 mm (¾ in) opening can be used for any of the above if making or filling a large shell, as well as for larger biscuits.

Star tube: There are different sizes available for different needs.
- Opening slightly larger than 6 mm (¼ in) can be used for fillings, and borders on small cakes.
- 12 mm (½ in) opening can be used for cake decorations, kisses, borders and fillings, as well as for shaping small moulded biscuits.
- 18 mm (¾ in) opening can be used for making biscuits that contain seeds, dried fruit pieces, or nuts for cake borders or for filling large pie shells or pies.

Ribbon tube: This can be used for making biscuits as well as for cake decorating. This is a flat tube with one serrated edge having an opening about 18 mm (¾ in) long. Press out dough into one long ribbon, and break into 5-7 cm (2-3 in) lengths before baking.

Coupling: With this attachment, you can interchange decorating tubes without having to empty the bag. It also prevents filling from squirting out of the side of the bag.

Revolving cake-decorating stand: You will find this tool to be very useful when decorating and icing cakes. It allows you to remain stationary as you decorate, giving you more flexibility in your designs.

TECHNIQUES FOR USING A PASTRY BAG: FILLING AND DECORATING

Filling the Pastry Bag

1. Insert the coupling into the pastry bag, fitting it into the small end of the tube.
2. Place the tube over the coupling.
3. Screw the coupling nut onto the coupling.
4. Hold the bag in one hand, and, keeping it open, fold the edge over the other hand.

Alternative Method for Filling

1. Fit the pastry bag into a large jar, folding the edge over the lip of the jar.
2. Using a rubber spatula, spoon the filling into the pastry bag. Remove excess filling from the spatula by pinching the bag as you withdraw the spatula.
3. Fold over the top or flap of the bag, squeeze down filling, then fold the sides of the bag near the top and twist until a little filling is forced through the tube. *Never put too much filling into the bag.* Leave enough room so that the top may be folded down securely to prevent any filling from oozing out at the top.

Decorating with Pastry Bag

With your dominant hand, press down on the top of the twisted bag and squeeze out the filling. Use the other hand to guide the end of the bag. *Do not press the lower end of the bag.* Retwist the top as the bag empties.

Alternative Method

Press down on the top of the twisted bag to squeeze out filling. Use the other hand to guide the dominant hand.

Biscuits: For shaping round biscuits, hold the pastry bag vertically above the baking sheet with the tip about 6 mm (¼ in) away from the sheet. Without moving the bag, squeeze out the filling into a 2.5 or 5 cm (1 or 2 in) round. Pull the bag away quickly. Try other shapes and sizes when you feel comfortable working with the bag.

Cream puffs: For shaping cream puffs, hold the bag vertically above the baking sheet with the tip about 18 mm (¾ in) away from the sheet. Squeeze out batter, raising the bag slightly, to form a high mound about 5 cm (2 in) in diameter.

Borders: For making fancy borders on cakes use a star tube with 18 mm (¾ in) opening. Hold the pastry bag at an angle about 3 mm (⅛ in) away from the cake. Squeeze out the filling by moving the bag back and forth, so that each layer of icing partly covers the previous one. Or, holding the bag vertically, squeeze out filling quickly, finishing each movement by abruptly drawing the bag away straight up. The more you squeeze, the bigger the star.

Drop tubes into a glass of water after using, so the icing does not harden in the tubes.

First practise using a pastry bag, filled with an inexpensive ingredient (e.g., potatoes) on sheets of wax paper, upside-down bowls, pans and cardboard boxes until you get the hang of it.

FORGET ME KNOTS

1. The amount of liquid necessary for the proper consistency of each recipe will vary according to the moisture and temperature of the flour and the room, the size of the eggs and the general weather of the day. Remain flexible and adjust liquid content accordingly.
2. Any fruit juice may be substituted for liquid in any recipe. If more sweetness is desired, add a few tablespoons of sweetener (see chart, p. 12), decreasing the liquid content accordingly.
3. When diluting arrowroot in liquid, stir again *immediately before* adding it to the mixture, as arrowroot tends to settle to the bottom rather quickly.
4. Kuzu may be substituted for arrowroot in any recipe (use two-thirds the amount).
5. Using agar-agar, arrowroot or kuzu with acid fruits (lemons, tangerines, oranges, strawberries) may cause the mixture to set less firmly. Add 1-2 tablespoons more agar-agar, or ½ tablespoon more arrowroot or kuzu, according to the amount of fruit used and the acidity of the fruit.
6. Double boilers are better to use for heating delicate icing ingredients (especially with eggs), which tend to cook rather quickly and burn.
7. Never cook liquid vanilla, rum, brandy or citrus rind, as doing so will decrease their flavour.

ICINGS

The consistency of icings can vary, depending upon what you want to do with it. A firm icing is necessary if you want to pipe it onto a cake for decoration. A softer icing is better to use for spreading around the sides of a cake, especially if you want to roll the sides of the cake in nuts, seeds or rind. A delicate, soft, creamy butter icing is nice to make when you are planning to fill or cover the top. Then, over this layer you can pipe fluted edges or write with a firmer contrasting coloured icing or frosting.

Tips

1. Add a little extra Chestnut Cream (p. 90) or nut butter to make the icing stiffer.

2. After adding nut butter or puree, chill several hours before using (icings made with arrowroot flour, however, should be used immediately).

3. To soften icing, add a little warm liquid before using.

4. If icing is too thick, mix with a little sweetener or juice.

5. Nut butter icing that is going to be used for piping or writing should be made several hours in advance to make it stiffer, so it will maintain its shape after piping. If the icing becomes too stiff and tends to crack, beat in a few drops of hot liquid, or use for marzipan.

GLAMOROUS ICING

EF GF

1/2-1 tablespoon arrowroot or kuzu flour
1 cup fruit juice
2 tablespoons maple syrup
2 tablespoons any nut butter
1 teaspoon vanilla or 1/2 teaspoon rose water

1. Dissolve arrowroot flour in 2 to 3 tablespoons juice and maple syrup and set aside.

2. In a heavy saucepan, combine the rest of the juice and nut butter. (For piping, use less juice.) Add arrowroot mixture and stir rapidly until mixture comes to the boil, thickens and turns clear. Remove from heat, add vanilla or rose water. Cool slightly and decorate.

MOCHA ICING

EF GF

Follow the recipe for Glamorous Icing. Add 2 tablespoons grain coffee or carob flour to juice and nut butter. Remove from heat and stir in 1/2 teaspoon cinnamon, 1 teaspoon lemon juice and rum or brandy to taste.

WHITE FLUFF

If you ever have an occasion to decorate a wedding cake, here is an icing that will have everyone's attention before it is eaten and will be long remembered afterwards. It comes from a traditional Shaker recipe.

GF
1 1/4 cups maple syrup
1-2 egg whites (room temperature)
Pinch of sea salt

1. Place the maple syrup in a heavy saucepan (oil the rim of the pan to keep the syrup from overflowing). Attach a confectionary thermometer and cook until it registers 115°C (239°F), stirring occasionally.

2. Beat the egg whites and sea salt together until peaked. As soon as the syrup has reached 115°C (239°F), begin to drip it very slowly into the egg whites, beating with an electric mixer for best results. (A hand beater will achieve the same results, but you will need assistance and more time.) Keep beating until the icing begins to thicken. Lift a little of the icing up with a wooden spoon. When it has a very stiff, threadlike appearance, it is ready.

3. Ice the cake immediately with a spatula, sweeping it with an upward motion around the sides and top. Decorate with real flowers, nuts, rind, etc.

RICH ICING

EF   GF
1 cup tahini, almond or cashew butter
1/2 to 1 cup Chestnut Cream (p. 90) or Cashew Cream (p. 89) to taste
2 tablespoons carob flour
1 teaspoon orange or lemon rind
Pinch of sea salt
1 teaspoon vanilla

1. Blend together tahini, Chestnut Cream and carob.

2. Add rind, sea salt and vanilla. Keep blending until desired consistency is reached (the longer you blend, the thicker it becomes). Use hot juice to adjust consistency.

Sugar

The amount of sugar primitive people could eat was limited by the amount of food from natural sources their stomachs and intestines could hold. When they ate sugar they also were eating protein, vitamins, minerals and other valuable foods along with it. Because their sugar supply came mainly from natural fruits and vegetables, their bodies were able to break down the sugar into glucose gradually without straining.

Today, we eat kilogram after kilogram of refined sugar without being restrained by any natural fibre. Not getting any nutrients with it, especially those which are necessary to help metabolize the sugar, we strain our pancreas and other internal organs by eating sugar in the form of sucrose. The stress of bypassing the natural digestive process of breaking sugar down into glucose causes undue strain on the body and can lead eventually to severe illness.

A number of other ill-effects can be produced in the body by sugar. Dr Denis P. Burkitt of the Medical Research Council of London has stated that refined sugar alters the bacteria in the lining of the intestines. Such altered bacteria are capable of breaking down bile salts to form cancer-producing material. Dr Burkitt said, 'You can put the whole thing down to food – especially white flour and sugar.'

Our grandparents were led to believe that 'raw' sugar was inferior to the refined, white product because it was dark and full of impurities. Actually the reverse was true: the dark vibrant colour was proof of the presence of natural minerals. But in 1898, certain sugar refiners procured a chemist who was willing to say that upon examination 'raw' sugar was found to contain 'disease producing insects'. It was then proposed that only refined sugar be sold because 'those terrible creatures' do not occur in refined sugar of any quality, and a law prohibiting the sale of unrefined sugar in the U.S. was passed. Today, much of the 'raw' and even 'brown' sugar is made by processing white sugar one step further – putting molasses back into it for colour and flavour.

According to Dr McCracken of the University of California, 'pure or almost pure sugar (sucrose) such as refined sugar is the worst of all foods. It is absorbed so rapidly into the body through the bloodstream that it may trigger an over production of insulin; this reduces the blood sugar to harmfully low levels, a condition known as hypoglycemia. However, sugar obtained from natural foods, such as grains and vegetables, is absorbed into the bloodstream gradually and does not upset the delicate balance of high and low blood sugar levels. Thus it gives the body more energy to work with.'

There is ample evidence to prove that refined sugar encourages bacteria to eat up B vitamins and kills certain bacteria that help produce vitamins and enzymes in the body. In order to digest sugar (which has lost its own vitamins during the refining process), the body must take vitamin B and minerals such as calcium from the heart, liver, kidneys and nervous system, resulting in other deficiencies as well. The instant energy or 'sugar rush' occurring immediately upon sugar entering the system paralyses the stomach until acids are mobilized to neutralize it. This over-production of acids is counteracted by an emergency mobilization of stored minerals. Calcium is the first mineral to be used and is therefore the most easily depleted mineral in the body.

Furthermore, when we have an excess of sugar in our bodies, the liver stores it. When the liver is overloaded, it returns the excess sugar to the blood in the form of fatty acids. These are circulated throughout the body.

They are stored as accumulated solid fat in the thighs, buttocks and other less active areas.

Other symptoms have been related to the overconsumption of sugar. These include loss of appetite, fatigue, tooth decay, depression, difficulty in thinking, rheumatism due to a calcium-phosphorus imbalance and even mental illness. Refined sugar irritates the mucous membranes, blood vessels, glands and digestive organs because it is unnaturally concentrated.

Choose an unrefined sweetener such as sun-dried fruits, barley malt, rice syrup, fructose, fruit juice, maple syrup, molasses, fruit juice concentrate (e.g. apple) or, on rare occasions, honey. (Of course too much of anything, including unrefined sugars, may also be harmful to the body.) Carrots, beets, parsnips and other vegetables, fruits and grains contain many valuable nutrients as well as natural sugars. So bake and cook with unrefined ingredients. They will make your food taste better and your family and friends feel more vital.

SUGAR IN POPULAR FOODS

The approximate sugar content of popular foods expressed in teaspoons. 1 level teaspoon sugar has approximately 84 kilojoules (20 calories).

		tsp sugar
Confectionery		
Chocolate bar	1 average size	7
Chocolate cream	1 average size	2
Chocolate fudge	4 cm (1½ in) square	4
Chocolate mints	1 medium	3
Marshmallow	1 average	1½
Chewing gum	1 stick	½
Biscuits and Cakes		
Chocolate cake	1/12 cake	15
Angel food cake	1/12 cake	6
Sponge cake	1/10 cake	6
Doughnut, plain	8 cm (3 in) diameter	4
Gingersnaps	1 medium	1
Ice-Cream	½ cup	5-6
Pies		
Apple	1/6 medium pie	12
Cherry	1/6 medium pie	14
Raisin	1/6 medium pie	13
Soft Drinks		
Sweet carbonated beverage	180 ml (6 fl oz) bottle	4⅓
Ginger ale	180 ml (6 fl oz) bottle	3⅓
Milk Drinks		
Chocolate	1 cup	6
Cocoa	1 cup	4
Spreads and Sauces		
Jam	1 tablespoon	3
Marmalade	1 tablespoon	3
Syrup, maple	1 tablespoon	2½
Honey	1 tablespoon	3
Chocolate sauce	1 tablespoon	4½
Cooked Fruit		
Peaches, canned in syrup	2 halves, 1 tablespoon syrup	3½
Apple sauce	½ cup	2
Prunes, sweetened	4 medium	8
Dried Fruits		
Apricots	4-6 halves	4
Prunes	3-4	4
Dates	3-4 pitted	4½
Figs	2 small	4
Raisins	¼ cup	4
Fruits and Fruit Juices, Sweetened		
Orange juice	½ cup	2
Pineapple juice	½ cup	2⅗
Grapefruit juice	½ cup	2⅕

SUGAR CONSUMPTION BY NATION
Annual kilograms per capita

Ireland	57.15
Netherlands	55.3
Australia	52.1
United Kingdom	50.3
New Zealand	49.8
Denmark	48.08
Israel	47.6
Switzerland	47.1
United States	46.2
Canada	46.2

Taken from Australian Bureau of Statistics

CAROB ICING

EF GF

1/2 cup sweetener (p. 12)
1/2 cup carob flour
1/3 cup tahini or peanut butter
1/4 teaspoon sea salt
1 teaspoon anise or coriander
2 teaspoons vanilla
Fruit juice as necessary

1. Heat sweetener in a heavy saucepan until warm. Stir in carob flour (sift if lumpy).

2. Add next three ingredients, stirring as you go. Remove from heat and mix in vanilla. Stir until creamy and smooth adding juice as necessary. Use immediately for icing, filling or topping. It can also be used as a fudge. If you are using greaseproof paper, oil it first so that the fudge doesn't stick.

Coconut *(Cocos nucifara)*

Coconuts, the fruit of the coconut palm (*Cocos nucifera*), grow in large clusters among giant, feather-like leaves. About twelve new leaves appear each year, and an equal number of compound flower stalks push out from the base of the older leaves. Thirty female flowers, and ten thousand male flowers appear on each stalk, maturing at different times, thereby assuring cross-pollination. Flowering begins when the tree is about five years old, and continues thereafter.

Each coconut has a smooth, light coloured rind, under which is found a 1.2 or 2.5 cm (1 or 2 in) thick tough husk of brownish-red fibres. The rind and husk surround a brown woody shell that has three soft spots or 'eyes' at one end. The rind and husk are usually discarded before the coconuts are shipped to market.

The coconut seed lies inside the shell in the shape of a crisp white ball of coconut meat, surrounded by a tough, brown skin. Its hollow centre contains a sugary liquid referred to as coconut 'milk'. The coconut seed is one of the largest of all seeds, measuring 20-30 cm (8-12 in) long and 15-25 cm (6-10 in) across. It requires about one year to ripen.

Coconut fruits float easily and have been dispersed widely by ocean currents throughout the tropics. The native home of the coconut palm is unknown. It flourishes best close to the sea on low-lying areas a few metres above water where there is circulating ground water and ample rainfall.

Most of the world's coconuts are produced in the Philippines, Indonesia, India, Ceylon and Malaysia.

GLAZES

Glazes give cakes or pastries a smooth, shiny appearance. If you want the glaze to drip down the sides of the cake, thin it by adding more liquid. If you want to use the glaze as a filling, decrease the liquid. See Poppy Seed Fruit Puree (p. 84), for advice on handling arrowroot flour. Kuzu may be substituted for arrowroot (p. 25), using slightly more liquid and only two-thirds the amount of flour. Recipes may also be augmented with natural flavourings, spices, fruits, nuts or seeds. Try using soy or nut milk in place of fruit juice. Add sweetener to taste.

SESAME GLAZE

EF GF
1 cup any fruit juice
Pinch of sea salt
1/2-1 tablespoon arrowroot flour
2 tablespoons any fruit juice
1/4 cup roasted sesame seeds

1. Bring 1 cup juice and sea salt to the boil.
2. Dissolve arrowroot flour in 2 tablespoons fruit juice and add to the boiling liquid, stirring rapidly until it boils again, thickens and turns clear. Remove from heat immediately and stir in seeds. Pour over dessert and serve.

ORANGE GLAZE

EF GF

Follow the recipe for Sesame Glaze, reducing the cup of juice to 3/4 cup. Add 1/4 cup orange juice and substitute 2 tablespoons tangerine, orange or lemon rind for sesame seeds.

VARIATIONS FOR SESAME GLAZE
EF GF

Coffee glaze: Bring fruit juice and sea salt to the boil. Before adding arrowroot mixture, add 2-3 tablespoons grain coffee and boil until coffee dissolves.

Spice glaze: Follow directions for Coffee Glaze, adding 1/2-1 teaspoon cloves, ginger or cinnamon (or a combination) after cooking. Stir and let sit 2-3 minutes before using.

Fruit glaze: Soak 1/4 cup dried fruit in fruit juice to cover until soft. Drain and save liquid, adding enough liquid to measure 1 cup. Dice fruit, combine with liquid and boil 10 minutes. Add arrowroot mixture and follow Sesame Glaze recipe.

Fresh fruit glaze: After cooking, add 1 teaspoon lemon rind and 3 cups diced strawberries, blueberries, apples, pears or other fruit. Stir well. (Decrease liquid accordingly.)

Raisin-orange glaze: Add ½ cup soaked raisins to Orange Glaze before cooking.

Peppermint glaze: Place 2 mint-tea bags in 1 cup fruit juice and boil. Remove bags, add dissolved arrowroot and stir rapidly. Continue as with Sesame Glaze.

Vanilla glaze: Add 1 teaspoon vanilla extract (or to taste) after removing pan from heat. Or use vanilla bean (see pp. 29-30).

Nut or seed glaze: Add 1 cup roasted sunflower seeds, blanched almonds, walnuts, pecans, peanuts or chestnuts to glaze after cooking.

Nut butter glaze: Blend 2 tablespoons of any nut butter into juice after cooking. This glaze will not be as clear, but it will still be shiny.

Coconut glaze: Add 4 tablespoons shredded coconut to glaze after cooking.

BLUEBERRY SOY GLAZE

EF GF
1 cup Soy Milk (p. 233)
Pinch of sea salt
1 tablespoon arrowroot or kuzu flour as needed
Sweetener to taste (p. 12)
1 teaspoon vanilla
½-1 cup chopped blueberries

Follow instructions for Cherry Almond Glaze, substituting vanilla and blueberries for lemon juice, lemon rind and cherries.

CHERRY ALMOND GLAZE

EF GF
1 cup Almond Milk (p. 232)
Pinch of sea salt
1-2 tablespoons arrowroot or kuzu flour
2 tablespoons sweetener (p. 12)
2 teaspoons lemon juice
1-1½ teaspoons lemon rind to taste
½-1 cup chopped, pitted cherries

1. Heat ¾ cup Almond Milk and sea salt together in heavy saucepan over medium heat until almost boiling.

2. Dissolve arrowroot flour and sweetener in ¼ cup Almond Milk. Add this to Almond Milk, stirring constantly, until mixture boils, thickens and turns clearer.

3. Remove from heat, add lemon juice and rind, and cherries and stir. Use immediately.

VARIATION

Almond coffee mint glaze: Follow recipe for Cherry Almond Glaze. Add 2-3 tablespoons grain coffee before boiling and ¼ teaspoon dried mint to Almond Milk after boiling. If you prefer, cook 2 mint-tea bags in juice or Almond Milk until liquid boils, add grain coffee and let simmer 2-3 minutes. Then add other ingredients, except cherries and follow recipe.

PEACH COCONUT GLAZE

EF GF
1 cup Coconut Milk (p. 233)
Pinch of sea salt
1 tablespoon kuzu or arrowroot flour as needed
Sweetener to taste
2 teaspoons orange juice
2 teaspoons rum or vanilla
¹/2-1 cup skinned, stoned and chopped peaches

Follow instructions for Cherry Almond Glaze, p. 80, substituting orange juice, rum or vanilla, and peaches for lemon juice, rind and cherries.

CRUMB GLAZE

EF
4 tablespoons sweetener (p. 12)
4 tablespoons oil
1 cup cake or biscuit crumbs
¹/2 teaspoon cinnamon
1 cup ground nuts

Combine ingredients and spoon on cake before or during baking.

NUT GLAZE

GF
¹/4 cup sweetener (p. 12)
2 tablespoons oil
1 unbeaten egg white
2 tablespoons sweetener (p. 12)
¹/2 cup crushed nuts
¹/2 teaspoon cinnamon

Blend first three ingredients together. Add the rest of the ingredients and spread on top of dessert before baking.

PUREES

BASIC VEGETABLE PUREE

EF GF

6-8 cups chopped squash, carrots, sweet potato, parsnips, pumpkin, beets or yams*
3 tablespoons oil
Pinch of sea salt
2 tablespoons sweetener (optional)

*Squash, pumpkin and yams contain more liquid, so use a larger quantity of these vegetables.

1. If using squash, pumpkin or yams, remove skins before cooking.
2. Heat oil in a heavy skillet. Sauté vegetables on a low heat for 5 minutes, stirring occasionally. Add sea salt, cover and cook until tender. Add sweetener if desired.
3. Puree in food processor or blender.

ALTERNATIVE METHOD

Cut squash, pumpkin, sweet potato or yam into thin strips or wedges (like melons). Baste with *tamari* and oil. Heat oven to 180°C (350°F). Place in casserole, add water 6 mm (¼ in), cover and bake until tender. Uncover 5 minutes before removing from oven (to allow excess water to evaporate). These vegetables sometimes taste sweeter if baked.

Squash and Pumpkin

(Cucurbitaceae)

The squash, cucumber, melon and pumpkin are all members of the same family. They are all trailing or climbing herbs, with tendrils and large, lobed leaves. The flowers are usually yellow and the berry-like fruit is generally oval or round in shape.

The most familiar kind of pumpkin grown in northern America is usually orange, maturing in October just before Halloween. Another kind of pumpkin, called *natawari* (from the Japanese for 'to split with an axe') was first grown in Hokkaido, a northern island of Japan. Unlike its relative, it is greenish-blue on the outside and deep yellow on the inside. It has a strong sweet taste that is excellent for the traditional pumpkin pie.

Some Australian and New Zealand varieties that are good in desserts are butternut, winter squash and Queensland blue. Most of these are very sweet if used in season. Winter Luxury and Small Sugar are popular in the United States; as are Hubbard, Gold Nugget and Hundredweight in the United Kingdom.

FANCY VEGETABLE PUREE

EF GF
2 cups vegetable puree
2 tablespoons tahini, sesame, almond or peanut butter
2-3 tablespoons arrowroot flour (see Poppy Seed Fruit Puree, p. 84)
¼ cup sweetener (p. 12) or fruit juice
1 teaspoon orange or lemon rind
1 teaspoon cinnamon

1. Prepare vegetable puree; allow to cool.
2. Place puree and nut butter in a saucepan and cook on a medium heat until mixture boils.
3. Dilute arrowroot in sweetener or juice. Add arrowroot combination to puree and stir constantly until it comes to the boil and thickens.
4. Remove from heat. Stir in rind and cinnamon.

VARIATIONS FOR VEGETABLE PUREES
EF GF
Combine two different vegetables and/or fruits together in ratios such as:

carrot – beet	3:1
carrot – squash	1:1
carrot – parsnip	3:1
apricot – yam	1:1
beet – parsnip	1:2
parsnip – yam	1:2
pumpkin – parsnip	2:1
pear – parsnip	2:1
carrot – raisin	2:1

See also variations for Oat Cream (p. 91).

Parsnip *(Pastinaca sativa)*

This strong yellowish-white root vegetable is found in most parts of Australia and New Zealand as well as England, Europe and the United States. Cultivated since Roman times, it contains large quantities of sugar and starch and has been used for feeding man as well as livestock. If used sparingly in desserts, it will enhance the flavour of any dish.

CHESTNUT PUREE

EF GF

Chestnut Puree is widely used in European pastries because of its delicate taste and texture.

To prepare with dried chestnuts: Soak in liquid to cover overnight. Add more liquid to cover if necessary before cooking. Bring to a boil and then simmer, covered, until tender. Drain off liquid,* cool, and puree in a food processor or blender, or mash like potatoes.

To prepare with fresh chestnuts: Cut a cross with a knife on the flat side of each chestnut. Place in a saucepan and cover with cold liquid. Bring to a boil. Remove from heat. Take out chestnuts (a few at a time) and peel off outer and inner skins while warm. Cover the chestnuts with liquid. Simmer until tender. Drain, reserving liquid. Cool, then mash, blend, or puree in a food processor. Leftover liquid can be used as flavouring in other desserts.

* Reserve liquid and use as fruit juice.

POPPY SEED FRUIT PUREE

EF GF

1¹/₂ cups dried mixed fruit
Fruit juice or water
¹/₂ cup poppy seeds
2 tablespoons arrowroot flour (1 tablespoon per ¹/₂ cup of pureed fruit)
Pinch of sea salt

1. Soak fruit in liquid to cover until soft. Add more liquid if necessary to cover fruit. Add poppy seeds, simmer in a covered pan 30 minutes.

2. Strain off extra liquid and set aside. Allow liquid to cool. Puree. When cooking liquid is cool, dilute arrowroot flour in ¹/₂ cup liquid.

3. Combine arrowroot mixture, sea salt, and puree, adding more liquid if necessary to make 2 cups. Place in a saucepan and cook on medium heat, stirring until mixture comes to the boil and thickens.

FRUIT PUREE

EF GF

1 cup dried apricots, currants, dates, figs, sultanas, etc.
Fruit juice or water
1 teaspoon vanilla
Pinch of sea salt

Put fruit in a saucepan with enough juice to almost cover. Bring to the boil, lower heat and simmer uncovered until no liquid remains. Remember that each type of fruit is different; some may require more liquid or soaking, some less. Adjust accordingly.

Make a larger quantity and keep it refrigerated until you want to use it.

FRESH FRUIT PUREE

EF GF

To use fresh fruit, follow the recipe for Basic Vegetable Puree (p. 82), substituting fruit for vegetables. When using arrowroot flour, remember quantity needed is ¼-½ tablespoon per cup of liquid. When you combine arrowroot flour with Fruit or Vegetable Puree, it may be necessary to add a few more tablespoons of puree or some fruit juice per tablespoon of arrowroot flour because of the thicker consistency of the puree.

See Oat Cream Variations (p. 91) for other suggestions.

Apple or Prune Butter or Sugarless Fruit Jam may be substituted for any fruit puree.

Pineapple *(Ananas comosus)*

One of the most popular and delicious of the tropical fruits, the pineapple is native to South America, with commercial production occurring also in Hawaii, Australia, Malaysia and a number of other tropical countries. Only fruit ripened before the picking is very sweet. Avoid pineapple with discoloured dried-out leaves. Due to their high sugar content and delicious flavour they are an ideal dessert fruit which has the added bonus of also containing vitamins A and C.

FILLINGS

TOFU FRUIT COTTAGE CHEESE

EF GF
1 cup blanched mashed tofu
1/2 teaspoon cinnamon
1/2 teaspoon ground coriander
1 teaspoon vanilla
3/4 cup chopped mixed fresh fruit
1/2 cup chopped mixed dried fruit
1/2 cup almond butter

Mix all ingredients until well combined. Use as a filling.

LEMON NUT

EF GF
3 tablespoons oil
250 g (1/2 lb) roasted, crushed sesame seeds
3-4 cups roasted blanched ground almonds
1/2 cup sweetener (p. 12)
1 tablespoon lemon rind
1 teaspoon cinnamon
Pinch of sea salt
1 teaspoon lemon juice

Cook all ingredients except lemon juice for 5 minutes, mixing occasionally. Remove from heat, add lemon juice, toss lightly.

RAISIN NUT

*Gluten free if using coconut.

EF GF*
4 tablespoons whole wheat breadcrumbs or desiccated coconut *
1/4 cup sweetener (p.12)
1 1/2 cups roasted ground almonds or macadamia nuts
1/4 cup tahini
1/2 cup raisins or sultanas
1 teaspoon orange or lemon rind
Pinch of sea salt
1 teaspoon vanilla

Combine breadcrumbs or coconut with sweetener, stir in nuts, tahini, fruit, rind, sea salt and vanilla. Use as filling for pastry sheets, tarts, strudels.

WALNUT MANGO

EF GF

1 1/2 cups lightly roasted ground walnuts
1/2 grated mango
1/2 cup oil
1/2 cup raisins or sultanas
2 teaspoons orange rind
1 teaspoon vanilla
Pinch of sea salt
1 teaspoon cinnamon

Combine the above ingredients. Mix well. Use for pastry sheets, tarts, strudels.

ALMOND NUT

EF GF

4 cups blanched roasted ground almonds
2 teaspoons cinnamon
1 teaspoon cardamom or coriander
1 1/2 cups oil
1/4 teaspoon sea salt

Sauté nuts and spices in oil for 5 minutes, stirring occasionally. Cool and fill pastry sheets, tarts, strudels, etc.

Cloves *(Eugenia aromatica)*

Cloves are produced from a tree that is native to Indonesia. They are the dried flower buds of the tree. The trees, which grow to about 12 m (4 ft) in height, begin to bear at about 8 or 9 years old, and have a life span of about 60 years. The buds are picked by hand and dried in the sun for several days. Cloves are mainly used as a spice for cakes, biscuits, pies and pastry.

APPLE APRICOT

EF GF
4 apples
1/2 cup sultanas
2 cups dried apricots
1/2-1 cup apple juice
1 teaspoon cinnamon
1/2 teaspoon ginger
1/2 teaspoon coriander
1 tablespoon miso

Core and chop apples. (Peel if not organic.) Combine apples, sultanas, apricots and enough juice to cover fruit in saucepan. Bring to the boil, add the next three ingredients, cover and simmer 15 minutes. Remove cover and boil off excess liquid. Cream in miso, cool and use as a filling.

TOFU CRUMB

GF
2 cups pressed tofu
3 tablespoons oil
Pinch of sea salt
1 beaten egg
1 teaspoon vanilla, rum or brandy
1/4 cup sweetener (p. 12)
Grated rind of 1/2 lemon or orange
1/2 cup raisins or sultanas
1/4 cup roasted chopped almonds or hazelnuts

1. Break tofu into small pieces. In a warm skillet, lightly sauté tofu, oil and sea salt. Set aside 5 minutes to cool.

2. Combine lightly beaten egg, tofu, vanilla, sweetener, rind and raisins. Mix together until all ingredients are combined. Add nuts. This texture is good for strudels (p. 136).

Opposite: Party Tarts
(page 132)

CREAMS

VANILLA CREAM

Spoon this over your favourite dessert, torte or pastry.

EF GF
1 tablespoon arrowroot flour
1/2 cup Nut or Soy Milk (pp. 232-3)
1/2 cup grape or other fruit juice
2 teaspoons vanilla
1 quantity Tofu Whip Cream (p. 94)
2 cups minced strawberries or other fruit in season

Dissolve arrowroot in Nut or Soy Milk and add juice. Cook, stirring continuously until mixture comes to the boil. Remove from heat, and cool. Refrigerate. Prepare Tofu Whip Cream. Before serving beat in vanilla and whip cream into first mixture. Fold in strawberries and use as desired.

CASHEW NUT CREAM

Prepare as for Nut Milk (p. 232), but do not add as much liquid and do not strain.

VARIATIONS
Add soaked dried fruit or fresh fruit in season.

Apricot *(Prunus armeniaca)*

The apricot comes from a tree 7-9 m (20-30 ft) high, with white and sometimes pink flowers, which bloom in spring before the leaves appear. Under proper conditions, the apricot tree can be grown from discarded stones. The trees are found mainly in warm, temperate climates. Some of the fruits are pale yellow, but they may range from yellow to deep orange with a freckled skin.

Opposite: Rum-Scented
Rock Melon Tart
(page 135)

CHESTNUT CREAM

EF GF

1 cup dried chestnuts soaked overnight in 2 cups fruit juice
Extra fruit juice, as needed
3-4 tablespoons tahini or almond butter
2 tablespoons sweetener (p. 12)
Pinch of sea salt
1 teaspoon cinnamon
1 teaspoon vanilla

1. Add enough fruit juice to cover chestnuts. Bring to the boil and simmer covered until tender.

2. If pressure-cooking, pressure-cook for 45 minutes in enough liquid to cover.

3. Drain off liquid from chestnuts and reserve.

4. While they are still hot, blend the chestnuts together with the next five ingredients. (If you want a thinner consistency, thin with reserved cooking liquid.)

If you blend or cream the chestnuts when they get cold, it will be almost impossible to get a good creamy consistency because of their high fat content.

CHESTNUT CREAM MOULD

EF GF

1 quantity Chestnut Cream (above)
4 tablespoons agar-agar flakes
2 cups fruit juice

1. Combine agar-agar and juice, and bring to the boil. Lower heat, cover and simmer 5 minutes. Blend together with Chestnut Cream.

2. This mixture will set when cold. It can be used for various desserts, such as pies, or ice-cream. For ice-cream you would have to freeze, whip and freeze again for best results.

OAT CREAM

EF
1 cup rolled oats
4-6 cups fruit juice
1/4 cup nut butter
Pinch of sea salt, to taste
1/4 cup sweetener (p. 12)
1 teaspoon cinnamon
1 teaspoon vanilla

1. Roast oats until lightly browned. Combine juice, nut butter and oats in a heavy pot. Add sea salt and sweetener, and bring to the boil, stirring occasionally. Lower heat, cover and simmer at least 20 minutes.

2. After cooking, add cinnamon and vanilla. Blend until creamy and smooth. Adjust liquid content until desired texture is attained. This can be kept under refrigeration for several weeks.

VARIATIONS

1. Add 4 tablespoons grain coffee or carob flour before cooking.

2. Add 1 teaspoon cinnamon, ½ teaspoon ground ginger and 1 teaspoon orange, tangerine or lemon rind after cooking.

3. Add 2 teaspoons mint before cooking.

4. Add the juice and grated rind of 1 orange, tangerine or lemon after cooking.

5. Add ½ cup cooked chestnuts (follow instructions in Chestnut Cream, p. 90) after cooking, and before or after blending.

6. Add ½ cup chopped, roasted nuts or seeds after blending.

7. Add 1 to 2 teaspoons more vanilla after cooking, or vanilla bean before cooking.

8. Add ½ cup sweetener before or after cooking.

9. Substitute whole wheat cake or pastry flour, chestnut or cornflour for oats.

ALMOND CREAM

GF

1 cup blanched ground almonds
Fruit juice, as needed
2 eggs, beaten
2 tablespoons warm almond butter
1 tablespoon lemon juice
Rind of 1/4 lemon
4 tablespoons maple syrup
Pinch of sea salt
Vanilla, rum or brandy to taste

Blend almonds with a little fruit juice until smooth. Add eggs, warm almond butter and the rest of the ingredients. Blend until smooth. Cook over a double boiler until thickened. Flavour with vanilla, rum or brandy after removing from the heat. Adjust consistency as necessary.

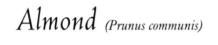

Almond *(Prunus communis)*

Almonds are one of the fruits of the rose family. Originally, the almond is thought to have come from one of the Mediterranean countries, where it is still widely grown.

The tree is medium-size, related to the peach and grown chiefly for its nuts. The beautiful pinkish-white blossoms open in early spring before the long, pointed leaves appear. The edible seed or nut is enclosed within a small dry shell.

Almonds contain a large percentage of oil, and are also made into almond butter, used in baking and cooking. There are two kinds of almonds: sweet and bitter. Sweet almonds, a popular delicacy, are eaten roasted or salted, or are used in the cooking and baking of pastries.

The bitter almond is a variety of the common almond, but is usually not considered edible. Because of the large quantity of hydrocyanic acid it contains, the oil is most frequently used in medicines, or as a flavouring extract (almond extract) for baking, after the acid has been removed.

CUSTARD CREAM

3 tablespoons whole wheat cake or pastry flour
1 1/2-2 cups fruit juice
4 tablespoons sweetener (p. 12)
3 egg yolks
Pinch of sea salt
2 teaspoons orange rind
1 tablespoon oil
2 teaspoons vanilla or rum

1. Roast flour until lightly browned. Set aside to cool.
2. Heat juice. Cool.
3. Place sweetener, yolks, flour, sea salt and rind in double boiler. Pour juice slowly into the sweetener mixture, beating with rotary beater or wire whisk.
4. Cook over low heat for 5 minutes or until thickened, stirring occasionally. Remove from heat, add oil and flavouring, mix well.

See variations for Oat Cream (p. 91).

BASIC TOFU CREAM

EF GF
2 cups tofu
1/2 cup fruit juice
1/2 cup tahini or almond butter
Pinch of sea salt
1/2 tablespoon arrowroot flour
1/2 cup sweetener (p. 12)
3 tablespoons fruit juice
1 teaspoon vanilla

1. Blanch tofu in boiling water for 2 minutes. Drain and blend until creamy. Add next three ingredients. Dissolve arrowroot in sweetener and juice.
2. Place tofu mixture in pan, and when almost boiling, add arrowroot mixture, and bring to the boil. Remove from heat. Stir in vanilla.

See variations for Oat Cream (p. 91).

MINUTE TOFU CREAM

EF GF

2 cups blanched tofu (p. 93)
1 cup Date Puree (p. 85) or 1/2 cup maple syrup
1/2 cup tahini, or almond butter
1 teaspoon vanilla, rum or brandy
Pinch of sea salt

Combine tofu with remaining ingredients, blending until creamy. Add fruit juice blending to desired consistency.

TOFU WHIP CREAM

EF GF

1 cup blanched tofu (p. 93)
1/4 cup sweetener (p. 12)
4 tablespoons oil or nut butter
Pinch of sea salt
1/2 cup fruit juice
3 tablespoons agar-agar flakes
1 teaspoon vanilla or almond essence
1/2 tablespoon grated lemon rind

1. Blend tofu, sweetener, oil or nut butter and sea salt together until creamy. Set aside.

2. Pour fruit juice over agar-agar and bring to the boil; lower heat and simmer until agar-agar dissolves. Stir occasionally. Remove from heat.

3. Add vanilla and lemon rind to tofu cream mixture. Beat until smooth and creamy. Set aside to gel. When the mixture has almost set, beat again. Set aside for a few hours to mellow.

4. Chill if not using immediately. To freshen, beat again before using.

See variations for Oat Cream (p. 91).

TOFU SOUR CREAM

EF GF
1 cup tofu
Juice of 1 lemon (2-3 tablespoons)
1/2-1 teaspoon sea salt
1/4-1/3 cup oil

1. Drop tofu into boiling salted water. Drain and discard cooking water.
2. Place tofu in a blender, add lemon juice and salt. Blend until creamy. Slowly drip in oil till creamy and smooth. Taste. If it is too sour, add more salt or hot water to counteract lemon.

FRUIT TOFU SOUR CREAM

EF GF
1/2 teaspoon cinnamon
1/2-1 teaspoon vanilla
1 cup Tofu Sour Cream (above)
1 cup diced apples or peaches
1/4 cup raisins or sultanas

Blend cinnamon and vanilla with Tofu Sour Cream; add fruit and mix together. Use as a filling or cake topping.

VARIATIONS

1. Use any fresh fruit in season in place of apples.
2. Use any dried fruit; soak and dice.
3. Add roasted chopped nuts or seeds, before or after blending.
4. Add 1 to 2 teaspoons sweetener and 1 teaspoon lemon juice to fruit.
5. Allow to marinate for several hours before mixing with cream.
6. Also see variations for Oat Cream (p. 91).

CRUMB TOPPINGS

Crumbs
There are many ways to convert leftover breads, cakes or biscuits into crumbs. To dry out, place them on a baking sheet in a 140°C (275°F) oven before making crumbs. Bake until dry, but not browned. Crush them or chop and then roll between two sheets of paper. Substitute crumbs for flour in any of the following recipes.

Any of these crumb topping recipes may be used as fillings, pastry dough, or snacks as well.

OAT CRUMB

EF
1/2 cup whole wheat flour
1 cup rolled oats
1 cup roasted ground sesame or sunflower seeds
2 teaspoons instant grain coffee
Pinch of sea salt
1/4 cup oil
1/4 cup maple syrup
1/4-1/2 cup fruit juice

Combine all dry ingredients. Rub oil and sweetener into dry mixture, adding more liquid if necessary. Use as for Macadamia Coffee Crumb.

ORANGE PINE NUT CRUMB

EF
2 cups rolled oats
1 cup lightly roasted ground pine nuts
2 teaspoons cinnamon
2 tablespoons orange or lemon rind
Pinch of sea salt
1 teaspoon vanilla or orange flower water
Fruit juice as needed
1/4 cup oil
Maple syrup to taste

Follow directions for Macadamia Coffee Crumb.

MACADAMIA COFFEE CRUMB

EF
1 cup whole wheat flour
1 cup rolled oats
1/4 cup corn or maize meal
1 cup crushed macadamia nuts
2 tablespoons cinnamon
Pinch of sea salt
1/2 cup oil
1/4 cup maple syrup
1 tablespoon vanilla or rum or 1/2 teaspoon rose water
Fruit juice to bind

1. Combine all dry ingredients together.
2. Beat oil, maple syrup and vanilla together, and combine with dry mixture. Mix until it becomes sticky, adding a few drops of juice if necessary. Do not saturate with too much juice – texture should resemble a crumble.
3. Sprinkle on top of dessert and bake, or sprinkle onto baking tray and bake, until firm and lightly browned. Cool and store in jar if not using immediately.

This recipe can also be used for a pie crust or biscuits. Add enough juice to bind. Press into pre-oiled pan, and bake.

Macadamia *(Macadamia ternifolia)*

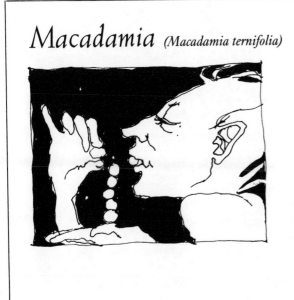

The macadamia nut is a large round seed that grows on a tropical Australian evergreen tree and is the sole commercial food crop native to Australia. Macadamia trees were brough to Hawaii in the late 1800s and today it is one of Hawaii's most important crops.

The macadamia nut has such a hard shell that it has to be cracked by a special machine. The white kernels are usually roasted in oil, and then very often canned and salted. Their taste is similar to a Brazil nut. They can be used in various ways and are most adaptable in cakes, confectionery and ice-cream. The macadamia tree grows more than 12 m (40 ft) tall and has dark green, leathery leaves and creamy-white flowers.

GRAIN SYRUP

EF GF

1. Pressure-cook or boil 2 cups brown rice without salt, in 5 cups water for 45 minutes. Place in a bowl (not metallic) and cool to 60°C (140°F) (use a confectionary thermometer).

2. To the cooked rice, add freshly made grain sprouts* which have been crushed or blended.

3. Cover and keep in a warm place, so that temperature of the rice-sprout mixture is maintained at 50°-60°C (120°-140°F) for 4-5 hours. (You can place it on a warm stove, or rest it in a pan of hot water.) Remove cover and taste. If it is not sweet enough, cover and let sit another few hours, tasting often.

4. Squeeze liquid through cheesecloth into pan. Reserve grain for puddings, etc. Add a pinch of sea salt and cook until desired consistency is reached.

VARIATION

For a different texture, do not squeeze liquid through cheesecloth. Blend. This can be used over cakes, or as a warm drink, or to sweeten recipes.

Amazake may be used instead of grain syrup.

*Use 1 tablespoon unsprouted grain to every 1½ cups cooked rice. Place in a glass jar, put a cheesecloth over the top of the jar and secure. Soak at least 12 hours in springwater to cover. Drain through cheesecloth, rinse with fresh water and drain again. Place jar on its side in a warm, dark place. Rinse and drain each day to maintain moisture.

The grain will sprout in 3-5 days, depending on the grain used and the temperature; the warmer the temperature, the shorter the time needed.

4. SHAPING SIMPLY:
Pastries, Tarts, Pies and Strudels

'Delicious… fragrant… a crust so flaky that it melts in your mouth.'
These and many more compliments from friends and family will surround
you when you have baked pastries from the recipes that follow.

PREPARING THE DOUGH

Methods for Adding the Oil
Choose one of the following.

1. Drip the oil into the dry ingredients in a spiral motion. Using two metal utensils (knives, forks or spoons), cut into the dry mixture until it resembles tiny breadcrumbs.

2. Drip oil into dry ingredients in a spiral motion. Rub oil in with your hands until it resembles tiny breadcrumbs.

3. Drip oil into dry ingredients in a spiral motion. Mix with an electric mixer, but only until the flour resembles tiny breadcrumbs.

4. Beat hot liquid and oil together. Add to the dry ingredients, mixing as you go until a ball of pastry is formed.

Rolling Out
Choose a table which is a comfortable height, neither too low so that you must bend over, nor too high so that you cannot give the rolling pin proper weight.

Temperature of the dough: If the dough is too cold (especially oily dough), it may be too hard to roll out. If the dough is too warm, it may be too soft to shape. The dough should be firm when you press your finger into it, but should not stick.

For oily dough, roll out, shape, place in pan, cover and chill 30 minutes before baking. For non-oily dough, wrap and chill 30 minutes before rolling and shaping.

Method: Cover the rolling surface with canvas, muslin cloth, or greaseproof paper large enough to hang over the sides. Flour lightly with arrowroot. (Arrowroot flour is good to use when the pastry is thin and delicate. It helps to keep the dough from tearing or splitting.) If you over-flour the surface, the pastry may become tough and hard to work with.

1. Shape dough into the desired form with your hands before rolling out.

2. Divide dough into several pieces if necessary. Cover and set aside until ready to roll out.

3. Place dough in centre of cloth or rolling surface so that there is plenty of room for expansion.

4. Sprinkle the top of the dough and rolling pin with arrowroot flour.

5. Roll from the centre outward with quick, light, short strokes, not pressing too hard. Rotate the dough occasionally.

6. Lift the dough occasionally with a spatula or your hand and flour underneath it lightly to prevent it from sticking.

7. Roll out the dough to desired shape and thickness, 5 cm (2 in) larger than the size of the form.

Alternative method: Lay a piece of greaseproof paper over the rolling surface. Divide dough, shape, cover with paper, roll out into the desired shape and size.

TECHNIQUES FOR PIES AND TARTS

Transferring Pastry Dough to Pie Dish (Choose one technique)
1. After rolling out pastry dough to desired shape and size, roll one-third of it around the rolling pin and lift into the pie or tart dish. Allow pastry dough to fall naturally. Do not stretch pastry, otherwise the dough will shrink during baking.

Be sure that the pastry dough overlaps the edge of the pie dish 2.5 to 5 cm (1 to 2 in) to form a decorative edge (see p. 102), if the pie or tart has no cover.
2. After rolling out pastry dough to desired shape and size between pieces of greaseproof paper, peel off the top layer of paper and invert pastry dough onto an oiled pie or tart dish. Peel off the bottom layer of paper. Allow the dough to drop naturally into pan. Do not stretch it.

Section Pie or Tart I
For 4-section pie or tart, cut a long strip of dough and roll it into a rope.
1. Use this rope to divide the shell into four sections. Secure it to the bottom crust by brushing with egg white.
2. Chill 15 minutes.
3. Bake at 220°C (425°F) 10 minutes, and 180°C (350°F) 10-15 minutes longer.
4. Fill and serve, or fill after baking 10 minutes with different-coloured purees and fillings, return to oven and bake 10-15 minutes longer at 180°C (350°F) or until set.

Section Pie or Tart II
When filling a prebaked pie shell with cream, reserve half of the filling for the topping, and prepare a fruit topping.
1. Divide the pie into six or eight slices. Do not cut through.
2. Place cream in a pastry bag and squeeze out design on each alternate slice, leaving every other side empty.
3. Spoon fruit mixture on the remaining sections.
4. Chill before serving.

FANCY COVERS FOR PIES AND TARTS

Lattice Tops
Cut plain strips 12 mm (½ in) wide and 8-10 cm (3-4 in) longer than the pie shell. Roll then twist 12 mm (½ in) rope-like pieces. Place them crisscross or weave them together.

Full Cover
Fold the pastry top in half. Cut one pattern on the fold with a small biscuit cutter. (This allows steam to escape.) Place top crust over pie, unfold, seal edges, glaze and bake.

Fancy Free
Roll out excess pastry dough to 6 mm (¼ in) thickness. With a biscuit cutter, glass bowl or cup, cut out several pieces (six or seven, depending upon the size of the cutters and pie) to cover the top of the pie. Lie the pieces over the filling touching each other (try a yeasted dough also with this technique). Seal the edges.

MAKING EDGES FOR PIE AND TART CRUSTS

1. Make an attractive edge by pressing the back of a spoon or fork around the edge of the pie.
2. Press the prongs of a fork around the edge of the pie.
3. *Fluted:* Double the edge of the crust. Use your index finger or the handle of a knife to make the indentations, and the thumb and index finger of your other hand as a wedge to push against, making scallops.
4. *Crisscross:* Trim the crust at the edge of the pan. Cut the rolled pastry into 12 mm (½ in) wide strips. Moisten the edge of the pastry in the dish. Interlace two strips on the edge of the pie. Keep the strips flat, do not twist, turn over or stretch them. To seal, press rounded edge on both sides of crisscrossed strip tightly against moistened edge with your finger.

FINISHED LOOK

For added colour in yeasted or unyeasted pastry, brush with egg white, yolk or whole egg, combined with 1 teaspoon of cold water, before baking.

For a hard crust and shiny look, brush with any glaze (p. 79) or sweetener (p. 12) several times while baking, or brush with juice or sweetener immediately after removing pastry from the oven.

For a clear glaze just before the pastry has finished baking, brush with ¼ cup sweetener (dissolve in a small amount of liquid if too thick to apply).

After glazing with any of the above, decorate with crushed roasted nuts.

BAKING A SINGLE UNFILLED PIE CRUST

There are three ways to bake an unfilled pie shell:

1. Prick the pastry shell with a fork all over before baking. This allows steam to escape and prevents the bottom from rising or buckling.

2. The second way produces a more evenly shaped pie crust, but the bottom does not brown as much as the rim. Place a large piece of brown paper on the crust. Fill the paper with enough uncooked, oiled rice or beans to hold paper in place. Bake in 190°C (375°F) oven 12-15 minutes or until crust browns lightly. This will prevent the crust from puffing up. Remove the paper and beans or rice a few minutes before the crust is done.

3. Choose either 1 or 2 from above, glaze with egg white and a few drops of water before baking to prevent crust from becoming soggy after filling.

Corn or Maize *(Zea mays)*

Originally a food crop of the Western Hemisphere, corn was taken to Europe by Columbus and has spread all over the temperate zone of the world. It has long been the staple of the American Indians and was supplemented in their diet by beans, sweet potatoes and squash.

The people of Latin America and southern and eastern Africa use ground cornmeal. In Latin America, cornmeal is cooked into flatcakes called *tortillas*; in Africa, it is boiled with water into a cereal resembling the Italian *polenta*.

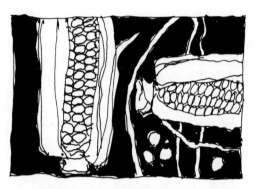

In many Western countries today, white and yellow cornmeal is commonly used as a cereal; as cornflour, it goes into breads, pancake batters and desserts.

FORGET ME KNOTS

1. The amount of liquid and oil necessary for the proper consistency of each recipe will vary according to the moisture and temperature of the flour and the room, the size of the eggs, and the general weather of the day. Remain flexible, and adjust liquid and oil content accordingly.

2. When preparing an unyeasted cold water pastry dough, handle it as little and as delicately as possible. This will inhibit the development of gluten and prevent the dough from becoming tough. Never knead it. After combining all the ingredients with a wooden spoon, lightly shape it into the desired form with your hands before rolling it out.

3. Whole wheat cake or pastry flour makes the most tender pastry dough because it contains less gluten than bread flour.

4. For flakier pastry doughs, liquids and oils should be cold when used, because cold ingredients tend to expand more quickly in the heat of the oven, helping the pastry to be light and flaky.

5. Any fruit juice, cider, herbal tea or equal parts juice and tea may be used interchangeably for liquid in any recipe.

6. When rolling out a thin, delicate pastry dough, sprinkle arrowroot flour before rolling to prevent the pastry from splitting or tearing.

7. Cut pie dough at least 5 cm (2 in) larger than pie dish to allow for shrinkage and edges.

8. Chilling dough after rolling prevents shrinkage during baking.

9. Fill a baked shell with a filling of the same temperature, or slightly warmer; other-

wise, the shell may crack.

10. Bake pies in oven-glass pie plates or dull metal dishes for browner crusts.

11. When completely prebaking a pie shell, prick the bottom and sides with a fork before baking to allow the steam to escape, and oil the rim of the crust to prevent burning.

12. If the filling is juicy, before baking lightly brush the bottom crust with an egg white mixed with a few drops of water or a kuzu-water paste (dilute kuzu to pasty consistency). This will prevent the crust from becoming soggy from the filling.

13. Roll a small tube of wax or heavy paper and insert it into a slit in the centre of the top crust of a fruit pie to release the steam and prevent the juices from leaking out.

14. One and one-half cups flour will make a single pie crust; 2½ cups will make a double-crust pie 20 cm (8 in).

15. Four cups of filling are necessary to fill a 20 cm (8 in) pie shell.

16. For a lighter-coloured crust, place a sheet of paper over the pie crust the last 10 minutes of baking time.

17. To make a pastry dough light and puffy when deep-frying, add 1 or 2 teaspoons lemon or orange juice, brown rice vinegar or apple cider vinegar to the pastry dough before adding liquid.

18. Cool all pastries, pies and tarts on a rack so that air can circulate completely around them. This prevents moisture from accumulating on the bottom.

19. Remove pastries from baking sheets immediately after baking to cool more efficiently.

APPLE DUMPLINGS

1 quantity Strudel Pastry (p. 136)
6 apples
1 cup raisins or sultanas
Pinch of sea salt
¹/₂ cup tahini, almond or peanut butter
1-2 teaspoons cinnamon
1-2 cups fruit juice

1. Prepare pastry dough; cover and set aside. Peel and core apples. Mix rest of ingredients together except juice. Stuff the apples with filling.

2. Roll out pastry 6 mm (¹/₄ in) thick and cut into six squares large enough to cover a whole apple. Set an apple on each piece of pastry. Wrap pastry around apple, covering it completely.

3. Score top. Place dumplings in deep oiled dish. Cover and chill 20 minutes.

4. Preheat oven to 180°C (350°F). Spoon 1 or 2 tablespoons juice over top of each dumpling and bake, basting every 10 minutes with fruit juice until browned.

5. Serve with Basic Tofu Cream (p. 93).

VARIATION

Substitute peaches, pears or apricots (whole or slices), for apples. Do not score top. Heat oil and deep-fry until browned.

APPLE TOFU DELIGHT

1 quantity Eclairs (p. 109)
2-3 cups Basic Tofu Cream (p. 93)
1 apple, thinly sliced
2 teaspoons cinnamon
¹/₂ cup sliced almonds

1. Preheat oven to 190°C (375°F). Oil and lightly flour an 18 cm (7 in) circle on a baking sheet. Spread a thin layer of eclair pastry, about 6 mm (¹/₄ in) thick, within the outline of the circle. Spoon remaining pastry around the layer to make a border, or use a pastry bag instead of a spoon. Bake in a preheated 220°C (425°F) oven 20-25 minutes.

2. Spoon Basic Tofu Cream into the centre of the shell. Spread over pastry. Arrange apple slices (peel if not organic) on top of cream. Sprinkle cinnamon on top of apples, and almonds on top of cinnamon. Bake 10 minutes longer.

VARIATION

Substitute Chestnut Cream for Tofu Cream.

BAKLAVA

Baklava was created by the Persians, who originally had a nut filling scented with pussy-willow blossoms or jasmine inside the pastry.

Around the sixth century, the Greeks discovered the art of making fine, thin pastry (phyllo) and adopted Baklava as their traditional New Year's dessert.

EF

HOT WATER PASTRY DOUGH
²/₃ cup oil
1 teaspoon sea salt
1¹/₂ cups fruit juice
4 cups whole wheat cake or pastry flour
SYRUP
¹/₂ cup oil
6 tablespoons sweetener (p. 12)
2 teaspoons cinnamon
Grated rind of 1 orange
Grated rind of 1 lemon
Juice of 1 lemon (1 tablespoon)
FILLING
3 cups crushed walnuts
1 tablespoon plus 1 teaspoon cinnamon
1 teaspoon dried mint
Pinch of sea salt

HOT WATER PASTRY DOUGH

1. Heat oil, salt and liquid together. Remove from heat and beat by hand for a few minutes. Add this to flour and knead until a soft, sticky dough is formed. Knead about 5 minutes longer, place in an oiled bowl, cover and set in a warm place about half an hour.

2. Cut dough into five pieces, the size of an orange, dip in arrowroot flour, cover and let sit in a warm place half an hour.

SYRUP

Place oil in saucepan and warm. Add sweetener, cinnamon, rind and bring to the boil. Turn off heat, add lemon juice and cool.

FILLING

Mix together walnuts, cinnamon, mint and sea salt. Set aside.

PREPARING THE PASTRY

1. Sprinkle rolling surface with arrowroot. Roll out pastry very thin. (It should be almost transparent when held up to the light.) You should have five layers. Set three layers aside for top.

2. Place two layers of pastry in bottom of rectangular baking dish. Baste in between with oil. Sprinkle some of the walnut mixture over it.

3. Take the three layers that were set aside and brush oil in between each layer. Place on top of the filled pastry.

4. With a sharp knife, score into the top layer. This will allow the top to bake more evenly, as well as decorate it.

5. Pour the cooled syrup over the pastry. Preheat the oven to 190°C (375°F) and bake 30-45 minutes or until top is browned and crisp.

CANNOLI

This is a famous old Italian delicacy passed down from generation to generation. Here is my version of this delightful dessert.

3 cups sifted whole wheat cake or pastry flour
1 teaspoon cinnamon
Pinch of sea salt
2 tablespoons oil
2 eggs
¹/₄ cup sweetener (p. 12)
1 teaspoon lemon or orange juice, or vinegar*
Oil for deep-frying (pp. 18-19)
1 quantity Basic Tofu Cream (p. 93)

*Lemon juice, orange juice or vinegar make the pastries puff up while being deep-fried.

1. Combine, flour, cinnamon and salt together, in a mixing bowl. Cut in oil. Beat eggs, add sweetener, lemon or orange juice, or vinegar.

2. Stir into dry mixture, and knead until dough is smooth (adjust flour-liquid content accordingly).

3. Sprinkle arrowroot flour on pastry cloth or wooden surface and roll out dough until it is very thin. Cut into 10-12.5 cm (4-5 in) ovals or circles.

4. Fold dough over 2.5 x 12.5 cm (1 x 5 in) wooden or metal cylindrical form, and press the ends together in the centre only as if sealing an envelope. Do not overlap too far. (If ends do not stick together, brush with water or egg yolk before pressing together.)

5. Heat oil. Deep-fry until delicately brown. (Forms may separate from cannolis. Remove them immediately from oil.) Drain and cool. Remove form.

6. Fill with Basic Tofu Cream just before serving. Unfilled cannolis may be kept in a cool dry place for several days before using.

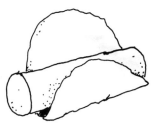

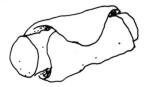

Walnut (Juglans regia)

The walnut tree is valuable not only for its fruit, but also for its timber. Oil is extracted from the nuts and is important for its edible qualities, as well as being a preparation used in paints for artists. The walnut grows up to 30 m (100 ft) high, with green fruit sometimes picked before it hardens, and eaten pickled in vinegar. If allowed to harden, the fruit is then picked and used as nuts.

PROFITEROLES

2/3-1 cup fruit juice
1/4 cup oil
Pinch of sea salt
1 cup whole wheat cake or pastry flour
4 eggs
FILLING
2-4 cups ice-cream (pp. 205-7), sherbet (p. 216) or Tropical Vanilla Fluff
TROPICAL VANILLA FLUFF
(Good also as a light pudding)
3 tablespoons arrowroot or kuzu flour
1 1/2 cups Soy or Nut Milk (pp. 232-3)
1/4 cup mashed banana, mango or paw-paw
1/4-1/3 teaspoon lemon juice
1 tablespoon vanilla
1/2 quantity Basic Tofu Cream (p. 93) or Tofu Whip Cream (p. 94)
TOPPING
CAROB ICING
1/4 cup oil or roasted cashew or almond butter
1/3 cup mashed fruit (banana, mango or very ripe blended peaches
or apricots)
1/4 teaspoon lemon juice to taste
1 teaspoon vanilla, rum or brandy to taste
1/4 cup carob flour
1/4 cup sweetener (p. 12)
Boiling fruit juice as needed

1. Preheat oven to 220°C (425°F). Oil baking sheet.

2. Combine fruit juice, oil and salt in a saucepan and then bring to the boil.

3. Remove from heat immediately and add the flour all at once. Stir fast and hard until mixture leaves the sides of the saucepan and forms a ball. Cool slightly (2-3 minutes).

4. Add eggs one at a time, beating after each addition.

5. Drop large teaspoons of batter onto baking sheet and bake 5 minutes.

6. Lower heat to 190°C (375°F) and bake another 15 minutes or until puffs are firm and golden. Turn off oven and leave door slightly ajar till coolish. Remove to a wire rack and cool completely.

7. Meanwhile prepare filling and topping.

TROPICAL VANILLA FLUFF

1. Dissolve arrowroot in milk. Cook mixture, constantly stirring until it almost comes to the boil. Remove from heat.

2. Beat together mashed fruit, lemon juice and vanilla until smooth. Add to first mixture. Cover and refrigerate.

3. Before using, whip Basic Tofu Cream and beat chilled vanilla mixture until smooth. Fold in Basic Tofu Cream.

CAROB ICING

1. Warm oil or nut butter to make it soft and easier to handle.

2. Beat together mashed fruit, lemon juice, oil or nut butter and flavouring until creamy.

3. Add carob, sweetener and gradually add boiling fruit juice as needed, beating until mixture is smooth, thick and creamy. Use immediately or chill till ready to use.

4. Cut off top of puffs and set aside as lids. Fill puffs with ice-cream, sherbet or Tropical Vanilla Fluff.

5. Replace lids. Cover with Carob Icing and serve at once.

ECLAIRS

¹/₃ cup oil
1 cup fruit juice
1 cup sifted whole wheat cake or pastry flour
Pinch of sea salt
4 eggs
FILLING
2-3 cups Tofu Whip Cream (p. 94)
TOPPING
Carob Icing (p.78)

1. Combine oil and juice in saucepan. Cook on a medium heat until boiling. Lower heat and add sifted flour and sea salt, continuously stirring until a ball forms in pan.

2. Remove from heat and add 3 eggs (one at a time), beating after each addition. Beat the last egg, and add it to the mixture slowly. Preheat oven to 220°C (425°F). Fill a pastry bag with batter. Squeeze out eclair shape onto oiled baking tray.

3. Bake for 20-25 minutes. Turn off oven, open door slightly and leave 10-15 minutes longer, otherwise the rapid change in temperature may cause them to fall and become soggy. Slit the side of the pastry open with scissors to allow steam to escape. Allow to cool.

4. Whip the cream filling. Fill pastry bag with cream and squeeze into eclairs just before serving (use a tube with a large opening).

5. Prepare Carob Icing. Top before serving.

FRENCH PUFFS

¹/4 cup sweetener (p. 12)
¹/4 cup oil
¹/2-³/4 cup boiling fruit juice
Pinch of sea salt
1¹/2 cups sifted whole wheat cake or pastry flour
2 eggs
1 teaspoon vanilla
Oil for deep-frying (pp. 18-19)

1. Combine sweetener, oil, juice and salt in a heavy saucepan. Bring to the boil on a medium heat, stirring occasionally. Add flour to pan all at once, stirring quickly, until thickened.

2. Remove from heat, add eggs immediately, one at a time, beating thoroughly after each addition. Add vanilla. Consistency should be that of a very thick, heavy batter. Adjust flour-liquid content accordingly.

3. Fill pastry bag (p. 72). Oil wax paper. Squeeze batter onto paper in the shape of circles. Heat oil, drop circles in by turning paper at an angle or upside-down so that they slide off. Fry until golden, and drain.

4. Dip into roasted chestnut flour, coconut, crushed nuts, carob or cinnamon after frying.

Cinnamon
(Cinnamomum zeylanicum)

Cinnamon is mainly used as a spice in flavouring desserts such as pies, biscuits, cakes, custards and pastries. It came originally from South India and Ceylon, and is cultivated only in warm tropical climates.

Planted as a seed, after 2 years it is ready to be harvested. The bark is removed in strips. The outer skin of the bark is scraped off, and the strips are dried very slowly. They are pale brown in colour and as they dry they curl into each other forming what we know as 'cinnamon sticks'. There are many different grades of cinnamon, the quality depending on where it is grown and the various colours, ranging from light to dark brown.

POPPY SEED CREPES

POPPY SEED FILLING
EF GF
$^1/_3$ cup poppy seeds
$^2/_3$ cup raisins or sultanas
Fruit juice to cover seeds and fruit
$^1/_4$ teaspoon sea salt
1 teaspoon vanilla
1 teaspoon orange rind
CREPE
2 eggs room temperature
2 tablespoons oil
$1^1/_2$ cups Soy Milk (p. 233)
1 cup whole wheat cake or pastry flour
Sea salt to taste

POPPY SEED FILLING

1. Simmer first four ingredients in an uncovered saucepan for 10 to 15 minutes, or until most of the liquid has evaporated.

2. Blend with vanilla and orange rind until creamy.

CREPE BATTER

(This can be prepared the night before.)

1. Combine all the ingredients and puree quickly for about 30 seconds.

2. Chill for best results for at least 30 minutes. If the batter thickens, thin it out with water till desired consistency is reached.

PUTTING IT ALL TOGETHER

1. Heat crepe pan – the temperature is correct when the batter sizzles when ladled into the pan.

2. Ladle the batter and quickly tilt the pan so that the batter covers the bottom entirely with a thin coating.

3. Pour the excess back into the bowl. Cook one side 1-2 minutes, or until holes appear. Turn over and cook slightly on the other side.

4. Remove crepe by turning pan upside-down and flipping crepe onto a cloth. Cover and set aside. Repeat with remaining batter. Fill and serve. (Place filling in centre, fold both ends toward the centre, overlapping, and fasten with a toothpick.)

CREPE CORNUCOPIA

CREPE BATTER
1/3 cup whole wheat cake or pastry flour
1 egg
1/2-3/4 cup Soy Milk or Nut Milk (pp. 232-3) as needed
FRUIT FILLING
EF GF
1 1/2 cups fresh strawberries
1/2 cup fresh raspberries
1 cup fresh blackberries or blueberries
1/2 teaspoon dry ginger or 2 teaspoons freshly grated ginger juice*
1 tablespoon rum, brandy or cognac or 2 teaspoons vanilla
1/2 cup fruit juice
1/2 cup maple syrup to taste
1 1/2 tablespoons arrowroot or kuzu flour
Pinch of sea salt
TOPPING
Few pine nuts
Plain yoghurt

* Grate fresh ginger on smallest side of grater. Squeeze out ginger to obtain juice.

CREPE BATTER

Place flour in a mixing bowl. Add egg in the centre and slowly incorporate the milk stirring with a fork until a thin batter is obtained. You may have to adjust the liquid content several times as each type of flour needs a different amount. Cover and let batter stand for 15 minutes.

FRUIT FILLING

1. Wash all fruit. Sprinkle with dry ginger or fresh ginger juice and spoon over rum, brandy, cognac or vanilla. Set aside for a few minutes.

2. Combine fruit juice, maple syrup, arrowroot or kuzu and salt and stir till flour is well dissolved. Place in a saucepan and begin to cook, stirring continuously till mixture comes to the boil.

3. Remove from the heat, add the fruit mixture and stir well. (You may find that you need more liquid or arrowroot, so adjust accordingly.) Spoon into cool dish and set aside.

PUTTING IT ALL TOGETHER

1. Heat crepe pan, and brush with oil. Add 2 tablespoons of the batter and swirl the pan to coat evenly. Cook until underside is golden. Turn crepe over and cook a few seconds more. Repeat with remaining batter.

2. Shape crepes into a triangle, cup in your hand and fill. Place on dish, sprinkle with pine nuts and spoon yoghurt over the top just before serving.

HORNS I

EF

3 cups whole wheat cake or pastry flour
1 teaspoon cinnamon
Pinch of salt
1/4 cup cold oil
Apple juice, or any fruit juice or water to form soft, firm dough
3-4 cups Tofu Whip Cream (p.94)

1. Sift all dry ingredients. Cut oil in gradually until mixture resembles tiny breadcrumbs. Combine liquid with mixture and mix until dough is formed.

2. Roll out pastry 3 mm (1/8 in) thick on arrowroot flour.

3. Oil horn-shaped forms. For a 12 cm (5 in) form, the dough should be 4-5 times as long. Wind each strip around a form, starting at the narrowest end, slightly overlapping the edges. Wind the dough around form until it is 12 mm (1/2 in) from the top. This space will allow you to remove the form easily after baking.

Do not stretch the pastry as you roll it around the tube; this will cause it to shrink and break while baking.

4. Cover and chill dough 30 minutes.

5. Preheat the oven to 180°C (350°F). Place the horns on an oiled baking sheet. Bake 45 minutes, or until browned. Remove from oven and cool slightly before removing horns (twist to remove).

6. Before serving, fill pastry bag with Tofu Whip Cream and fill horns.

HORNS II

EF

Follow recipe for Horns I, substituting Yeasted Pastry (p. 142). Wind dough around horns. Cover and set in a warm place to rise until it is one-third larger. Bake at 180°C (350°F) for 30-40 minutes, or until horns are lightly browned.

HORNS III

EF

Follow recipe for Horns I or II. Add 2 teaspoons lemon or orange juice, or vinegar to liquid before combining it with dry mixture.

Heat oil for deep-frying (pp. 18-19). Deep-fry horns until lightly browned. Drain and cool. Remove forms.

TEIGLACH

Adapted from a traditional Jewish recipe my mother always used.

2 cups whole wheat cake or pastry flour
1/4 teaspoon ground ginger
Pinch of salt
2 eggs
2 tablespoons oil
Raisins and nuts (optional)
Fruit juice
GINGER SYRUP
1 cup sweetener (p. 12)
2 teaspoons dry ginger

1. Sift flour, ginger and salt together. Place in a mixing bowl. Add eggs, oil, raisins, nuts and enough fruit juice to form a soft dough.

2. Roll dough into a log, and cut into 12 mm (½ in) pieces.

SYRUP

1. Combine sweetener and ginger in a heavy saucepan, and bring to the boil. Drop pieces of dough in, cover and simmer about 30 minutes. Stir occasionally for even browning; cook until all are browned. Inside should be crisp and dry.

2. Remove from heat and add 2 tablespoons boiling water to pan to keep Teiglach from sticking. Remove from pan and place on a large sheet or platter so they are not touching. Roll in cinnamon, roasted chestnut flour, coconut or roasted crushed nuts or seeds.

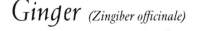

Ginger *(Zingiber officinale)*

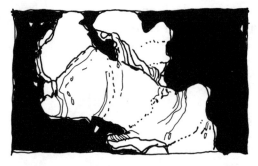

Ginger is a tropical plant, native to Asia, where it has been cultivated since ancient times. The roots, or rhizomes, are dug up when the plant is about 10 months old.

The Chinese traditionally use ginger as an external remedy for cataracts. It is also used to treat dyspepsia, or to settle a nauseous stomach, to strengthen the heart, and to improve circulation.

Dried ginger is made by a complicated process of washing, soaking or boiling, peeling and drying.

Ginger is grown throughout the tropics, including tropical Australia for local consumption, and is exported from West Africa, Jamaica and India. With care it can be grown in temperate areas. It is widely used all over the world for its pungent flavour, and is a major ingredient in curry powders, making ginger beer and gingerbread. Dried ginger is very concentrated and should be used sparingly in all baking.

PIES: SWEET AND SAVOURY

APPLE PIE

EASY DOUBLE CRUST PASTRY
2¹/₂ cups whole wheat cake or pastry flour
¹/₂ cup brown rice flour (optional) or ¹/₂ cup whole wheat cake or pastry flour
¹/₄ teaspoon sea salt
¹/₂ teaspoon cinnamon
1 teaspoon ground ginger
2-3 tablespoons instant grain coffee (or to taste)
¹/₂ cup cold fruit juice, cider or water
¹/₂ cup cold oil
¹/₂ teaspoon vanilla or orange blossom water
1 egg white
FILLING
8-10 cups chopped apples* or ¹/₂ dried fruit and ¹/₂ fresh
1 teaspoon cinnamon
¹/₂ teaspoon sea salt or 1 tablespoon miso
3-4 tablespoons arrowroot flour
¹/₄ cup fruit juice
1 egg yolk
TOPPING
1 quantity Vanilla Cream (p. 89)

*When using dried fruit, soak in liquid to cover until soft. Measure fruit after soaking.

1. Combine cake or pastry flour, brown rice flour, salt, spices and grain coffee in a mixing bowl. Set aside. Mix liquid, oil and vanilla together.

2. Slowly add liquid mixture to dry combination, mixing with a wooden spoon until a ball of dough begins to form. Press together with your hands. Divide dough into two pieces. Keep one piece covered with a damp cloth. Roll out bottom crust, very thin (see p. 100 for techniques).

3. Preheat oven to 190°C (375°F). Oil a pie dish and line with pastry; baste with egg white. Prebake 7 minutes.

4. Combine fruit, spice and salt. Dissolve arrowroot flour in juice and stir until well combined. Pour arrowroot mixture over fruit mixture and toss. Let sit about 10 minutes.

5. Place filling in pie shell, piling up fruit in the shape of a pyramid.

6. Roll out top crust. Cover and secure edge. (Brush egg white around the rim of the base if the top crust does not adhere to the bottom.) Prick top crust. Glaze with egg yolk water combination (p. 102).

7. Bake at 190°C (375°F) for 15 minutes, lower temperature to 180°C (350°F) and bake 20 minutes longer, or until fruit is soft. (Test centre of pie with a toothpick.)

INSTANT APPLE PIE

EASY DOUBLE CRUST PASTRY
2¹/2 cups whole wheat cake or pastry flour
¹/2 cup brown rice flour (optional) or ¹/2 cup whole wheat cake or pastry flour
¹/4 teaspoon sea salt
¹/2 teaspoon cinnamon
1 teaspoon ground ginger
2-3 tablespoons instant grain coffee (or to taste)
¹/2 cup cold fruit juice, cider or water
¹/2 cup cold oil
¹/2 teaspoon vanilla or orange blossom water
1 egg white
FILLING
8-10 cups chopped apples* or ¹/2 dried fruit and ¹/2 fresh
1 teaspoon cinnamon
¹/2 teaspoon sea salt or 1 tablespoon miso
Kuzu as needed
Fruit juice as needed

1. Make pastry following instructions for Apple Pie (p. 115).

2. Roll out bottom crust. Brush with egg white and prebake. Reserve extra pastry for another pie base.

3. Cook fruit and spices together until soft. Use more fruit as the liquid will evaporate.

4. When the fruit is almost tender, dilute 1 tablespoon kuzu (p. 25) for every 1¹/4 cups of cooked fruit in ¹/2 cup fruit juice. (The more liquid or acid that the fruit filling contains, the more kuzu will be needed to thicken the fruit.)

5. Stir into fruit mixture and cook, stirring continuously, until fruit filling thickens and turns clearer.

6. Place in warm pie shell and allow to set before cutting.

APRICOT CREAM PIE

EF
1 quantity Nut Pie Crust (p. 123)
3 cups Basic Tofu Cream (p. 93) or Chestnut Cream (p. 90)
1 cup Apricot Puree (p. 85)
1/2 cup Crumb Topping (p. 96)

1. Preheat oven to 190°C (375°F). Prepare pastry dough. Prebake shell 10 minutes.

2. Lower oven temperature to 180°C (350°F). Pour the cream into shell. Cover with puree. Sprinkle with Crumb Topping.

3. Bake 15-20 minutes or until set.

ALTERNATIVE METHOD

Combine puree and cream. Pour into half-baked shell. Bake until set.

Apple (Malus spp.)

The most common fruit in the Western world, the apple can be cultivated in most temperate regions. They have been grown for 3000 years and until the twentieth century hardly any other fruit was available in the winter. Apples can be eaten fresh (known as dessert apples) or they can be cooked (cooking apples). These categories do overlap. A vast range of varieties is available from country to country, all varying in acidity, sweetness, bitterness and scent. Apples and their juices impart a sweetness to many desserts without overpowering other flavours.

BULGUR PARSNIP PIE (SAVOURY)

EF
1 cup uncooked bulgur wheat
4 tablespoons oil
3 cups fruit juice
Pinch of sea salt
1 cup diced parsnips
1 grated apple
1 quantity Pressed Pastry (p. 119)
Crushed roasted nuts

1. Roast bulgur wheat in 2 tablespoons oil until lightly browned. Boil juice. Add salt and bulgur. Reduce heat, cover and cook 15 minutes.

2. Sauté diced parsnips in 2 tablespoons oil. Cover and cook until soft.

3. Puree parsnips and bulgur together. Add grated apple.

4. Prepare pie crust. Preheat oven to 190°C (375°F). Oil a pie dish. Press crust into dish and prebake 10 minutes.

5. Spread bulgur-parsnip mixture in shell and bake 10 minutes longer. Sprinkle crushed roasted nuts on top after baking.

6. Place on rack to cool before serving.

ALTERNATIVE METHOD

Puree parsnips. Set aside. Puree cooked bulgur. Spread one layer of bulgur, then grated apple and cover with parsnip puree. Sprinkle on Crumb Topping (p. 96) and bake 10-15 minutes or until firm.

Place on a rack to cool before serving.

VARIATIONS

1. Substitute 1 cup carrot puree for parsnips (p. 82).

2. Substitute 1 cup half-and-half squash-carrot puree for parsnips.

3. Substitute ½ cup carrot puree for ½ cup parsnip puree.

4. Substitute 1 cup couscous or semolina for bulgur.

5. Top with fruit puree before baking (p. 85).

6. To make pie more firm, add 2 tablespoons roasted cake or pastry or chestnut flour to parsnip-bulgur mixture after blending.

7. Adjust liquid content accordingly.

CHRISTMAS MINCEMEAT PIE

EF

PRESSED PASTRY
1 cup rolled oats
1/2 cup whole wheat cake or pastry flour
Pinch of sea salt
1/2 cup roasted ground nuts
1/3 cup oil as needed
Enough fruit juice to bind crust
MINCEMEAT FILLING
1 cup raisins or sultanas
Fruit juice to soak dried fruit
1 cup Apricot Puree (p. 85)
2 cups diced apples
Juice and rind of 1/2 lemon
Juice and rind of 1/2 orange
1 teaspoon cinnamon
1/4 teaspoon cloves
1/4 teaspoon ground ginger
1 1/2 tablespoons miso

PRESSED PASTRY

1. Combine oats and cake or pastry flour in a mixing bowl. Add sea salt and nuts. Rub oil in slowly until it resembles breadcrumbs. Put a handful of mixture in the palm of your hand, make a fist and open hand. If the mixture almost sticks together, then the amount of oil is sufficient.

2. Moisten with juice until it binds together. Press into oiled dish.

3. Preheat oven to 190°C (375°F). Bake crust 10-15 minutes.

MINCEMEAT FILLING

1. Soak fruit in juice to cover until soft. Reserve liquid. Prepare Apricot Puree.

2. Combine juice, rinds of lemon and orange, and spices with the Apricot Puree. Combine the miso and apricot puree mixture. Fold in the diced apples and raisins.

3. Place Mincemeat Filling in the pastry shell and bake 10 minutes.

CANDIED YAM PIE

Soul food developed out of the slaves' necessity to keep alive on the meagre fare allowed them by plantation owners. They lived mainly on vegetables, and used much skill and ingenuity to turn them into the tastiest dishes possible. This is probably how they developed such delicacies as Candied Yam Pie.

EF

1/2 quantity Easy Double Crust Pastry (p. 115) or Pressed Pastry (p. 119)
YAM FILLING
Fruit juice to cover yams
8-10 yams (6-7 cups chopped)
2 tablespoons oil
1-2 cups chopped carrots
3-4 tablespoons sweetener (p. 12)
Pinch of sea salt
1 teaspoon cinnamon
1/2 teaspoon ginger
1-2 cups Almond or Soy Milk (pp. 232-3)
1 teaspoon vanilla
3 tablespoons kuzu or arrowroot flour
TOPPING
1/2 cup unroasted macadamia nuts

1. Bring fruit juice to the boil. Drop in yams, turn off heat and let sit for a few minutes. Drain, then rinse under cold water immediately. Peel yams and chop. (Save skin for bread or soup if organic.)
2. Heat oil. Sauté chopped carrots for a few minutes. Add yams, sweetener, salt and spices. Add Almond Milk to almost cover vegetables.
3. Cover pan and simmer until soft.
4. After cooking, drain liquid from vegetables and reserve.
5. Prepare pie crust. Oil a 20 or 22.5 cm (8 or 9 in) pie dish. Preheat oven to 190°C (375°F).
6. Prebake pastry 10-12 minutes.
7. Blend or puree half to three-quarters of the yam mixture. Stir in vanilla.
8. Combine arrowroot with 2 tablespoons of cool reserved liquid. Mix until creamy and smooth. Stir this mixture into puree and cook until thickened. Combine with unpureed vegetables.
9. Fill pie crust with yam mixture and sprinkle crushed macadamias on top. Return to the oven and bake 15-20 minutes longer at 160° (325°F), or until crust is browned and filling is set. Remove, allow to cool and serve.

ALTERNATIVE METHOD

Brush yams with shoyu (naturally fermented soy sauce) and oil. Cover and bake in a 180°C (350°F) oven until soft. Peel. Proceed as in recipe.

Opposite: Crepe Cornucopia

CHESTNUT-APPLE PIE

EF
1 1/2 cups dried chestnuts
Fruit juice
1 quantity Pressed Pastry (p. 119)
8 cups peeled, cored and sliced apples
2 tablespoons oil
Pinch of sea salt
2 teaspoons orange rind
3 tablespoons roasted cornflour

1. Soak chestnuts in juice to cover overnight. Bring to the boil, cover pot, and simmer until tender (about 1 hour). Prepare pastry.

2. Preheat oven to 190°C (375°F). Prebake shell for 15 minutes.

3. Heat oil in a heavy skillet. Add apples and sauté for 5 minutes on a low heat. Add salt, cover and cook until soft.

4. Combine chestnuts and apples. Add orange rind and flour.

5. Puree half of chestnut-apple mixture until creamy. Combine puree and other half of mixture. Pour into pie shell.

6. Bake at 180°C (350°F) for 10-15 minutes.

Yam *(Dioscorea spp.)*

There are many species of yams, some of them dating back to ancient times. The air potato yam is one of the few true yams cultivated for food. Yams have thick tubers, generally a development at the base of the stem, from which protrude long, slender annual climbing stems, varying in colour from white to yellowish-orange.

The thick roots of yams are a major food crop in many tropical countries. They contain mostly water. Much of the solid matter is starch and sugar. The root has less starch than the white potato, but more sugar. Some kinds of yams are not fit to eat, but they produce substances called sapogenins that can be used to make drugs such as cortisone.

In many West African countries, the consumption of yams is so great that it is regarded as a staple food. About 20 million tonnes of yams are grown for food each year. Half of them are grown in the countries of West Africa.

Yams are also grown in India, South-East Asia, the Caribbean, Australia and New Zealand.

Opposite: Apple Pie
(page 115)

CHIFFON PIE

1 quantity Easy Double Crust Pastry (p. 115)
3-4 tablespoons agar-agar flakes
2 cups fruit juice (mango is lovely)
2 egg yolks
1 cup Cashew or Soy Milk (pp. 232-3)
4 tablespoons sweetener (p. 12)

1. Prebake pie shell.
2. Combine agar-agar and juice. Bring to the boil. Lower heat and cook until agar-agar dissolves.
3. Combine milk, sweetener and cooked agar-agar.
4. Take a few teaspoons of mixture, stir in egg yolks and return yolk combination to mixture. Cook until thickened in a double boiler, stirring continuously. *Do not boil.* Remove from heat, spoon into crust and cool.

PEAR CREAM PIE

EF
1 quantity Pressed Pastry (p. 119)
2 cups Basic Tofu Cream (p. 93)
4-6 tablespoons agar-agar flakes
2 cups fruit juice
4 cups sliced pears
Vanilla
Crushed roasted nuts

1. Prebake pie shell. Prepare Basic Tofu Cream.
2. Combine agar-agar and fruit juice and bring to the boil. Lower heat and simmer until the agar-agar dissolves.
3. Add half of the pears and vanilla to agar-agar mixture. Stir well.
4. Fold half of Basic Tofu Cream into agar-agar mixture. Cook on a low heat for 3 minutes, stirring constantly. Spoon mixture into pre-baked shell.
5. Chill until almost firm, then add remaining pears to remaining cream, and spread over top.
6. Garnish with crushed roasted nuts. Chill until firm.

ORANGE CREAM PIE

NUT PIE CRUST
EF
1¹/2 cups sifted whole wheat cake or pastry flour
1 teaspoon cinnamon or mint
¹/4 teaspoon sea salt
¹/4 cup ground roasted nuts or seeds
¹/4 cup oil
¹/2-1 cup fruit juice
ORANGE CREAM
GF
4-6 tablespoons agar-agar flakes
¹/2 cup fruit juice
2¹/2 cups Cream (pp. 89-93)
1 egg, separated
2 tablespoons sweetener (p. 12)
1 teaspoon vanilla
Juice and rind of ¹/2 orange
¹/2 teaspoon cinnamon
¹/4 teaspoon sea salt

NUT PIE CRUST

1. Combine all dry ingredients. Cut the oil through the dry mixture until it looks like fine breadcrumbs. Do not knead or overwork the flour. Too much movement activates the gluten, resulting in a hard crust.

2. Add enough juice to form a soft dough. Roll out pastry. Place in oiled pie dish and bake in preheated 190°C (375°F) oven 15-20 minutes.

FILLING

1. Combine agar-agar and ¹/2 cup juice, bring to a boil and cook on a medium heat until agar-agar dissolves. Add Cream, lower heat and simmer 5 minutes longer.

2. Combine egg yolk, sweetener, vanilla, orange juice and grated rind. Beat until fluffy. Combine with Cream mixture and blend until smooth and creamy, adding cinnamon gradually.

3. Beat egg white and sea salt together until peaked. Fold egg white into cream gently. Place entire mixture into half-baked crust and bake at 190°C (375°F) for 20-30 minutes.

4. You may substitute lemon juice and rind for orange juice and rind.

MELON CREAM PIE

EF

1 quantity Pressed Pastry (p. 119)
FILLING
4 cups diced melon
2 tablespoons oil
Pinch of sea salt
3 tablespoons tahini or almond or hazelnut butter
4 cups fruit juice
4-6 tablespoons agar-agar flakes
1-2 teaspoons cinnamon
1/2-1 teaspoon ground ginger
4 tablespoons arrowroot flour
TOPPING
1 quantity Basic Tofu Cream (p. 93)
Strawberries for garnish

1. Prebake pie shell. Set aside to cool.

2. Sauté melon in oil over a medium heat for 5 minutes. Add salt and simmer uncovered about 5 minutes longer.

3. Blend tahini, half of melon mixture, and half of the fruit juice together, until creamy and smooth.

4. Combine agar-agar with remaining 2 cups juice and bring to the boil. Lower heat and simmer until agar-agar dissolves. Blend melon-tahini mixture and spices with agar-agar.

5. Dilute arrowroot in a little juice and stir into mixture rapidly until it boils again and begins to thicken. Remove from heat and set aside to cool.* Prepare Basic Tofu Cream. Set aside.

6. Pour cool melon mixture into shell before it gels. Set aside until firm. (You may chill at this time, but it is advisable to wait until it is completely cool.)

7. Spoon Basic Tofu Cream over the top of the pie after the pie has set. Garnish with strawberries. Chill before serving.

*Pie shells have a tendency to crack if they have not cooled completely before being filled, or if filling is at a different temperature from crust.

POPPY SEED-APRICOT LAYER PIE

EF

1 quantity Pressed Pastry (p. 119)
3 tablespoons arrowroot flour
Fruit juice, as needed
2 cups Apricot Puree (p. 85)
2 cups Poppy Seed Fruit Puree (p. 84)

1. Prebake pie shell at 190°C (375°F) for 10-15 minutes. Dissolve arrowroot in a few tablespoons of cold juice.

2. Combine Apricot Puree with arrowroot mixture and cook, stirring constantly, until mixture begins to boil.

3. Pour into prebaked shell. (The shell should be the same temperature as the filling.)

4. Top with Poppy Seed Fruit Puree. (This mixture should contain almost no liquid.) Allow to set. Chill before serving.

LEMON MERINGUE PIE

1 quantity Pressed Pastry (p. 119)
FILLING
4 cups fruit juice
Pinch of sea salt
4-6 tablespoons agar-agar flakes
1 tablespoon sweetener (p. 12)
6 tablespoons arrowroot flour
Juice of 1 1/2 lemons or grated rind and juice of 1/2 lemon
1 teaspoon vanilla
MERINGUE
2-3 tablespoons sweetener (p. 12)
2 egg whites
Pinch of sea salt
1/2 teaspoon vanilla
1 teaspoon lemon or orange rind or mint

1. Prepare pastry.

2. Preheat oven to 190°C (375°F). Bake crust 10-15 minutes or until lightly browned (not quite completely baked).

FILLING

1. Combine 3 1/2 cups fruit juice, sea salt and agar-agar and bring to the boil.

2. Reduce heat and simmer until agar-agar dissolves.

3. Dilute arrowroot in remaining 1/2 cup juice and sweetener. Add arrowroot to agar-agar and, stirring constantly, bring to boil. Stir in lemon juice and vanilla, remove from heat and let set 5 minutes.

4. Pour lemon/agar-agar filling into shell. Allow to cool.

MERINGUE

1. Cook sweetener in a heavy saucepan or double boiler until it reaches 130°C (265°F). Use a confectionary thermometer.

2. Beat egg whites and sea salt together. Slowly drip the sweetener into the whites, while beating. Beat until stiff. Add vanilla and other flavouring, and beat until peaked.

3. Spread on top of dessert. Bake at 110°C (225°F) for 45 minutes, at 160°C (325°F) for 25 minutes or at 200°C (400°F) for 10 minutes.

4. Turn off oven, leave oven door slightly ajar and leave inside at least 15 minutes longer.

SPINACH PIE (SAVOURY)

PHYLLO PASTRY
2 cups whole wheat cake or pastry flour
Pinch of sea salt
2/3 cup water
1/4 cup olive oil
FILLING
500 g (1 lb) spinach
3 cups pressed* and mashed tofu
Sea salt
2 cups diced onion
4 tablespoons olive oil
1 teaspoon dill seed (crush for more flavour)
2-3 tablespoons white miso creamed in small amount of warm water or sea salt to taste
3 beaten eggs

*Remove tofu from container and place on wooden board which has been covered with a tea towel. Fold the tea towel over the tofu and cover with another board. Put a heavy weight on top and set aside for 15 minutes. Dry and use as suggested.

PHYLLO PASTRY

1. Combine flour and salt together. Heat water until warm. Combine with oil and beat together until cloudy. (Adjust liquid as required.)

2. Make a well in the centre of the flour. Pour the liquid and oil in all at once and mix until the dough comes away from the sides of the bowl.

3. Knead 10 minutes. After shaping into round ball, cover the dough with oil. Place cloth on top and set aside at room temperature for 1 hour.

FILLING

1. Blanch spinach in boiling salted water for 2 minutes. Drain off liquid and discard. Rinse spinach under cold water and squeeze out liquid. Chop finely and set aside.

2. Heat skillet and dry roast tofu without oil, sprinkling in sea salt as you roast to help evaporate water more quickly. Move tofu continuously until dry and cheese-like. Set aside.

3. Dice onion. Heat skillet; add oil and sauté onion on a medium heat until lightly browned. Mix in the spinach and tofu. Cook 5 minutes. Sprinkle in crushed dill seed, mix and remove from heat.

4. Cream in miso and stir until well combined with spinach-tofu mixture. Cool. When mixture is at room temperature, stir in beaten eggs.

ROLLING OUT PASTRY DOUGH

1. Roll out pastry into log. Divide into five pieces, covering four with cloth until ready to use.

2. Shape pastry into rectangle.

3. Oil rectangular 25 x 30 cm (10 x 12 in) dish.

4. Preheat oven to 200°C (400°F).

5. Sprinkle arrowroot flour on cloth or greaseproof paper. Begin to roll out pastry to the shape of baking dish. Make the pastry slightly larger than the size of the dish.

6. Roll the pastry around rolling pin making sure that the pastry is well floured. (This helps to make sure that the pastry does not stick to itself or the rolling pin.)

7. Unroll into baking dish. Trim off excess so that pastry just fits into the bottom of the dish (no sides).

8. Brush pastry with a lot of oil.

9. Repeat with one more layer, brushing with oil.

10. Spread on filling and cover with three more layers of pastry, brushing with oil in between each layer. Score.

11. Brush top layer with oil. Sprinkle cold water on top.

12. Bake 40-45 minutes or until lightly browned. Serve while still warm.

SUNSHINE PIE (SAVOURY)

EF

1 quantity Pressed Pastry (p. 119)
4 cups Yam or Sweet Potato Puree (p. 82)
2 tablespoons arrowroot flour or kuzu, dissolved in a few tablespoons of fruit juice
4 tablespoons almond butter
1 teaspoon dry ginger
1/2 teaspoon cinnamon
1/2 teaspoon sea salt or 1 tablespoon white miso
1/4 cup sweetener (optional) (p. 12)
1/2 cup unroasted crushed pecans
Roasted pecan halves

1. Preheat oven to 180°C (350°F). Prepare crust and prebake 10-15 minutes.

2. Combine puree, arrowroot flour, nut butter, ginger, cinnamon, salt and sweetener in a saucepan. Cook, stirring constantly, until thickened. Fill shell with mixture and bake 20-25 minutes, or until crust is golden brown.

3. Sprinkle crushed pecans on top of pie 10 minutes before removing from oven. Place the pecan halves on top for decoration after baking.

Sweet Potato *(Ipomoea batatas)*

A vegetable of the morning glory family, its large, fleshy roots are a popular food. Juicy sweet potatoes are often called yams, but the yam belongs to another family and grows mostly in the tropics. Sweet potatoes may be yellow or white. The yellow ones grow mostly in warm temperate zones; white sweet potatoes come from more tropical zones. Originally known as kumara in New Zealand, other commercial varieties are more popular today.

Some kinds of sweet potato plants have pale green vines with green pointed leaves. Others have purple vines with large leaves.

PEAR AND GINGER CRISP

EF
¹/2 cup raisins
2-3 cups Almond or Soy Milk (pp. 232-3)
10 cups sliced pears
1 teaspoon ground ginger
¹/2 cup brown rice flour
¹/2 teaspoon sea salt
1 teaspoon cinnamon
1 teaspoon vanilla
1¹/2 cups Crumb Topping (p. 96)

1. Soak raisins in milk to cover until soft.

2. Roast the flour in a dry skillet until it begins to smell sweet and is lightly browned. Set aside to cool. Preheat oven to 180°C (350°F).

3. Combine the roasted flour and milk combination, cinnamon and vanilla. Place pears in baking dish, cover with milk mixture, cover and bake 30 minutes. Remove cover, sprinkle on Crumb Topping and bake until browned.

VARIATIONS

1. Add 1 tablespoon orange rind.

2. Dilute 2 tablespoons tahini or almond butter in fruit juice before adding it to flour combination.

3. Substitute any fresh fruit in season for pears.

Pear *(Pyrus communis)*

There are many different varieties of pears found all over the world. They resemble the apple in many ways, but have a more elongated fruit. The tree grows wild in most parts of Europe, but more in the warmer southern parts than in the north. Many different kinds of pears are cultivated today, varying from round to top-shaped to oval shape, and red, brown, green, yellow or golden russet in colour.

The fruits may be eaten raw, stewed, cooked like apple sauce, or used in dessert making for pastries, pies or cakes.

TARTS

A tart is a delicate small or large open pie, made from deep-fried or baked pastry. It can be filled with cooked or raw fruit, vegetables, custards, creams, jellies or a combination of these.

Any pie filling can be used for tarts, and vice versa. Tarts can be kept for several weeks before filling.

LINING TART FORMS

Place 12 small tart forms touching one another in rows of four. Roll out pastry to 6 mm (¼ in) thick to a size 8-10 cm (3-4 in) larger than the area covered by the forms.

1. Fold the dough back twice, until you have a long, narrow piece of dough, which you can lift and place on top of the forms.

2. Place dough on forms nearest you and unfold outward to cover the others. Let pastry stand 10 minutes to settle naturally. It will stretch and fall into forms.

3. Cover pastry-lined forms with a towel or canvas cloth, and run a rolling pin over the top of the forms.

4. Form a small ball the size of a walnut from the leftover scraps of pastry dough. Use this to press pastry firmly into forms.

Cover and chill 30 minutes before baking.

PREPARATION

UNFILLED TARTS

To bake unfilled tarts, place them on a baking sheet and bake 10-15 minutes at 190°C (375°F). Then fill three-quarters full and bake 15 minutes longer, or until they begin to bubble (with fruit filling), or get firm (creams and custards), or get dry (purees).

FILLED TARTS

To bake prebaked tarts, fill three-quarters full and place on a baking sheet. Bake until the fruit fillings begin to get juicy and bubbly, or until the creams or custards get firm, or until the purees get dry.

VARIATIONS

1. Bake or deep-fry unfilled. Cool. Place 1 tablespoon cream (p. 89) in each tart. Allow to set for a few minutes. Cover with slices of cooked fruit or vegetables. Brush with apricot glaze (see Fruit Glaze, p. 79) and serve.

2. Line form with pastry, cover and chill 30 minutes. Heat oil. Deep-fry pastry dough and shell together. They will separate in the hot oil. Remove form and continue frying dough until lightly browned, and the oil has almost completely stopped bubbling around the edges of the tart. Drain and cool. Fill with filling the same temperature as the tart (preferably cool).

FRUIT FLAN

1 1/2 cups whole wheat cake or pastry flour
1/2 cup ground skinned hazelnuts or blanched almonds
Sea salt to taste
1/4-1/3 cup oil
Maple syrup or fruit juice concentrate to bind
1 whole egg (optional)
CREAM
1/2 cup maple syrup to taste
2 cups fruit juice
3 egg yolks
1-2 tablespoons whole wheat cake or pastry flour
1 cup mirin (sweet rice wine) or sherry
1 tablespoon rum
Selection of fresh fruit*
Kuzu cream** for glazing or sugarless fruit jam

* Strawberries, bananas, pineapple, kiwifruit, grapes (green and black) in season.
** 1 cup fruit juice dissolved with 2 teaspoons kuzu. Cook till thickened. Brush over fruit.

1. Mix flour and nuts together. Add a pinch of sea salt to taste. Beat oil, sweetener and egg together for 3 minutes. Add flour mixture. Shape into ball.

2. Oil flan tin, roll out pastry and line. Bake in a preheated oven 190°C (375°F) for 20 minutes.

3. Whip maple syrup, juice and egg yolks together. Add flour and mirin. Cook in a double boiler until almost boiling, whisking until smooth and creamy. Add rum. When cool, fill the tart and decorate with fruit. Brush fruit with kuzu cream or jam.

FIG AND WALNUT TART

1 quantity Pressed Pastry (p. 119)
1 cup walnuts
1 teaspoon cinnamon
1 cup Fig Puree (p. 85)
3 eggs, separated
1 teaspoon vanilla
Pinch of sea salt
1/4 cup hot sweetener (p. 12)
1/4 cup whole wheat cake or pastry flour
1/4 cup arrowroot or kuzu flour

1. Prepare pastry. Oil a 23 or 25 cm (9 or 10 in) tart form 2.5 cm (1 in) deep, or tart forms. Line with pastry, cover and chill at least 30 minutes.

2. Preheat oven to 190°C (375°F).

3. Roast the walnuts; while they are warm, grind finely. Mix with cinnamon, and press into the bottom of the chilled pastry.

4. Prebake 10 minutes. Spread Fig Puree on top of pastry.

5. Stir yolks lightly to break them up. Add vanilla and set aside.

6. Beat egg whites and salt until foamy. Slowly begin to drip in sweetener, beating continuously. Fold one-quarter of whites into yolks. Sift flours.

7. Combine yolk mixture and whites, and slowly fold together, sprinkling flour in as you fold. *Do not overmix.* Place on top of fruit puree. Bake 10-15 minutes, or until lightly browned.

APRICOT LATTICE TART

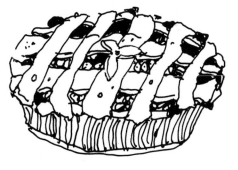

EF
PASTRY
2¼ cups whole wheat pastry or cake flour
½ teaspoon sea salt
1 teaspoon cinnamon
⅓ cup cold oil
¼ teaspoon almond extract or vanilla
Fruit juice as needed
FILLING
10 cups chopped fresh peeled and stoned apricots or 5 cups dried,
unsulphured apricots soaked in water to cover
1 teaspoon lemon juice
⅓ cup arrowroot or kuzu flour
1 teaspoon ground coriander
¾ teaspoon cinnamon

PASTRY

1. Combine flour, sea salt and cinnamon.

2. Beat together oil, extract and several tablespoons fruit juice.

3. Add remainder of liquid at once mixing until a ball of dough just forms. Adjust liquid as necessary.

4. Roll out two-thirds of the pastry on a sheet of greaseproof paper or rolling cloth to fit a 25 cm (10 in) dish. Flip over into dish, peel off paper or cloth, allow pastry to settle before trimming sides.

5. Prebake in a preheated 200°C (400°F) oven for 10-15 minutes.

6. Toss together apricots, with lemon juice, flour and spices. Spread evenly into pastry-lined dish.

7. Roll out remaining pastry to a 3 mm (⅛ in) thickness. Cut into 12 mm (½ in) wide strips and top with pastry.*

8. Bake in preheated 200°C (400°F) oven for 30 minutes or until lightly browned. Cool on a wire rack before serving.

*Brush the top of the tart with an egg yolk and water wash (1 teaspoon water to 1 egg yolk) before baking.

PARTY TARTS

PASTRY
1 1/2 cups whole wheat cake or pastry flour
1/2 cup ground hazelnuts
Pinch of sea salt
1/4-1/2 cup oil
Maple syrup or fruit juice to bind
1 whole egg (optional)
FILLING
1 recipe Tofu Whip Cream (p. 94)
1/4-1/3 cup fresh strawberry or raspberry juice
or
1 quantity Fluffy Snow (set and blended) (p. 218)
DECORATIONS
Sliced almonds
Coconut strands, marinated in strawberry or raspberry juice for colour
Pecans
Kiwifruit
Strawberry halves
Blackberries
Grapes
Peaches
Passionfruit

1. Combine flour and nuts. Add a pinch of sea salt to taste. Combine the oil, maple syrup and egg together and add to flour mixture (adjust liquid accordingly).

2. Shape into a ball, cover and chill for 15 minutes.

3. Oil little tart forms, and preheat oven to 200°C (400°F). Roll out pastry and line forms. Glaze with egg white mixed with a few drops of water. Prebake the pastry 10-12 minutes.

4. Spoon filling into cooled pastry, allow to set for a few minutes before decorating. You may want to glaze with arrowroot or kuzu fruit juice glaze; for this see Melon Tofu Cheesecake (p. 62).

PECAN CARROT TART

EF
8-10 medium-sized carrots (4 cups cooked)
2 tablespoons oil
1 teaspoon grated ginger
Pinch of sea salt
1/4 cup fruit juice
3 tablespoons chestnut or whole wheat cake or pastry flour
1 quantity Pressed Pastry (p. 119)
1/2 cup any nut filling (pp. 86-7)
1 cup chopped pecans

1. Dice carrots. Sauté in oil. Add ginger, salt and juice. Cover and cook until tender. Puree.

2. Roast flour. Set aside to cool. Preheat oven to 190°C (375°F).

3. Prepare pastry. Roll out dough and place in oiled forms. Sprinkle nut filling and nuts in tarts.

4. Cut strips for lattice top.

5. Combine cooled roasted flour with carrot puree.

6. Prebake tarts 10 minutes. Spoon filling into them. Bake another 15 minutes.

CHERRY CHEESE TART

This tart can also be made with peaches, kiwifruit, apricots, pears or any fresh fruit in season.

1 quantity Phyllo Pastry (p. 126)
2 eggs
1 cup Tofu Sour Cream (p. 95)
3 tablespoons sweetener (p. 12)
1/2 teaspoon vanilla
3 cups pitted chopped cherries

1. Prepare pastry. Oil a 23 or 25 cm (9 or 10 in) dish about 2.5 cm (1 in) deep, or 9-12 tart forms. Line with pastry. Cover and chill 30 minutes.

2. Preheat oven to 190°C (375°F). Prebake pastry 10 minutes.

3. Beat eggs with Tofu Sour Cream, sweetener and vanilla. Arrange fruit in tarts. Pour egg mixture over fruit, and bake on lowest rack in oven for 15 minutes, or until custard is firm.

VARIATIONS

1. Substitute any fresh or dried fruit for cherries.

2. Substitute any cream for Tofu Sour Cream.

Cherry *(Prunus cerasus)*

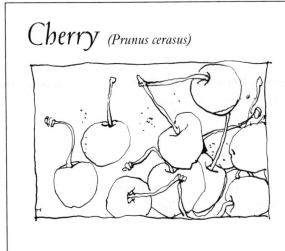

There are many different varieties of cherries, ranging from sour to sweet. Cultivated cherries are either dark red-black or pale yellow, covered with a red hue. There are beautiful white or pinkish flowers which are produced in clusters, bearing forth shiny fruit on long flower stalks. The cherry tree grows up to 23 m (75 ft) in height in well-drained woodlands. Used as a fresh fruit dessert in the summertime, the cherry is also traditionally used for cherry pie, tarts and custard.

LATTICE APPLE TARTS

EF
1 quantity Easy Double Crust Pastry (p. 115)
2 tablespoons oil
2 kg (4 lb) sliced apples
Juice and rind of 1 lemon
1 tablespoon white miso or 1/4 teaspoon sea salt
1 cup dried fruit
1 cup Crumb Topping (p. 96) (optional)
1/2-1 cup Apricot Glaze (see Fruit Glaze, p. 79)

Prepare pastry. Oil 12 tart forms. Line the forms with pastry. Save the extra dough for the top. Cover and chill at least 30 minutes.

FILLING

1. Heat oil in a heavy skillet or pan. Sauté apples for a few minutes, add lemon juice, rind, and miso. Cover and cook 2 minutes; remove cover, add dried fruit and cool.

2. Preheat oven to 190°C (375°F). Prebake pastry 10 minutes. Fill with apple mixture.

LATTICE TOP

1. Roll out a strip of dough 3 mm (1/8 in) thick. Brush with oil, and sprinkle with Crumb Topping to make it adhere better.

2. Cut into strips 6 mm (1/4 in) wide. (To cut strips, use a pastry wheel to give a fluted edge.)

3. Lattice the pastry strips on top of the apple filling.

4. Bake in 180°C (350°F) oven for 30 minutes or until filling begins to bubble in the centre. In the last 10 minutes of baking time, place the tarts on a higher rack in the oven to brown the lattice top.

5. Prepare Apricot Glaze. Remove tarts from oven, and cool on rack.

6. While still warm, brush with hot glaze.

MORE APPLE IDEAS

1. Follow directions for Lattice Apple Tarts. Toss apples in the juice of 1 lemon and 1 teaspoon vanilla. Drain off liquid. (Use for glazes, fillings, cake liquid.) Sauté half of the apple mixture until soft. Place in one large dish.

2. Arrange the remaining apples overlapping each other on top of apple filling.

3. Bake in 180°C (350°F) oven for 30 minutes. Sprinkle chopped nuts on top the last 10 minutes of baking time.

4. Remove from oven and cool on rack.

RUM-SCENTED ROCK MELON TART

1 quantity Nut Pie Crust (p. 123)
(use macadamia nuts; brush bottom of shell with egg white before baking to seal)
LEMON FILLING
1/2 cup sweetener (p. 12)
1 tablespoon oil
8 tablespoons whole wheat cake or pastry flour
2/3 cup freshly squeezed lemon juice
1 tablespoon grated lemon rind
4 eggs, separated
3/4-1 cup Nut or Soy Milk (pp. 232-3)
Pinch of sea salt
FRUIT TOPPING
1 cup Fruit Glaze (p. 79)
(strawberry is a good colour)
3-4 ripe rock melons
1 tablespoon brandy
Shredded coconut dipped in beetroot juice for colour (p. 21)

1. Preheat oven to 190°C (375°F).
2. Bake the unfilled pastry shell till almost cooked (10-15 minutes).
3. Beat together sweetener and oil. Add the flour, lemon juice and rind. Beat in the yolks. Add the milk and stir till well blended.
4. Beat egg whites and sea salt until peaked. Fold into lemon mixture, spoon into pre-baked shell and bake till set (30 minutes).

PUTTING IT ALL TOGETHER

1. Prepare Fruit Glaze. Add rum, cool slightly.
2. Scoop out melons with small ice-cream scoop. Place melon on cooled tart, spoon over glaze and sprinkle with shredded, coloured coconut. Set before serving.

Rock Melon *(Cucumis melo)*

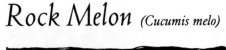

Many kinds of melon exist today. The flesh of a melon consists of about 90 to 95 per cent water and only about 5 per cent sugar. Melon plants have hairy stems, bearing many leaves which are quite large in size. An annual trailing plant, which probably originated in the tropics, it has given rise to many forms, and many cultivated varieties have been developed, varying in size, shape, colour and taste. Rock melons have deep grooves on the outside running vertically around the whole melon. Mainly used as the first or last course in a meal, they can be incorporated into many different desserts.

STRUDELS

APPLE WALNUT STRUDEL

FILLING
1 cup dried fruit
Fruit juice
2 cups chopped apples
2-3 cups chopped roasted walnuts
1 tablespoon cinnamon
STRUDEL PASTRY
2 cups whole wheat cake or pastry flour or 1 cup whole wheat cake or pastry flour
and 1 cup sifted whole wheat flour
$^1/_2$ teaspoon sea salt
$^1/_4$ cup oil
1 tablespoon orange or lemon juice
2 egg whites
$^2/_3$-1 cup lukewarm fruit juice
Arrowroot flour
3-4 tablespoons tahini or almond butter
1 cup Crumb Topping (p. 96)

FILLING

Soak dried fruit in fruit juice to cover until soft. (Drain off liquid and use for dough.) Mix apples with fruit, walnuts and cinnamon. Set aside.

STRUDEL PASTRY

1. Place flour and sea salt in a mixing bowl. Cut in oil. Add orange or lemon juice, and egg whites. Pour in juice gradually until a very soft, sticky dough is formed.

2. Knead on a floured surface until smooth and elastic. Place in an oiled bowl, brush the top of the dough with oil. Cover and set in a warm place. If there is no warm spot, place bowl in a pan of hot water until dough becomes lukewarm.

FILLING THE STRUDEL

1. Preheat oven to 190°C (375°F). Oil baking sheets.

2. Cover surface of dough with a pastry cloth or greaseproof paper. Sprinkle arrowroot onto surface. Roll out dough in rectangular shape until 3 mm (⅛ in) thick. Brush entire surface with oil. Allow dough to rest 5-10 minutes. Trim edges.

3. Spread surface of dough with nut butter, leaving a 5 cm (2 in) border on the two vertical ends. Sprinkle some apple-walnut filling and Crumb Topping over surface.

4. Fold over edges that do not have any filling on them toward the centre. Brush with oil.

5. Lift up the edge of the pastry cloth nearest you and begin to flip the dough over on the filling.

6. Continue until the dough is completely rolled around itself. Flip the dough onto a well-oiled baking sheet. Slit the top and bake 30-45 minutes, glazing before or after baking.

CHERRY TOFU STRUDEL

Substitute 4 cups pitted fresh chopped cherries and 2 cups Tofu Sour Cream (p. 95) for apple-walnut filling. Combine tofu and cherries. Fill.

MINCEMEAT STRUDEL

Substitute Mincemeat Filling (p. 119) for apple-walnut filling.

CHESTNUT ORANGE STRUDEL

Any yeasted or unyeasted dough
1-2 cups Chestnut Cream (p. 90)
2 teaspoons orange rind
1/2 teaspoon rose water
Egg yolk mixed with a few drops of water

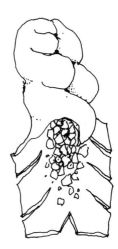

1. Roll out dough on pastry cloth or greaseproof paper.
2. Combine, Chestnut Cream, orange rind and rose water.
3. Place an 8 cm (3 in) strip of filling across the bottom end of strudel.
4. Fold in the end of the pastry on both sides. Brush with oil.
5. Lift up the end of the cloth nearest the filling, and fold the dough over onto the filling.
6. Raise the pastry cloth or greaseproof paper and continue until the dough is completely rolled.
7. Flip the dough onto a well-oiled baking sheet. Slit top, glaze with egg yolk. Bake in preheated 190°C (375°F) oven 30-40 minutes.

VARIATION

Fruit-filled slit strudel: Prepare yeasted dough (p. 142). Roll into rectangle 12 mm (½ in) thick. Place filling in the centre third of dough. Slit both sides of unfilled dough diagonally 12 mm (½ in) apart, from filling to edge.

Fold strips alternately over filling, stretching and twisting slightly. Allow to rise until almost double in size. Brush with egg yolk/water combination and bake in a preheated 190°C (375°F) oven 30-40 minutes.

Cinnamon-Almond Strudel

EF
1 cup chopped walnuts
1/2 cup blanched ground almonds
1 teaspoon cinnamon
2 quantities Hot Water Pastry Dough (p. 106)
1 cup olive oil
CINNAMON SYRUP
1/4 cup sweetener (p. 12)
1 cinnamon stick or 1 teaspoon cinnamon
1 teaspoon lemon juice

1. Combine walnuts, almonds and cinnamon. Set aside. Prepare dough. Roll into thin sheets.

2. Brush half of an 18 x 30 cm (7 x 12 in) pastry sheet with oil. Fold over the other half, and brush with more oil. Sprinkle with 1 tablespoon nut mixture.

3. Roll dough very tightly. Cut strudel in half, making two rolls.

CINNAMON SYRUP

1. Combine sweetener and cinnamon stick or cinnamon. Cook 10 minutes over a low heat. Add lemon juice and remove from heat.

2. Preheat oven to 180°C (350°F). Oil a baking sheet lightly. Place strudel on baking sheet. Slit top. Bake 25-30 minutes, or until browned. Remove from oven and place on a cooling rack with a dish underneath to catch drippings, and pour warm cinnamon syrup over pastry.

5. HIGHER AND HIGHER: Yeasted Pastries

The fine art of baking was first enhanced by the use of yeast in Egypt around 4000 B.C. Yeast, a living bacteria, feeds on natural sugar from grain, as well as from added sugar. The natural, simple sugars in flour are usually not enough to let the yeast work quickly, so sugar obtained from cane, syrups, and various fruits and juices is added. Braiding, twisting and swirling are only a few of the many ways in which you can have fun working with yeasted dough.

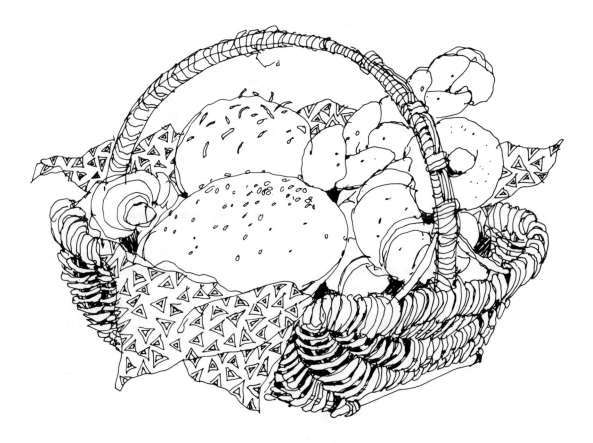

WORKING WITH YEAST

*T*HERE are many ways to prepare yeasted doughs or batters for pastries and cakes. The recipes in this section usually begin by first preparing a 'sponge', or first-rise batter. The advantage of this method is that the yeast will get activated more quickly and easily in the absence of the other ingredients, especially salt, which can delay or inhibit the yeasted batter or dough's rising action. However, if you are pressed for time, the first-rise batter may be omitted.

Sponge Preparation

*This liquid, which contains natural sugar, helps the yeast to work quickly.

Dissolve the yeast (dry or cake) in a small amount ($\frac{1}{2}$ cup) of lukewarm fruit juice, 24-32°C (75-90°F).* Stir until all the lumps have dissolved, and set aside for about 5 minutes, or until it begins to bubble. Add enough whole wheat flour or whole wheat cake or pastry flour to yeasted mixture to obtain a thin batter. Beat for several minutes with a wooden spoon or wire whisk. Cover with a damp cloth and set in a warm place to rise until it is doubled. Beat down, add the rest of the ingredients and follow the recipe.

Kneading

Kneading does not refer only to bread-making. This process develops the gluten in flour, allowing the dough to rise, and forming lighter, moister cakes or pastries. This kneading technique is used when the yeasted mixture is too thick to be beaten with a wooden spoon. If your dough is soft and sticky to the touch, you can knead it directly in the mixing bowl.

Kneading Soft Dough in a Bowl

Flour your hands. Pull the soft dough over and over from the side of the bowl to the centre, holding the bowl steady as you pull. Knead dough until it begins to pull away from the side of the bowl (10 to 15 minutes).

Kneading Heavier Dough on a Flat Surface

Flour your hands if the dough is sticky.

Knead dough on a pastry cloth or wooden board lightly dusted with arrowroot flour. Using the heels of your hands, press down firmly, folding the dough in half. Press down again with the heels of your hands, rotating it slightly. Repeat over and over again until the dough feels smooth and elastic. Do not be afraid to press firmly and punch the dough, because it is this movement that will activate the gluten in the flour and make the dough rise. When the dough is smooth, place it in a large oiled bowl; oil the top of the dough to prevent it from drying out. Cover and place in a warm spot, let rise until doubled.

FORGET ME KNOTS

1. Rising times will vary according to the temperature and moisture of the room, the gluten content of the flour, the ingredients in the dough or batter, the shape of the dough and the general weather of the day.

2. The amount of liquid necessary for each dough or batter will vary according to the temperature and moisture of the room, the coarseness of the flour and the general weather of the day.

3. *Compressed Yeast:* Compressed yeast cakes contain live active yeast plants. Use lukewarm liquid to dissolve compressed yeast. A drop of liquid which feels comfortable when placed on the inside of the wrist is lukewarm.

4. *Dry Yeast:* Dry yeast is prepared by mixing the plant with starch, pressing the mixture and then drying it at a low heat. In order to grow again, the yeast must be dissolved in a warm liquid (such as fruit juice).

    Dry yeast, unlike fresh yeast, may be kept refrigerated in a well-sealed container for many months without losing its rising powers. It cannot decay or mould since it contains no moisture.

    Use slightly warmer liquid, 32°-38°C (90°-100°F) to dissolve active dry yeast. Place your finger in the liquid; if you are able to keep your finger there without discomfort it is the right temperature.

5. A temperature of 62°C (145°F) will make yeast inactive.

6. Fill pans, forms or sheets only halfway, to allow batter or dough to rise.

7. Always slit the top of a yeasted pastry before it rises, to allow for greater expansion.

8. When covering the pan containing the yeasted batter or dough for the final rise, use a glass bowl as cover. This will enable you to see the rate of expansion so that the dough does not over-rise, and allows room for expansion.

9. Oil the rim of the bowl used for covering dough or batter, so that the dough or batter does not stick to it when rising.

10. To test dough for rising: a slight impression will remain when you press the dough lightly with your fingers. To test batters for rising, touch the batter lightly with finger. If sufficiently risen, the batter should stick to your finger, and air holes should be visible when finger is removed.

11. If the dough or batter has over-risen, it will fall while baking. In this event, it is best to prepare the dough or batter all over again because the yeast has probably died (become inactive).

12. To retard rising, place the dough or batter in an oiled pan or bowl, oil the surface of the dough, cover with a damp cloth and chill until ready to use.

13. The consistency of yeasted batters should be that of thick pancake batter dropping with difficulty from a wooden spoon.

14. Glaze yeasted dough before rising, or before, during or after baking (p. 102). If using an egg glaze, it is best to glaze immediately before or during baking to avoid slowing down the rising process.

15. Add dried fruit, crushed nuts, seeds or extra spices to dough after the first rise.

16. Shape dough into desired form before rolling out.

17. Ready or not: tap pastry lightly on the bottom. There will be a hollow sound when done. Pastry will be firm but not hard.

18. The sweeter the dough, the more oil it will absorb when deep-frying.

19. Try interchanging unyeasted and yeasted pastry doughs (see Chapter 5).

20. To preserve yeasted cakes or pastries, place a small, damp paper napkin with the yeasted products. Keep container tightly sealed and in a cool place.

YEASTED PASTRY

1 tablespoon dry yeast
³/₄-1¹/₂ cups fruit juice
2-4 tablespoons sweetener (p. 12)
2 beaten eggs
3 cups whole wheat cake or pastry flour
¹/₂ cup oil
¹/₂ teaspoon sea salt
1 teaspoon vanilla
2 teaspoons cinnamon
1 tablespoon orange and lemon rind

1. Dissolve yeast in ¹/₂ cup lukewarm fruit juice, add sweetener. Stir and set aside 5 minutes or until mixture bubbles.

2. Add eggs and enough flour to form a thin batter. Beat until smooth and not lumpy. Clean down the sides of the bowl with a rubber spatula. Cover and let rise in a warm spot until it is almost doubled in size.

3. Beat in oil, salt and vanilla. Combine the rest of the dry ingredients, reserving ¹/₂ cup of flour, and beat into yeasted mixture until it is too hard to beat. Add only enough fruit juice to form a soft sticky dough.

4. Knead dough on a lightly floured surface, kneading in the reserved flour if necessary to make the dough perfectly smooth. Place in an oiled bowl, cover and let rise in a warm spot until doubled in size. (After rising, it should feel soft and puffy.)

5. Roll and shape the dough into desired form. Place it on an oiled baking tray, cover with another tray to allow room for expansion. Let rise until almost double in size. Punch down, shape and bake.

VARIATION

All recipes which use Yeasted Pastry dough can be made substituting Eggless Yeasted Pastry Dough (p. 161). Many of these recipes would then be suitable for those on egg-free diets.

BOW TIES

1 quantity Yeasted Pastry (p. 142)
Any fruit puree (p. 85) or nut butter icing (pp. 74-5)
Nut filling (pp. 86-7)

1. Shape dough into rectangle. Roll out dough 6 mm (¹/₄ in) thick and cut away uneven edges. Cut into 5 × 13 cm (2 × 5 in) strips. Brush with puree or nut butter icing, and sprinkle over nut filling.

2. Twist each end of the strip from the centre in the opposite direction so that a bow is formed and fillings are face up. Place on an oiled baking sheet. Cover and let rise until almost doubled in size.

3. Preheat the oven to 180°C (350°F). Glaze before or after baking (p. 102). Bake 20-30 minutes, or until brown.

FRUIT PIZZA

There are many ways to make a sweet pizza, and each province in Italy has its own speciality. This pizza has been adapted from the Sicilian 'fruit pizza'.

1 quantity Yeasted Pastry (p. 142)
2 tablespoons orange juice
1 tablespoon orange rind
FILLING
2 cups Apricot Puree (p. 85)
3 cups sliced kiwifruit
TOPPING
Crumb Topping (p. 96)

1. Oil a 20 cm (8 in) round pizza tray. Prepare dough. Add juice and rind. Press out to 6 mm (¼ in) thickness and place on the bottom of the tray. Cover and let rise.

2. Preheat oven to 180°C (350°F). Prebake crust 10 minutes. Spread puree over dough, and place kiwifruit on top. Sprinkle Crumb Topping over filling. Bake 10 minutes longer, or until dough is lightly browned.

BLUEBERRY PEACH PIZZA

1 quantity Yeasted Pastry (p. 142)
2 tablespoons orange juice
1 tablespoon orange rind
FILLING
5 medium-sized peaches
3 cups blueberries
1 teaspoon ginger
1 teaspoon lemon juice
1 tablespoon tahini or almond butter
TOPPING
1 quantity Crumb Topping (p. 96)
1/2 cup unsweetened coconut (optional)

1. Blanch and peel peaches (p. 20) slice into 6 mm (¼ in) pieces. Prepare dough. Combine peaches, blueberries, ginger, lemon juice and tahini or nut butter in a mixing bowl. Toss lightly until fruit is coated. Set aside for 15 minutes. Prepare topping. (Add coconut if desired.) Set aside.

2. Preheat oven to 180°C (350°F). Oil a round 20 cm (8 in) pizza tray. Follow Fruit Pizza method.

BOWKNOTS

1 quantity Yeasted Pastry (p. 142)
Oil for deep-frying (pp. 18-19)
Roasted chestnut flour or carob flour for dusting

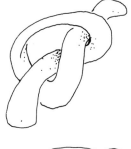

DEEP-FRYING FOR UNYEASTED OR YEASTED DOUGH

1. Prepare dough. Sprinkle pastry cloth or wooden surface with arrowroot flour. Divide dough into four parts. Cover three parts of the dough with a damp cloth and set aside. Roll remaining piece of dough into thin log.

2. Cut into strips 15 × 2.5 cm (6 × 1 in). Tie in bowknots.

3. Repeat procedure until all the dough is shaped. (For yeasted dough, cover and let rise until almost double in size.)

4. Heat oil. Deep-fry until delicately brown. Drain, dust with flour immediately and cool.

BAKING FOR UNYEASTED OR YEASTED DOUGH

1. Roll out into desired shape. Place on a baking sheet, cover and let rise in a warm place until almost double in size. (For unyeasted dough, bake immediately after shaping.)

2. Bake at 180°C (350°F) for 25-30 minutes, or until lightly browned. Brush with sweetener (p. 12) immediately after baking.

BLUEBERRY-PEACH TURNOVERS

2-3 cups sliced peaches
2-3 cups blueberries
1 teaspoon cinnamon
1 teaspoon orange rind plus 1 tablespoon ground kuzu or arrowroot flour
Pinch of sea salt
1 quantity Yeasted Pastry (p. 142)

1. Mix peaches with blueberries, cinnamon, orange rind, kuzu and salt. Let sit at least 30 minutes. Prepare dough.

2. Flour surface with kuzu or arrowroot, sprinkling cinnamon over flour. Shape dough into square before rolling. Roll out to 6 mm (¼ in) thickness. Trim edges. Cut pastry into 10 or 13 cm (4 or 5 in) squares.

3. Drain excess liquid from fruit mixture. Place a teaspoon of filling in the centre of each square. Fold over one corner of the square to make a triangle.

4. Press dough firmly around edges of pastry with the back or front of a fork. Oil a shallow pan or baking sheet. Place pastries on sheet 5 cm (2 in) apart. Slit each diagonally twice to allow steam to escape.

5. Cover and set in a warm place to rise until almost double in size.

6. Preheat the oven to 180°C (350°F). Glaze before or after baking (p. 102). Bake about 30-40 minutes, or until turnovers are browned.

Date Cinnamon Rolls

4-6 cups raisins, sultanas or apricots
Fruit juice
1 quantity Yeasted Pastry (p. 142)
Date Puree (p. 85) as needed
Cinnamon
TOPPING
1 cup Tofu Sour Cream (p. 95)
1/4 cup sweetener (p. 12)
1 teaspoon vanilla

1. Soak dried fruit in juice to cover until soft. Squeeze out excess liquid. Divide the dough in half.

2. On a *lightly* floured board, cloth or greaseproof paper, roll out half of the dough to a rectangle. Brush with oil. Spread Date Puree over dough. Sprinkle cinnamon liberally over the Date Puree.Cover with fruit. Roll up from the side like a jam roll (see Chestnut Carob Cake, p. 57). Cut into 2.5 cm (1 in) slices and place cut side up on an oiled baking sheet, or in muffin tins.

3. Repeat procedure with other half of the dough. Cover and let rise in a warm place until almost doubled in size.

4. Preheat oven to 180°C (350°F). Bake 15 minutes.

5. Combine Tofu Sour Cream with sweetener and vanilla. Spoon over the rolls. Bake 10-15 minutes longer.

Date Palm *(Phoenix dactylifera)*

This plant, an important crop of very ancient origin in the Middle East, dates back to at least 3000 B.C. It grows to a height of about 24 m (80 ft). The male and female trees are different, and it is only necessary for the grower to plant one male tree to 50-100 females. Palms may begin to bear fruit about 4 or 5 years after they are planted; but they reach a full bearing age at about 15 years, and continue to bear fruit to about 80 years of age. An average yield for one tree is about 50 kg (100 lb) of fruit per year.

Dates are grown in desert oases; they are important in the diet of Arab people. There are three kinds of dates: soft dates are eaten raw or used in confectionery; semi-dry dates are sold boxed with the fruits still attached to their strands; dried dates can be preserved for a long period of time. They are quite hard and can even be ground into flour or softened by steeping in water. The chief nutritional value of dates is their high sugar content, which varies from 60 to 70 per cent. They also have some vitamin A, B_1, B_2, and nicotinic acid.

COVERED TWISTS

Cut Yeasted Pastry (p. 142) into strips 5 × 25 cm (2 × 10 in). Brush with puree or icing and sprinkle filling on top. Fold strips over lengthwise, making them half as long. Slit the centres. Twist each end of strip in the opposite direction until a bow is formed.

CARROT PINWHEELS

1 tablespoon dried yeast
3¹/2-4 cups whole wheat cake or pastry flour
¹/2 teaspoon sea salt
¹/2 cup sweetener (p. 12)
¹/4 cup hot fruit juice or water
¹/4 cup soy milk or water
¹/3 cup oil
1 egg
FILLING
1 tablespoon oil
1 cup minced or grated onions
4-5 cups grated carrots
2 tablespoons mirin (sweet rice wine)
Sea salt to taste
1 teaspoon kuzu
Cold water
1-2 tablespoons orange rind
Sesame seeds (optional)
1 egg yolk and 1 tablespoon soy milk for glazing

1. Combine the yeast, ¹/2 cup flour and salt together.

2. Heat the sweetener, juice, soy milk and oil together. Add this to the dry ingredients and beat 1-2 minutes. Add the egg and enough flour to make a soft dough. Turn onto board and knead 5-10 minutes.

3. Heat skillet, add oil and sauté vegetables lightly. Add the mirin and salt and cook 4-5 minutes.

4. Dissolve the kuzu in cold water, add rind and stir into vegetables. Sprinkle with sesame seeds if desired. Cool.

5. Divide the dough into 3 pieces. Roll out to 30 × 25 cm (12 × 10 in) rectangles. Spread with filling. Roll up. Cut each roll into 12 slices.

6. Place slices on oiled baking sheet. Cover and let rise in warm place until doubled. Brush with mixture of egg yolk and milk. Bake at 190°C (375°F) 20-25 minutes. Cool and remove from baking sheet.

CRUMB SWIRL

1 quantity Yeasted Pastry (p. 142)
1 quantity Crumb Topping (p. 96)
Sweetener (p. 12)
Oil

1. Prepare Yeasted Pastry. Roll Yeasted Pastry into a large square 6mm (¼ in) thick. Brush with oil and sprinkle Crumb Topping over dough. Roll up like a jam roll. Cut roll into six even slices. Combine 2 parts sweetener to 1 part oil and use in the bottom of the loaf pan for a sweeter swirl.

2. Place slices, cut side down, in oiled 18 × 13 × 8 cm (7 × 5 × 3 in) loaf pan. (Squeeze them in if necessary.) Cover, set in a warm place until dough doubles in size. Bake in preheated 180°C (350°F) oven about 30 minutes, or until lightly browned. Glaze before or after baking.

SWEET CROISSANTS

Croissants (crescent rolls) were created in Hungary about 1686, to commemorate the withdrawal of the invading Turks. Bakers working at night heard the Turks tunnelling into the city and sounded the alarm which helped to defeat the Turkish troops. As a reward, the bakers were commissioned to produce a special pastry, shaped like a crescent, which is the emblem of Turkey.

1 quantity Yeasted Pastry (p. 142)
3-4 cups Fruit Puree (p. 85)
1 cup sweetener (p. 12)
2 cups ground almonds, walnuts or pecans

1. Prepare dough. Flour pastry cloth. Shape and roll out dough into circle 3mm (⅛ in) thick. Cut into triangles.

2. Place a teaspoon or less of puree on the widest side of the triangle, or spread over the whole triangle. Roll toward the pointed end and shape into croissants.

3. Oil a large baking sheet. Place croissants on sheet. Cover and let rise in a warm spot until almost double in size.

4. Preheat the oven to 180°C (350°F). Glaze with sweetener before or after baking (p. 102). Bake 25-35 minutes, or until browned. Sprinkle nuts on top after baking.

TWO FINGERS

1 quantity Yeasted Pastry (p. 142)
Rich Icing (p. 75)
Walnut Apple Filling (p. 87)

1. Prepare dough. Shape and roll out into a 15 × 40 ×0.6 cm (6 × 16 × ¼ in) strip.

2. Spread dough with icing. Sprinkle Walnut Apple Filling over it. Fold lengthwise toward the centre so that the two folded parts meet in the centre. Then fold again to make a long six-layer roll. Cut into 12 mm (½ in) slices. Place on an oiled biscuit sheet.

3. Spread the two halves of each slice slightly so they have room to expand. Cover, and set in a warm place to rise until almost doubled in size.

4. Bake at 180°C (350°F) in a preheated oven for about 30 minutes (you may wish to turn the slices over after 20 minutes).

FIRESIDE KUCHEN

3 cups diced apples or other fruit in season or 1½ cups dried fruit
Fruit juice as needed
½ quantity Yeasted Pastry (p. 142)
1 egg
1 teaspoon lemon rind
½ cup Crumb Topping (p. 96)

1. If using dried fruit, first soak fruit in fruit juice to cover. Cover and cook until soft. Squeeze out liquid, and dice. Be sure that the fruit has enough moisture to prevent it from drying up. Reserve juice.

2. Preheat oven to 160°C (325°F). Oil a 28 × 40 cm (11 × 16 in) sheet. Roll out dough, and place on an oiled sheet. Cover and let dough rise in a warm place until it becomes puffy, but not doubled in size.

3. Brush with a beaten egg. Arrange diced fruit on top. Combine rind and Crumb Topping, and sprinkle over fruit.

4. Bake in preheated oven 45 minutes, or until browned.

FRUIT AND HAZELNUT DUMPLINGS

1 quantity Yeasted Pastry (p. 142)
2-3 cups fruit juice or stewed fruit
1 cup crushed roasted hazelnuts

1. Prepare pastry dough. Roll into little balls.
2. Place fruit juice or stewed fruits in the bottom of a deep baking dish. Add the dumplings. (Cover, and set in a warm place to rise before baking.) Preheat oven to 190°C (375°F). Bake 1½-2 hours covered. Do not lift the cover off during the first hour of baking time.
3. When all of the liquid has been absorbed, and they begin to smell sweet, remove from oven.
4. Garnish with nuts. Serve immediately.

GRANDMA'S RUGELACH

3 cups whole wheat cake or pastry flour
1 tablespoon dried yeast
1 cup oil
3 egg yolks
1 cup Tofu Sour Cream (p. 95)
1 cup ground walnuts
1 cup carob flour
2 teaspoons cinnamon
1 egg yolk and 1 teaspoon cold water for glazing

1. Combine flour and yeast in large bowl. Add the oil, mixing until flour is crumbly. Stir in egg yolks. Blend in Tofu Sour Cream. Flatten dough into disc.
2. Cover and chill, preferably overnight.
3. Preheat oven to 180°C (350°F).
4. Combine walnuts, carob and cinnamon in a bowl. Sprinkle quarter of the mixture into a 20 cm (8 in) circle on work surface. Divide the dough into 4 equal portions. Place 1 portion on top of nut mixture. Roll out into circle 25 cm (10 in) in diameter, lifting the dough as you roll and pushing nut mixture back underneath. Cut circle into 16 wedges. Roll each triangle up from outside edge to point, then bend to form crescent. Repeat for other 3 portions of mixture and dough. Transfer to baking sheet. Brush on egg yolk and water mixture. Bake until puffed and golden, about 20-25 minutes.

FRUIT STOLLEN

I once baked four of these for a Christmas dinner, and never even tasted a crumb.

EF

1 cup mixed dried fruit
1/4 cup raisins or sultanas
Fruit juice to cover fruit
1 1/2 tablespoons dried yeast
1 cup warm fruit juice
1/4 cup sweetener (p. 12)
3 1/2 cups whole wheat cake or pastry flour
1/2 cup oil
1/2 cup pecans or other chopped nuts
1 teaspoon cinnamon
1/2 teaspoon sea salt

1. Soak dried fruit and raisins or sultanas in juice. Squeeze out liquid and dice (set aside liquid for batter).

2. Dissolve yeast in warm fruit juice. Combine with sweetener. Add enough flour to form a thin batter. Cover and let rise in a warm spot until doubled in size.

3. Mix in other ingredients, and knead about 5-10 minutes. Punch down, and roll into an oval. Fold over lengthwise, and place on an oiled sheet or in a bread tin. Slit top. Cover and let rise.

4. Preheat oven to 200°C (400°F). Glaze before or after baking (p. 102). Bake 10 minutes, turn down to 180°C (350°F), and bake 25-30 minutes longer. Remove from oven and place on a rack to cool.

Pecans (Carya illinoinensis)

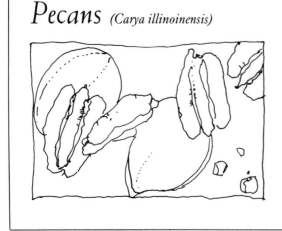

Considered queen of the nuts in their native home of North America due to the rich aromatic flavour, pecans are high in potassium, B vitamins and kilojoules. Pecans thrive on riverbanks which are their natural habitat, and grow well in areas of low humidity with plentiful water supplies. Pecans are a delicious treat for those special occasions.

DOUGHNUTS

Doughnuts were traditionally tossed in the air for children to catch on 'Fat Tuesday' (mardi gras), the day before Lent.

1 recipe Yeasted Pastry dough, substituting 2 tablespoons oil for ½ cup (p. 142)
½ cup orange juice and rind
Oil for deep-frying (pp. 18-19)
TOPPING
Carob Icing (p. 78)

1. Add orange juice and rind to spices in dough. Prepare a soft moist dough, just firm enough to handle. Knead. Cover and chill 15 minutes.

2. Prepare Carob Frosting.

3. Roll out or pat dough to 12 mm (½ in) thickness on a floured cloth. With a well-floured doughnut cutter, cut into rings or logs 12 mm × 10 cm (½ × 4 in).* Twist the logs gently and bring the ends together.

4. Place on well-oiled greaseproof paper, cover with a damp cloth and let rest 20 minutes.

5. Heat oil. Deep-fry about 3 minutes (1½ minutes on each side) or until lightly browned. Drain and cool.

6. Glaze, dip into cinnamon, roasted chestnut flour, grated unsweetened coconut or crushed roasted seeds or nuts.

*For doughnuts cut with a doughnut cutter, or a large cutter with a smaller one for the centre hole. If you do not have a cutter, roll into logs.

SUGGESTIONS

For more tender doughnuts, have all ingredients at room temperature.

Add dried fruits, nuts, seeds, spices to dough before resting it.

Add a few whole cloves to hot oil before deep-frying for additional flavour.

JAM DOUGHNUTS

1 quantity Yeasted Pastry (p. 142)
Apple butter, or any puree (pp. 84-5) or sugarless jam

1. Prepare dough. Cut into 8 cm (3 in) rounds instead of rings.

2. Place 1 teaspoon apple butter or any fruit puree or jam into the centre of one round. Brush the edge of the round with egg white. Place another round on top. Press the edges together. Repeat with the rest of the dough. Cover and set aside 30 minutes on a lightly floured board.

3. Deep-fry 3-5 minutes. Drain.

4. Follow directions in Doughnuts for glaze and topping.

JOHN IN THE SACK

2 cups chopped fruit
1 cup chopped dried pears or peaches
1/2 cup chopped walnuts or hazelnuts
2 teaspoons orange rind
1 teaspoon cinnamon
Pinch of sea salt
1 quantity Yeasted Pastry (p. 142)
Fruit juice for boiling pastries

*To remove excess liquid from fruit, cut into small pieces and sprinkle with salt. Toss lightly, allow to sit at least 30 minutes. Pour off excess liquid.

1. Choose fruit that has little liquid content.*
2. Combine fruits, nuts, rind, spices and salt. Set aside.
3. Prepare Yeasted Pastry. Roll out dough. Cut out circles about 8 cm (3 in) in diameter or 8 × 10 cm (3 × 4 in) squares.
4. Place a tablespoon of fruit filling in the centre, wrap and tie securely. Place on oiled baking sheet. Cover and let rise in a warm place until almost doubled in size.
5. Boil juice. Drop into boiling juice and cook 20-30 minutes or until pastry has been cooked.

ALTERNATIVE METHODS

1. Bake at 180°C (350°F) 35-45 minutes.
2. Deep-fry until brown. Drain immediately.
3. Steam 30 minutes.

PUFF PIES

1 quantity Yeasted Pastry (p. 142)
FILLING
2 cups Date Puree (p. 85)
1/2 cup crushed walnuts
1 tablespoon orange rind
Oil for deep-frying
Roasted chestnut flour, cinnamon or carob for dusting

1. Sprinkle arrowroot flour on rolling surface.
2. Roll out dough to 6 mm (1/4 in) thickness and cut out 8 cm (3 in) circles. Combine Date Puree, walnuts and orange rind to make filling. Place a spoonful of filling in the centre of one of the circles. Moisten the edge of the dough all around the filling with water or egg. Place another circle on top, and press edges firmly together. Repeat until all dough is used.
3. Cover and set in a warm place for about 20 minutes.
4. Heat oil. Deep-fry until browned on both sides. Drain, and sprinkle with roasted chestnut flour, carob or cinnamon while still warm.

Opposite: Yeasted pastries: Bow Ties (page 142), Date Cinnamon Rolls (page 145) and Sweet Croissants (page 147)

OLYKOECKS (HUDSON VALLEY DOUGHNUTS)

FILLING
EF   GF
4 finely chopped apples
3 tablespoons lemon rind
1¹/₂ cups chopped pitted dates or other dried fruit
2 tablespoons cinnamon
DOUGH
1¹/₂ tablespoons dried yeast
¹/₄ cup warm fruit juice
4 cups whole wheat cake or pastry flour
1 egg
¹/₂ teaspoon sea salt
¹/₂ teaspoon cinnamon
¹/₂ teaspoon dry ginger
¹/₄ cup sweetener (p. 12)
2 tablespoons oil
¹/₄ cup cold juice as needed
Fruit juice to form dough
Oil for deep-frying
Maple syrup
Desiccated coconut

1. Add rind, dates and cinnamon to apples. Mix well. Set aside.

2. Dilute yeast in warm juice. Add enough flour to form a thin batter. Cover and set in a warm place to rise until doubled in size.

3. Beat egg. Add salt, cinnamon and ginger. Set aside.

4. Beat down batter. Add egg mixture, sweetener, oil and the rest of the flour to batter. Adjust liquid-flour content accordingly. Knead until dough is smooth and elastic. Cover and let rise in a warm place until almost doubled in size.

5. Punch down. Pinch off a small piece of dough and roll into a ball. Make a depression in the centre and place some of the fruit mixture in the centre of each ball; cover with dough. Roll into ball. Place on a floured board. Cover, set in a warm place to rest.

6. Heat oil. Remove doughnuts from board and roll again to make them round. Drop into hot oil and deep-fry about 5 minutes, rotating each ball after first few minutes. Drain.

7. Brush with maple syrup and sprinkle with coconut.

VARIATION

Substitute any fresh fruit in season or any dried fruit for apples.

Opposite: Pumpkin Crumb Muffins (page 158)

MISO TAHINI BRAID

EF
1/4 cup lukewarm fruit juice
1 tablespoon yeast
1/2 cup sweetener (p. 12)
1/3 cup oil
2 cups whole wheat cake or pastry flour
1/4 teaspoon sea salt
FILLING
GF
1/4 cup tahini
1/4 cup white miso
1/4 cup sweetener (p. 12)
1 tablespoon orange rind
1 teaspoon ground coriander

1. Place juice in bowl and sprinkle yeast over it. Add sweetener and oil, and mix until creamy. Cover and place in a warm spot to bubble.

2. Add flour and salt, stirring briskly until mixture begins to thicken and forms a dough. Knead mixture 10 minutes. (Adjust liquid.) Cover and set in a warm place to rise (30-40 minutes).

FILLING

Combine all filling ingredients together and mix until smooth paste forms. (Add small amount of warm liquid to help cream.)

ROLLING OUT

1. Divide dough into quarters. Keep unused sections covered with a damp cloth.

2. Roll dough into large square 6 mm (1/4 in) thick. Brush with oil and spread filling over dough. Roll up very tightly into a thin log.

3. Continue until four logs are formed. Braid strips together to make loaf. Place in oiled and floured loaf tin or on baking sheet. Cover and set in a warm spot until dough doubles in size.

4. Preheat oven to 180°C (350°F). Brush dough with egg wash before baking (p. 102), or sweetener (p. 12) just after baking.

Sesame *(Sesamum indicum)*

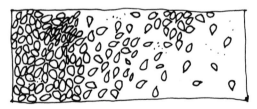

The sesame was originally from Africa, although today it is grown in Mexico, California, and other tropical or subtropical climates.

The plant grows up to 2 m (6 ft) high, taking 3 to 5 months to mature. The different varieties have many flowers, such as white, pink or mauve. When harvested, the whole plants are cut and stacked upright to dry. As they dry, the seed capsules split open and the plants are usually turned upside-down and shaken out onto a cloth. These seeds contain 45 to 50 per cent oil, which is used in various ways in desserts. The seeds can be used for nut butters in fillings and for decoration in cooking and baking.

SWEET PUFFS

2 teaspoons dried yeast
1/2-1 cup warm water or fruit juice
1 cup flour (chickpea or whole wheat)
1/2 cup whole wheat cake or pastry flour
1 egg (optional)
TOPPING
2 cups maple syrup
2 tablespoons lemon juice
1/2 teaspoon cinnamon and cardamon
Coconut for topping (optional)

1. Dissolve the yeast in the warm water or juice. Set aside, till mixture bubbles.

2. Combine the dry ingredients in a bowl, add the yeast mixture, stirring well. Add egg (if using), enough water or juice until a soft dough is formed that falls from the edge of the spoon. Set aside to rise.

3. Heat oil for deep frying. Drop teaspoons of batter into the hot oil. Fry 3-4 minutes turning over as necessary. Drain and repeat with the rest of the batter.

4. Heat maple syrup, lemon juice, cinnamon and cardamon. Simmer 5 minutes. Dip in puffs. Stack on a large platter and sprinkle with cinnamon and serve immediately. Sprinkle with coconut if desired.

SAUCERS

1 quantity Yeasted Pastry (p. 142)
3-4 cups Chestnut Cream (p. 90)
Sweetener as needed (p. 12)
2-3 teaspoons cinnamon

1. Prepare dough. Flour surface and roll out dough 6 mm (1/4 in) thick. Cut out circles 10-15 cm (4-6 in) in diameter.

2. Oil baking tray. Place half of the circles on sheet. Spread with filling, leaving 12 mm (1/2 in) all around edges of circle. Using a small knife or razor blade, score remaining circles with arcs radiating from the centre of the circle. Place over filling. Press edges to seal in filling.

3. Cover and set in a warm place to rise until almost double in size. Brush top with sweetener, and sprinkle on cinnamon.

4. Preheat oven to 180°C (350°F). Bake 45-60 minutes or until pastry is browned.

VARIATIONS

1. Add 2 teaspoons orange or lemon rind to dough.
2. Substitute any vegetable or cream filling.
3. Unyeasted pastry dough may be substituted for yeasted dough.

HAMENTASCHEN

Purim, a Jewish feast, celebrates the victory of the beautiful Queen Esther over the evil Haman. The traditional Hamentaschen, poppy seed or prune-filled triangles of pastry, are said to represent Haman's hat.

1 quantity Yeasted Pastry (p. 142)
PRUNE RAISIN FILLING
500 g (1 lb) prunes
1 cup sultanas or raisins
Fruit juice to cover
Pinch of sea salt
Juice and rind of 1/2 orange
2 tablespoons lemon rind
1/2 cup chopped roasted almonds

1. Soak prunes and sultanas or raisins in fruit juice to cover for 10 minutes. Bring to a boil, add sea salt, and boil down until there is no more liquid left. Stone prunes.

2. Blend cooked fruit together with the rest of the ingredients except almonds. Fold in nuts.

3. Roll out dough to 6 mm (1/4 in) thickness. Cut into squares about 10 × 10 cm (4 × 4 in).

4. Make a depression in the centre of each square. Spoon in 1 tablespoon filling. Pinch each corner together, leaving about 3-5 cm (1 1/2 in) of the filling exposed.

5. Sprinkle with cinnamon. Place on oiled sheet, cover and set in a warm spot to rise until pastry has almost doubled in size.

6. Glaze before or after baking (p. 102). Bake in a preheated 180°C (350°F) oven 30-45 minutes, or until browned.

SWEET BUNS

1 quantity Yeasted Pastry (p. 142)
1 cup soaked raisins, currants or other dried fruit
1/2 cup sweetener (p. 12)

1. Follow directions for Yeasted Pastry, adding fruit after first rise. Cut off small pieces of dough and shape.

2. Place in oiled cupcake tins after shaping, cover, and let rise until almost doubled in size.

3. Preheat oven to 180°C (350°F). Bake 20-30 minutes or until browned. (Tap on bottom and top of bun. When it sounds hollow, it is done.)

4. Remove from oven, brush with sweetener and chill immediately.

VARIATIONS

1. Bring fruit juice to the boil, add 4 tablespoons grain coffee (p.

24). Cool juice to warm before adding yeast. Add 1 teaspoon ginger to dry mixture before adding oil.

2. Add 1 cup roasted chopped walnuts or pecans to flour mixture.

3. Add juice and rind of 1 grated orange to flour mixture after the first rise.

SCHNECKEN

1 quantity Yeasted Pastry (p. 142)
¹/4 cup oil
2 tablespoons maple syrup
Pecans as needed
1 quantity Crumb Topping (p. 96)
Raisins
Nuts

1. Prepare Yeasted Pastry. Set aside.

2. Combine oil with maple syrup. Oil muffin tins or cupcake tins with this mixture. Place a few pecans in each cup.

3. Roll dough into a long rectangle 6 mm (¹/4 in) thick. Sprinkle Crumb Topping, raisins, and nuts over dough. Roll up dough tightly like jam roll, sealing the seam with water or egg.

4. Stretch out the roll if it is too thick for the tins, or compress it if it is too thin. Slice into small pieces and fill the cups halfway.

5. Cover, set in a warm place until dough doubles in size.

6. Bake in preheated 180°C (350°F) oven about 25-30 minutes, or until lightly browned.

7. Turn pans upside-down on cake rack immediately (place baking sheet underneath pan to catch the drippings) to remove schnecken and allow glaze to drip over the sides.

UPSIDE-DOWN PECAN SWIRLS

1 quantity Yeasted Pastry (p. 142)
3-4 cups Apricot Puree (p. 85)
2-3 cups Crumb Topping (p. 96)
1 teaspoon vanilla
¹/2-1 cup sweetener (p. 12)
Roasted pecan halves

1. Follow rolling and shaping directions for Date Cinnamon Rolls (p. 145).

2. Pour sweetener into oiled cupcake tins. Place pecans in tins. Cut dough into 2.5 cm (1 in) slices. Swirl over pecans.

3. Cover, and let rise till almost doubled in size.

4. Preheat oven to 180°C (350°F). Bake 25-30 minutes.

PUMPKIN CRUMB MUFFINS

GF*

¹/4 cup oil
2¹/2 cups grated pumpkin
*2 cups fine wholemeal breadcrumbs or 2 cups ground nuts ***
¹/2 cup unsweetened shredded coconut or ¹/2 cup chopped nuts
1 teaspoon ground coriander
1 teaspoon cinnamon
Pinch of sea salt
4 eggs, separated
¹/2 cup sweetener (p. 12)
1¹/2 teaspoons vanilla
2 tablespoons grated orange rind
Whole, blanched almonds

* Gluten free if using ground nuts.

1. Preheat oven to 180°C (350°F). Then oil and lightly flour 15 muffin tins.

2. Heat skillet, add oil and sauté the pumpkin 2-3 minutes. Remove from the heat. Combine the breadcrumbs, coconut, coriander, cinnamon and sea salt in a mixing bowl. Stir in the pumpkin.

3. Beat the egg yolks with sweetener, vanilla and orange rind. Blend into the pumpkin mixture.

4. Beat egg whites with a pinch of sea salt till peaked. Fold into pumpkin mixture. Adjust liquid content here to form a thick batter.

5. Spoon into muffin tins, two-thirds full, and place almond on top, and bake 30-40 minutes or until skewer inserted comes out dry. Remove from oven, and place on rack to cool. Remove from pan, glaze with sweetener before serving. Serve with favourite sugar-free jam or jelly.

SESAME MUFFINS

¹/₂ cup oil
2 eggs
¹/₃ cup maple syrup
1 tablespoon lemon juice or orange juice
1 tablespoon grated lemon or orange rind
¹/₄ cup Tofu Sour Cream (p. 95) or yoghurt, optional (if using omit lemon juice)
¹/₃ teaspoon sodium bicarbonate and ²/₃ teaspoon cream of
tartar or 2 teaspoons dried yeast
1 cup whole wheat cake or pastry flour
1¹/₂ cups rolled oats
¹/₂ cup toasted sesame seeds
1 teaspoon cinnamon

1. Beat together oil, eggs and maple syrup till creamy. Set aside.
2. Combine the lemon juice, rind, Tofu Sour Cream or yoghurt and sodium bicarbonate and cream of tartar or dried yeast. Add to oil mixture. If using yeast allow to rise until mixture bubbles.
3. Combine flour and rolled oats, sesame seeds and cinnamon. Fold into wet mixture.
4. Oil muffin tins. Pre-heat oven to 180°C (350°F). Fill tins two-thirds full. Bake 15-20 minutes. Cool.

Baking Soda and Baking Powder

Both of these common leavening agents have been used for a great number of years. However, sometimes these leavening agents have proved detrimental to people's health.

Many natural food stores have begun to carry a range of different kinds of low sodium baking powder that contain no lime or aluminium compounds. For best results try making your own (see p. 21).

MILLET APPLE MUFFINS

2 teaspoons dried yeast
1/2 cup warm fruit juice
1 tablespoon whole wheat cake or pastry flour
1 tablespoon oil
2 sliced apples
1 teaspoon cinnamon
1/3 cup hulled millet
1 egg (room temperature)
1/4 cup warm oil
1/3-1/2 cup maple syrup
1 teaspoon cinnamon or coriander
1 teaspoon crushed fennel seeds
2 tablespoons orange rind
Juice of 1 orange
1 cup sifted whole wheat cake or pastry flour

1. Combine the first three ingredients and set aside until the mixture bubbles.

2. Meanwhile, heat skillet, add oil and sauté the apples and cinnamon. Set aside.

3. Wash and roast millet till lightly browned. Cool.

4. Beat together the egg, oil and maple syrup till creamy. Add all the remaining ingredients except the flour. Blend well. Fold in the flour.

5. Oil muffin tins, and preheat the oven to 190°C (375°F). Place cooked apples on the bottom of each tin and cover with batter, until two-thirds full. Set aside to rise 30 minutes or until almost doubled. Bake 30 minutes and test if done. Remove from oven and tins and place on a cake rack to cool.

Cashew *(Anacardium occidentale)*

The cashew is only grown in frost-free areas. Originally found in America it is now extensively cultivated in India, eastern Africa and does well in parts of Australia. After picking, the nut has to be roasted and then shelled (a time-consuming process). The shell contains a caustic irritant oil that is painful to the skin. Therefore, the cashew is never eaten in a truly raw state. Containing 45 per cent fat and 20 per cent protein, their rich oily flavour makes them a perfect dessert nut.

TOFU CRUMB ROLL

EF

EGGLESS YEASTED PASTRY DOUGH
1 tablespoon dried yeast
³/4-1¹/2 cups fruit juice
2-4 tablespoons sweetener (p. 12)
3¹/2 cups whole wheat cake or pastry flour
¹/2 cup oil
1 teaspoon vanilla
¹/2 teaspoon sea salt
2 teaspoons cinnamon
1 tablespoon orange or lemon rind
FILLING
3-4 tablespoons cashew or other nut butter
3 cups Tofu Crumb Filling (p. 88)

1. Dissolve yeast in ¹/2 cup lukewarm fruit juice; add sweetener here if desired. Stir and set aside 5 minutes or until mixture bubbles.

2. Add enough flour to form a thin batter. Beat until smooth and not lumpy. Clean down the sides of the bowl with a rubber spatula. Cover and let rise in a warm spot until it is almost doubled in size. Beat in oil and vanilla. Combine the rest of the dry ingredients, reserving ¹/2 cup of flour, and beat into yeasted mixture until it is too thick to beat. Add only enough fruit juice to form a soft sticky dough.

3. Knead dough on a lightly floured surface, kneading in the reserved flour if necessary to make the dough perfectly smooth. Place in an oiled bowl, cover and let rise in a warm spot until doubled in size.

4. Roll out dough to 6 mm (¹/4 in) thickness.

5. Spread nut butter and sprinkle Tofu Crumb Filling evenly over dough. Roll up into roll.

6. Cut roll in half. Place each loaf in an oiled 23 × 13 × 8 cm (9 × 5 × 3 in) loaf pan. Cover, set in a warm place until dough doubles in size. Bake in preheated 180°C (350°F) oven 45 minutes or until browned.

7. Glaze before or after baking (p. 102).

DANISH RING

1 quantity Yeasted Pastry (p. 142)
Fruit Puree (p. 85)

1. Prepare Yeasted Pastry. Roll out dough into a rectangle approximately $15 \times 50 \times 0.6$ cm ($6 \times 20 \times \frac{1}{4}$ in).

2. Spread dough with Fruit Puree. Fold to make strip one-third of its previous width. Roll with a rolling pin to lengthen and flatten.

3. Cut into dough with a knife, making three incisions lengthwise, equally spaced apart, almost the entire length of the strip, leaving 2.5 cm (1 in) uncut at both ends. Take one end in each hand. Turn and twist the ends in opposite directions to form a long twist, stretching dough slightly as you twist.

4. Hold ends, shaping into a ring. Cross the ends, and press them firmly together. Press down with thumbs or hand on crossed ends, and flip over the ring to conceal the ends.

5. Place on oiled baking tray. Cover. Set in a warm place until dough doubles in size.

6. Bake in a preheated 180°C (350°F) oven 30-40 minutes.

6. MUNCHIES:
Biscuits, Cookies and Slices

Wouldn't it be nice to always have your biscuit jar filled to the brim with mouth-watering tastes that please anyone's sweet tooth? Well, now that fantasy can come true with a little effort on your part by experimenting with various-shaped cutters, natural colourings, flavourings and a variety of techniques, as well as combining wholesome flours to make rolled, chewy, nut, drop biscuits, cookies or bars. It's a good idea to sample the batter or dough before baking, and adjust the seasoning to suit your taste. Bake an extra-special batch for the holidays, and try to keep your jar filled with tasty treats all year round.

FORGET ME KNOTS

1. The amount of liquid necessary for each recipe will differ each time, according to the texture of the flour and the humidity of the air, the size of eggs and the general weather of the day.
2. Always preheat the oven 10-15 minutes before baking.
3. In making any kind of munchies, never beat or knead the dough after the flour has been added or they may be tough. Eggs used in dough should be at room temperature.
4. Do not roll dough in excessive amounts of flour. Instead roll out on a lightly arrowroot floured board, or between two sheets of greaseproof paper. This technique usually produces flakier biscuits.
5. Keep the dough covered and chilled until you use it.
6. Dust cutters with flour, carob or cinnamon before using them. Use glasses, bowls, cups etc., for unusual designs.
7. Baking sheets may be oiled with beeswax or use deep-frying oil in place of fresh oil.
8. Use a flat baking sheet or the bottom of a reversed baking pan, so that the heat can circulate directly and evenly over the biscuit tops.
9. Dark baking sheets absorb heat, and biscuits may brown more on the bottom. Old baking sheets have shiny baking surfaces, and specially dulled bottoms to produce more even browning.
10. A pan with high sides will deflect the heat and make the biscuits difficult to remove after baking.
11. A baking sheet should be at least 5 cm (2 in) shorter and narrower than the oven rack, so that the air can circulate around it.
12. Baking sheets should always be cold when you put the biscuits on them so they will not lose their shape.
13. Transfer rolled or moulded biscuits from rolling surface to sheet with a spatula.
14. Drop biscuits tend to spread more than other biscuits, so leave 5 cm (2 in) between them. Try to make them the same size, so they will bake in the same time.
15. Watch biscuits carefully because ovens tend to overheat. The later batches tend to cook more quickly.
16. When a baking sheet is only partially filled, the heat is drawn to the area where the biscuits lie, and they may burn on the bottom before they are baked. If there is not enough batter or dough to fill a baking sheet, use a reversed pie pan or small baking tin instead.
17. If two racks are used, the heat circulates unevenly so that the bottoms of the biscuits on the lower rack and the tops of those on the upper rack brown too quickly, so change position of sheets.
18. During baking, turn the baking sheets around for a more even baking.
19. After baking, remove the biscuits from the sheet immediately, or they will continue to cook.
20. Always cool biscuits spread out on a rack, and not overlapping.
21. When deep-frying biscuits, seeds and nuts have a tendency to separate from the batter or dough unless finely ground.
22. *Do not store crisp and soft biscuits together.*
23. Store crisp biscuits in a jar with a loose-fitting cover in a cool place. If they soften, put them in a slow oven for five minutes before serving.
24. Keep soft biscuits moist by storing them in a cool place in a covered jar. If they dry out, put a piece of bread, an apple, an orange or a clove-studded lemon in the jar with them to help maintain the moisture.

SHADES OF THINGS TO COME

PINWHEELS

EF

1 1/2 cups whole wheat cake or pastry flour
2 cups chestnut, brown rice or sweet brown rice flour
1 tablespoon orange rind or mint
Pinch of sea salt
1/2 cup oil
1/2 cup sweetener (p. 12)
Vanilla
1 egg (optional)
Fruit juice to moisten as necessary
1/3 cup grain coffee or 1 teaspoon cloves plus 1/3 cup flour
or 1/3 cup carob flour

1. Combine dry ingredients, except grain coffee. Cut oil in until mixture resembles tiny breadcrumbs. Add sweetener, vanilla and beaten egg. Mix with wooden spoon.

2. Divide mixture in half. Add grain coffee or carob powder to one half. Add juice to each mixture until two doughs are formed.

3. Roll out light dough into a large rectangle between two sheets of greaseproof paper. Roll dark rectangle the same way. Remove paper, and invert dark dough on light dough. Roll up like a jam roll. Wrap in wax paper, sealing the ends well. Chill at least 1 hour.

4. Preheat oven 180°C (350°F). Slice 12 mm (½ in) thick. Bake 10-12 minutes, or until lightly browned.

VARIATION

Substitute ingredients for Rolled Biscuits. Follow directions for Pinwheels.

BULL'S EYE

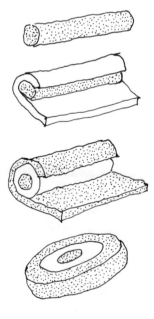

1. Prepare two doughs, one plain, one dark. For basic dough, see Pinwheels (p. 165). (Add grain coffee, carob or raisin puree for dark colour.) Form a quarter of the dark dough into a log 2.5 cm (1 in) thick and 15 cm (6 in) long. Wrap in wax paper and chill 2 hours.

2. Roll three-quarters of the plain dough into a 10 × 15 cm (4 × 6 in) thick, and roll around dark dough. Reverse with the remaining dough. Wrap in paper and chill at least 2 hours.

3. Slice into 12 mm (½ in) pieces and bake at 180°C (350°F) 12-15 minutes.

HALF AND HALF

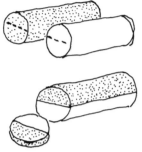

1. Prepare two logs, one plain, one dark (see Bull's Eye, p. 165). Wrap in wax paper and chill.

2. Cut lengthwise through the centre of each log. Brush surfaces with sweetener and press together, the plain against the dark. Wrap in wax paper and chill at least 2 hours.

3. Slice 6-12 mm (¼-½ in) thick and bake at 180°C (350°F) 12-15 minutes (see Rolled Biscuits, p. 169).

CRISSCROSS

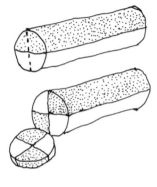

1. Prepare Half and Half logs. Cut lengthwise through the centre again. Brush cut surface with sweetener. Turn one of the halves around and place it end to end with the other half. Press together. Wrap and chill at least 2 hours.

2. Slice 6-12 mm (¼-½ in) thick and bake at 180°C (350°F) 12-15 minutes (see Rolled Biscuits, p. 169).

MARBLE EFFECT

1. Prepare 2 logs of different colours. Wrap and chill. Pinch off small pieces from each log, and roll them out together in one large circle. Cut with biscuit cutter.

2. Combine a few pieces from each colour dough, shape into one log, wrap and chill at least 4 hours. Slice into 6 mm (¼ in) biscuits. Place on an unoiled sheet, and bake at 190°C (375°F) 10-12 minutes.

BLACK AND WHITE BISCUITS

1. Use leftover dough from Pinwheels or any of the two-tone biscuits.

2. Roll out, cut with favourite biscuit cutters and bake 10-12 minutes. Cool.

3. Prepare Carob Mousse (p. 216) or Carob Icing (p. 78) and dip in one side of the biscuit. Set aside to dry on rack.

ALPHABET BISCUITS

1. Use same leftover dough as listed above.
2. Cut out different letter shapes and bake 7-10 minutes. Cool.

SESAME NUGGETS

1 1/2 cups whole wheat cake or pastry flour
1/6 teaspoon sodium bicarbonate
1/3 teaspoon cream of tartar
3/4 teaspoon ground aniseed
4-7 tablespoons maple syrup to taste
5 tablespoons oil
1 small egg, beaten to blend
1 1/2 teaspoons vanilla
1/2-3/4 cup sesame seeds

1. Preheat the oven to 180°C (350°F). Combine the dry ingredients in bowl.
2. Blend in maple syrup, oil, egg and vanilla with a wooden spoon. Press dough together with your hands.
3. Roll out about ½ cup dough into a thick rope. Cut into 2.5 cm (1 in) lengths. Roll in sesame seeds to coat completely.
4. Arrange biscuits on an unoiled baking sheet spacing about 2.5 cm (1 in) apart. Bake until biscuits are lightly golden, about 15-20 minutes. Cool on wire rack.

VARIATIONS

Add 2 teaspoons freshly grated orange rind to dough.

Peppermint (Mentha piperita)

This herb is mostly used for its essential oil, obtained by distilling the fresh plants. The oil is secreted by glands which are often visible to the eye as translucent dots on the leaf of the plant. It can also be used to make tea. If used in jelly-type desserts, puddings or custards, it will enhance the flavour.

ROLLED BISCUITS AND COOKIES

Holiday biscuits and cookies usually take a shape associated with the occasion being celebrated: Christmas trees for Christmas, rabbits for Easter, hearts for Valentine's Day. By using special cutters to form such shapes as these, any holiday cookies can be made.

The trick to making successful biscuits and cookies is simple. The dough must not be too soft. Excess flour must not be added when rolling out. Too much flour can make them too tough to eat. (Always use arrowroot flour for rolling out doughs.)

Helpful Hints

1. Divide large amounts of dough into a few pieces.

2. Doughs that contain neither sweeteners nor eggs may be less firm than sweetened dough. Wrap and chill overnight, and roll out dough on greaseproof paper floured with arrowroot.

3. Substituting chestnut flour or brown rice flour for half of the whole wheat pastry flour will also produce a firmer, crisper dough.

4. Dough that contains sweeteners can be chilled a shorter length of time than non-sweetened doughs. Extra-long chilling can make this dough too firm and difficult to roll out. (Dough that contains both sweeteners and eggs can be chilled longer.) If dough becomes too firm, unwrap and let sit at room temperature until easier to work with (about 1 hour).

5. Roll out on an arrowroot floured surface or between two sheets of greaseproof paper.

6. Flour cutters only if the dough is soft and sticky.

7. If the dough is not too floury, re-roll and use the scraps.

Lemon Tree (Citrus limon)

The lemon tree is native to south-eastern Asia, but it is grown commercially in the countries around the Mediterranean Sea, in southern California and in many parts of Australia. The tree is a small evergreen with spreading branches that give it an irregular shape. It has long, pointed, pale green leaves and large fragrant flowers that usually grow in clusters. The buds tend to be reddish purple, but the flower petals are white.

ROLLED BISCUITS

¹/₂ cup cold oil
1 teaspoon vanilla
¹/₂ cup sweetener (p. 12)
¹/₂-1 cup cold fruit juice
Pinch of salt
1 teaspoon cinnamon
³/₄ teaspoon ground ginger
3 cups whole wheat cake or pastry flour
¹/₂ cup ground toasted nuts
1 egg and water (for glazing)

1. Mix together oil, vanilla, sweetener and fruit juice, and stir until smooth. Sift dry ingredients together and add the liquid mixture, mixing with a wooden spoon until a ball of dough begins to form. Divide into three pieces. Cover and chill at least 60 minutes before rolling. While shaping, keep unused dough covered with a damp cloth until ready to use.

2. Preheat oven to 190°C (375°F).

3. Roll out dough to 6mm (¹/₄in) thickness. Cut with any shape cutters; brush with beaten egg and sprinkle with one of the following: chopped nuts, cinnamon, or sesame seeds.

4. Place on a sheet and bake 10-15 minutes, or until crisp. Place on a rack to cool.

5. If dough becomes too soft and warm after cutting, cover sheet and chill about 30 minutes before baking; this will make them more crisp.

ALTERNATIVE METHOD

Follow directions for Rolled Biscuits. Experiment by shaping the dough into different forms – logs, squares, balls, etc.

Heat oil in a deep pot. Deep-fry biscuits until lightly browned. Drain on paper towels or paper bags before serving.

VARIATIONS

Lemon-walnut: Add grated rind, juice of ¹/₂ lemon and ¹/₂ cup crushed walnuts to dry ingredients.

Orange-almond: Add grated rind and juice of ¹/₂ orange and ¹/₂ cup crushed almonds. (Decrease oil by ¹/₄ cup.)

Poppy-seed-lemon: Add 1 cup poppy seeds to mixing bowl before adding flour. Add grated rind and juice of ¹/₂ lemon to liquid mixture.

Lemon-walnut-mint: Follow directions for Lemon-walnut Biscuits, adding 2-3 teaspoons mint to dry mixture before combining with liquid.

Mint-walnut: Follow directions for Rolled Biscuits. Add 1 teaspoon mint to dry ingredients, and press in crushed walnuts.

Sweet Orange-mint: Follow directions for Rolled Biscuits, substituting 1 tablespoon mint for ginger, and adding orange rind to taste to dry ingredients.

Sesame-mint: Add 1 tablespoon mint and ¹/₂ cup roasted sesame seeds to oil mixture before adding dry ingredients.

Sweet Mint Drops: Substitute 1 tablespoon mint for ginger, and add enough juice to form a stiff batter. Drop onto baking sheet, and bake 10-15 minutes, or until brown.

Wafers: Dip a piece of cheesecloth in water, wring it out and tie it securely around the bottom of a glass. Press into dough to make a patterned design.

RAINBOWS

EF

One Thanksgiving I was invited to Michio and Aveline Kushi's house for dinner. I baked an assortment of biscuits (Half and Half, Crisscross and Rainbows), placed them in a box and gave them to the lady of the house.

2 cups whole wheat cake or pastry flour
1 cup chestnut flour, brown rice or arrowroot flour
1 teaspoon sea salt
1/2 cup oil
2 teaspoons vanilla
COLOURS
1/4 cup beetroot juice
1/4 cup carrot or mango puree
1/4 cup instant grain coffee
1/4 cup carob flour

1. Sift flours, add salt. Place in a mixing bowl. Cut oil into flour mixture until it looks like tiny breadcrumbs. Add vanilla. Divide mixture into four equal portions and place in separate mixing bowls.

2. Add one colour to each bowl, mixing with a wooden spoon until a ball of dough begins to form (add fruit juice if the mixture is too dry).

3. Roll out each piece of dough between two sheets of greaseproof paper into a rectangle. Chill 2 hours.

4. Cut each piece of dough in half lengthwise, cutting through the paper. Peel off top sheets.

5. Brush the top of one strip with sweetener. Place another strip, paper side up, on top.

6. Peel off paper.

7. Repeat procedure with the remaining dough strip, alternating colours, to make eight layers.

8. Press lightly together. Cut stack lengthwise to make two narrow stacks. Wrap in paper and chill 30 minutes.

9. Preheat oven to 190°C (375°F). Cut dough into 2.5 cm (1 in) slices. Bake 10-15 minutes or until lightly browned on bottom.

EVERYONE'S FAVOURITE BISCUIT

EF
1 cup blanched ground almonds
1 cup rolled oats
1 cup whole wheat cake or pastry flour
1/2 teaspoon cinnamon
Pinch of sea salt
1/2 cup maple syrup
1/3-1/2 cup oil
Fruit juice as needed

1. Preheat oven to 190°C (375°F).
2. Mix together all dry ingredients.
3. Beat together maple syrup and oil and add all at once to dry mixture. Add fruit juice if necessary to form a dough.
4. Roll out and cut with biscuit cutters. Place on oiled sheet and bake 15-20 minutes. Brush on maple syrup. Cool on wire rack.

DIAMONDS

EF
1/4 cup sweetener (p. 12)
1/4 cup plus 2 tablespoons oil
Juice and rind of 1/2 lemon
Juice and rind of 1/2 orange
1 cup slivered blanched almonds
1 tablespoon cinnamon
1 teaspoon ground cardamon
Pinch of sea salt
1 1/2 cups whole wheat cake or pastry flour
1/4 cup arrowroot flour
Fruit juice to form dough
Sweetener for glazing (p. 12)

1. Beat together sweetener and oil until creamy. Add next three ingredients.
2. Sift dry ingredients. Combine with first mixture and add enough fruit juice to form a dough.
3. Shape into rectangle and roll out to 12 mm (1/2 in) thickness on oiled greaseproof paper. Place paper and dough onto baking sheet. Cut halfway into dough, forming diamonds.
4. Bake in preheated 160°C (325°F) oven 20-25 minutes or until lightly browned and almost firm. Remove from pan, peel off paper and place on cooling rack. Glaze with sweetener immediately.

CHRISTMAS CANES

2 cups whole wheat cake or pastry flour
1 cup ground nuts
Pinch of sea salt
3 teaspoons dried mint
2 tablespoons carob flour
1/2 cup sweetener (p. 12)
2 teaspoons vanilla
1/3 cup oil
2 eggs
1/4-1/2 cup beetroot juice
Fruit juice to form dough
Sweetener for glazing (p. 12)

1. Prepare two mixing bowls, divide the first four ingredients in half and sift into separate bowls. Add carob to one.

2. Divide the next three ingredients in half, beat and add to each bowl of sifted flour.

3. Whisk each egg separately. Add beetroot juice to one egg, mixing well. Add each beaten egg to each mixture, and form two soft doughs, using fruit juice if necessary.

4. Roll each dough into a log and divide into six pieces. Cover. Roll out two pieces, one of each colour into a log 15 cm (6 in) long. Place strips side by side, pressing the ends together, and twist. Place on unoiled sheet about 2.5 cm (1 in) apart, and bend the tops of the twists into a cane shape.

5. Bake in preheated 180°C (350°F) oven 15-20 minutes or until almost firm and browned on the bottom. Glaze with sweetener immediately after removing from oven.

6. If you want to hang them on the tree, insert wooden or metal skewer into the end of the curved part of the cane before baking to form a hole for the string.

JOE FROGGERS

Joe Froggers is the name of a cookie that the fishermen of Marblehead, U.S.A., took with them on their long trips. These big, fat cookies are named after the big, fat frogs that sit on top of lily pads in New England ponds.

EF

3 cups whole wheat cake or pastry flour
1 tablespoon cinnamon
1 teaspoon ground ginger
1 teaspoon cloves
1/4 teaspoon ground coriander
Pinch of sea salt
1/4 cup instant grain coffee or carob flour
1/2 cup ground nuts or seeds
1/2 cup oil
1/2 cup sweetener (p. 12)
2 teaspoons vanilla or orange blossom water
1/2-1 cup fruit juice

1. Combine first eight ingredients together. Set aside.

2. Whisk together all liquid ingredients. Sift dry ingredients, add beaten liquid mixture and stir until a soft dough is formed. (Adjust liquid content accordingly.) Wrap in paper and chill at least 1 hour.

3. Roll out on greaseproof paper to 12 mm (1/2 in) thickness. Cut out with 10 cm (4 in) cutters into different shapes.

4. Place on oiled sheet, and bake in 190°C (375°F) pre-heated oven 12-15 minutes or until lightly browned and almost firm. Glaze with sweetener (p. 12) immediately after removing from oven. Cool on rack.

SESAME SEED BISCUITS

EF
1 cup unhulled sesame seeds
1 1/2 cups whole wheat cake or pastry flour
1 teaspoon cinnamon
Pinch of sea salt
1 cup cracked rolled oats
1/2 cup cold oil
1/2-1 cup fruit juice
2 tablespoons tahini or almond butter
1 teaspoon vanilla or 1/2 teaspoon rose water

*Suribachi – A suribachi is a bowl with ridges on the inside. It is used with a pestle to crush seeds, nuts and to cream salad dressings. It is much like a mortar and pestle, but more versatile. (Can be purchased in most Japanese and some health food stores.)

1. Lightly roast sesame seeds in a dry skillet until they just begin to pop. Crush immediately. (Use blender or *suribachi**.)

2. Combine next three ingredients and sift. Add rolled oats and sesame seeds. Set aside.

3. Beat next four ingredients together until creamy. Add wet mixture to dry mixture and stir until ball of dough forms. (Adjust liquid-flour content.)

4. Roll dough into log, wrap in paper, and chill for 30 minutes or until firm.

5. Preheat oven to 200°C (400°F) and oil baking sheets. Slice off into 12 mm (1/2 in) pieces, or roll out to 6 mm (1/4 in) thickness and cut into different shapes with cutter. (Keep dough refrigerated until using.)

6. Bake 20-25 minutes or until slightly browned on bottom and almost firm. Remove from pan, brush with sweetener if desired.

VARIATION

Substitute any crushed nut or seed for sesame seeds. Add 1 teaspoon dry ginger to dry ingredients.

Peanut *(Arachis hypogaea)*

The peanut is an annual herb of the pea family, its fruit being a pod and not a nut. Peanuts are native to South America; the Indians were growing peanuts there at least 1000 years ago. Today, they are grown in semi-arid regions as well as in other parts of the world and have the ability to endure long drought and grow when the rain comes.

The peanut contains kilo for kilo more protein than sirloin steak, more carbohydrates than potatoes, and one-third as much fat as butter.

Peanut hulls have the food value of coarse hay, and the thin skin that covers the nut is sometimes used in place of wheat bran in cattle fodder. Also the roots of the plant, if left in the soil, enrich it with valuable nitrogen products.

APRICOT-PEANUT COOKIES

EF

1/4-1/2 cup apricot juice or cider
2 tablespoons peanut butter
1/2 cup sweetener (p. 12)
1 teaspoon lemon rind
1 teaspoon orange rind
1 tablespoon mint
3/4 teaspoon ground ginger
1 teaspoon cinnamon
1 cup crushed roasted peanuts
2 1/4 cups whole wheat cake or pastry flour
1/2 cup millet or oat flour
Pinch of sea salt
Sweetener for glazing (p. 12)

1. Blend juice, peanut butter, and sweetener together. Heat in saucepan, add rinds, mint and spices. Cool.

2. Combine peanuts with flours and salt, and gradually stir in wet mixture until a ball of dough forms. (Adjust liquid content.) Wrap and chill.

3. Preheat oven 180°C (350°F) and oil baking sheets. Roll out dough to 12 mm (1/2 in) thickness, cut into shapes and bake 20-25 minutes or until lightly browned. Remove and brush with sweetener immediately.

TWISTS

1 1/2 cups whole wheat cake or pastry flour
1 egg
1/4 cup oil
1/4 cup maple syrup to taste
1 1/2 tablespoons rum, brandy or vanilla
Fruit juice as needed
Oil for frying
Poppy or sesame seeds for decoration

1. Place flour on a wooden board and make a well in the centre. Break egg into the well and beat lightly with a fork. Add oil, maple syrup, rum, brandy or vanilla and fruit juice. Mix well with egg. Using your hands for best results, gradually add the flour, starting from the inside of the well and work into a ball. Cover and chill 30-40 minutes.

2. Roll out dough 6 mm (1/4 in) thick. Using a pastry wheel or sharp knife, cut dough into strips 2.5 cm (1 in) and 15 cm (6 in) long. Twist the dough into different shapes. Heat oil. Drop the twists into the hot oil a few at a time, turning over when necessary. Remove and drain. Sprinkle with poppy seeds, sesame or drizzle with maple syrup.

CHRISTMAS SANDWICHES

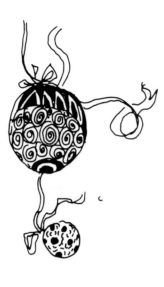

1 cup ground macadamia nuts
2 cups whole wheat cake or pastry flour
1 teaspoon cinnamon
1/2 teaspoon ground coriander
1/2 teaspoon sea salt
1/2 cup sweetener (p. 12)
3 eggs
3/4 cup oil
1 teaspoon rum or brandy
CASHEW-POPPY FILLING
EF GF
1/3 cup poppy seeds
2/3 cup raisins or sultanas
Pinch of sea salt
2 tablespoons grain coffee
1 cup orange juice
1/2 cup cashew butter
1 teaspoon lemon rind
1 teaspoon cinnamon

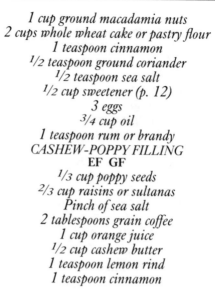

1. Sift first five ingredients together. Set aside.

2. Beat sweetener and eggs together until creamy. Slowly drip in oil and continue beating until fully absorbed. Add rum or brandy.

3. Place dry ingredients on board. Make a well in the centre, and put egg mixture in. Begin to mix dry ingredients toward centre incorporating both together until dough forms. (Adjust liquid content accordingly.) Cover and chill 30 minutes.

CASHEW-POPPY FILLING

1. Cook poppy seeds, dried fruit, sea salt, grain coffee and orange juice together until most of the liquid has evaporated.

2. Add remaining ingredients and blend until creamy. (You may have to add more liquid to get a creamy consistency.) Set aside.

3. Preheat oven to 180°C (350°F) and oil baking sheets. Roll out dough to 6 mm (1/4 in) thickness and cut out with biscuit cutters. Bake 15-20 minutes or until bottom is lightly browned. Cool on rack. Spread filling in between, sandwich together, and glaze.

VARIATIONS

1. Press centre of biscuit with thumb and insert drop of fruit puree or halved almond before baking.

2. Use Carob Icing (p. 78) for filling.

ODDS AND ENDS

Use any leftover dough (pies, biscuits, strudel, pastries). Roll out on greaseproof paper and cut with cutters into different shapes.

Preheat oven to 180°C (350°F), place on oiled sheet and bake 10 minutes. Brush with shoyu and bake another 5-10 minutes.

SHAPED BISCUITS

German and Danish biscuits are so appealing because they are pressed with wooden moulds or rollers which have quaint designs and shapes carved into them.

No matter what kind of technique you use for moulding – biscuit presses, wooden moulds, carved rollers or just your hands – you won't be able to keep up with the demand.

ALMOND BALLS

EF GF
1 cup roasted sweet brown rice flour or brown rice flour
1/2 cup arrowroot flour
4 tablespoons oil
Pinch of sea salt
1 teaspoon vanilla
1/4 cup sweetener (p. 12)
2 tablespoons almond butter
1/4-1/2 cup fruit juice

1. Sift flours together. Combine oil, sea salt, vanilla, sweetener, almond butter and ¼ cup juice together. Stir until creamy. Stir into dry mixture and add more liquid if necessary until mixture begins to stick together.

2. Prepare steamer (p. 18). Shape mixture into little balls. Cover and steam 10 minutes. Cool on wire rack before serving. Roll in crushed, roasted nuts or carob flour, for added effect.

ALTERNATIVE METHOD

Roll mixture into log. Cut into even pieces, press out and place on oiled sheet. Bake at 190°C (375°F) 10-12 minutes or until lightly browned.

FINGERS

1 quantity Rolled Biscuits dough (p. 169)
Crushed nuts

1. Follow directions for Rolled Biscuits. Shape dough into fingers, wrap individually in paper and chill overnight. Preheat oven to 190°C (375°F).

2. Roll fingers in crushed nuts and place on unoiled sheet. Bake 10-12 minutes or until lightly browned. (Brush fingers with egg white if nuts do not adhere to dough.)

VARIATION

Shape dough into long, thin rolls, and twist into pretzel shape. Brush with egg yolk and bake 15-20 minutes.

SPIRALS

1/4 cup oil
1/4 cup sweetener (p. 12)
2 egg whites
Pinch of sea salt
1 teaspoon vanilla
1 1/4 cups sifted whole wheat cake or pastry flour

1. Combine oil and sweetener, beating well until creamy. Beat whites and sea salt together until stiff peaks form. Add vanilla and combine with oil and sweetener mixture.

2. Sift flour, and fold into egg mixture. Stir until a very thick, moist dough is formed.

3. Fill pastry bag and press out into spiral shapes on oiled sheet. Leave 5 cm (2 in) between shapes for expansion.

4. Bake 8-12 minutes in preheated 200°C (400°F) oven. Cool on a wire rack.

VARIATIONS

1. Add 2 tablespoons carob flour to oil-sweetener combination before folding in flour.

2. Add 1 tablespoon cinnamon and 3/4 teaspoon dry ginger to flour before sifting.

SESAME ALMOND FLAKES

4 tablespoons sesame or hazelnut butter
1/4 cup sweetener (p. 12)
1/4 cup oil
1 egg
1 3/4 cups sifted whole wheat cake or pastry flour
1 tablespoon lemon rind
Pinch of sea salt
Fruit juice to form dough
Blanched almond halves

1. Combine sesame butter, sweetener and oil. Beat until thick and creamy. Keep beating and drop in egg. Continue beating until smooth.

2. Combine flour, rind and salt, and fold into first mixture. Add juice if necessary to form soft dough.

3. Preheat oven to 190°C (375°F). Shape dough into little balls, place on unoiled sheet and press half an almond in centre. Bake 10-15 minutes or until almost firm.

LEMON DROPS

EF

1/4 cup sweetener (p. 12)
1 tablespoon oil
2 tablespoons lemon juice
2 cups whole wheat cake or pastry flour
1 tablespoon lemon rind
1/4 cup crushed peanuts
Pinch of sea salt
1 teaspoon ground cardamon
Fruit juice to form dough
Oil for deep-frying

1. Combine first three ingredients together. Whisk until well combined.

2. Place flour, rind, crushed nuts, salt and cardamon in mixing bowl, and combine with first mixture. Stir well. Add enough juice to form a soft dough. Roll out into a log, cut into equal sections and roll into balls.

3. Heat oil and deep-fry until lightly browned. Drain well and roll in cinnamon, carob flour, roasted chestnut or crushed nuts while still warm.

ALTERNATIVE METHOD

Roll dough into a log, wrap in wax paper and chill at least 60 minutes. Remove from refrigerator, cut into 6 mm (1/4 in) pieces and bake at 180°C (350°F) 10-12 minutes.

Honey

Variations in honey today are due in part to adulterants, usually glucose, a type of sugar syrup sweeter than sugar itself. As honey has almost twice the sweetness of sugar, this greatly affects and alters flavour. Add a pinch, 1/12 to 1/5 teaspoon, of baking soda to neutralize the acidity of honey.

DROP COOKIES AND BISCUITS

Most of these are made by the teaspoon or tablespoon method. Some batters fall easily from the spoon, expanding and flattening while baking. When chilled before baking, some of these batters can actually be formed into balls or logs and baked as is, or flattened with a lightly oiled glass or biscuit cutter.

Stiffer doughs can be shaped and formed through a pastry bag fitted with a large plain star or ribbon-type tube (p. 71). Make sure that the tube is large enough to allow chopped fruits and nuts or seeds to pass through easily.

PASTRY BAG METHOD
Fill pastry bag half full of batter. Seal in the batter by twisting the top of the bag (p. 72).

Line the baking sheets with greaseproof paper. Oil paper.

Hold the bag vertically with the tip of the tube 12 mm (½ in) away from the baking sheet, and press out rounds, kisses or strips of batter directly onto paper. Cut off dough with wet knife or quick upward movement.

LEMON CURRANT COOKIES

EF

1 cup toasted, cracked rolled oats or barley
½ cup whole wheat cake or pastry flour
½ cup brown rice flour
¼ cup ground sunflower seeds
1 tablespoon lemon rind
2 teaspoons cinnamon
Pinch of sea salt
½ cup chopped currants
¼-½ cup fruit juice
½ cup sweetener (p. 12)
½ cup oil
1 teaspoon vanilla

1. Combine first eight ingredients.

2. Heat juice and sweetener together. Remove from heat and beat in oil. Combine with dry ingredients and stir until mixture resembles a thick batter that drops with difficulty from a wooden spoon. Add vanilla. (Adjust liquid content accordingly.)

3. Drop onto oiled baking sheet. Do not press down. Bake in 190°C (375°F) oven 20-25 minutes or until firm and lightly browned on bottom. Cool on wire rack.

WALNUT KISSES

3 tablespoons almond butter
1/4 cup sweetener (p. 12)
2 egg whites
Pinch of sea salt
1 teaspoon vanilla
1/2 cup arrowroot flour
3/4-1 cup whole wheat cake or pastry flour
1 1/4 cups ground walnuts
Blanched almond halves

1. Beat together almond butter and sweetener until creamy and light. Beat egg whites and sea salt until stiff peaks form. Fold in nut-butter combination very gently. Add vanilla.

2. Sift flours and add ground walnuts; then add to first mixture. Stir gently, until a smooth, moist dough is formed.

3. Using a pastry bag and medium sized tube (pp. 71-2), fill the bag with moist dough and press out into 5 cm (2 in) kisses on oiled sheet, leaving about 5 cm (2 in) between each one. Press almond halves into the centre of each.

4. Bake in preheated 200°C (400°F) oven 10-12 minutes or until edges begin to lightly brown. Cool on rack.

COCONUT MACAROONS

GF
4 egg whites
Pinch of sea salt
1 teaspoon lemon juice
1/4 cup sweetener (p. 12)
1 teaspoon lemon rind
1/2 teaspoon cinnamon
1 cup roasted ground almonds
1/2 cup desiccated coconut
1 teaspoon vanilla
1/4-1/2 cup arrowroot flour

1. Beat whites with sea salt until stiff peaks form. Combine lemon juice and sweetener together. Drop into egg whites slowly and keep beating. Fold in rind, cinnamon, almonds, coconut, vanilla and arrowroot. Drop onto oiled paper, or pipe through pastry bag.

2. Preheat oven to 190°C (375°F). Bake 10-15 minutes or until lightly browned and almost firm. Cool on a wire rack.

ALMOND CRUMBLES

EF GF

1 cup sweetener (p. 12)
2/3 cup oil
1 cup roasted ground almonds
3 cups brown rice flour
Pinch of sea salt
2 teaspoons cinnamon
1 teaspoon ground ginger
Hot fruit juice or soy milk

1. Whisk together first two ingredients until creamy and fluffy. Add roasted ground almonds and beat again.

2. Sift flour and combine with next three ingredients. Fold into first mixture. Add hot juice or milk to make drop consistency.

3. Preheat oven to 180°C (350°F). Drop onto oiled baking sheet. Bake 25 minutes or until edges are lightly browned. Cool on a wire rack.

ANISE NUT CRUMBLES

EF

3/4 cup sweetener (p. 12)
2/3 cup oil
1/2 cup roasted ground sunflower seeds
3 cups whole wheat cake or pastry flour
Pinch of sea salt
2 teaspoons ground anise

1. Beat together first two ingredients until creamy and light. Add roasted seeds and beat again.

2. Sift flour and next two ingredients, and fold into first mixture. Drop onto oiled baking sheet and bake 25 minutes at 180°C (350°F). Cool on a wire rack.

TROPICAL CAROB COOKIES

EF
2 cups mango or pineapple juice
1 cup currants
1/4 cup carob flour
1 cinnamon stick
Pinch of sea salt
1/2 teaspoon orange rind
1/4 cup oil
1 tablespoon grain coffee (optional)
1 tablespoon maple syrup
3 cups rolled oats
1 cup whole wheat cake or pastry flour
2/3 cup toasted, ground, sunflower seeds
Carob Icing (p. 78)

1. Bring to the boil juice, currants, carob flour, cinnamon stick and salt and simmer covered for 15 minutes. Remove cinnamon stick and transfer mixture to a bowl. Add orange rind, oil, coffee and maple syrup and whisk till well mixed.

2. In another bowl mix oats, flour and sunflower seeds. Make a well in mixture and add the wet ingredients; mix thoroughly to form a thick batter.

3. Oil baking trays and place tablespoons of batter onto trays. Bake at 180°C (350°F) for half an hour. Spread icing over cookies.

JUMBLES

EF

1/4 cup dried pitted dates or apricots
Fruit juice to cover fruit
1/4 cup oil
1/4 cup sweetener (p. 12)
1 cup whole wheat cake or pastry flour
1 cup barley or oat flour
1 teaspoon anise
1 teaspoon cinnamon
1/2 teaspoon ground ginger
1 tablespoon lemon rind
Pinch of sea salt
3 tablespoons instant grain coffee
1 teaspoon vanilla

1. Soak fruit in juice until soft. Drain and squeeze out moisture. Reserve juice and dice fruit.

2. Combine oil and sweetener. Sift flours, add other dry ingredients and dried fruit. Combine wet mixture with dry mixture, add vanilla and enough reserved juice to form a thick batter.

3. Preheat oven to 160°C (325°F). Drop batter onto baking sheet and bake 15-20 minutes or until edges are browned. Cool on a wire rack.

ORANGE COOKIES

EF

1 1/2 cups chopped apples or pears
3 cups sweet brown rice or brown rice flour
Pinch of sea salt
2 tablespoons orange rind
1 1/4 cups rolled oats
1 1/4 cups roasted ground hazelnuts or cashews
1 teaspoon cinnamon
1 teaspoon ground ginger
1/2 cup oil
3/4 cup sweetener (p. 12)
Juice of two oranges
1 teaspoon vanilla
Fruit juice as necessary

1. Combine first eight ingredients. Beat together oil, sweetener, orange juice and vanilla. Stir in dry mixture, adjust liquid if necessary until mixture drops with difficulty from the end of a wooden spoon.

2. Preheat oven to 180°C (350°F). Oil paper and drop batter by tablespoon onto paper. Bake 15-20 minutes or until lightly browned. Cool on a wire rack.

Opposite: Assorted biscuits and cookies; Twists (page 175), Pinwheels (page 165), Half and Half (page 166), Crisscross (page 166), Black and White Biscuits (page 166) and Alphabet Biscuits (page 167)

PEANUT BUTTER COOKIES

EF
1 cup brown rice flour
1 cup rolled oats
Pinch of sea salt
2 teaspoons cinnamon
1 teaspoon ground ginger
1 cup chopped dried bananas
1 cup roasted chopped peanuts
2 teaspoons lemon rind
1 cup orange or apple juice
4 tablespoons peanut butter
¼ cup oil
¼ cup sweetener (p. 12)

1. Combine first eight ingredients together.

2. Heat next four ingredients, and stir until creamy. Cool and stir into dry mixture.

3. Preheat oven, drop cookies onto oiled sheet and bake at 180°C (350°F) for 15-20 minutes or until browned. Cool on wire rack.

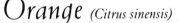

Orange *(Citrus sinensis)*

Oranges are given their distinctive colour by cold weather. They have an outer skin that is green until ripened. The fruit is not necessarily naturally ripened, even if it is orange.

When oranges are put into the store to be sold, they have to be orange, otherwise they will not sell. Gas is sometimes used to turn a green fruit orange, or an orange fruit brighter. Fruit from warmer areas is frequently gas ripened.

The Navel orange is widely available and is popular in many parts of the world.

Opposite: Vanilla Ice-Cream (with kiwi-fruit) (page 205), Mango-Strawberry Ice-Cream (page 206) and Peach Tofu Ice-Cream (page 205)

POPPY SPICE

EF

1/2 cup dried fruit
Fruit juice to cover
1 grated apple or pear
1 teaspoon cinnamon
3/4 teaspoon ground ginger
1 tablespoon lemon juice
1 tablespoon lemon rind
1/2 cup whole wheat cake or pastry flour
1/2 cup cornflour or oat flour
1/4 cup brown rice flour
Pinch of sea salt
1/2 cup poppy seeds
1/3 cup oil

1. Soak dried fruit in juice to cover. Add next five ingredients and stir well. Set aside.

2. Sift flours and salt together. Drain juice off fruits, and combine with dry mixture.

3. Roast poppy seeds in dry skillet until they begin to pop. Combine with dry mixture, add oil and enough reserved juice to form a thick batter. Drop onto oiled paper and bake in preheated 190°C (375°F) oven for 20 minutes or until lightly browned. Cool on a wire rack.

ALTERNATIVE METHOD

Combine dried fruit, poppy seeds and juice in a heavy saucepan; cook on a medium heat until moisture evaporates and mixture is almost dry. Add 1/2 cup more juice and blend until creamy. Combine with the rest of the ingredients and follow recipe.

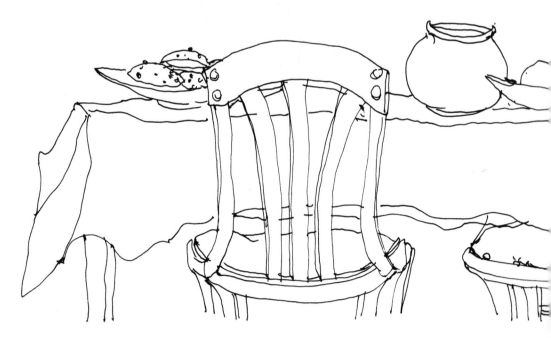

FANCY OAT-NUT COOKIES

1/2 cup ground walnuts or pine nuts
2 cups rolled oats
1 1/2 cups whole wheat pastry or cake flour
1/2 teaspoon baking soda (sodium bicarbonate)
3/4 cup oil
1 cup sweetener (p. 12)
2 eggs
1/2 teaspoon vanilla
1/2 teaspoon almond extract

1. Preheat oven to 180°C (350°F). Oil baking sheets or line with greaseproof paper and then oil.

2. Blend together walnuts and oats for 2 minutes. Add flour, baking soda and mix well. Set aside.

3. Combine oil and sweetener and process until well creamed.

4. Add eggs and flavourings and blend well in.

5. Add flour mixture and mix by hand till well combined.

6. Drop batter onto baking sheet making sure there is at least 2.5 cm (1 in) between each to allow for expansion.

7. Bake 10-12 minutes or until well browned. (They will still be somewhat soft, however when they cool they will firm up.)

8. Cool on wire racks.

SPICE DROPS

2 cups chopped figs
Fruit juice to cover
2-3/4 cups whole wheat cake or pastry flour
Pinch of sea salt
1 teaspoon ground ginger
1/2 teaspoon cloves
1 teaspoon cinnamon
1 cup crushed roasted walnuts
1/4 cup sweetener (p. 12)
2-3 eggs
1/2 cup oil

1. Soak figs in juice to cover until soft. Drain, chop figs and reserve liquid.
2. Sift next five ingredients together. Add nuts and figs to dry mixture. Set aside.
3. Combine sweetener and eggs together and beat until light and creamy. Slowly drip in oil and continue beating until oil is absorbed.
4. Fold one-third of egg mixture into dry ingredients, then combine rest of egg mixture with it. Add reserved liquid, if necessary, to form thick batter.
5. Preheat oven to 180°C (350°F) and oil baking sheets. Drop batter from spoon onto sheets. Bake 15-20 minutes or until lightly browned. Cool on a wire rack.

GINGER DROPS

1 1/2 cups whole wheat cake or pastry flour plus 1/4 cup maize meal
Pinch of salt
1 teaspoon cinnamon
2 teaspoons ground ginger
1/2 teaspoon ground coriander
1/4 cup oil
1/4 cup sweetener (p. 12)
1 egg

1. Sift all dry ingredients together. Beat together the last three ingredients until light and creamy. Fold first mixture into wet mixture, and mix only until flour is no longer visible. Drop onto oiled sheet.
2. Bake in preheated 190°C (375°F) oven for 10 minutes, then reduce temperature to 180°C (350°F) and bake 5-10 minutes longer. Cool on a wire rack.

SOMETHING SPECIAL

GF*
³/4-1 cup oil
³/4 cup sweetener (p. 12)
2 eggs
2 cups brown rice or whole wheat pastry or cake flour*
1 cup arrowroot flour
2 cups finely ground pumpkin seeds
2 teaspoons cinnamon or ground coriander
¹/2 cup blueberry, strawberry or raspberry sugarless jam

* Gluten free if using brown rice flour.

1. Combine oil and sweetener and beat till light and creamy.
2. Add eggs and mix well.
3. Sift together the flour and arrowroot, add the creamed mixture and blend well. Mix in pumpkin seeds and cinnamon.
4. Preheat oven to 180°C (350°F) and oil several baking sheets.
5. Drop mixture onto the sheets by tablespoon.
6. Bake 12-15 minutes or until lightly browned.
7. Remove from oven and cool on a wire rack.
8. When they are cool, spread half of the biscuits with the jam on the bottom side, and top with one of the remaining biscuits again with the bottom side.

BIG CURRANT COOKIES

1¹/4 cups oil
³/4-1 cup sweetener (p. 12)
2 eggs
1 teaspoon vanilla
2¹/2 cups whole wheat cake or pastry flour
¹/2 teaspoon bicarbonate of soda
1¹/2 cups currants

1. Preheat oven to 180°C (350°F) and oil a baking sheet.
2. Combine oil and sweetener together and beat till light and fluffy. Add eggs and vanilla and continue beating another 2-3 minutes.
3. Sift flour and bicarbonate of soda twice and add to first mixture.
4. Add currants and mix well.
5. Drop the batter onto the baking sheet with a large tablespoon and spread it out into a large 10 cm (4 in) circle. Repeat with remaining batter making sure there is at least 2.5 cm (1 in) between them.
6. Bake 10-12 minutes. Remove from the oven while cookies are still somewhat soft and cool on a wire rack.

VARIATIONS

1. Use any other minced dried fruit or a combination.
2. Add ¹/2-1 cup chopped nuts, seeds or coconut and fruit juice.

FRUIT AND NUT SLICES

All children love finger things: any sweet or savoury food that they can pick up and eat in their hands. Slices have the appeal of both biscuits and cakes. They are quick to make, easy to handle and fun to eat.

Slices, because they are usually unleavened, should be baked in rectangular or square baking pans only 4-5 cm (1½-2 in) deep; otherwise they will not bake in the centre. For parties, try baking them in shallow cupcake or muffin tins. Any way you serve them, children as well as adults will keep coming back for more. They are a big hit when kids discover them in their lunch boxes.

BASIC FRUIT SLICE

Use any pie, pastry or rolled biscuit dough recipe. Divide the dough and roll out on greaseproof paper 2.5 cm (1 in) larger than the size of the pan. (Keep other piece of dough covered until ready to use.)

Place dough in oiled pan on bottom only. *Do not stretch.* Bake in preheated 190°C (375°F) oven for 10 minutes.

Blueberry *(Vaccinium* spp.*)*

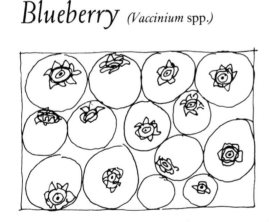

Blueberries grow wild in many parts of the world. However, the U.S. and Canada supply most of the blueberries used by the food indus-try. British gardeners can now buy and cultivate American plants. Australians and New Zealanders are now acquiring a taste for blueberries and are growing the fruit on a small but increasing scale.

The food industry uses two main kinds of blueberries, lowbush and highbush. Lowbush blueberry shrubs grow wild and measure about 15 to 45 cm (6-18 in) tall. Farmers generally gather the wild berries and sell them for processed foods.

The highbush berries make up most of the fresh blueberries sold in grocers'. Ripe blueberries range in colour from light blue to black and have a waxy, powdery-grey coating. They have green leaves and white or pink flowers, and the fruits are generally available in the summertime.

Spread fruit puree over base. Roll out remaining piece of dough the same way. Cover fruit puree with dough, slit dough with knife to allow steam to escape.

Brush with beaten egg yolk and bake at 190°C (375°F) for 20-25 minutes.

Remove from oven, place on rack; cut slices and cool before removing from pan.

CAROB BLUEBERRY BROWNIES

1/2 cup sweetener (p. 12)
1/3 cup oil
1/2 cup fruit juice as needed
2 teaspoons vanilla
2 eggs
1 tablespoon grain coffee (optional)
1/2 cup whole wheat cake or pastry flour
2 cups rolled oats or rolled barley
Pinch of sea salt
1/2 cup carob flour
2 tablespoons orange or lemon rind
1 cup currants or sultanas
3/4 cup chopped walnuts
BLUEBERRY SUPREME
EF GF
1 tablespoon kuzu or arrowroot flour
1 1/2-2 cups fruit juice
1 teaspoon ground ginger
Pinch of sea salt
1 cup fresh blueberries
2 teaspoons orange flower water or vanilla

1. Preheat oven to 190°C (375°F). Oil baking sheet.
2. Beat liquid ingredients together.
3. Combine all the dry ingredients and add to the liquid ingredients folding until well combined. Adjust liquid to form thick batter.
4. Spoon onto oiled sheet. Bake 20 minutes or until centre is firm to the touch and cake tester comes out clean when inserted into centre.
5. Cover with Blueberry Supreme just before serving.
BLUEBERRY SUPREME
1. Dissolve kuzu in fruit juice.
2. Add ginger, salt and bring to the boil stirring continuously.
3. When it thickens and boils remove from the heat, add blueberries and flavouring.

CHESTNUT SLICE

I created this recipe for one of my first cooking classes. Diana, one of the people in the class, was especially fond of it, perhaps because the bulgur wheat reminded her of her mother's home cooking.

Today, roasted bulgur and nuts cooked in olive oil make a favourite eggplant stuffing among Middle Eastern people.

EF
1 cup raisins, sultanas or apricots
3-4 cups fruit juice
1 cup uncooked bulgur
¹/4 cup oil
Pinch of sea salt
1 tablespoon orange or tangerine rind
2 cups Chestnut Puree (p. 84)
2 cups brown rice flour

1. Soak dried fruit in juice to cover until soft. Drain and chop. Reserve liquid. Roast bulgur in oil for a few minutes over medium heat. Add fruit, sea salt and 2 cups boiling juice. (Use juice from soaking fruit.) Cover and cook 15 minutes on a low heat.

2. Preheat the oven 160°C (325°F). Oil a small pan and sprinkle it lightly with flour. Combine orange rind and Chestnut Puree. Add the flour to the bulgur, mix in Chestnut Puree and slowly add remaining juice until a thick pancake-like batter is formed. Mix well. Place in pan, cover, and bake 1 hour. Remove cover and bake 15-20 minutes longer or until firm. Cool before slicing.

VARIATION

Add 2 well-beaten eggs to the batter after mixing in Chestnut Puree. Decrease liquid content accordingly. *Do not pat down.* Do not cover while baking.

FIG COCONUT SLICE

EF
3 cups Crumb Topping (p. 96)
2-3 cups Fig Puree (p. 85)
2 cups desiccated coconut

1. Preheat oven to 180°C (350°F). Oil baking sheet.

2. Add just enough fruit juice to moisten crumb mixture so that it can be pressed onto baking sheet.

3. Prebake 7 minutes. Cover with a layer of Fig Puree. Bake 10-15 minutes or until fruit is almost dry. Sprinkle on coconut and bake another 5 minutes. Cool on a wire rack.

PECAN-GINGER SLICE

EF
1/4 cup semolina
4 tablespoons oil
1 cup dried fruit
2 teaspoons cinnamon
1 tablespoon ground ginger
Pinch of sea salt
1/2 teaspoon cloves
3-4 cups boiling fruit juice
2 cups grated carrots or pumpkin
1/2 cup whole wheat cake or pastry flour
1 cup maize flour
1/2 cup oil or 1/4 cup tahini
1 1/2 cups roasted chopped pecans
APPLE SAUCE TOPPING
EF GF
8-9 medium-sized sliced apples
1 teaspoon cinnamon
1/2 teaspoon cloves
1/2 teaspoon ground ginger
Pinch of sea salt
2 teaspoons lemon juice
1/2 cup currants

1. Sauté semolina in 2 tablespoons oil. Add fruit, cinnamon, ginger, sea salt, cloves and 3 cups boiling juice; cover and cook for 10 minutes. Sauté grated carrots or pumpkin in 2 tablespoons oil. Combine with cooked semolina. Fold flours and oil into the mixture.

2. Preheat the oven to 180°C (350°F); oil and lightly flour a shallow rectangular baking pan.

3. Add the nuts and more fruit juice as necessary until the batter is thick enough to drop with difficulty from a wooden spoon.

4. Pour batter into pan. Cover and bake about 45 minutes; uncover and bake 15 minutes longer or until slice pulls away from the sides of pan. Remove from the oven and cool on a wire rack.

TOPPING

1. Combine apples, spices, sea salt and lemon juice in a pot. Cover and cook until apples are soft. Blend. Add currants and cool.

2. If desired, add arrowroot diluted in 2 tablespoons fruit juice to sauce after blending and return to heat. Cook, constantly stirring, until mixture comes to the boil. (Use 1/2 tablespoon arrowroot per cup of apple sauce.) Spoon over each slice before serving.

COUSCOUS VARIATION

Substitute 1 cup couscous for semolina. Sauté couscous in 1/4 cup oil. Combine dried fruit, cinnamon, sea salt, cloves, and 2 cups warm juice with couscous. Set aside for 30 minutes. Combine this mixture with 2 cups more juice and bring to the boil. Add the rest of ingredients and proceed as in recipe.

Pecan Slice

EF

3 cups raisins or sultanas
2-3 cups cider to cook fruit
3 cups whole wheat cake or pastry flour
4 cups chopped apples
2 tablespoons miso
1/2 cup oil or 1/4 cup sesame butter or almond butter
3 tablespoons orange juice
2 teaspoons orange rind
2 teaspoons brandy or rum
1 teaspoon cloves
1 1/2 cups lightly roasted chopped pecans

1. Combine the raisins or sultanas in a saucepan with enough cider to cover. Bring to a boil, cover, and simmer about 10 minutes.

2. Roast the flour in a dry skillet until it begins to brown lightly. Set aside to cool. Toss apples together with flour.

3. Preheat the oven to 160°C (325°F); oil and lightly flour the baking pan.

4. Dissolve the miso in a small amount of the warm cider from the boiled fruit. Combine with next six ingredients. (You may boil fruit with a vanilla bean.) Add this mixture to the flour-apple combination, folding in until a thick batter has formed.

5. Spoon into pan, cover and bake 40 minutes. Remove cover and bake about 20 minutes longer or until slice pulls away from the sides of the pan. Remove from the oven and place on a wire rack to cool.

PUMPKIN CRUMB SLICE

2-3 eggs, separated
¹/2 cup sweetener (p. 12)
¹/3 cup tahini
1 teaspoon vanilla
2¹/2 cups breadcrumbs or ground oats
1 cup ground roasted sesame or sunflower seeds
1 teaspoon cinnamon
1 teaspoon ground ginger
1 cup chopped dried fruit
2 cups grated pumpkin
Pinch of sea salt
TOPPING (OPTIONAL)
2 tablespoons oil
2-3 sliced apples
Cinnamon to taste
Sweetener to taste (p. 12)

1. Preheat oven to 190°C (375°F). Oil baking dish.

2. Combine egg yolks, sweetener and tahini and beat until creamy and smooth. Add vanilla. Combine the remaining dry ingredients (except sea salt) and pumpkin. Beat egg whites and sea salt until peaked. Combine first and second mixtures, fold in egg whites and spoon into baking dish. Bake 30 minutes.

TOPPING

Heat skillet, add oil and sauté sliced apples. Add cinnamon and sweetener. Spoon over slice and grill several minutes after baking, or add to slice for the last 5 minutes of baking time.

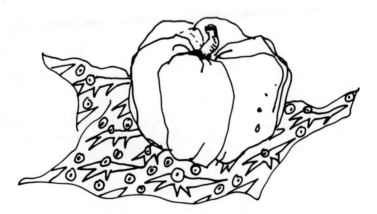

CARROT SLICE

3 tablespoons oil
6 tablespoons maple syrup
1 egg
1/2 cup Tofu Sour Cream (p. 95) or yoghurt
1 cup rolled oats
1/2 cup whole wheat cake or pastry flour
1 teaspoon cinnamon
1/2 cup grated carrots
1/4 cup grated apples
1/4 cup currants
3 tablespoons desiccated coconut

1. Cream together oil and maple syrup until thick. Add egg and yoghurt or Tofu Sour Cream and mix until well incorporated. Stir in oats and flour, cinnamon, carrots, apples, currants and coconut.

2. Oil a 23 × 18 cm (9 × 5 in) pan and spoon mixture in.

3. Pre-heat the oven to 180°C (350°F) and bake 30-40 minutes or until golden brown. Cool. Spread with icing if desired.

LAYERED ALMOND SLICE

BASE
EF

2 cups whole wheat cake or pastry flour
Pinch of sea salt
1/3 cup oil
Fruit juice to form dough
FIRST TOPPING
GF
2 eggs
2 tablespoons sweetener (p. 12)
Pinch of sea salt
1 1/2 teaspoons vanilla or orange blossom water
2 cups chopped almonds
SECOND TOPPING
EF GF
1 1/2 cups fruit juice
2 tablespoons sweetener (p. 12)
2 tablespoons carob flour
3 tablespoons agar-agar flakes
4 tablespoons almond butter
Ground almonds

BASE

1. Place flour and salt in a mixing bowl. Add oil, cutting it in until it looks like breadcrumbs. Preheat oven to 190°C (375°F) and oil rectangular baking pan.

2. Add enough liquid to form a dough. Roll out on oiled grease-proof paper and place in baking pan.* Prick base with fork and bake 10 minutes.

> *The baking pan should be deep enough to accommodate the other layers.

FIRST TOPPING

1. Beat eggs, sweetener, salt and flavouring. Add chopped nuts.

2. Remove crust from oven, spread egg mixture over it and bake 10 minutes or until set. Cool.

SECOND TOPPING

1. Blend juice, sweetener, carob together. Add agar-agar and bring to the boil. Lower heat and simmer 5 minutes. Blend in almond butter.

2. Pour mixture on first layer and sprinkle with ground almonds. Cool and set. Cut into bars when cold.

GINGER BY THE SEA

1 cup dried pears or peaches
2 cups cornflour
2 cups whole wheat cake or pastry flour
1/2 teaspoon sea salt
1 teaspoon ground ginger
1/2 cup oil
1 egg yolk
3/4 cup maple syrup
1/4-1/2 cup fruit juice
APPLE TOPPING
GF
2 cups apple sauce
1 egg white
Pinch of sea salt

1. Soak the fruit in liquid to cover until soft. Preheat the oven to 180°C (350°F).

2. Combine fruit and next four ingredients. In a separate bowl, beat together oil, yolk, and maple syrup until thick and creamy. Fold first mixture into oil and syrup combination.

2. Combine fruit and next four ingredients. In a separate bowl, beat together oil, yolk, and maple syrup until thick and creamy. Fold first mixture into oil and syrup combination. Add juice if necessary.

4. Prepare apple sauce. Beat egg white and sea salt until peaked. Fold egg white into sauce.

5. During the last 5 minutes of baking, place topping on slice and bake at 200°C (400°F). Cool on a wire rack.

BANANA-PEACH SLICE

EF

2 cups dried bananas
Fruit juice to cover fruit
1 cup couscous
1 cup roasted brown rice flour
2 cups whole wheat cake or pastry flour
1 teaspoon cinnamon
1/2 teaspoon cloves
2 teaspoons orange, tangerine or lemon rind
Pinch of sea salt
1/2 cup oil
3 cups diced peaches or apricots

1. Soak bananas in juice until soft. Reserve liquid.

2. Combine all dry ingredients. Add oil to dry mixture, rubbing with your hands until oil is fully absorbed.

3. Boil reserved juice. Add fruits to the dry mixture and slowly pour boiled juice over the mixture until the consistency is pancake-like – thick enough to drop from a wooden spoon. Add more boiled liquid if necessary.

4. Pour batter into pan, cover and bake in a preheated 180°C (350°F) oven for 1 hour. Remove cover and bake 15-20 minutes longer or until slice is set and lightly browned.

AZUKI-BEAN SLICE

EF GF*

1 cup dried soaked chestnuts
1 cup uncooked soaked azuki *beans* **
Fruit juice to cover
1 cup raisins or sultanas
Apricot or strawberry-apple juice as needed
Pinch of sea salt
1/2 cup roasted chopped walnuts
1/4 cup chestnut or whole wheat flour *
1 1/4 teaspoons vanilla

* Gluten free if using chestnut flour.
** *Azuki* beans are very small red beans which can be found in most natural food shops, Chinese, Korean or Japanese stores.

1. Soak chestnuts and *azuki* beans overnight in fruit juice to cover. Reserve liquid from beans and chestnuts.

2. Pressure-cook beans, chestnuts and 1/2 cup dried fruit together in 5 cups soaking liquid for 30 minutes. Add sea salt and simmer 20 minutes longer. Toss 1/2 cup dried fruit and nuts lightly in flour and set aside. Oil a rectangular pan. Preheat the oven 190°C (375°F). Drain off excess liquid from bean-chestnut combination.

3. Puree half of the cooked mixture in a food processor or blender. Combine all mixtures and add vanilla. (Adjust liquid-flour content to form a heavy batter.) Spoon into pan. Bake 45 minutes or until firm. Cool on a wire rack.

PINE NUT SLICE

3 eggs
1/2 cup sweetener (p. 12)
1/2 cup oil
3 cups sifted whole wheat cake or pastry flour
1 teaspoon cinnamon
1/2 teaspoon cloves
2 teaspoons orange rind
1 teaspoon lemon rind
2 cups chopped pine nuts
Pinch of sea salt
1 teaspoon vanilla
Juice and rind of 1 orange
Fruit juice to form thick batter

1. Combine eggs and sweetener together, and beat until creamy and light. Slowly drip in oil and continue beating until absorbed. Set aside.

2. Combine next seven ingredients. Mix vanilla, orange juice and rind together, add to egg mixture. Combine wet mixture with dry mixture.

3. Stir until batter is thick. (Adjust liquid content accordingly.)

4. Preheat oven to 190°C (375°F) and oil baking sheet. Spoon onto sheet, and bake 25-35 minutes or until slice pulls away. Test by inserting a skewer into the centre of the slice. If it comes out clean, slice is done.

Pine Nut *(Pinus pinea)*

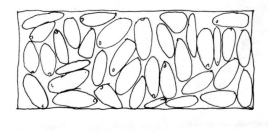

Native of the Mediterranean, pine nuts are the seeds of the stone pine. The tree, which is easily grown in a range of soils, is quite attractive and is growing in popularity. The sweet seeds are found in the cones which are unusually beautiful and are used in floral designs. The nuts can be eaten raw, roasted or steamed.

APPLE SAUCE SLICE

EF
2 cups apple sauce
¹/2 cup sweetener (p. 12)
·¹/2 cup oil
¹/2 cup dried fruit
¹/2 cup roasted chopped walnuts or sunflower seeds
3 cups sifted whole wheat cake or pastry flour
2 teaspoons cinnamon
³/4 teaspoon cloves
2 teaspoons ginger
¹/2 teaspoon sea salt

1. Whisk together apple sauce and sweetener. Slowly drip in the oil, beating continuously.

2. Preheat the oven to 180°C (350°F). Oil baking pan.

3. Toss dried fruit and nuts with a small amount of the flour.

4. Sift the remaining ingredients, add to the apple sauce mixture, and stir until batter is smooth and creamy. Fold in raisins and nuts. The consistency should be thick and pancake-like. Adjust flour-liquid content accordingly.

5. Pour into baking pan, cover and bake 30 minutes, remove cover and bake until slice pulls away from the sides of the pan and is springy to the touch. Cool on a wire rack.

O'GEORGE BARS

While baking for stores and restaurants in New York City, I created this recipe. I sold these bars on a push-cart which I wheeled around Central Park in the summertime. It was my most popular item.

EF

4 cups sweet brown or sweet white rice flour
1 cup rolled oats
1 1/2 cups sesame seeds
2 teaspoons cinnamon
1 tablespoon orange rind
Pinch of sea salt
2 cups raisins or sultanas
3 cups roasted crushed nuts
1/2 cup peanut butter
1/2-1 cup fruit juice
1 teaspoon vanilla
1/2 cup hot sweetener (p. 12)

1. Combine all dry ingredients. Blend peanut butter, 1/2 cup juice, vanilla and sweetener until smooth and creamy.

2. Combine dry mixture with liquid mixture, adding more juice if necessary to form a thick batter.

3. Preheat oven to 180°C (350°F) and oil baking pan. Spoon batter into pan, cover, and bake 45 minutes. Remove cover and bake until firm. Cool on wire rack and brush with sweetener to add a glaze on top.

VARIATIONS

1. Substitute any nut butter for peanut.

2. Use any dried fruit.

PEACH AND APRICOT WALNUT CRISP

EF

1/2 cup soy milk
1/2 tablespoon vanilla or rum
3 tablespoons tahini or other nut butter
1 tablespoon orange or lemon rind
2 teaspoons cinnamon
1 tablespoon grated fresh ginger
1 kg mixed sliced peaches and apricots
TOPPING
1 cup chopped walnuts
3/4 cup chopped rolled oats
1/4 cup whole wheat cake or pastry flour
Pinch of sea salt
1/2 cup sweetener (p. 12)
1/3 cup oil
Fruit juice as needed
EXTRAS FOR TOPPING
1/4 cup carob flour
1 tablespoon orange rind
1 teaspoon ground coriander
Pinch of allspice

1. Preheat the oven to 180°C (350°F).

2. Blend together the soy milk, vanilla, tahini, orange rind, cinnamon and grated ginger. Toss sliced fruit with the blended mixture. Oil a baking dish, spoon in fruit mixture and set aside.

3. Combine all the dry ingredients for the topping. Beat together the oil and sweetener and mix into the dry ingredients. Add a little fruit juice until the topping is a thick batter-like consistency.

4. Spoon over the sliced fruit pressing around the edges of the dish to seal. Bake 20-30 minutes or until the fruit is soft, and the top is brown and crisp. Serve warm or cool with Tofu Whip Cream (p. 94).

7. REFRESHINGLY LIGHT:
Cooling Desserts

FORGET ME KNOTS

1. Most cold desserts can best be frozen if they contain agar-agar.
2. When freezing desserts in refrigerator trays, they should be frozen to a fairly solid consistency, beaten until fluffy and then quickly returned to the freezer to freeze again. This is the best method for ice-cream.
3. To convert your favourite recipes, instead of cow's or goat's milk, use soy milk, coconut or any nut milk, as the base.
4. French ice-cream uses egg yolks to obtain its richness in addition to cream, sugar, salt and flavouring – 6 yolks to 4 cups cream.
5. Italian ice-cream uses both yolks and whites beaten separately, folding in whites at the end, before freezing.

Ice-Cream

When Nero was emperor of Rome, one of his favourite desserts was created by adding honey and fruit juice to snow. This was probably the first form of sherbet recorded in history. Eventually, a recipe was brought out of China whereby milk was substituted for snow, but since it had to be frozen, only a handful of people could enjoy it.

What is the ice-cream like today which we all eat too much of? In Australia, New Zealand and the United States, the average person consumes between 17 and 20 litres ($3\frac{3}{4}$ and $4\frac{2}{5}$ gallons) of ice-cream annually. The figures for the United Kingdom are lower. In the good old days, when ice-cream was made from whole eggs, milk and sugar with natural flavouring added, it was a rare treat which the family tediously cranked together and shared maybe once a week. Today, many ice-creams are synthetic from start to finish. Here is a little example of what you may expect to find in some of them:

1. *Ethyl acetate* – used to give a pineapple flavour. It is used as a cleaner for textiles and leather goods; highly toxic vapours have been known to cause chronic liver, lung and heart damage.
2. *Amyl acetate* – used for banana flavouring and paint solvent.
3. *Diethylen glucol* – a chemical used as an emulsifier in addition to or in place of eggs. It is the chemical that is used in anti-freeze and paint removers.
4. *Benzyl acetate* – used for strawberry flavouring and as a nitrate solvent.
5. *Butyraldehyde* – used for its nut flavouring abilities. It's also used to make rubber cement.

So, now you may be looking at the ice-cream you eat with different eyes. Be discriminating, and if you can't find any 'real' ice-cream, try making some of your own.

ICE-CREAMS AND ICE-BLOCKS

VANILLA ICE-CREAM

EF GF
4 tablespoons agar-agar flakes
1 cup fruit juice
1 cup blanched ground almonds
2 cups hot Soy or Nut Milk (pp. 232-3)
1/2 cup sweetener (p. 12)
Pinch of sea salt
1 teaspoon cinnamon
1 teaspoon dried mint
1 tablespoon vanilla
1/4 cup oil or 2 egg yolks

1. Bring agar-agar and fruit juice to a boil, cover and simmer 5 minutes.

2. Blend together juice and almonds until creamy. Add the rest of the ingredients except oil. Slowly drip in oil as you beat or blend until creamy.

3. Place in freezer until frozen, whip and freeze again, or use ice-cream machine.

You may also serve this without freezing. Quite refreshing!

ICE-CREAM FLAVOURS

1. Add 3-4 tablespoons carob flour to any ice-cream recipe and cook with agar-agar mixture.

2. Add 1 cup desiccated coconut while blending.

3. Substitute 1 cup fresh fruit in season for 1 cup soy milk.

4. Substitute 1/2 cup nut butter for 1 cup nuts.

PEACH TOFU ICE-CREAM

EF GF
2 cups peeled and chopped peaches
Juice of one lemon
1/2 cup maple syrup
1 cup Soy Milk or Coconut Milk (pp. 232-3)
345 g (11 oz) tofu
1/4 cup maple syrup
2 tablespoons vanilla
Pinch of sea salt

1. Marinate the peaches in the lemon juice in the refrigerator for one hour.

2. Combine with the rest of the ingredients and blend till creamy and smooth. Freeze in ice-cream maker or place in freezer until frozen. Whip and freeze again.

MANGO-STRAWBERRY ICE-CREAM

EF GF

4 tablespoons agar-agar flakes
1 cup mango juice
1/2 cup Date Puree (p. 85) or 1/4 cup maple syrup
1/2 cup hot Soy Milk or Almond or Coconut Milk (pp. 232-3)
2/3 cup roasted cashews
2 tablespoons carob flour
Pinch of sea salt
1 teaspoon ground ginger
1 tablespoon lemon rind
2 teaspoons vanilla
1 cup strawberries

1. Combine agar-agar and juice. Bring to the boil. Lower heat, cover and simmer 5 minutes. Set aside.

2. Combine Date Puree or maple syrup with the rest of the ingredients, blending until smooth and creamy. (Reserve some of the strawberries for topping.)

3. Whip in agar-agar mixture and blend again quickly. Freeze, then whip and freeze again, or use ice-cream machine.

AMBROSIA JUBILEE

BANANA ICE-CREAM
EF GF

2 tablespoons agar-agar flakes
1 1/2 cups orange juice
2 cups pureed banana
2 tablespoons crushed nut

1. Dissolve the agar-agar in the orange juice and bring to the boil. Simmer till the agar-agar dissolves.

2. Blend with the pureed bananas, adding the crushed nuts. Pour the mixture into the bowl of an ice-cream machine and freeze 20-25 minutes. Or freeze until firm, blend, and freeze again.

BANANA YOGHURT
EF GF

1 cup banana puree
3 tablespoons fresh lemon juice
1/2-3/4 cup maple syrup to taste
1 cup yoghurt

Puree all the ingredients till smooth.

STRAWBERRY ICE-CREAM
GF
1¹/2 cups strawberry puree
³/4 cup Soy Milk (p. 233)
³/4 cup maple syrup
2 egg yolks
1 tablespoon lemon juice

1. Combine all the ingredients together and blend till smooth.

2. Pour the mixture into the bowl of an ice-cream machine and freeze 20-30 minutes. Or freeze till almost firm, blend, then freeze again.

CAROB MAPLE ICE-CREAM
GF
2 cups Soy Milk (p. 233)
¹/2 cup maple syrup
4 egg yolks
¹/2 cup yoghurt
¹/2-1 cup carob flour (to taste)

1. Combine the Soy Milk and maple syrup in a saucepan and heat.

2. Place the egg yolks in a bowl and whisk briefly. Still whisking, slowly pour in about 1 cup of the liquid. Add the yoghurt and when the mixture is smooth, slowly pour it into the saucepan, whisking constantly. Cook until the mixture thickens slightly. Don't boil.

3. Combine with the carob flour (sift the flour if lumpy), mixing well till smooth.

4. Pour the mixture into the bowl of an ice-cream machine and freeze 20-25 minutes, or freeze until firm, blend and freeze again.

PUTTING IT ALL TOGETHER
Coconut
Nuts
Banana
Blackberries or blueberries
Raspberries
Grapes
Strawberries
Orange
Kiwifruit
Any fruit in season
Banana Yoghurt
Tofu Whip Cream (p. 94)
Few sprigs of fresh mint

1. Layer the coconut, nuts, fruit, Banana Yoghurt and Tofu Whip Cream to form a nice bed so that the ice-cream can sit on top.

2. Scoop out one scoop of each flavour and decorate with fruits and mint sprigs. Serve immediately.

FIG SUPREME

Try any 'ice-cream' with fresh or dried fruit or other toppings and Tofu Whip Cream.

EF GF
1 cup chopped fresh figs or 1/2 cup dried figs
1/3 cup maple syrup
1/4 cup chopped walnuts
2 cups any ice-cream (p. 205)
Tofu Whip Cream (p. 94)

1. Cook figs and maple syrup for 3-4 minutes or until almost dry and shiny. Add walnuts and chill.

2. Arrange alternate layers of ice-cream and fig sauce in parfait glasses. Top with Tofu Whip Cream.

BANANA YOGHURT ICE-BLOCKS

EF GF
2 cups plain yoghurt
2 cups sliced banana or other fruit
1 1/2 cups fruit juice or chopped fresh fruit
1 teaspoon vanilla

1. Blend ingredients together and pour into small paper cups or moulds. Freeze.

2. Place an iced lolly stick or plastic spoon in each cup when yoghurt mixture is half frozen. Continue freezing.

3. To serve, turn cup or mould upside-down and run hot water over it until the ice-block slides out.

WATERMELON ICE-BLOCKS

EF GF
1/2 cup blended watermelon
1 cup orange juice
1/4 cup of water

1. Blend, pour into moulds or paper cups. Place in freezer and when part frozen insert iced lolly stick or plastic spoon in each cup. Continue freezing.

2. To serve pour hot water over bottom of cup or mould.

CUSTARDS

CINNAMON RUM CUSTARD

GF
2 cups Nut or Soy Milk (pp. 232-3)
4 egg yolks
3 tablespoons kuzu or arrowroot flour
Pinch of sea salt
2 tablespoons oil
2 teaspoons rum
1 teaspoon cinnamon

Whip together Nut or Soy Milk, yolks, flour and salt until smooth. Cook in a double boiler stirring continuously until mixture thickens (5-8 minutes). Remove from heat, add oil, rum and cinnamon. Use as desired.

ORANGE CUSTARD

GF*
2 tablespoons whole wheat cake or pastry, corn or chestnut flour *
2 tablespoons oil
1/2 cup sweetener (p. 12)
Juice and grated rind of 1 orange
1 egg
2 teaspoons rum or brandy
Pinch of sea salt
Fruit juice, as needed

* Gluten free only if using corn or chestnut flour.

1. Roast flour in oil until lightly browned. Set aside to cool.

2. Combine flour and sweetener together. Add juice and rind, and cook in a heavy saucepan over a medium heat, stirring constantly until mixture boils.

3. Beat egg slightly. Add rum or brandy and sea salt. Combine this with the flour mixture, and cook 5 minutes in a double boiler until thickened.

STRAWBERRY ALMOND CUSTARD

EF GF
4 tablespoons agar-agar flakes
3 cups fruit juice
1 cup Soy Milk (p. 233)
2 tablespoons almond butter
2 cups chopped strawberries
1-2 tablespoons arrowroot
1 tablespoon almond essence or 1/2-1 teaspoon rose water

1. Combine agar-agar with 2 cups juice. Bring to the boil on a medium heat. Lower heat and cook until agar-agar dissolves.

2. Blend 1 cup Soy Milk and almond butter until creamy. Add to agar-agar mixture. Stir in strawberries.

3. Dissolve arrowroot in remaining 1 cup juice and add to custard. Stir until mixture boils and thickens. Remove from heat, add flavouring and cool.

SOY CUSTARD

GF
1 tablespoon oil
2 cups soy milk, scalded
2 eggs, beaten
1/4 cup sweetener (p. 12)
1-2 teaspoons vanilla, rum or brandy to taste
Pinch of sea salt to taste

1. Combine oil, soy milk. Beat eggs and sweetener till foamy. Gradually add the hot milk in a thin stream. Add the flavouring.

2. Pour the mixture into an oiled baking dish or into small individual moulds. Place in a shallow pan of water and bake at 160°C (325°F) for 30-40 minutes or until a tester inserted into the middle comes out clean. Eat warm or cool.

LEMON CUSTARD

2¹/₂ tablespoons whole wheat cake or pastry flour
1 tablespoon oil
1 egg, separated
1 cup fruit juice
3 tablespoons lemon juice
Pinch of sea salt
3 tablespoons lemon rind

1. Roast flour in oil until lightly browned. Set aside to cool.

2. Stir yolk with a fork. Combine flour with 2 tablespoons juice and stir into a smooth and creamy batter. Remove all lumps. Combine with egg yolk and remaining juice. Cook in a double boiler, stirring constantly for 5 minutes.

3. Beat egg white and sea salt together until peaked. Add lemon juice, rind, and egg white to the cooked mixture. Fold in gently. *Do not overmix.*

VARIATIONS

Add any one or a combination of the following.

1. 2-3 tablespoons instant grain coffee, before cooking.

2. Mint to taste, before or after cooking.

3. 1 teaspoon cinnamon, after cooking.

4. ¼ cup crushed roasted nuts or seeds before folding in egg white.

5. ½ cup fresh diced fruit to yolk mixture, after cooking.

Also see variations for Oat Cream (p. 91)

Strawberry *(Fragaria spp.)*

The strawberry is a plant native to North America. It is now cultivated throughout the temperate zones of the world. It radiates stems or runners which take root and grow into new plants. It has a thick, dark foliage, and bears white or pinkish flowers. Male and female flowers are borne on separate plants; female plants will not flower into fruit unless planted with males. Used mainly as a dessert fruit, strawberries can also be made into jam and used in pies, cakes and tarts.

CARROT CURRANT CUSTARD

EF GF
¹/₃ cup oil
¹/₂ cup grated carrots
Pinch of sea salt
3¹/₂ cups soy milk or ¹/₂ fruit juice and ¹/₂ milk
¹/₂ cup maple syrup or other sweetener (p. 12)
4-5 tablespoons agar-agar flakes
¹/₂ cup currants
1 teaspoon ground cardamon to taste
1 tablespoon arrowroot (optional)
¹/₂ cup ground nuts or seeds
1 teaspoon vanilla or ¹/₂ teaspoon rose water
Mint when available

1. Heat skillet, add oil and sauté the carrots with sea salt for a few seconds.

2. Combine with 2¹/₂ cups soy milk combination, sweetener, agar-agar, currants and cardamon. Bring to the boil, lower heat till agar-agar dissolves.

3. Dissolve the arrowroot in remaining milk, stir into custard adding the nuts. Bring to the boil, remove from the heat, add vanilla and spoon into moulds. Freeze or chill before serving. If freezing, whip before serving. (You may omit arrowroot if freezing.) Garnish with mint.

Paw-Paw *(Carica papaya)*

Recognised as papaya in its native home in southern Mexico, the paw-paw grows well in the tropics and is now found widely throughout the warmer regions of the world. In equatorial regions the fruit can be found all year round but it is somewhat more limited in more temperate areas where flowering and fruit set ceases in winter. A rich source of vitamins A and C, they are believed to aid in digestion owing to the enzyme papain contained in the flesh. The small black seeds (which make an attractive garnish) contain an enzyme, pepsin, which is another digestive aid. When ripe the paw-paw has a bright yellow skin with a deep yellow flesh that contains about 7-9 per cent sugar. They are fairly low in kilojoules making them a great sweet for the weight-conscious.

MAGNIFICENT MOUSSES

RUM BANANA MOUSSE

EF GF

2 tablespoons agar-agar flakes
1/4 cup fruit juice
2 cups mashed banana
1 teaspoon lemon juice
1 tablespoon rum
1 tablespoon carob flour
1 cup Tofu Whip Cream (p. 94)
Fresh fruit for garnish

1. Combine agar-agar and fruit juice and bring to the boil. Simmer till agar-agar dissolves. Meanwhile beat mashed banana, lemon juice, rum and carob until light and fluffy.

2. Add agar-agar mixture and continue beating until smooth and creamy. Chill until mixture is slightly thicker than unbeaten egg white. Prepare Tofu Whip Cream. Fold into banana mixture and chill to set. Garnish with fresh fruit.

BLACK AND WHITE MOUSSE

EF GF

6 tablespoons agar-agar flakes
6 cups fruit juice
4 tablespoons tahini or hazelnut butter
2 tablespoons grain coffee or carob flour
Pinch of sea salt
Kiwifruit and berries for layering and topping
Mint for garnish

1. Combine 3 tablespoons agar-agar with 3 cups fruit juice in one saucepan and the remaining flakes and juice in another. Bring each mixture to the boil, lower heat, cover and simmer 5 minutes. Put instant grain coffee or carob flour and sea salt into blender, add 3 cups boiled juice-agar-agar combination, 2 tablespoons tahini and whip until creamy.

2. Repeat with other juice-agar-agar mixture, adding 2 tablespoons tahini and whip until creamy and smooth. Cool in separate bowls until firm. Blend each one separately, pour into rinsed parfait glasses, alternating layers – black and white – placing fruit in between and on top. Top with fresh mint.

WINTER WONDERLAND MOUSSE

EF GF
3 cups fruit juice
1 cup mirin (sweet rice wine) or sherry
4 tablespoons agar-agar flakes
1 cup cooked pears
1/2 cup almond butter
1 teaspoon grated lemon rind
1 teaspoon grated orange rind
Few drops ginger juice
Mandarin segments for garnish

1. Combine juice, wine and agar-agar and bring to the boil. Lower heat and simmer till agar-agar is dissolved. Blend the rest of the ingredients, except the mandarins, with the agar-agar mixture until smooth and creamy.

2. Set aside till firm. Before serving whip in blender and top with mandarin segments.

STRAWBERRY MOUSSE

GF
6 tablespoons agar-agar flakes
2 cups fruit juice
1/4 cup maple syrup (to taste)
1 egg white, room temperature
2 tablespoons tahini
2 cups strawberries (250 g, 8 oz) washed and trimmed
1-2 teaspoons vanilla extract
Sliced strawberries

1. Combine the agar-agar flakes, juice and bring to the boil. Lower heat and simmer till agar-agar dissolves.

2. In another saucepan, heat the maple syrup. Beat the egg white till peaked and slowly drip in the hot maple syrup. Add the tahini to the juice mixture, and the strawberries and vanilla. Fold the egg white mixture into the strawberry mixture.

3. Place in serving dish and set aside to cool or chill. Whip before serving. Decorate with sliced strawberries.

CAROB CASHEW MOUSSE

EF GF
2 cups grape juice
1 cup dates
1 cup tofu
1 cup lightly roasted ground cashews
3 tablespoons carob flour
1 tablespoon orange rind
Pinch of sea salt
1 teaspoon vanilla
Fresh fruit for garnish

1. Cook together juice and dates until they are soft. Drop tofu into boiling water, bring to the boil and drain.
2. Blend together juice, dates, and roasted cashews until creamy. Add warm tofu and the rest of the ingredients. Blend again until smooth and light in texture.
3. Place in parfait glasses alternating with fresh fruit. Serve chilled.

PEACH STRAWBERRY MOUSSE

EF GF
3 peaches, peeled and stoned
4 tablespoons agar-agar flakes
5 cups mango juice
4 tablespoons arrowroot flour
4 tablespoons juice or 2 tablespoons sweetener (p. 12) and 2 tablespoons juice
Pinch of sea salt
2 teaspoons lime juice
1 cup roasted ground nuts
1 cup halved strawberries

1. Slice the peaches into thin vertical strips.
2. Combine agar-agar with the 5 cups mango juice. Cook the juice-agar-agar combination together until liquid comes to the boil. Lower heat and cook until agar-agar dissolves. Blend in peaches till creamy and smooth.
3. Dissolve arrowroot in 4 tablespoons juice or juice-sweetener combination. Add this to agar-agar mixture and bring to the boil, stirring constantly. Add sea salt, lime juice and nuts.
4. Alternately spoon the mixture and berries into parfait glasses. Allow to cool at room temperature, or chill until set.

STRAWBERRY MILK SHERBET IN CAROB MOUSSE

GF
SHERBET
EF
1 1/2 cups washed, halved strawberries
1/2 cup Soy Milk (p. 233)
1/3 cup maple syrup
1/4 cup tahini, almond or cashew butter*
3/4 tablespoon lemon juice (to taste)
CAROB MOUSSE
6 egg yolks
1/2 cup maple syrup to taste
1 cup carob flour
1/2 cup strong grain coffee (optional)
1/4-1/2 cup almond, cashew or sesame butter
1-2 tablespoons brandy or rum
6 egg whites (beaten till peaked)
Thin strips of lemon rind soaked in cold water till soft

*2 egg yolks may be substituted for tahini, almond or cashew butter.

SHERBET

1. Puree the strawberries, add the Soy Milk and maple syrup, tahini, almond or cashew butter and lemon juice.

2. Pour the mixture into the bowl of an ice-cream maker and freeze for 20-25 minutes. If you do not have an ice-cream maker, freeze till almost solid, whip again and freeze or serve as is.

CAROB MOUSSE**

**Can also be baked in a 220°C (425°F) oven for 12-15 minutes in individual cups.

1. Beat the egg yolks. Combine the maple syrup, carob flour and almond butter together and beat with the egg yolks till creamy and smooth.

2. Add the brandy or rum to the carob mixture and fold in the beaten egg whites till they almost disappear. Refrigerate till well set.

3. Place some sherbet in a tall glass; add a layer of mousse. Top with a scoop of sherbet. Decorate with thin strips of lemon rind.

Opposite: Ambrosia Jubilee (page 206)

Milk Sherbet In Carob Mousse (page 216)

Fluffy Snow
(page 218)

PARFAITS

A parfait is a mixture of beaten eggs or egg whites into which cooked syrup or fruit puree is whipped. Fruits and cream can also be folded in and it can be chilled or frozen till ready to serve.

ALMOND PARFAIT

GF
4 eggs plus pinch of sea salt
1 cup sweetener (p. 12)
2 cups Almond Whip Cream (below)
Fruit puree or fresh fruit

1. Add sea salt to eggs and beat until yolks and whites are well blended. Heat sweetener to boiling, lower heat and simmer 3-4 minutes. Pour in a steady stream into eggs, beating constantly. Cook in a double boiler until thick, stirring continuously. Cool. Prepare Almond Whip Cream.

2. Fold almond cream into first mixture. Fill glasses alternating with fruit puree or fresh fruit. Refrigerate or freeze until ready to serve.

ALMOND WHIP CREAM

£F GF
Blend 2 cups blanched roasted almonds with warm apple juice and vanilla until thick and creamy. (It should drop reluctantly from the edge of a wooden spoon.) Or use almond butter and thin to desired consistency with fruit juice and vanilla.

Carob (Ceratonia siliqua)

In its appearance, the tree which bears the carob pod looks very much like an apple tree with small flowers. It is a dark evergreen tree, which grows wild in the countries that border the Mediterranean Sea and on the islands off the east coast of Spain. The carob grows a brown, leathery pod, 10-25 cm (4-10 in) long. It is the pod that contains a sticky pulp that is fed to horses and cattle and sometimes eaten by people. Carob pod is said to have been eaten by John the Baptist when he lived in the wilderness, and is sometimes referred to as 'St John's Bread'.

Opposite, from left: Berry Shake (page 235), Kiwi Shake (page 235) and Carob Shake (page 236)

FLUFFY SNOW

GF

4 tablespoons agar-agar flakes
1 1/2 cups peach or grape juice
1/2 cup maple syrup
2 egg whites
Pinch of sea salt
1 teaspoon grated lemon or orange rind
1 tablespoon lemon or orange juice
Yoghurt for decoration and topping or Tofu Whip Cream (p. 94)

1. Combine the agar-agar with the juice and bring to the boil. Simmer till agar-agar dissolves.

2. Add the syrup and cook until liquid is reduced by one-third. Cool.

3. Beat the egg whites with a pinch of sea salt until stiff.

4. Add the lemon or orange rind and juice and beat this whole mixture into the cool agar-agar mixture.

5. Place in rinsed parfait glass and allow to set at room temperature.

6. Spoon some yoghurt or Tofu Whip Cream down along the sides of the filled parfait glass. Top with some more yoghurt or tofu cream. Decorate with fresh fruit. Serve immediately.

Banana (Musa paradisiaca)

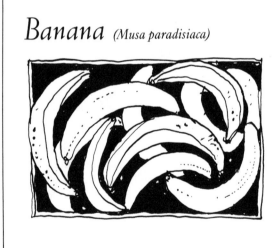

The banana plant, often referred to as a 'tree', is actually a giant herb whose stem is composed of overlapping bases of the leaves above. It originated in the region spanning India to New Guinea. Now the banana is cultivated throughout the tropics with many varieties available worldwide. When the banana fruits are green they are 20 per cent starch and 2 per cent sugar. They should not be used until their skin has turned yellow and speckled brown as this is when they are ripe and they then contain 20 per cent sugar and 2 per cent starch. At this stage they are more digestible and tastier.

MORE COOLING DESSERTS

SORBET BANANA

EF GF

2 cups pureed bananas
2 tablespoons agar-agar
1 1/2 cups fresh orange juice
2 tablespoons or more crushed nuts (almonds)
Strawberries, cherries, kiwifruit for garnish
Fresh mint

1. Blend bananas. Dissolve the agar-agar in orange juice and bring to the boil. Simmer 5 minutes.

2. Blend with banana puree, adding the crushed nuts. Freeze until firm. Blend and serve with fresh fruit topping, or freeze again, blend and serve, garnished with fruit and fresh mint.

STRAWBERRY DIVINE

GF

5 tablespoons agar-agar flakes
1 1/2 cups fruit juice or 1 cup juice and 1/2 cup mirin (sweet rice wine)
1/4 cup maple syrup
1/2 cup tofu
1 tablespoon tahini
2 cups strawberries, cut in half
1 egg white (room temperature)
Sliced strawberries

1. Combine agar-agar flakes and juice and bring to the boil. Cook till agar-agar dissolves.

2. Meanwhile begin to cook the maple syrup and simmer until almost caramelized.

3. Combine tofu, tahini, strawberries and cooked juice mixture and blend till creamy and smooth.

4. Beat egg white dripping in hot maple syrup, mix a little of the strawberry mixture into the egg white, then fold into strawberry mixture.

5. Place in serving dishes and chill. Decorate with sliced strawberries.

GRILLED PEARS

EF GF

3 ripe pears, halved, cored and peeled
4 tablespoons mirin (sweet rice wine) or sherry
1/2 cup chopped nuts
2-3 tablespoons chopped sultanas or currants
2-3 tablespoons tahini
1 teaspoon anise powder
1 teaspoon white miso or sea salt
CAROB SAUCE COVER
1 tablespoon sesame oil
1-2 teaspoons arrowroot flour or kuzu
1 tablespoon carob flour
1 cup Soy Milk (p. 233)
1/3 cup maple syrup, to taste
1 teaspoon vanilla or brandy

1. Preheat oven to 180°C (350°F). Arrange pears cored side up in baking dish. Scoop out some of the centre.

2. Blend the remaining ingredients for stuffing and fill fruit cavities. Bake, covered, 15-20 minutes.

CAROB SAUCE COVER

1. Warm pan, add oil and combine the flour and carob, stirring into the oil.

2. Slowly add the Soy Milk and maple syrup, stirring continuously until thickened. Simmer 2-3 minutes.

3. Take off heat and stir in vanilla or rum. Spoon over pears just before serving. Serve hot or cold.

CHERRY CAROB PUDDING

EF GF*
4 tablespoons agar-agar flakes
2 cups fruit juice
3 tablespoons arrowroot or kuzu (dissolved in a few tablespoons of the fruit juice)
Pinch of sea salt or 1 teaspoon white miso
4 tablespoons tahini or cashew butter
5 tablespoons maple syrup
*3 tablespoons maltose (optional) or rice syrup **
4 tablespoons roasted carob flour
2 teaspoons vanilla or orange rind
1/4 cup chopped almonds or walnuts
500 g (1 lb) fresh, pitted cherries

* Gluten free only if using rice syrup.

1. Combine the agar-agar and fruit juice in a saucepan and bring to the boil. Lower heat and simmer till agar-agar dissolves. Then add the dissolved arrowroot, sea salt or miso, tahini, sweeteners and carob and simmer 5 minutes.

2. Remove from the heat and stir in the vanilla, chopped nuts and cherries. Serve hot or cold.

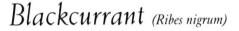

Blackcurrant *(Ribes nigrum)*

The blackcurrant, known to be one of the richest natural sources of vitamin C, is thought to have been found wild centuries ago and grows across the whole of Europe and northern Asia. In Australia, Tasmania is a main area of production. The blackcurrant is also grown in New Zealand. At any season the blackcurrant is easily recognized by the distinctive aroma of its stems and leaves. By early summertime its fruit appears hanging in loose bunches from the leafy shrub.

SUMMER PUDDING

EF

14 slices fresh whole wheat bread
500 g (1 lb) mixed berries (strawberries, raspberries, blueberries, redcurrants,
blackcurrants and gooseberries)
1/2 cup dried currants
1/2 cup fruit juice
1/4 cup sweetener (p. 12)
4 tablespoons agar-agar
1 tablespoon arrowroot flour dissolved in 1 tablespoon juice
Fresh berries for garnish
1 quantity Tofu Whip Cream (p. 94)

1. Cut crusts off bread. Oil a 1 litre (4 cup) mixing bowl or pudding basin and place a circle of foil in the bottom. Place a slice of bread over the foil and line the sides with overlapping slices or strips of bread.

2. Wash and prepare fruit, hull strawberries, top and tail redcurrants and gooseberries.

3. Place fruit, juice, sweetener and agar-agar in a saucepan and bring to the boil. Simmer till agar-agar dissolves. Stir in arrowroot mixture and bring to the boil. Remove from the heat, and spoon fruit mixture into bowl until half full, cover with slices or strips of bread.

4. Place remaining fruit mixture on top and then cover completely with more slices or strips of bread. Place a circle of foil on top of the bread, and cover with a saucer. Put some weights on the saucer and refrigerate until set (overnight for best results).

5. To serve, remove weights, saucer and foil, cut down the sides of the bread if necessary until they are level with the rest of the pudding. Loosen the edge with a palette knife or round-bladed knife, place a serving plate on top, and turn out onto the plate by turning the mixing bowl and serving plate upside-down. Serve with reserved berries and Tofu Whip Cream.

8. LITTLE NIBBLES:
Sweet Treats

*There will always be those times when you feel like a 'little nibble'
and would give your weight in gold for there to be a snack within reach. The
following ideas are intended to stimulate your creativity and whet your appetite.
This section is filled with wholesome treats that can be used as a quick treat
for anyone in the family or when the unexpected guest drops in. However,
don't get too stuck in this chapter which is easy to do because
they are quite delicious indeed!*

FORGET ME KNOTS

1. The amount of liquid necessary for each recipe will differ each time, according to the moisture in the ingredients (especially *nut butters*), humidity in the room, acidity of the fruit, water content in the sweetener, and how finely you are able to grind your seeds and nuts.
2. Use all ingredients at room temperature,

unless otherwise instructed.
3. Try to obtain dried fruits without sulphur dioxide or sorbic acid.*
4. Choose a sweetener according to the consistency of the recipe you are preparing as well as the taste.
5. Allow confectionery to harden before serving.

*Sulphur dioxide is used as a preservative in dried fruit to prevent browning and oxidation of fruit, mould growth and loss of vitamin C after drying.

Sorbic acid is used as a preservative in dried tree fruit.

PINE NUT BALLS

EF GF
1/2 cup pine nut meal
1/4 cup roasted and chopped pine nuts
1/4 cup tahini or cashew butter
3-4 tablespoons maple syrup
1/2 teaspoon rose water
1 tablespoon carob powder
Coconut or toasted seeds

1. Combine the meal, chopped nuts, tahini, maple syrup, rose water and carob. Knead together or process until firm (add liquid if necessary).
2. Roll into log and shape into balls. Roll in coconut or toasted seeds.

FRUIT AND NUT BALLS

EF
1 1/4 cups sprouted wheat
2 1/4 cups pitted dates
1/4 cup currants
1 cup minced walnuts or almonds
1/2 cup roasted sesame seeds
1/2 tablespoon miso to taste
1/4 cup sweetener (p. 12)
2 tablespoons hazelnut butter
1 1/2 tablespoons lemon rind
1 teaspoon ground coriander
Almonds, halved
Desiccated coconut for outside coating (optional)

Blend first two ingredients together. Add the rest of the ingredients, slowly working them into fruit mix. Form into balls and press half an almond in the centre of each ball. Roll in coconut if desired.

ALMOND POPCORN

EF GF *
4 tablespoons oil
1/2 cup unpopped popcorn
Pinch of sea salt
1 1/2 cups unblanched chopped almonds
1/2 cup sweetener (p. 12)
1/2 cup barley malt, maltose or rice syrup *
1/4-1/2 cup almond butter
1 teaspoon vanilla

* Gluten free only if using
rice syrup.

1. Preheat oven to 120°C (250°F).
2. Heat oil in heavy pot. Add corn and salt. Place lid on pot slightly ajar allowing a little crack so that excess steam can escape. Cook over high heat, turning pot around as corn pops until all corn is popped.
3. In a large pan combine popcorn and almonds and place in oven. Oil the side of a heavy saucepan, combine sweetener and malt. Bring to the boil. Stir continuously for 5 minutes or until mixture reaches the soft ball stage on a confectionary thermometer. Remove from heat, stir in almond butter and vanilla till creamy. Immediately pour over popcorn mixture, stirring to coat. Cool, and break into bite-sized pieces.

Rice *(Oryza sativa)*

Rice was a staple food of China as early as 2800 B.C. Most rice is produced and used in Asia, and is grown from the equator to as far north as Japan. It is also grown commercially in Australia. Rice, usually grown in water, forms a hollow stem that lets oxygen pass downward and reach the roots in the wetted soil. In the milling process, the inedible outer husk is first removed.

This leaves brown rice, containing the bran, where all of the essential vitamins and minerals are stored. It is an excellent nutritious food that can be cooked easily by simply boiling. Another variety, known as 'glutinous' or sweet brown rice (which may be difficult to buy in Australia), is sweeter and stickier than brown rice. It is used in Japan and China mainly for festive occasions, in the form of sweet white rice.

'White' rice is brown rice with most of the valuable part of the grain – the bran – removed. Milled to remove the bran, the rice is then subjected to a process known as pearling, leaving a white grain. It is then coated with glucose and talc to preserve the whiteness and marketed.

Rice, whether it be boiled, steamed, baked or fried, is a basic dish in many countries. Served in Asia with vegetables, in India with curry, and in Spain with fish, rice also provides the Japanese with their staple grain *sake* (rice wine) made from fermented grains, and rice paper made from the stems.

FIG AND RUM TREATS

*Gluten free only if using rice.

EF GF*
2 cups sprouted rice or wheat *
2 cups dried chopped figs
1/2 cup dried chopped apricots
1/2 cup desiccated coconut
1 cup roasted ground cashews
1/2 cup almond or roasted cashew butter
1 1/2 tablespoons orange rind
1/2 tablespoon lemon rind
1 tablespoon cinnamon
2 tablespoons carob flour
1 tablespoon rum or brandy
Pinch of sea salt

Blend or grind first four ingredients together. Add the rest of the ingredients and mix until stiff. Shape into logs, wrap in greaseproof paper and chill.

SPICE AND NUT SQUARES

GF EF
3/4 cup maple syrup
1/2 cup carob flour
1 cup roasted ground hazelnuts
1/2 cup roasted chopped almonds
1/2 cup desiccated coconut
1/2 cup roasted ground sunflower seeds
1/2 tablespoon miso to taste
1 teaspoon ground coriander or cinnamon
1 teaspoon ground ginger
1 teaspoon orange flower water

Combine all ingredients mixing well. Oil pan and spread out 12 mm (1/2 in) thick. Set in refrigerator to harden. Cut when firm.

CARROT BALLS

EF GF

1/2 cup grated carrot or pumpkin
3/4-1 cup nut butter
1 cup sweetener (p. 12)
2 cups roasted chopped macadamia nuts
4 tablespoons desiccated coconut
1 teaspoon cinnamon
Pinch of sea salt
Coconut for rolling

Mix all ingredients together in an oiled bowl. Shape into little balls and roll in additional coconut before serving.

CASHEW-ALMOND LOGS

EF GF

1/4 cup maple syrup
1/2 cup tahini or almond butter
1/2 cup carob flour
1/2 cup roasted ground cashews
1/2 cup roasted ground almonds
1/2 cup finely chopped dates or figs
1/2 tablespoon miso or pinch of sea salt
1 teaspoon ground coriander
1 teaspoon cinnamon
1 tablespoon lemon rind
1 tablespoon rum or brandy

1. Combine maple syrup and nut butter in a heavy saucepan, and cook over a low heat until creamy. Remove from heat and immediately stir in the rest of the ingredients.

2. Shape into logs and set aside to rest for at least 1 hour. Roll in coconut if desired, or top with Carob Glaze that follows.

CAROB GLAZE

EF GF
1/2 cup sweetener (p. 12)
1/3 cup carob flour
1/3 cup tahini
Pinch of sea salt
1 tablespoon to taste vanilla, rum or brandy

1. Heat sweetener in heavy saucepan until warm. Stir in carob (sift if lumpy).

2. Add next two ingredients. Remove from heat and stir in flavouring.

3. Place logs on oiled greaseproof paper and spoon glaze over immediately. Roll or sprinkle on crushed roasted nuts or seeds. (If you wait to cover logs, the glaze will harden into fudge.)

ALMOND ROLLS

EF GF
1/2 cup blanched roasted, ground almonds
1/4 cup almond butter
4 tablespoons sweetener (p. 12)
1/2 cup dried chopped fruit
1 teaspoon vanilla or 1/2 teaspoon rose water to taste
1/4 teaspoon miso or pinch of sea salt
1 1/2 tablespoons carob flour
1 1/2 tablespoons grated lemon rind
Roasted unhulled sesame seeds

1. Combine first five ingredients and beat until ball forms.

2. Stir in next three ingredients and knead several minutes.

3. Place mixture on greaseproof or waxed paper and roll into log. Allow to set 15 minutes before cutting into small pieces. Roll in sesame seeds before serving.

MACADAMIA DELIGHTS

EF GF

1/4 cup sweetener (p. 12)
1/2 cup roasted cashew butter
1/2 cup carob flour
1/2 cup roasted finely chopped macadamia nuts
3/4 cup finely chopped currants or figs
2 teaspoons ground coriander
1/2 tablespoon miso or pinch of sea salt
1/2 cup desiccated coconut

1. Combine sweetener and cashew butter in a saucepan, and cook over a low heat until melted. Remove from heat, and immediately stir in remaining ingredients except coconut.

2. Press mixture into oiled and paper lined (greaseproof is best) tray. Sprinkle surface with coconut, and press in. Cover and chill until firm. Cut into squares or diamond shapes to serve.

CAROB FUDGE

EF GF

1/2 cup carob flour
4 tablespoons agar-agar flakes
1/2 cup fruit juice
1/2 cup maple syrup
1/2 cup tahini
1/2 cup fruit juice
1 1/2 tablespoons arrowroot flour
1 tablespoon vanilla
1/2 cup chopped walnuts

1. Sift flour. Combine agar-agar, juice and maple syrup and bring to the boil. Simmer till clear.

2. Combine all the rest of the ingredients, except vanilla and walnuts, mix with first juice mixture and cook till thick. Stir in vanilla and walnuts. Pour into mould and chill.

Salt

Salt has always been one of the most common and important ingredients of life. Thousands of years ago, it was one of the only preservatives used by man. At one time it had religious significance, for it was the symbol of purity among the ancient Hebrews, who rubbed newborn babies with it to ensure their good health. The Old Testament tells the story of Elisha throwing salt into a spring to purify its waters (2 Kings, 2:19-22). In the Near East, salt used at meals is a sign of friendship and hospitality. The Arabs say, 'There is salt between us,' meaning we have eaten together and are friends. Salt was once so precious that Caesar's soldiers received part of their pay for the purpose of buying common salt; it was known as their *salarium*, which is where our word *salary* comes from.

All salt was at one time essentially sea salt. Today, there are three main kinds of salt on the market: unrefined sun-dried sea salt, iodized salt, and refined table salt. Salt found inland, in rock deposits or in springs that flow through them, can be traced back to the ocean that covered the earth millions of years ago. Earth movements isolated parts of this ancient sea uncovering these beds of rock.

Unrefined, sun-dried, white sea salt contains many minerals that are not found in refined table salt: gold, iron, copper, calcium, and magnesium, which are important to our digestive processes, are present in small quantities.

In ancient times, people kept crude, grey sea salt in a jar for at least one year. During that time, the magnesium absorbed water from the air and went to the bottom of the jar. The top salt became less salty and purer, and was used in cooking and baking. Usually this salt was roasted to make it drier and ground into a fine powder before it was used.

Most salt found in the stores today has had the trace minerals removed, supposedly to make it taste 'saltier' and look purer. The refining process subjects salt to great pressure and steam heat, causing it to crystallize instantly. Although this method saves money, the crystal produced is not only devoid of its trace minerals but also slow to dissolve and difficult to digest.

Try this experiment to see if your salt has been refined. Place a teaspoon of salt in a glass of water and stir it once. Look at it a little while later to see if there is any sediment. Natural, unrefined sea salt has a tendency to disappear in the water within a few minutes, leaving the liquid clear (a residue or cloudiness in the water may indicate the presence of impurities), but the refined table salt will take longer to dissolve.

Commercial table salt may also contain additives. Calcium bicarbonate is added to keep it dry and pourable, and iodine, which is commonly used to prevent goitre,* may also be added. Dextrose, a simple sugar, is added to stabilize the iodine, because it is very volatile and oxidizes in direct sunlight. Other additives are used to keep the salt looking white.

It is important to use salt that is as pure and unrefined as nature intended it, salt that has not been treated with chemical additives, but has been extracted from the sea and allowed to dry naturally in the sun. Therefore, when you buy salt, remember that while it may be the smallest ingredient you use in quantity, it is just as important, or even more important, than the other ingredients in your cooking and baking. It can bring out the delicate flavours of other ingredients, sometimes actually making them sweeter.

---

* *Iodine is naturally supplied by the following, in order of highest iodine content: kelp, agar-agar, swiss chard, turnip greens, summer squash, mustard greens, watermelon, cucumber, spinach.*

9. FANTASTICALLY FAST FILLERS

*I know that there are those impatient moments when you can't
be bothered waiting for a dessert to bake, cool or set, because there just isn't
enough time. That's why I have created some 'fast' food ideas, which
can be used in place of a dessert.
One shouldn't gulp down any food, let alone sweets, but sometimes time
gets in the way of your better judgment; so, 'drink it instead'.
These drink ideas are filling enough for a meal in themselves, or for
a quick summer refresher on a hot day. They are also handy when you
just want a quick pick-me-up!*

FORGET ME KNOTS

1. The amount of liquid necessary for each drink will differ each time, according to the fat and oil content of each nut, seed, bean or grain, the moisture in the room, the weather of the day and how fine you are able to grind and strain your 'milk' base.

2. When nuts are warm, always blend them with warm liquid.

3. Use a small amount of liquid when blending nuts or seeds at first, so they can break down into a creamy consistency.

4. You can prepare 'milk' several days in advance and keep it refrigerated until you want to flavour it.

5. Experiment with different fruits when they come into season for a nice refreshing change.

6. These drinks with thick nut, seed, grain, or bean bases, can be turned into delightful, creamy pies by just adding agar-agar. Follow one of the recipes. Mix agar-agar into ½ cup juice, cook until it dissolves and combine with the rest of the ingredients. Pour into pre-baked pie shell and cool until set! Allow 4-6 tablespoons agar-agar for every 4 cups liquid. If the puree is thick use half the amount of agar-agar.

MILK BASES: NUT, SEED, GRAIN AND BEAN

These 'milks' can be used in the same way as goat's or cow's milk with much the same results. In some recipes, you may want to adjust the flavouring to compensate for the difference in taste.

ALMOND MILK

EF GF
2 cups blanched almonds
4 cups fruit juice or water (boiling)
3-4 tablespoons sweetener (p. 12)
Dash of vanilla to taste

Combine almonds and ½ cup boiling juice or water. Blend until creamy, slowly adding the remaining liquid, sweetener and vanilla. Strain and use as desired. As a variation blend a very ripe banana with Almond Milk.

CASHEW MILK

EF GF
2 cups lightly roasted cashews
4 cups boiling fruit juice or water
3-4 tablespoons sweetener (p. 12) to taste

Follow recipe for Almond Milk.

SOY MILK

(Buy it commercially or try making your own)

Soy milk may be used for hot or cold drinks; but when added to boiling liquid, it has a tendency to curdle.

EF GF
1 cup soybeans
8 cups water
4 cups water

1. Soak beans at room temperature in 8 cups of water until they are three times the original size (6-8 hours in warm weather or 10-12 hours in cold weather). Drain the beans, and combine them with 2-2⅔ cups of water and puree until very smooth. Heat ½ cup water in large pot; when water is very hot, add pureed beans.

2. Cook on medium heat, stirring constantly or beans will stick to the bottom of the pot. When foam suddenly rises to the top, turn off immediately and pour through muslin or cheesecloth, twist closed, and press sack of beans against colander or strainer to press out milk.

3. Pour milk into another pot and bring to the boil, stirring constantly to prevent sticking. Reduce heat and simmer 7-10 minutes. Taste and season. Serve hot or cold. If you are using organic soybeans, the milk may be slightly bitter. Add 10 per cent tahini, as well as other flavourings, to cancel bitterness.

The part that is left over after making the milk is called *okara* and is very rich in nutrients. Try using it in breads, cakes, burgers, casseroles, soups, and pies.

COCONUT MILK

EF GF
3-4 cups boiling water or fruit juice
Sweetener to taste (p. 12)
2 cups desiccated coconut or 6 cups freshly ground coconut

Add boiling liquid (including sweetener) to the desiccated coconut. Let stand for at least 20 minutes, then strain through muslin or cheesecloth. You can re-use the coconut for a weaker milk. Use in place of milk.

OAT MILK

EF
2-3 cups fruit juice or water
1/4 cup rolled oats
2-4 tablespoons sweetener (p. 12)
Pinch of sea salt

1. Bring juice to the boil. Add oats, cover and simmer over low heat for 20 minutes.
2. Blend sweetener, salt and oats together while still hot.

SEED MILK

EF GF
1 cup sunflower or sesame seeds
4 cups boiling fruit juice or water
4 tablespoons Fruit Puree (p. 85) to taste
Vanilla to taste

Follow same method as Almond Milk.

Milk

Milk is a transitionary food that is secreted by female mammals to help their offspring adjust from the womb to the outside world. Cow's milk, which is richer in protein, fats and minerals than human milk, helps to build the strong bones essential for calves. However, humans first develop a strong nervous system which is aided by human milk because of its rich, easily digestible fats, more digestible protein and more alkaline factors.

No other mammal uses milk after infancy. The arrival of teeth transforms infants from a liquid to a solid state eating mammal – time to forget about drinking milk. In fact, we tend to lose the ability to digest milk as we grow older. About 80 per cent of the adults in the world lack the enzyme *lactase* needed to digest lactose (sugar in milk). Undigested milk has been known to form mucus which can clog the system and cause disease and allergies.

Milk, both cow's and goat's, was traditionally consumed when people were nomadic with no fixed crops to live on and needed food that was rich in saturated fats to keep warm. However, the amount of milk, butter and cheese consumed was very small in comparison with today's figures. The consumption of dairy foods in the last fifty years has just about doubled, but the quality of our dairy products today is very different. Cattle are not allowed to live a natural existence mainly because of economic reasons. The residues of chemical sprays and pesticides, and the hormones that are fed to cattle to fatten them and stimulate milk production, are all passed into the milk of the cow in a more concentrated form. The lack of exercise and restricted diet of modern cattle have changed the balance of the fats in their milk and meat.

SHAKES

ORANGE SHAKE

GF
2 glasses 'milk'
Juice of 1 orange
1 teaspoon orange rind
2 egg yolks
1 teaspoon vanilla
2 tablespoons Fruit Puree (p. 85) or maple syrup

Blend all ingredients together.

BERRY SHAKE

EF GF
2 glasses sweetened 'milk'
1 cup berries
2 tablespoons tahini
1 teaspoon cinnamon
Pinch of sea salt
1/3-1/2 cup maple syrup to taste

Blend all ingredients together. (Berries may thin out shake, so use less liquid when making 'milk'.) Pour out, decorate with fresh fruit and serve.

KIWI SHAKE

EF GF
2 glasses 'milk'
1 cup sliced kiwifruit
2 tablespoons freshly chopped mint
1/4-1/3 cup maple syrup to taste

Blend all ingredients together. Pour out, decorate with fresh fruit and serve.

CAROB SHAKE

EF GF
2 glasses 'milk'
3 tablespoons sweetener (p. 12) to taste
2 tablespoons tahini
1/4 cup carob flour
1 teaspoon cinnamon
1 teaspoon vanilla
1/3-1/2 cup maple syrup to taste
Pinch of sea salt
Pinch of coconut

Blend all ingredients together, pour, decorate with fresh fruit and serve.

FRUIT COMBINATIONS FOR SHAKES AND SMOOTHIES
Apple – strawberry
Apple – carrot juice – date
Apple – date – sultana
Melon – mango – apple
Apple – peach – fig
Apricot – date – nectarine
Pear – mint – apple
Lemon – apple
Orange – pear
Pear – apple

Mango (Mangifera indica)

Belonging to the family Anacardiaceae, the mango is related to the cashew, pistachio and hog plum, and finds its origins in the Indo-Burmese region. Today, often referred to as 'king of the fruits', the mango is widely grown in almost every tropical country. The mango tree produces a fine fruit that is an excellent source of vitamin A and also contains vitamin C, iodine, niacin, potassium, calcium, phosphorus and sodium. The ripe mango should have a smooth skin with a slightly rosy blush and when pressure is applied to the fruit the flesh should yield slightly to the touch. They are best eaten at this point as texture and sweetness are at their peak.

SMOOTHIES

These drinks are thinner than shakes as they are made by blending a combination of fruits with fruit juice or 'milk', spring water or natural carbonated water and seasoning to taste.

APPLE PEAR LEMON

EF GF
1 cup Cashew Milk (p. 232)
1 cup fruit juice
1/2 cup chilled grated apples
1 cup chilled chopped pears
1 teaspoon cinnamon
1 teaspoon lime rind
1 tablespoon lime juice
Pinch of sea salt or shoyu

Blend all ingredients together.

APRICOT PEACH

EF GF
1 cup Almond or Soy Milk (pp. 232-3)
1 cup fruit juice
3/4 cup chopped apricots
1/2 cup chopped peaches
1 teaspoon cinnamon
2 tablespoons sweetener (p. 12) to taste
Pinch of sea salt

Blend all ingredients together.

PUMPKIN SMOOTHIE

EF GF
1 cup Soy or Nut Milk (pp. 232-3)
1 cup sliced apple and banana combination
2-4 tablespoons cooked pumpkin
Cinnamon to taste
Ginger to taste

Blend together until foamy.

OTHER DRINKS

NATURAL SODAS

EF GF

A thinner drink for those who are so inclined! Just combine sparkling mineral water and fruit juice concentrate or fruit juice together. For extra flavour, try adding lemon, lime, orange rind, or vanilla, to taste.

AMAZAKE DRINK

EF

If your time is short, you can buy prepared amazake in most health food stores.

2 cups freshly cooked sweet brown or brown rice
4 cups water
2 cups koji (yeast) rice

1. To freshly cooked rice, add 4 cups water and bring to the boil. Lower heat and simmer 5 minutes. Let cool to 100°C (200°F), then add 2 cups yeast rice to the first mixture.

2. Cover and place in a 100°C (200°F) oven for 8-10 hours. Taste for sweetness. Leave longer if not sweet enough.

3. Pour into saucepan, add the same amount of water, bring to the boil and serve.

4. To use as a sweetener, after allowing rice to ferment, boil down until thick. Refrigerate until ready to use. Amazake can be blended for a smoother texture, and served with cakes and slices.

VARIATION

Carob Milk: Add ½ cup carob flour to ingredients before blending.

ROCK MELON COOLER

EF GF
2 cups chopped rock melon
¹/4 cup sweetener (p. 12)
1 cup Soy or Nut Milk (pp. 232-3)
4 strawberries for garnish

Blend until foamy. Slit open strawberries and slip on side of glasses.

Appendices

INGREDIENT MEASUREMENT CHART

Because the density of ingredients varies, this table gives equivalent cup measurements for a standard weight or volume.

Almonds, whole, shelled	3 cups	500 g (1 lb)
Almonds, ground	2¾ cups	500 g (1 lb)
Almonds, slivered	3 cups	500 g (1 lb)
Almond butter	1¾ cups	500 g (1 lb)
Apples, cored and sliced	3-4 cups	500 g (1 lb)
Apricots, dried	3 cups	500 g (1 lb)
Arrowroot	3½ cups	500 g (1 lb)
Brown rice flour	3½ cups	500 g (1 lb)
Chestnut flour	3 cups	500 g (1 lb)
Oats (rolled)	4 cups	500 g (1 lb)
Oil	2 cups	500 g (1 lb)
Peanuts, shelled	2¼ cups	500 g (1 lb)
Peanut butter	1½ cups	500 g (1 lb)
Pecans, shelled	3½ cups	500 g (1 lb)
Raisins	3½ cups	500 g (1 lb)
Sea salt	1 cup	500 g (1 lb)
Sesame butter	2 cups	500 g (1 lb)
Strawberries	2-3 cups	2 punnets
Tahini	2 cups	500 g (1 lb)
Walnuts, shelled, whole	4 cups	500 g (1 lb)
Water	2 cups	500 mL (16 fl oz)
Whole wheat flour	3¾ cups	500 g (1 lb)
Whole wheat cake or pastry flour	4 cups	500 g (1 lb)

EQUIVALENT INGREDIENT MEASUREMENT CHART

This table gives approximate equivalent measurements for ingredients in different forms; e.g. 3-4 tablespoons of lemon juice can be obtained from 1 medium lemon.

Apples (raw)	1.75-2 kg (3½-4 lb)	500 g (1 lb) dried
Dried fruit	1 cup (dried)	2 cups, soaked
Eggs (whole)	1 cup	4-5 eggs
Agar-agar	2 bars	8 tablespoons flakes
Lemon rind (dried)	½-1 tablespoon	1 medium lemon
Lemon rind (fresh)	1-2 tablespoons	1 medium lemon
Lemon juice	3-4 tablespoons	1 medium lemon
Mint tea (leaves)	1 teaspoon	3-4 cups
Mu tea	1 packet	8-10 cups
Orange rind (dried)	1-2 tablespoons	1 medium orange
Orange rind (fresh)	2-3 tablespoons	1 medium orange
Orange juice	6-8 tablespoons	1 medium orange
Vanilla (pure liquid)	1 teaspoon	6 cm (2½ in) bean
Whole wheat cake or pastry flour	1 cup (unsifted)	1⅓ cup, sifted
Yeast	2 teaspoons (dried)	30 g (1 oz), compressed

DRIED FRUIT COOKING GUIDE

Dried fruit	Cover with water & simmer uncovered for (minutes)	Increase in volume when cooked
Apples	20	4 times
Apricots	25	double
Bananas	20	double
Chinese dates	20	double
Currants	10	double
Dates	15	double
Figs	20	double
Mangoes	25	triple
Nectarines	25	double
Paw-paws	30	triple
Peaches	25	triple
Pears	25	triple
Pineapples	20	double
Prunes	30	double
Raisins & sultanas	10 to 15	double

TEMPERATURES FOR BAKING PIES

Pie	*Minutes*	*Oven Temperature* *Celsius (Fahrenheit)*
Unfilled pie shells	15-20	190°-200°C (375°-400°F)
Filled one-crust cream or custard type half baked shell	25-30	180°C (350°F)
Filled one-crust cream or custard type	15-20	180°C (350°F)
Filled two-crust cream or custard type	40-50	180°C (350°F)
Filled one-crust fruit, half baked shell	30-40	190°C (375°F)
Filled two-crust fruit, unbaked shell	45-60	180°-190°C (350°-375°F)
Filled lattice top half, baked shell	30-45	180°C (350°F)
Meringues	45	110°C (225°F)
	25	160°C (325°F)
	10-12	200°C (400°F)

Baking time will vary according to the material of the pie dish. If you use enamelware or glass, reduce the baking time indicated by one quarter; if using stoneware, increase the baking time by one half.

WHERE TO SHOP

HEALTH FOOD STORE Wholemeal flours, seeds, expeller-pressed unrefined oils, miso, *shoyu*, sea salt, kuzu, arrowroot, nut butters, unsulphured dried fruits, sweeteners, teas, grain coffee, fruit juices, bean curd (tofu), soy milk, organic fruits and vegetables, free-range eggs, herbs, spices, natural flavourings, vitamin and mineral supplements, etc.
ORIENTAL FOOD STORE (JAPANESE, KOREAN, CHINESE) Kuzu flour, spices, herbs, maltose, nuts, seeds, oils, dried chestnuts, etc.
MIDDLE EASTERN STORE Herbs, spices, grains, dried beans, tahini, nuts, seeds, olive oil, goat or sheep cheese, etc.
ITALIAN DELICATESSEN Nuts, seeds, olive oil, grain, chestnut flour, fresh or dried herbs, etc.
SUPERMARKETS Wholemeal flour, nuts, seeds, nut butters, herbs, spices, fruit juice, cider, honey, maple syrup, etc.

Unfortunately, not every item that you may wish to purchase may be found under one roof, but more and more items are being made available in your local supermarkets and small shops. It will take you time to familiarize yourself with where to find what, but this basic guide was designed with the expectation that natural food items will become more accessible in a number of places. If you can't find something, please ask for it. By creating a demand, the supply will automatically come! Experiment, and try something new. If you don't know how to use it, just ask your shopkeeper who will usually be more than willing to explain how to work with it.

Suggestions for Further Reading

Aihara, Cornelia. *The Calendar Cookbook.* The George Ohsawa Macrobiotic Foundation, Los Angeles, 1979.

Ballentine, Rudolph, M. D. *Diet & Nutrition.* The Himalayan International Institute, Pennsylvania, 1978.

Barkie, Karen. *Fancy, Sweet & Sugar Free.* St Martins Press, New York, 1985.

Brown, Sarah. *Sarah Brown's Healthy Living Cookbook.* Doubleday, Sydney, 1986.

Brown, Sarah. *Sarah Brown's Vegetarian Cookbook.* Doubleday, Sydney, 1984.

Buist, Robert. *Food Intolerance.* Harper & Row, Sydney, 1984.

Deutsch, Ronald M. *Realities of Nutrition.* Bull Publishing Co., California, 1976.

Dufty, William. *Sugar Blues.* Warner Books, New York, 1976.

Duquette, Susan. *Sunburst Farm Family Cookbook.* Woodbridge Press Publishing Company, California, 1976.

Editors of the *East West Journal. Whole World Cook Book.* Avery Publishing Group, New Jersey, 1984.

Gouldstone, Selby. *Growing Your Own Food-Bearing Plants in Australia.* The Macmillan Company, Melbourne, 1983.

Hall, Dorothy, and Odell, Carol. *The Natural Health Cookbook.* Thomas Nelson, Melbourne, 1982.

Kenton, Leslie and Susannah. *Raw Energy.* Doubleday, Sydney, 1986.

Kenton, Leslie and Susannah. *Raw Energy Recipes.* Doubleday, Sydney, 1986.

Kushi, Michio. *The Book of Macrobiotics.* Japan Publications, Inc., Tokyo, 1977.

Kushi, Michio. *The Macrobiotic Way of Natural Healing.* East-West Publications, Boston, 1978.

Lindsay, Pat, and Cull, Brian. *Fruit Growing in Warm Climates.* A.H. & A.W. Reed Pty Ltd, Sydney, 1982.

Masefield, G.B., Wallis, M., Harrison, S.G., and Nicholson, B.E. *The Oxford Book of Food Plants.* Oxford University Press, London, 1969.

Nutrition Education Collective. *Through the Seasons: Autumn Harvest.* Aldebaran Press, Massachusetts, 1980.

Nutrition Education Collective. *Through the Seasons: Winter Tidings.* Aldebaran Press, Massachusetts, 1981.

Robertson, Laurel, Flinders, Carol, and Godfrey, Bronwen. *Laurel's Kitchen.* Bantam Books, Nilgiri Press, 1976.

Rohe, Fred. *The Complete Book of Natural Foods.* Shambhala, Boulder and London, 1983.

Schwantes, Dave. *The Unsweetened Truth about Sugar and Sugar Substitutes.* Doubletree Press, Washington, 1975.

Sussman, Vic. *The Vegetarian Alternative.* Rodale Press, Pennsylvania, 1978.

Weber, Marcea. *The Australian & New Zealand Book of Wholemeals.* Doubleday, Sydney, 1983.

Williams, Roger. *Nutrition Against Disease.* Pitman Publishing Group, New York, 1971.

INDEX

EF denotes egg free.   GF denotes gluten free.